HIGH LIFE
HIGHLAND LIBRARIES

KT-497-017

38001700876877

BERTRAMS	09/03/2018
THR	£12.99
AF	

M‍osh

LET
ME
LIE

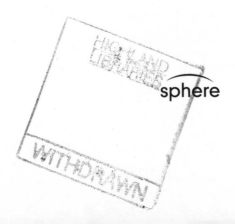

HIGHLAND LIBRARIES

WITHDRAWN

sphere

SPHERE

First published in Great Britain in 2018 by Sphere

1 3 5 7 9 10 8 6 4 2

Copyright © Clare Mackintosh 2018

The moral right of the author has been asserted.

All characters and events in this publication, other than those
clearly in the public domain, are fictitious and any resemblance to
real persons, living or dead, is purely coincidental.

All rights reserved. No part of this publication may be reproduced, stored in a
retrieval system, or transmitted, in any form or by any means, without the prior
permission in writing of the publisher, nor be otherwise circulated in any form of
binding or cover other than that in which it is published and without a similar
condition including this condition being imposed on the subsequent purchaser.

A CIP catalogue record for this book is available from the British Library.

Hardback ISBN 978-0-7515-6490-7
Trade Paperback ISBN 978-0-7515-6487-7

Typeset in Sabon by Palimpsest Book Production Ltd, Falkirk, Stirlingshire

Printed and bound in Great Britain by Clays Ltd, St Ives plc

Papers used by Sphere are from well-managed forests
and other responsible sources.

MIX
Paper from
responsible sources
FSC® C104740

Sphere
An imprint of
Little, Brown Book Group
Carmelite House
50 Victoria Embankment
London
EC4Y 0DZ

An Hachette UK Company

www.hachette.co.uk

www.littlebrown.co.uk

3800 17 0087687 7

HIGH LIFE HIGHLAND

Clare Mackintosh spent twelve years in the police force, including time on CID, and as a public order commander. She left the police in 2011 to work as a freelance journalist and social media consultant and is the founder of the Chipping Norton Literary Festival. She now writes full time and lives in North Wales with her husband and their three children.

Clare's debut novel, *I Let You Go*, was a *Sunday Times* bestseller and the fastest-selling title by a new crime writer in 2015, selling over one million copies worldwide. It won the Theakston Old Peculier Crime Novel of the Year in 2016 and was selected for ITV's *Loose Women*'s Loose Books. Clare's second novel, *I See You*, was a number one *Sunday Times* bestseller. *I Let You Go* and *I See You* were both selected for the Richard & Judy Book Club and have sold in over sixty international territories combined. *Let Me Lie* is Clare's third novel.

Clare is the patron of the Silver Star Society, an Oxford-based charity which supports the work carried out in the John Radcliffe Hospital's Silver Star unit, providing special care for mothers with medical complications during pregnancy.

For more information visit Clare's website www.claremackintosh. com or find her at www.facebook.com/ClareMackWrites or on Twitter @ClareMackint0sh #ILetYouGo #ISeeYou #LetMeLie

Also by Clare Mackintosh

I Let You Go
I See You

For Rob, who does everything.

Three may keep a secret if two of them are dead.

Benjamin Franklin

PART ONE

PART ONE

ONE

Death does not suit me. I wear it like a borrowed coat; it slips off my shoulders and trails in the dirt. It is ill-fitting. Uncomfortable.

I want to shrug it off; to throw it in the cupboard and take back my well-tailored clothes. I didn't want to leave my old life, but I'm hopeful for my next one – hopeful I can become someone beautiful and vibrant. For now, I am trapped.

Between lives.

In limbo.

They say sudden goodbyes are easier. Less painful. They're wrong. Any pain saved from the lingering goodbyes of a drawn-out illness is offset by the horror of a life stolen without notice. A life taken violently. On the day of my death I walked the tightrope between two worlds, the safety net in tatters beneath me. This way safety; that way danger.

I stepped.

I died.

We used to joke about dying – when we were young enough, still vital enough, for death to be something that happened to other people.

'Who do you think'll go first?' you said, one night when the wine had run dry and we lay by the electric fire in my rented Balham flat. An idle hand, stroking my thigh, softened your words. I was quick to answer.

'You, of course.'

You aimed a cushion at my head.

We'd been together a month; enjoying each other's bodies, talking about the future as though it belonged to someone else. No commitment, no promises – just possibilities.

'Women live longer.' I grinned. 'It's a well-known fact. Genetic. Survival of the fittest. Men can't cope on their own.'

You grew serious. Cupped my face in your hand and made me look at you. Your eyes were black in the half-light; the bars of the fire reflected in your pupils. 'It's true.'

I moved to kiss you but your fingers held me still; pressure on my chin as your thumb pushed against bone.

'If anything happened to you I don't know what I'd do.'

The briefest chill, despite the fierce heat from the fire. Footsteps on my grave.

'Give over.'

'I'd die too,' you insisted.

I put a stop to your youthful dramatics then, reaching to push aside your hand and free my chin. Keeping my fingers tangled with yours, so the rejection didn't sting. Kissing you, softly at first, then harder, until you rolled backwards and I was lying on top of you, my hair curtaining our faces.

You would die for me.

Our relationship was young; a spark that could be snuffed out as easily as coaxed into flames. I couldn't have known you'd stop loving me; that I'd stop loving you. I couldn't help but be flattered by the depth of your feeling, the intensity in your eyes.

You would die for me, and in that moment, I thought I might die for you, too.

I just never thought either of us would have to.

4

TWO

ANNA

Ella is eight weeks old. Her eyes are closed, long dark lashes brushing apple cheeks that move up and down as she feeds. One tiny hand splays across my breast like a starfish. I sit, pinned to the sofa, and think of all the things I could be doing while she feeds. Reading. Watching television. An online food shop.

Not today.

Today is not a day for the ordinary.

I watch my daughter, and after a while her lashes lift and she fixes navy eyes on me, solemn and trusting. Her pupils are deep pools of unconditional love; my reflection small but unwavering.

Ella's sucking slows. We gaze at each other, and I think how motherhood is the best-kept secret: how all the books, all the films, all the advice in the world could never prepare you for the all-consuming feeling of being everything to one tiny person. Of that person being everything to you. I perpetuate the secret, telling no one, because who would I tell? Less than a decade after leaving school, my friends share their beds with lovers, not babies.

Ella's still gazing at me, but gradually the focus in her eyes blurs, the way morning mist creeps over a view. Her lids drop once, twice, then fall closed. Her sucking – always so ferocious at first, and then rhythmic, relaxed – slows, until several seconds elapse between mouthfuls. She stops. She sleeps.

I lift my hand and gently press my index finger onto my

5

breast, breaking the seal between my nipple and Ella's lips, then pull my nursing bra back into place. Ella's mouth continues to move for a while, then sleep takes her deeper, her lips frozen into a perfect 'O'.

I should put her down. Make the most of however long she will sleep. Ten minutes? An hour? We are a long way from any kind of routine. *Routine.* The watchword of the new mother; the single topic of conversation at the post-natal coffee mornings my health visitor bullies me into attending. *Is she sleeping through yet? You should try controlled crying. Have you read Gina Ford?*

I nod and smile, and say *I'll check it out,* then I gravitate towards one of the other new mums. Someone different. Someone less rigid. Because I don't care about routine. I don't want to leave Ella crying while I sit downstairs and post on Facebook about my 'parenting nightmare'.

It hurts to cry for a mother who isn't coming back. Ella doesn't need to know that yet.

She stirs in her sleep, and the ever-present lump in my throat swells. Awake, Ella is my daughter. When friends point out her similarities to me, or say how like Mark she is, I can never see it. I look at Ella, and I simply see Ella. But asleep . . . asleep I see my mother. There is a heart-shaped face hiding beneath those baby-plump cheeks, and the curve of their hairline is so alike I know that, in years to come, my daughter will spend hours in front of a mirror, attempting to tame the one tiny section that grows differently to the rest.

Do babies dream? What can they dream of, with so little experience of the world? I envy Ella her sleep, not only because I am tired in a way I never experienced before having a baby, but because when sleep comes, it brings with it nightmares. My dreams show me what I can't possibly know. Supposition from police reports and coroner's court. I see my parents, their faces bloated and disfigured from the water. I see fear on their faces as they fall from the cliff. I hear their screams.

Sometimes my subconscious is kind to me. I don't always see my parents fall; sometimes I see them fly. I see them stepping into nothing and spreading their arms and swooping low above a blue sea that sends spray into their laughing faces. I wake gently then, a smile lingering on my face until I open my eyes and realise that everything is just the way it was when I closed them.

Nineteen months ago, my father took a car – the newest and most expensive – from the forecourt of his own business. He drove the ten minutes from Eastbourne to Beachy Head, where he parked in the car park, left the door unlocked, and walked towards the cliff top. Along the way he collected rocks to weigh himself down. Then, when the tide was at its highest, he threw himself off the cliff.

Seven months later, consumed with grief, my mother followed him, with such devastating accuracy the local paper reported it as a 'copycat suicide'.

I know all these facts because on two separate occasions I heard the coroner take us through them, step by step. I sat with Uncle Billy as we listened to the gentle but painfully thorough account of two failed coastal rescue missions. I stared at my lap while experts proffered views on tides, survival rates, death statistics. And I closed my eyes while the coroner recorded the verdict of suicide.

My parents died seven months apart, but their linked deaths meant the inquests were held the same week. I learned lots of things, on those two days, but not the only thing that mattered.

Why they did it.

If indeed they *did* do it.

The facts are unarguable. Except that my parents were not suicidal. They were not depressed, anxious, fearful. They were the last people you would expect to give up on life.

'Mental illness isn't always obvious,' Mark says, when I raise it, his voice giving no hint of impatience that the conversation is, once again, circling back to this. 'The most capable, the most upbeat people can have depression.'

Over the last year I've learned to keep my theories to myself; not to give voice to the cynicism that lies beneath the surface of my grief. No one else has doubts. No one else feels unease.

But then, maybe no one else knew my parents the way I did.

The phone rings. I let the answerphone pick up but the caller doesn't leave a message. Immediately I feel my mobile vibrate in my pocket, and I know even before I look that it's Mark calling.

'Under a sleeping baby, by any chance?'

'How did you guess?'

'How is she?'

'Feeding every half an hour. I keep trying to start dinner and not getting anywhere.'

'Leave it – I can do it when I get home. How are you feeling?' There's a subtle change of tone that no one else would notice. A subtext. How are you feeling *today, of all days?*

'I'm okay.'

'I can come home—'

'I'm fine. Really.'

Mark would hate to leave his course halfway through. He collects qualifications the way other people collect beer mats, or foreign coins; so many letters they no longer fit after his name. Every few months he prints new business cards, and the least important letters fall off the end into oblivion. Today's course is The Value of Empathy in the Client–Counsellor Relationship. He doesn't need it; his empathy was evident the second I walked through his door.

He let me cry. Pushed a box of tissues towards me and told me to take my time. To begin when I was ready, and not before. And when I stopped crying, but still couldn't find the words, he told me about the stages of grief – denial, anger, bargaining, depression, acceptance – and I realised I hadn't moved past first base.

8

We were four sessions in when Mark took a deep breath and told me he couldn't treat me any more, and I asked if it was me, and he said there was a conflict of interest and this was terribly unprofessional but would I like to have dinner some time?

He was older than me – closer to my mum's age than my own – with a confidence at odds with the nerves I now saw hovering beneath the surface.

I didn't hesitate. 'I'd love to.'

Afterwards he said he felt guiltier about interrupting my counselling than about the ethics of dating a patient. *Former* patient, I pointed out.

He still feels uncomfortable about it. People meet in all sorts of places, I remind him. My parents met in a London nightclub; his met in the frozen food section at Marks & Spencer. And he and I met in a seventh-floor apartment in Putney, in a consultation room with leather chairs and soft woollen throws, and a sign on the door that said MARK HEMMINGS, COUNSELLOR. BY APPOINTMENT ONLY.

'If you're sure. Give Ella-bella a kiss from me.'

'Bye.' I hang up first, and I know he has the handset pressed against his lips, the way he does when he's deep in thought. He'll have gone outside to make the call, forgoing coffee, or networking, or whatever thirty counsellors do when they're released from the classroom. In a moment he'll rejoin the others, and he'll be lost to me for the next few hours, as he works on displaying empathy for a made-up problem. Pretend anxiety. A fictional bereavement.

He'd like to work on mine. I don't let him. I stopped seeing a therapist when I realised all the talking in the world wasn't going to bring back my parents. You reach a point where the pain you feel inside is simply sadness. And there's no cure for that.

Grief is complicated. It ebbs and flows and is so multi-faceted

9

that unpicking it makes my head hurt. I can go for days without crying, then barely be able to breathe for the sobs that wrack my body. One moment I'll be laughing with Uncle Billy about something stupid Dad once did; the next I'll be filled with rage for his selfishness. If Dad hadn't killed himself, Mum wouldn't have done, either.

The anger is the worst part of all of this. The white-hot fury, and the guilt that inevitably follows.

Why did they do it?

I've gone over the days preceding my dad's death a million times; asked myself if we could have done anything to prevent it.

Your dad's missing.

I'd frowned at the text, looking for the punchline. I lived with my parents, but I was away overnight at a conference in Oxford, chatting over morning coffee with a colleague from London. I excused myself to call her.

'What do you mean, missing?'

Mum wasn't making sense. The words came slowly, as though she was dredging them up. They'd had an argument the night before; Dad had stormed off to the pub. So far, so normal. I had long since accepted the storminess of my parents' relationship; the squalls that would pass over as quickly as they blew in. Except this time Dad hadn't come home.

'I thought he might have slept at Bill's,' she said, 'but I'm at work now and Bill hasn't seen him. I'm out of my mind, Anna!'

I left the conference straight away. Not because I was worried about Dad, but because I was worried about Mum. They were careful to keep the causes of their arguments from me, but I'd picked up the aftermath too many times. Dad would disappear – off to work, or to the golf course, or to the pub. Mum would hide in the house, pretending to me she hadn't been crying.

10

It was all over by the time I got home. Police in the kitchen, their hats in their hands. Mum shaking so violently they'd called a paramedic to treat her for shock. Uncle Billy, white with grief. Laura, Mum's goddaughter, making tea and forgetting to add milk. None of us noticing.

I read the text Dad had sent.

I can't do this any more. The world will be a better place without me in it.

'Your father took a car from work.' The policeman was about Dad's age, and I wondered if he had children. If they took him for granted. 'The cameras show it heading towards Beachy Head late last night.' My mother let out a stifled cry. I saw Laura move to comfort her, but I couldn't do the same. I was frozen. Not wanting to hear, but compelled to listen all the same.

'Officers responded to a call-out around ten o'clock this morning,' PC Pickett stared at his notes. I suspected it was easier than looking at us. 'A woman reported seeing a man fill a rucksack with rocks, and place his wallet and phone on the ground, before stepping off the edge of the cliff.'

'And she didn't try to *stop* him?' I hadn't meant to shout, and Uncle Billy put a hand on my shoulder. I shook him off. Turned to the others. 'She just watched him jump?'

'It all happened very quickly. The caller was very upset, as you can imagine.' PC Pickett realised his poor judgement too late to bite his tongue.

'*She* was upset, was she? How did she think Dad was feeling?' I whirled round, searching for support in the faces around me, then fixing my gaze on the police officers. 'Have you questioned her?'

'Anna.' Laura spoke quietly.

'How do you know she didn't push him?'

'Anna, this isn't helping anyone.'

I was about to snap back, but I looked at my mother, leaning into Laura, moaning softly. The fight left me. I was hurting, but Mum was hurting more. I crossed the room and kneeled beside her, reaching for her hand and feeling tears wet my cheeks even before I knew they'd left my eyes. My parents were together for twenty-six years. They lived together – and worked together – and despite all their ups and downs, they loved each other.

PC Pickett cleared his throat. 'The description matched Mr Johnson. We were on scene within minutes. His car was recovered from Beachy Head car park, and on the edge of the cliff we found . . .' He tailed off, indicating a clear plastic evidence bag in the centre of our kitchen table, in which I could see Dad's mobile phone and his tan leather wallet. Out of nowhere I thought of the joke Uncle Billy always cracked, about the moths in Dad's jacket pockets, and for a second I thought I was going to burst into laughter. Instead I cried, and I didn't stop for three days.

My right arm, squashed beneath Ella, has gone to sleep. I slide it out and wiggle my fingers, feeling the tingle as the blood returns to the extremities. Suddenly restless, I extricate myself from beneath Ella's sleeping body with the newly acquired mothering stealth skills of a Royal Marine, and barricade her onto the sofa with cushions. I stand up, stretching out the stiffness that comes from too much sitting down.

My father had never suffered from depression or anxiety.

'Would he have told you, even if he did?' Laura said. We were sitting in the kitchen – Laura, Mum and me. The police, neighbours, everyone had gone, leaving us sitting numbly in the kitchen with a bottle of wine sour on our tongues. Laura's point was a valid one, even if I didn't want to acknowledge it. Dad came from a long line of men who believed talking about 'feelings' meant you were a 'poof'.

Whatever the reasons, his suicide came from nowhere, and plunged us all into grief.

12

Mark – and his replacement, once one had been found – encouraged me to work through the anger I felt in relation to my father's death. I seized upon five words uttered by the coroner.

While not of sound mind.

They helped me separate the man from the act; helped me understand that Dad's suicide wasn't about hurting those he was leaving. Rather, his final text message suggested a genuinely held belief that we might be happier without him. Nothing could have been further from the truth.

Harder than coming to terms with my dad's suicide was what happened next. Trying to fathom why – after experiencing first hand the pain of bereavement by suicide; of watching me cry for my beloved father – my mother would knowingly put me through it again.

Blood hums in my ears like a wasp trapped against glass. I walk into the kitchen and drink a glass of water, fast, then press my hands onto the granite worktop and lean over the sink. I hear Mum, singing as she washes up; nagging Dad to *clear up after yourself once in a blue moon*. Clouds of flour as I made clumsy cakes in Mum's heavy earthenware bowl. Her hands around mine – shaping biscuits, making pastry. And later, when I came back home to live; taking turns to lean against the Aga while the other made supper. Dad in the study, or watching TV in the sitting room. We women in the kitchen – through design, not default. Chatting as we cooked.

It's in this room I feel most close to Mum. In this room it hurts the most.

A year ago, today.

Grieving widow plunges to her death, read the *Gazette*. *Chaplain calls for media blackout on suicide hotspot*, read the unwittingly ironic *Guardian* headline.

'You knew,' I whisper, feeling sure that talking out loud is not the action of a sane mind, yet being unable to contain it for a second more. 'You knew how much it hurt, and you still did it.'

I should have listened to Mark, and planned something for today. A distraction. I could have called Laura. Had lunch. Gone shopping. Anything that didn't involve moping about the house, going over old ground, obsessing over the anniversary of Mum's death. There is no logical reason why today should be any harder than any other. My mother is no more dead than she was yesterday; no more dead than she will be tomorrow.

And yet . . .

I take a deep breath and try to snap out of it. Put my glass in the sink and tut loudly, as though an audible admonishment to myself will make a difference. I will take Ella to the park. We can go the long way around to kill time, and on the way back we'll pick up something for supper, and before I know it Mark will be home and today will be almost over. This abrupt decisiveness is a familiar trick, but it works. The ache in my heart lessens, and the pressure behind my eyes fades away.

Fake it till you make it, Laura always says. *Dress for the job you want, not the job you have* is another favourite. She means at work (you'd have to listen very carefully to pick up on the fact that her public-school accent is learned, not inherited) but the principle is the same. Pretend you're okay, and you'll feel okay. Before too long you really will be okay.

I'm still working on the last bit.

I hear the squeak that means Ella is awake. I'm halfway across the hall when I see something poking through the letterbox. It's either been delivered by hand, or it got caught in the letterbox when the postman did his rounds. Either way I didn't see it when I collected the post from the mat this morning.

It's a card. I received two others this morning – both from school friends more comfortable with grief when held at arm's length – and I'm touched by the number of people who note dates in this way. On the anniversary of Dad's suicide someone left a casserole on my doorstep with the briefest of notes.

Freeze or reheat. Thinking of you.

I still don't know who it's from. Many of the condolence cards that arrived after my parents' deaths came with stories of the cars they'd sold over the years. Keys handed to over-confident teens and over-anxious parents. Two-seater sports cars traded for family-friendly estates. Cars to celebrate promotions, big birthdays, retirements. My parents played a part in many different stories.

The address is typed on a sticker, the postmark a smudge of ink in the top right-hand corner. The card is thick and expensive – I have to wiggle it out of its envelope.

I stare at the image.

Bright colours dance across the page: a border of lurid pink roses with intertwined stems and glossy green leaves. In the centre, two champagne glasses clink together. The greeting is embossed and finished with glitter.

Happy Anniversary!

I recoil as if I've been punched. Is this some kind of sick joke? A mistake? Some well-meaning, short-sighted acquaintance, mistaken in their choice of missive? I open the card.

The message is typed. Cut from cheap paper and glued to the inside.

This is no mistake.

My hands shake, making the words swim in front of my eyes. The wasp in my ears buzzes louder. I read it again.

```
Suicide? Think again.
```

THREE

It wasn't the way I wanted to go. Not the way I always thought I'd go.

If I imagined my death I pictured a darkened room. Our bedroom. Pillows plumped behind my back; a glass of water touched to my lips once my own hands became too weak to hold it. Morphine to manage the pain. Visitors tiptoeing in single file to say their good-byes; you red-eyed but stoic, absorbing their kind words.

And me; gradually more asleep than awake, until one morning I never woke up at all.

I used to joke that in my next life I wanted to come back as a dog.

Turns out you don't get that much choice.

You take what you're given, whether it suits you or not. A woman just like you. Older, uglier. That or nothing.

It feels strange to be without you.

Twenty-six years, we were together. Married for almost as long. For better or for worse. You in a suit, me in an empire-line dress picked to hide a five-month-old bump. A new life together.

And now it's just me. Lonely. Scared. Out of my depth in the shadows of a life I once lived to the full.

Nothing worked out the way I thought it would.

And now this.

Suicide? Think again.

The words aren't signed. Anna won't know who they're from.

But I do. I've spent the last year waiting for this to happen, fooling myself that silence meant safety.

It doesn't.

I can see the hope on Anna's face; the promise of answers to the questions that keep her awake at night. I know our daughter. She never would have believed that you and I would have stepped off that cliff of our own free will.

She was right.

I see too, with painful clarity, what will happen now. Anna will go to the police. Demand an investigation. She'll fight for the truth, not knowing that the truth hides nothing but more lies. More danger.

Suicide? Think again.

What you don't know can't hurt you. I have to stop Anna going to the police. I have to stop her finding out the truth about what happened, before she gets hurt.

I thought I'd seen the last of my old life, the day I drove to Beachy Head, but I guess I was wrong.

I have to stop this.

I have to go back down.

FOUR

ANNA

I ring Mark back. Leave a message about the card that makes so little sense I have to stop, take a breath, then explain myself again.

'Call me as soon as you get this,' I finish.

Suicide? Think again.

The meaning is clear.

My mother was murdered.

The hairs on the back of my neck are still prickling and I turn slowly around, taking in the wide stairs behind me, the open doors on either side with their floor-to-ceiling windows. No one there. Of course there isn't. But the card in my hand has unnerved me as surely as if someone had broken into the house and put it directly into my hand, and it no longer feels as though Ella and I are alone in the house.

I stuff the card back into its envelope. I need to get out of here.

'Rita!'

There's a scuffle from the kitchen, followed by a skittering of claws on the tiles. The result of a rehoming appeal, Rita is part Cyprus poodle, part several other breeds. She has auburn whiskers that fall over her eyes and around her mouth, and in the summer, when she's clipped, the white patches on her coat look like snow. She licks me enthusiastically.

'We're going out.'

18

Never one to be asked twice, Rita races to the front door, where she cocks her head and looks at me impatiently. The pram is in the hall, tucked beneath the curve of the stairs, and I push the anonymous card into the shopping basket at the bottom, covering it with a blanket as though not seeing it changes the fact that it's there. I pick up Ella just as she's morphing from contentment to grouchiness.

Suicide? Think again.

I knew it. I've always known it. My mother had a strength I wish I had a tenth of – a confidence I covet still. She never gave up. She wouldn't have given up on life.

Ella roots for my breast again, but there's no time. I don't want to be in the house for another minute.

'Let's go and get some fresh air, shall we?'

I find the change bag in the kitchen, check for the essentials – nappies, wipes, muslins – and throw in my purse and the house keys. This is usually the point at which Ella will fill her nappy, or throw up her milk and require a full set of clean clothes. I sniff cautiously at her bottom and conclude that she's fine.

'Right, let's go!'

There are three stone steps that lead down from the front door to the gravelled area between the house and the pavement. Each step dips in the middle, where countless feet have trod over the years. As a child, I would jump off the bottom step, my confidence growing with my years until – accompanied by my mother's 'do be careful!' – I could leap from the top step and land square-footed on the drive, my arms raised before invisible applause.

Ella in one arm, I bounce the pram down the steps before putting her inside and tucking the blankets firmly around her. The cold snap shows no sign of lifting, and the pavements glitter with frost. The gravel makes a dull crunch as frozen clumps break apart beneath my feet.

'Anna!'

19

Our neighbour, Robert Drake, is standing on the other side of the black railings that separate our house from his. The properties are identical: three-storey Georgian houses with long back gardens and narrow outdoor passages that run from front to back between each house. My parents moved to Eastbourne in 1992, when my unexpected appearance had curtailed their London lives and launched them into married life. My late grandfather bought the house – two streets from where Dad had grown up – for cash ('it's the only currency people listen to, Annie') and, I imagine, for significantly less than Robert paid when he bought the neighbouring property fifteen years later.

'I've been thinking about you,' Robert says. 'It's today, isn't it?' He gives a sympathetic smile and tilts his head to one side. The action reminds me of Rita, except that Rita's eyes are warm and trusting, and Robert's . . .

'Your mother,' he adds, in case I'm not following. There's a touch of impatience in his voice, as though I should be more grateful for his compassion.

Robert is a surgeon, and although he has never been anything but friendly towards us, he has an intense, almost clinical gaze that makes me feel as though I'm on his operating table. He lives alone, mentioning the nieces and nephews who occasionally visit with the detachment of a man who has never had, and never wanted, children of his own.

I wrap Rita's lead around the handle of the pram. 'Yes. It's today. It's kind of you to remember.'

'Anniversaries are always tough.'

I can't listen to any more platitudes. 'I was just taking Ella out for a walk.'

Robert seems glad of the change of subject. He peers through the railings. 'Hasn't she grown?' There are so many blankets around Ella he couldn't possibly see, but I agree and tell him what percentile she's on, which is probably more detail than he needed.

'Excellent! Jolly good. Well, I'll let you get on.'

The drive is the width of the house, but only just deep enough for cars. Iron gates, never closed in my lifetime, lie flat against the railings. I say goodbye, then push the pram through the opening and onto the pavement. Across the street is a park, a grown-up space with complicated planting, and signs that keep you off the grass. My parents would take it in turns to walk Rita there, last thing at night, and she strains now at the lead, but I pull her back and push the pram towards town instead. At the end of the row of town houses, I turn right. I glance back towards Oak View, and as I do I realise Robert is still standing on his driveway. He looks away, and walks back into his house.

We walk along Chestnut Avenue, where glossy railings flank more double-fronted town houses; bay-tree sentries wrapped in twinkling white lights. One or two of the huge houses on the avenue have been turned into flats, but most are still intact, their wide front doors uncluttered by doorbells and letterboxes. Christmas trees are positioned in bay windows, and I catch glimpses of activity in the high-ceilinged rooms beyond. In the first, a teenage boy flops on a sofa; in the second, small children race around the room, heady with festive excitement. At number six an elderly couple read from their respective papers.

The door to number eight is open. A woman – late forties, I guess – stands in a French Gray hall, with one hand resting lightly on the door. I nod a hello, but although she lifts a hand in greeting, the laughing smile is directed towards a gently squabbling trio wrestling a Christmas tree from the car to the house.

'Careful, you're going to drop it!'

'Left a bit. Watch the door!'

A peal of laughter from the teenage girl; a wry grin from her clumsy brother.

'You'll have to lift it over the railings.'

Dad, directing proceedings. Getting in the way. Proud of his children.

For a second it hurts so much I can't breathe. I squeeze my eyes shut. I miss my parents so badly, at different times and in ways I could never have predicted. Two Christmases ago that would have been me and Dad with the tree; Mum mock-scolding from the door. There would have been tins of Roses chocolates, too much booze and enough food to feed the five thousand. Laura, arriving with a pile of presents if she'd just started a job; IOUs and apologies if she'd just left one. Dad and Uncle Billy, arguing about nonsense; flipping a coin to settle a bet. Mum getting emotional and putting 'Driving Home for Christmas' on the CD player.

Mark would say I'm looking at the past through rose-tinted glasses, but I can't be alone in wanting to only remember the good times. And, rose-tinted or not, my life changed for ever when my parents died.

Suicide? Think again.

Not suicide. Murder.

Someone stole the life I had. Someone murdered my mother. And if they murdered Mum, it follows that Dad didn't kill himself either. My parents were murdered.

I grip the handle of Ella's pram more tightly, unsteadied by a wave of guilt for the months I've raged against my parents for taking the easy way out – for thinking of themselves above those they were leaving behind. Maybe I was wrong to blame them. Maybe leaving me wasn't their choice.

Johnson's car showroom is on the corner of Victoria Road and Main Street, a beacon of light at the point where shops and hairdressers give way to flats and houses on the outskirts of town. The fluttering bunting I remember from my childhood has long gone, and heaven knows what Granddad would have made of the iPads tucked under the sales reps' arms or the huge flat screen scrolling that week's special deal.

I cross the forecourt, navigating Ella's pram between a sleek

Mercedes and a second-hand Volvo. The glass doors slide soundlessly open as we draw near, warm air luring us in. Christmas music plays through expensive speakers. Behind the desk, where Mum used to sit, a striking girl with caramel skin and matching highlights taps acrylic nails on her keyboard. She smiles at me and I catch the flash of diamante fixed to one of her teeth. Her style couldn't be more different to Mum's. Perhaps that's why Uncle Billy hired her; it can't be easy coming in to work, day after day. The same, but different. Like my house. Like my life.

'Annie!'

Always Annie. Never Anna.

Uncle Billy is Dad's brother, and the very definition of 'confirmed bachelor'. He has a handful of female friends, content with Friday night dinners and the occasional jaunt to London to see a show, and a regular poker night with the boys the first Wednesday of the month.

Occasionally I'll suggest Bev, or Diane, or Shirley join us for a drink some time. Billy's response is always the same.

'I don't think so, Annie love.'

His dates never become anything more serious. Dinner is always just dinner; a drink's always just that. And although he books the nicest hotels for his trips to London, and lavishes gifts upon his companion of choice, it's always months before he sees her again.

'Why do you keep them all at arm's length?' I demanded once, after too many of what's known in our family as a 'Johnson G&T'.

Billy winked at me, but his tone was serious. 'Because that way no one gets hurt.'

I wrap my arms around him and inhale the familiar mix of aftershave and tobacco, along with something indefinable that makes me bury my face in his jumper. He smells like Granddad did. Like Dad did. Like all the Johnson men. Only Billy left now.

I pull away. Decide to just come out with it. 'Mum and Dad didn't commit suicide.'

There's a look of resignation in Uncle Billy's face. We've been here before.

'Oh, Annie . . .'

Only this time it's different.

'They were murdered.'

He looks at me without saying anything – anxious eyes scanning my face – then he ushers me into the office, away from the punters, and settles me into the expensive leather chair that's been here since for ever.

Buy cheap, buy twice, Dad used to say.

Rita flops on the floor. I look at my feet. Remember how they used to dangle off the edge of the seat, and how, gradually, they stretched to reach the floor.

I did work experience here, once.

I was fifteen. Encouraged to think about joining the family business, until it became clear I'd have struggled to sell water in the Sahara. Dad was a natural. What is it they say? Ice to the Eskimos. I used to watch him sizing up customers – *prospects*, he called them. He'd take in the car they were driving, the clothes they wore, and I'd see him select the right approach like he was choosing from a menu. He was always himself – always Tom Johnson – but his accent would slide a few notches up or down, or he'd declare himself a devotee of Watford FC, The Cure, chocolate Labradors . . . You could pinpoint the moment the connection happened; the second the customer decided they and Dad were on the same wavelength. That Tom Johnson was a man to be trusted.

I couldn't do it. I tried mimicking Dad, tried working with Mum on the desk and copying the way she smiled at customers and asked after their kids, but it sounded hollow, even to me.

'I don't think our Annie's cut out for sales,' Billy said – not unkindly – when my work experience was up. No one disagreed.

24

Funny thing is, sales is exactly where I've ended up. That's what charity work comes down to in the end, after all. Selling monthly donations; sponsored children; legacies and bequests. Selling guilt to those with the means to help. I've been with Save the Children since I left uni, and it's never once felt hollow. Turns out, I just never felt that passionately about selling cars.

Billy's wearing a navy pinstripe suit, his red socks and braces lending him a Wall Street air I know is entirely deliberate. Billy does nothing by accident. On anyone else I'd find the bling crass, but Billy wears it well – even if the braces are straining over his stomach slightly – with a touch of irony that makes him endearing, rather than flashy. He's only two years younger than Dad, but his hairline shows no sign of receding, and what grey there might be around his temples is carefully touched up. Billy takes the same pride in his appearance as he does in the showroom.

'What's all this about, Annie?' He's gentle, the way he always was when I fell over, or when I'd had a spat in the playground. 'Tough day? I've been out of sorts myself today. Be glad when it's over, to be honest. Anniversaries, eh? Full of memories.' Beneath the brusqueness there's a vulnerability that makes me vow to spend more time with him. I used to come by the showroom all the time, but since Mum and Dad died I've made excuses, even to myself. I'm too busy, Ella's too small, the weather's too bad . . . Truth is, it hurts to be here. But that isn't fair.

'Come for supper tomorrow night?'

Billy hesitates.

'Please?'

'Sure. That would be nice.'

The glass between Billy's office and the showroom is tinted one way, and on the other side of it I see one of the salesmen shaking hands with a customer. He glances towards the office, hoping the big boss is watching. Billy nods approvingly, a mental note filed away for the next appraisal. I watch him, looking for the tell; trying to read his mind.

Trade's been slow. Dad was the driving force, and his death hit Uncle Billy hard. When Mum went too, there was a moment when I thought he was going to fall apart.

I'd not long discovered Ella was on the way, and I'd come down to the showroom to see Uncle Billy, only to find the place in disarray. The office was empty, and disposable coffee cups littered the low tables in the waiting area. Customers wandered unaccompanied between the cars on the forecourt. At reception, Kevin – a newish sales rep with a shock of ginger hair – perched on the desk, flirting with the receptionist, an agency temp who had started the week after Christmas.

'But where is he?'

Kevin shrugged. 'He didn't come in today.'

'And you didn't think to call him?'

In the car on the way to Billy's place, I ignored the rising panic in my chest. He'd taken a day off, that was all. He wasn't missing. He wouldn't do that to me.

I rang the bell. Hammered on the door. And just as I was fumbling in my bag for my mobile, my lips already forming the words familiar from my parents' inquest – *this is a fear for welfare* – Billy opened the door.

Fine red lines covered the whites of his eyes. His shirt was open; his suit jacket crumpled enough to tell me he'd slept in it. A waft of alcohol hit me, and I hoped it was from the previous evening.

'Who's running the shop, Uncle Billy?'

He stared past me to the street, where an elderly couple were making slow progress along the pavement, a wheeled shopping basket in their wake.

'I can't do it. I can't be there.'

I felt a surge of anger. Didn't he think I wanted to give up? Did he think he was the only one finding this hard?

Inside, the house was a mess. A greasy film covered the glass-topped coffee table in the sitting room. Dirty plates littered the kitchen surfaces; nothing in the fridge but a half-empty bottle of white wine. It wasn't unusual to find no proper meals in the house – Uncle Billy considered eating out to be the primary advantage of single life – but there was no milk, no bread. Nothing.

I hid my shock. Dumped the plates in the sink, wiped the counters and picked up the post from the hall floor.

He gave me a tired smile. 'You're a good girl, Annie.'

'You're on your own with the laundry – I'm not washing your underpants.' My anger had passed. This wasn't Billy's fault. It wasn't anyone's fault.

'I'm sorry.'

'I know.' I gave him a hug. 'You need to get back to work though, Billy. They're just kids.'

'What's the point? We had six punters show up yesterday; all tyre-kickers.'

'Tyre-kickers are just buyers who don't know it yet.' Dad's favourite saying brought a lump to my throat. Billy squeezed my arm.

'He was so proud of you.'

'He was proud of you, too. Proud of what the two of you achieved with the business.' I waited a beat. 'Don't let him down.'

Billy was back at work by lunchtime, putting a rocket up Kevin's arse and offering a bottle of champagne to the first rep to make a sale. I knew it would take more than champagne to get Johnson's Cars on an even keel, but at least Billy was at the helm again.

It was Dad who'd had the tinted glass installed, a few weeks after Granddad retired, and Billy and Dad had moved into the office, a desk on either side of the room.

'Keeps them on their toes.'

'Keeps them from catching you having forty winks, more like.' Mum could see through the Johnson boys. Always had.

Billy turns his attention back to me. 'I'd have thought that man of yours would have taken today off.'

'It's Mark, not *that man*. I wish you'd give him a chance.'

'I will. Just as soon as he makes an honest woman of you.'

'It's not the 1950s, Billy.'

'Fancy leaving you on your own today.'

'He offered to stay home. I said I was fine.'

'Clearly.'

'I was. Before this arrived.' I fish in the bottom of Ella's pram for the card and give it to Billy. I watch his face as he takes in the celebratory greeting, the carefully typed message stuck inside. There's a long pause, then he puts the card back in its envelope. His jaw tightens.

'Sick bastards.' Before I can stop him, he's ripped the card in two, and then in two again.

'What are you doing?' I leap out of my chair and snatch back the torn pieces of card. 'We need to take it to the police.'

'The police?'

'*Think again*. It's a message. They're suggesting Mum was pushed. Maybe Dad, too.'

'Annie, love, we've been through this a hundred times. You don't seriously believe your parents were murdered?'

'Yes.' My bottom lip wobbles and I clamp it shut for a moment to regain some control. 'Yes, I do. I've always thought something was wrong. I never thought either of them was capable of suicide, least of all Mum, when she knew how much Dad's death affected us all. And now—'

'It's someone shit-stirring, Annie! Some jumped-up prick who thinks it's funny to trawl the obituaries and torment grieving families. Like the shits who look through funeral listings to see when to go out burgling. They probably sent a dozen others at the same time.' Even though I know it's the sender of the card who's wound him up, it feels like his anger's directed at me. I stand up.

28

'Even more reason for me to go to the police with it, then. So they can find out who sent it.' My tone is defensive; it's that or bursting into tears.

'This family never used to run to the police. We used to sort out our own problems.'

'"Problems"?' I don't understand why Billy's being so obtuse. Doesn't he see this changes everything? 'This isn't a *problem*, Billy. It isn't some argument you can settle out the back of the pub. It could be *murder*. And I care what happened to my mum, even if you don't.' Too late, I bite my tongue. Billy turns away, but not before I've seen the hurt on his face. I stand helplessly for a while, looking at the back of his head and trying to say sorry, but the words won't come.

I push Ella's pram out of the office, leaving the door wide open. If Billy won't help me, I'll go to the police on my own.

Someone murdered my parents, and I'm going to find out who.

FIVE

MURRAY

Murray Mackenzie swirled a teabag around a polystyrene cup.

'Milk?' He opened the fridge and surreptitiously sniffed three cartons before finding one he could safely offer a member of the public in distress. And Anna Johnson was undoubtedly in distress. She was dry-eyed, but Murray felt uncomfortably certain crying was on the cards. He wasn't good with tears. He never knew whether to ignore or acknowledge them, or whether nowadays it was politically correct to offer a neatly pressed handkerchief.

Murray heard a quiet murmur that could have been the precursor to sobbing. Politically correct or not, if Mrs Johnson didn't have a tissue to hand he would come to her aid. He didn't use a handkerchief himself, but he had always carried one, like his father had done, for these very occasions. Murray patted his pocket, but when he turned around – the polystyrene cup overfull in one hand – he realised the half-hearted squeaking noise was coming from the baby, not from Mrs Johnson.

Murray's relief was short-lived, as Anna Johnson deftly whipped the baby from its carriage and positioned it horizontally across her lap, before pulling up her top and starting to feed. Murray felt himself blushing, which made him redden even more. It was not that he objected to women breastfeeding, it was simply that he never knew where to look while they did it. He had once adopted what he'd intended to be a supportive smile towards a

30

mother in the café above M&S, only to have her glare at him and cover up as though he were some sort of pervert.

He fixed his gaze somewhere above Mrs Johnson's left eyebrow as he put down her tea as reverently as if he were serving it in a bone china cup. 'I couldn't find any biscuits, I'm afraid.'

'Tea is lovely, thank you.'

As Murray had grown older he had become less and less able to judge other people's ages, with anyone the right side of forty looking young to him, but Anna Johnson definitely hadn't seen thirty yet.

She was an attractive young woman, with a slight wave to her sandy brown hair that made it bob about on her shoulders as she moved her head. Her face was pale, and showed the effects of new motherhood Murray remembered seeing in his sister when his nephews had been small.

They were sitting in the small area behind the front desk of Lower Meads police station, where a kitchenette had been installed for Murray and his colleagues to take their lunch breaks while simultaneously keeping an eye on whoever might come through the door. Members of the public weren't supposed to be on this side of the counter, but the station was quiet, and whole hours could go by without anyone coming in to report a lost dog, or to sign a bail sheet. Murray had enough time alone with his thoughts at home; he didn't need silence at work, too.

It was rare to see anyone above the rank of sergeant this far from headquarters, so Murray had thrown caution to the winds and shown Mrs Johnson through to the inner sanctum. You didn't need to be a detective to know that three feet of melamine counter weren't conducive to making a witness feel relaxed. Not that Mrs Johnson was likely to ever feel relaxed, given the purpose of her visit.

'I think my mother was murdered,' she'd announced on arrival. She had eyed Murray with a determined air, as though he might be about to disagree. Murray had felt a rush of adrenalin. A murder. Who was duty DI today? Oh . . . Detective Inspector Robinson. That was going to rankle, reporting to a whipper-snapper with fluff on his upper lip and five minutes in the job. But then Anna Johnson had explained that her mother had been dead a year, and that in fact a coroner had already ruled on the death and pronounced it to be suicide. That was the point at which Murray had opened the door at the side of the front desk and invited Mrs Johnson in. He suspected they were going to be some time. A dog trotted obediently at her feet, seemingly unfazed by its surroundings.

Now, Anna Johnson twisted awkwardly behind her and took a handful of paper from inside the pram. As she did, her T-shirt rode up to reveal an inch of soft stomach, and Murray coughed hard and stared fiercely at the floor, wondering how long it took to feed a baby.

'Today is the anniversary of my mother's death.' She spoke loudly, with a force Murray guessed was an attempt to override emotion. It made her voice strangely dispassionate, and at odds with her troubled eyes. 'This came in the post.' She thrust the bundle of paper at Murray.

'I'll get some gloves.'

'Fingerprints! I didn't think . . . will I have destroyed all the evidence?'

'Let's see what we've got first, Mrs Johnson, shall we?'

'It's Ms, actually. But Anna is fine.'

'Anna. Let's see what we've got.' Murray returned to his seat and stretched the latex over his hands, in a gesture so familiar it was comforting. Putting down a large plastic evidence bag on the table between them, he laid out the pieces of paper. It was a card, crudely ripped into four.

'It didn't come like that. My uncle . . .' Anna hesitated. 'I think he was upset.'

'Your mother's brother?'

'Father's. Billy Johnson. Johnson's Cars on the corner of Main Street?'

'That's your uncle's place?' Murray had bought his Volvo from there. He tried to remember the man who had sold it to him; pictured a smartly dressed fellow with hair carefully coiffured over a bald patch.

'It was my granddad's. Dad and Uncle Billy learned the trade with him, but they went off to work in London. That's where my parents met. When Granddad fell ill Dad and Billy went back to help him, then they took over the business when he retired.'

'And now the business belongs to your uncle?'

'Yes. Well, and me, I suppose. Although that's a mixed blessing.'

Murray waited.

'Trade's not great at the moment.' She shrugged, careful not to disturb the baby in her arms. Murray made a mental note to return to the detail of who had inherited what from Anna's parents. For now, he wanted to examine the card.

He separated the pieces of card from the sections of envelope, and laid them out together. He noted the celebratory image on the front of the card; the cruel juxtaposition with the anonymous message inside.

Suicide? Think again.

'Do you have any idea who might have sent this?'

Anna shook her head.

'How widely known is your address?'

'I've lived in the same house all my life. Eastbourne's a small place; I'm not hard to find.' She switched the baby expertly from one side to the other. Murray examined the card again, until he concluded it was safe to look up. 'After Dad died, we got a lot of post. Lots of sympathy cards, lots of people remembering cars he'd sold them over the years.' Anna's face hardened. 'A few weren't so nice.'

'In what way?'

'Someone sent a letter saying Dad would burn in hell for taking his own life; another one just said, "Good riddance". All anonymous, of course.'

'That must have been incredibly upsetting for you and your mother.'

Anna shrugged again, but it was unconvincing. 'Crackpots. People pissed off because of cars that didn't work out.' She caught the look on Murray's face. 'Dad never sold a lemon. Sometimes you get a dud, that's all. People want someone to blame.'

'Did you keep these letters? We could compare them to this one. See if it's from someone holding a grudge.'

'They went straight in the bin. Mum died six months later and . . .' She looked at Murray, her train of thought abandoned in favour of something more pressing. 'I came to see if you'd re-open the investigation into my parents' deaths.'

'Is there anything else that makes you suspect they were murdered?'

'What more do you want?' She gestured to the card, lying in pieces between them.

Evidence, Murray thought. He took a sip of his tea to buy himself time. If he passed this to DI Robinson now, it would be dismissed by the end of the day. CID were up to their necks in live investigations; it would take more than one anonymous note and a funny feeling to make them re-open a cold case.

'Please, Mr Mackenzie, I need to know for certain.' The control that Anna Johnson had shown all the time they'd been talking was starting to crack. 'I never believed my parents would kill themselves. They were full of life. Full of ambition. They had big plans for the business.' The baby had finished feeding. Anna propped it on her knee, one outstretched hand beneath its chin, the other rubbing circles on its back.

'Your mother worked there too?'

'She did the books and front-of-house.'

'Quite the family business.' Murray was heartened to hear there were still a few of them about.

Anna nodded. 'When Mum was pregnant with me, she and Dad moved to Eastbourne to be closer to Dad's parents. Granddad wasn't doing too well, and it wasn't long before Dad and Billy were running the show. Mum, too.' Tired now, the baby's eyes rolled in their sockets like drunks in the cells on a Saturday night. 'And when she wasn't working, she was raising money for her animal charity, or out campaigning.'

'Campaigning for what?'

Anna gave a short laugh. Her eyes glistened. 'Anything. Amnesty International, women's rights. Even bus services – although I don't think she ever took a bus in her life. When she got behind something she made things happen.'

'She sounds like a wonderful woman,' Murray said softly.

'There was a story on the news once. Years ago. I was at home with my parents, and it was on in the background. Some young lad who'd driven a moped off Beachy Head. They'd recovered the moped but not his body, and they showed his mum on the television, crying because she couldn't even give him a proper burial.' The baby strained uncomfortably and Anna shifted position and patted it on the back. 'We talked about it. I remember Mum watching with her hands over her mouth, and Dad being angry with the boy for putting his parents through it.' She tailed off, pausing her rhythmic patting to stare intently at Murray. 'They saw what that boy did to his mother, and they would never, ever have done it to me.'

Tears welled in the corners of Anna's eyes, finding the line of her narrow nose and running in tandem towards her chin. Murray held out his handkerchief, and she took it gratefully, pressing it against her face as though brute force alone could hold back the tears.

Murray sat very still. There was much he could have said about the impact of suicide attempts, but he suspected it wouldn't

35

help Anna. He wondered if she'd been offered the right support all those months ago. 'You should have been given a leaflet by the officers who dealt with your parents' deaths. There are charities that support people bereaved by suicide. Groups you can go to; people you can see on a one-to-one basis.'

Some people found shared experiences a lifeline. They thrived in group therapy sessions, walking out stronger and better equipped to deal with their emotions. A problem shared . . .

But suicide support groups didn't help everyone.

They hadn't helped Murray.

'I saw a grief counsellor.'

'Did it help?'

'I had a baby with him.' Anna Johnson gave a half sob, half laugh. Murray found himself laughing with her.

'Well, that does sound quite helpful.'

The tears had slowed. Anna's smile was weak, but steady. 'Please, Mr Mackenzie. My parents didn't commit suicide. They were murdered.' She pointed at the torn-up card. 'And this proves it.'

It didn't prove it. It didn't prove anything.

But it did ask a question. And Murray had never been one to ignore an unanswered question. Perhaps he could take a look himself. Pull out the original files, read through the coroner's reports. And when – if – there was something to investigate, he could hand over the package. He had the skills, after all. Thirty years in the job, and the best part of that on CID. You didn't hand in your knowledge along with your warrant card.

He looked at Anna Johnson. Tired and emotional, but determined, too. If Murray didn't help her, who would? She wasn't the type to give up.

'I'll request the files this afternoon.'

Murray had the skills, and he had the time. Lots and lots of time.

SIX

You're not allowed to go back. It upsets people. If there was a manual, that would be the first rule – never go back – swiftly followed by rule number two: never let yourself be seen.

You have to move on.

But it's hard to move on when you're a non-person; when you've left behind the life you knew and haven't yet begun a fresh one. When you're stuck in no-man's-land between this life and the next. When you're dead.

I followed the rules.

I disappeared into this half-life, lonely and bored.

I miss my old life. I miss our house: the garden, the kitchen, the coffee machine you bought on a whim. And, vacuous though it sounds, I miss manicures and six-weekly highlights. I miss my clothes; my beautiful walk-in wardrobe of pressed suits and carefully folded cashmere. I wonder what Anna's done with them all – if she's wearing them.

I miss Anna.

I miss our daughter.

I spent her last year of school filled with dread for her first one at college. I was afraid of the emptiness I knew she'd leave; the influence she'd never know she had on us both. I was afraid of being lonely. Of being alone.

People used to say she was the spit of me, and we'd turn to each other and laugh, not seeing it. We were so different. I loved parties; Anna hated them. I loved to shop; my daughter was thrifty, making do and mending. We had the same mousey hair

– I never did understand why she wouldn't go blonde – and the same build, with a tendency to plumpness that bothered me more than it did her. I wear my new lightness well, I think, although I confess I mourn the compliments of friends.

The journey down takes longer than I anticipated, but my tiredness dissipates the second I set foot on familiar ground. Like a prisoner on parole I drink in my surroundings, marvelling at how so much has changed for me, yet so much has stayed the same. The same trees, still bereft of leaves; a scene so identical to the one I left, it is as though I've only stepped away for a moment. The same busy streets and bad-tempered bus drivers. I catch sight of Ron Dyer, Anna's old head teacher, and shrink back into the shadows. I needn't have bothered – he stares right through me. People see what they want to see, don't they?

I walk slowly along quiet streets, revelling in the illicit freedom I've seized for myself. Every action has a consequence; I haven't broken these rules lightly. If I'm caught, I risk losing my next life, languishing instead in purgatory. A prison of my own making. But the buzz of being back is hard to ignore. My senses are tingling after so long away, and as I turn into the next street I feel a racing in my chest.

Nearly home. Home. I catch myself. Remind myself it's Anna's home now. I expect she's made changes. She always loved the bedroom at the back, with the pretty sprigs of blue on the wallpaper, but I suppose it's silly to imagine her there now. She'll have taken over our bedroom.

For a second my defences slide and I remember the day we went to see Oak View together. The previous owners, an elderly couple, had updated the electrics and connected the house to mains gas and waste, replacing the costly oil tank and the unpleasant septic tank still buried in the garden. Your father had already made an offer. All that was left for us to do was to breathe life into the place; to uncover the original doors and fireplaces, and free the windows long-since painted shut.

38

I slow my pace. Now that I'm here, I'm nervous. I focus on the two things I need to do: stop Anna going to the police and ensure that any evidence points to suicide, not murder.

But how?

A couple, walking arm in arm, turn into the street ahead of me. I step into a doorway, wait until they've passed, and use the time to calm myself. I need to make Anna understand the danger she'll be in if she starts to question what she thinks she knows. How can I do that yet stay invisible? I imagine a cartoon ghost, rattling chains and wailing in the dead of night. Ridiculous. Impossible. Yet how else do I get a message to her?

I'm here. Outside our – Anna's – house. I retreat to the opposite side of the street, and when even that feels too close I move into the gated park in the middle of the square, watching through the prickly branches of a holly bush. What if she isn't home? I could hardly have called in advance to check. What if the risks I've taken to come down were all in vain? I could lose everything. Again.

A noise along the street makes me retreat further behind the holly. I peer through the gloom onto the street. A woman, walking with a pram. She's on the phone, walking slowly. Distracted. I keep watching the house, scanning each window for signs of activity.

The pram's wheels make a rhythmic sound on the wet pavement. I remember pushing Anna around the forecourt at Johnson's, in and out of the cars, waiting for sleep to envelop her. We were just kids ourselves, barely scraping by on what your dad saw fit to pay us. The pram was a second-hand monstrosity, with a bouncing chassis that jerked Anna awake if we went over bumps. Nothing like the sleek modern affair this woman has.

She pauses by the house, and I tut, impatient for her to move on, in case I miss some movement beyond the open curtains.

But she doesn't walk by. And now I see that she isn't alone. She has a dog with her, trotting in the shadows beside her. I feel a sharpness in my chest.

Is it . . . ?

The pram wheels crunch over gravel as she pushes it through the gates and to the front door. The stained-glass panel in the front door glows a soft red from the light in the hall.

It is.

The woman's call ends and she slips her phone into a pocket. She takes out a key, and as she does so she pushes back her hood and I see mousey hair beneath the light above the door, and soft features above a mouth that was always quick to smile, only it isn't smiling now, and there's a pounding in my head, because it is her.

It's Anna.

And a baby.

Our daughter has a baby.

She turns around to pull the pram up the steps into the hall, and for a second she looks out into the park and it feels as though she's looking right at me. Tears glint on her cheeks. She shivers, pulls the baby into the safety of the hall, and closes the door.

Anna has a baby.

I have a grandchild.

And even though I know no one could have told me – that nothing cuts communication channels like a death certificate – I feel a rush of anger that this momentous transition from mother to grandmother has taken place without me knowing.

Anna has a baby.

This changes everything. It will change Anna. Motherhood will make her question everything she thought she knew; it will make her examine her life, her relationships.

My death. Yours.

Having a baby makes Anna vulnerable. She has something

40

now she loves more than anything else in the world. And when someone knows that, they can use it against you.

Don't look for answers, Anna. You won't like what you find.

If she goes to the police she'll put herself, and her baby, in danger.

She'll set something in motion that can't be stopped.

SEVEN

ANNA

I've been home for half an hour when the doorbell rings. Laura pulls me into a hug.

'Mark called me. He didn't want you on your own when you were upset.' She gives me another squeeze, then gently pulls away and looks at me, assessing the damage. Guilt seeps through me. I shouldn't have left that message for Mark – there's nothing he could have done and now he'll be worrying all afternoon, distracted from his course and from the drive home.

'I'm fine.'

'You don't look it. Can we go inside? It's bloody freezing out here.' There's nothing to Laura – she's tiny and skinny, with long blonde hair and a baby face that means she's still asked for ID to buy booze, despite being over thirty.

I call Rita, who is standing on the driveway, barking at nothing.

'What's up with her?'

'Invisible squirrels. She's been like this all day. Rita!' Reluctantly the dog comes inside, and I can shut the door. I realise Laura's in jeans, instead of the awful brown and orange uniform of the bank she started at a month ago. 'Shouldn't you be at work?'

'It didn't pan out.' She shrugs off my concern. 'It's fine, honestly. I wasn't enjoying it. Shall I put the kettle on?'

When the tea's made we sit at the island and I show Laura the photographs of the anonymous card. I took them at the police station, not having thought to do so sooner, and the light reflects off the evidence bags, making the contents hard to read.

'And that's all it said?'

'Just that one line.'

'Did the police take it seriously?'

'I think so.' I catch a look in her eyes. 'You don't think they should?'

'Of course they should! Look at it. Look at you – it must have been really upsetting.' She pauses. 'Didn't you get something like this when your dad died?'

'That was different. Those people were crazy.'

She raises an eyebrow. 'You think this is sane?'

I look out of the window for the longest while. I think about the searches Dad made on his phone, checking for high tide, for the best place to jump to his death. I think about the chaplain who listened to Mum cry over her husband's suicide. I think about my parents falling five hundred feet into ice-cold sea. And I wonder if someone pushed them. 'I just want answers, Laura.'

She stares into her tea for a long while before speaking. 'Sometimes they're not the ones we want.'

I was ten when Laura's mum died. I ran to answer the phone, knee-high socks slipping on the hall floor.

'Can I speak to your mum?'

'Laura! When are you coming to see us again?' As Mum's goddaughter, Laura was the big sister I never had. Seven years older, and everything I aspired to be, back when I thought it was important. Cool, fashionable, independent. 'I got Star of the Week today, and—'

'I need your mum, Anna.'

I'd never heard Laura like that. Serious. Sort of cross, I thought, although I realised afterwards she'd simply been trying to hold it all together. I took the phone to Mum.

My mother's crying jags were punctuated with bursts of anger.

I heard her rail at my dad, when I was in bed – supposedly asleep.

'That bloody flat. Damp in every room. Alicia must have told the council about it a hundred times. She found mushrooms in the bathroom. Mushrooms! Her asthma was bad at school, but . . . Mushrooms, for God's sake. No wonder it got worse.'

My dad. Soothing. Too low to hear.

'I mean, they've already said they'll move Laura into a new-build. If that's not an admission of guilt, I don't know what is.'

Only it wasn't. The housing association strenuously denied any liability. The coroner ruled death by natural causes; Alicia's asthma an unfortunate contributory factor.

'You still miss her?' I ask now. It isn't really a question.

'Every day.' Laura meets my eyes. 'I want to tell you it gets easier, but it doesn't.'

I wonder how I'll feel, sixteen years from now. Surely this jagged, raw pain in my chest won't still be choking me, all that time later? It has to ease. It has to. The nightmares will fade, along with the fresh sense of loss when I walk into a room and realise my father's chair is empty. It will get easier. Won't it?

I stand up and crouch beside Ella's bouncy chair. She's sleeping, but I need to distract myself from the surge of emotion. That's the key. Distraction. When Alicia died Laura had no one. I have Ella, and I have Mark. Mark who always knows what to say; always knows how to make me feel better.

My parents sent Mark for me. I know that sounds absurd, but I believe people walk into your life at precisely the right moment for you, and Mark is everything I never knew I needed.

A few days after Mum died I drove to Beachy Head. I had refused to go after Dad's death, even though my mother spent hours up there, walking the cliff tops, standing at the spot from where he was seen to have jumped.

When Mum died as well I wanted to see what my parents

had seen – wanted to try and understand what had gone through their heads. I parked my car and walked to the edge; looked at the sea as it crashed against the rocks. I felt a dizzying rush of vertigo, coupled with a terrifying, irrational urge to jump. I don't believe in an afterlife, but right then I felt close to my parents for the first time since their deaths, and I wished I knew unequivocally I would be reunited with my loved ones in heaven. If I knew that, I thought, I wouldn't hesitate.

The coroner said my mother's suicide was understandable – in so far as any death can be understood. She missed my father.

Dad's death sent Mum mad. She became nervous and paranoid, jumping at noises and refusing to answer the phone. I'd go downstairs in the middle of the night for a glass of water and find the house empty, my mother out for a walk in the early hours.

'I went to see your father.' A memorial stone lay in the churchyard, among the other marks of lost lives. I wept to think of her standing alone by his grave.

'You should have woken me. Wake me, next time.'

She never did.

They're vigilant at Beachy Head. Particularly on Christmas Eve, less than a week after a copycat suicide has been splashed across the national press. I was still staring at the rocks when the chaplain approached, calm and non-judgemental.

'I wasn't going to jump,' I told him afterwards. 'I just wanted to know how it must have felt.'

It wasn't the same chaplain who had spoken to my mother, up there on the cliff top. This man was older, wiser, than the young chaplain who had come to the police station six days before, shaking in his slip-on loafers as he described my mother's rucksack, heavy with rocks; the way her handbag and mobile phone were placed neatly on the grass, just as my father's wallet and phone had been seven months previously.

That chaplain had been close to tears. 'She . . . she said she'd changed her mind.' He kept his eyes resolutely turned from mine. 'She let me walk her back to the car.'

But my mother was a stubborn woman. An hour later she'd returned to the cliffs, set her bag and phone once again to one side, and – so the coroner ruled – killed herself.

The chaplain who spoke to me on Beachy Head last Christmas Eve wasn't taking any chances. He called the police, waiting until they took me gently away; until he could finish his shift knowing no one had died on his watch. I was grateful for his intervention. It scared me to realise we were all a single step from the unthinkable.

I wasn't going to jump, I'd told him. But the truth was I couldn't be sure of that.

When I got back home there was a leaflet stuffed through the letterbox: *Psychotherapy services. Smoking cessation, phobias, confidence. Divorce mediation. Grief counselling.* No doubt the whole street had been leafleted, but it felt like a sign, nonetheless. I phoned before I could change my mind.

I liked Mark instantly. Felt comforted before he'd even spoken. He is tall without being towering, broad-shouldered without being intimidating. His dark eyes have crow's feet that hint at wisdom, and when he listens, he is thoughtful, interested; taking off his glasses as though it will help him hear better. I couldn't have predicted, that first time, that we'd have ended up together. That we'd have a child together. All I knew was that Mark made me feel safe. And he's made me feel safe ever since.

Laura finishes her tea and takes her mug to the sink, where she rinses it and puts it upside down on the draining board. 'How's Mark taken to being a dad?'

I straighten. 'He's obsessed with her. Doesn't even stop to take his coat off when he gets in from work – he goes straight to Ella and takes over. It's just as well men can't breastfeed, or I'd never get a look-in.' I roll my eyes, but of course I'm not complaining. It's great Mark's so hands-on. You don't know what kind of father someone will be, do you? They say we instinctively search out the characteristics we need in a mate: honesty, strength, love. But you don't know whether they'll go out at 3 a.m. for the blackcurrant jelly you crave, or do their fair share of the night-feeds, and by the time you do it's too late to back out. I'm lucky to have Mark. Grateful he stuck by us.

My father never changed a nappy in his life, and as far as I know, Mum never asked him to. It was just the way things were, back then. I imagine Dad looking on as Mark burps Ella, or expertly switches a dirty babygro for a clean one, and I know he'd have made some quip about 'new men'. I push away the image. If I'm honest, I don't know if Dad would have liked Mark at all.

It shouldn't matter. It doesn't matter. Mark's a great dad to Ella, and that's all that counts.

I drank too much, that first date. It took the edge off my nerves and went some way to assuaging the guilt I felt at going out and enjoying myself, less than two months after Mum had died.

'I'm not normally like this,' I said, when we were back at Mark's flat in Putney, and the promised cup of coffee had been abandoned in favour of another glass of wine, the tour of the flat ending abruptly in the bedroom. It sounded like a line, but it wasn't. I'd never slept with anyone on a first date. Or a second or a third. But that night, I felt impetuous. Life was too short not to grab it by the horns.

In reality I was drunk, not empowered. Reckless, not spontaneous. Mark – perhaps a little less drunk, perhaps still conscious of the fine ethical line we were crossing – attempted to slow things down, but I wouldn't be swayed.

The guilt came the following morning. A burning shame that tore through my self-respect and pushed me out of Mark's bed before he woke.

He found me by the front door, putting on my boots.

'You're leaving? I thought we could go out for breakfast.'

I hesitated. He didn't look like a man who'd lost all respect for me, but memories of the night before made me wince. I had a sudden recollection of peeling off my knickers, in a low-grade strip-tease that ended when I lost my balance and toppled onto the bed.

'I have to go.'

'I know a great place around the corner. It's early, still.' The unspoken question – where did I have to be so urgently at eight o'clock on a Sunday morning? – made me say yes.

By nine my hangover had abated, along with my awkwardness. If Mark wasn't embarrassed, why should I be? We agreed on one thing, though: it had happened a little faster than either of us had expected.

'Shall we start again?' Mark suggested. 'Last night was fantastic, but . . . maybe we could have another first date. Get to know each other.'

It was another five weeks before we went to bed again. I didn't know it then, but I was already pregnant.

'Should I take it to the papers?' I ask Laura now.

'You might be jumping ahead a bit.' She winces at her poor turn of phrase. 'Sorry.'

'They wrote an article when Mum died. They might do a follow-up. Appeal for information.' I picture the card.

Suicide? Think again.

'No one came forward at the time, but if Mum was with someone that day – someone who pushed her off the cliff – they must have come across other people.'

'Anna, the chaplain saw your mum.'

I fall silent.

'He talked her back from the edge. She said she wanted to kill herself.'

I want to put my fingers in my ears. *La la la la la.* 'He wasn't there when she actually went over, though, was he? He didn't see if she was alone when she came back.'

There's a pause before Laura speaks. 'So, Caroline's on Beachy Head. She's ready to jump. The chaplain talks her down, then, an hour later, someone murders her?'

She doesn't have to point out how absurd it sounds.

'She could have been trying to get away from someone. Thought that killing herself was better than being killed. Only she couldn't go through with it, and when the chaplain thought he was taking her to safety he was actually delivering her to . . .' I tail off, the pity in Laura's eyes too much to take.

'To who?'

Ella's awake. She's making tiny mewing sounds and pushing her bunched fist into her mouth.

'Who killed her, Anna? Who would have wanted Caroline dead?'

I chew my bottom lip. 'I don't know – one of those idiots who blame everyone else when their car breaks down?'

'Like the idiots who sent the anonymous letters after your dad died?'

'Exactly!' I'm triumphant, thinking she's proved my point, then I see her face and somehow, it's me who's proved hers. The mews become full-blown wails. I take Ella from her bouncy chair and start to feed her.

'Look at you – quite the pro now.' Laura smiles.

In the early days, I could only breastfeed in one particular chair, with a precise arrangement of cushions around me, and no one else in the room to distract Ella from latching on. Nowadays I feed one-handed. Standing up, if I need to.

I don't let Laura change the subject. Her question is an important one. Who would have wanted Mum dead? Some of the car dealers my parents and Billy crossed paths with made no attempts to hide their shady practices. Could Mum and Dad's deaths have been the result of a bad business deal?

49

'Will you help me go through Mum and Dad's study?'

'Now?'

'Is it a problem? Do you need to go?' If Laura can't help, I'll do it on my own. I'm wondering if Mum's campaigning is the key. When I was in my teens she got involved in protests against animal testing at the University of Brighton, earning herself a smattering of hate mail from employees and their families as a result. I don't recall her campaigning against anything more contentious than planning applications and cycle lanes in recent years, but maybe I'll find something in the study that suggests otherwise.

'I don't mean that – I just meant . . . are you sure you want to do it now?'

'Laura, you've spent the best part of a year nagging me to do it!'

'Only because it's ludicrous to have been working at the kitchen table when you could have been using that lovely study. And I wasn't nagging. Although I do think it would have been cathartic, whatever Mark said.'

I keep my response light. 'He does do this sort of thing for a living, you know.'

'What's healthy about shutting everything away and pretending it isn't there?'

'He didn't tell me to pretend it wasn't there, just that I should deal with it when I felt ready.'

'When *he* said you were ready?'

'No. When *I* felt ready.' Firmer now. I know Laura's loyalties – like Uncle Billy's – lie with me, first and foremost, but I wish they were less protective.

It was too fast, that was the problem. Mark and I haven't even been together a year, and our baby is eight weeks old. We're still finding out each other's favourite foods, movies, books. I've only met his mother twice. We're like teenagers, caught out the first time they have sex, except that I'm twenty-six and Mark's forty.

That's part of it, too.

'He's old enough to be your father,' Billy said when I'd got all the announcements over in one go. *I've met someone, he's moving in with me, oh and by the way our baby's due in October.*

'Barely. And Dad was ten years older than Mum.'

'And look how that turned out.'

'What's that supposed to mean?'

But he wouldn't be drawn, and I was secretly glad. I didn't want to know. I'd never wanted to know. When you're young you think your parents are perfect. Perhaps they shout at you a bit too often, or withhold pocket money till your room's been tidied, but they're your parents. They love you. You love them.

I was at university when I realised not everyone's parents were like mine. That not everyone's mum and dad had screaming rows; not everyone's mum and dad took daily trips to the bottle bank. The insight was enough – I didn't want more. I didn't want to know how my parents' marriage worked. If it worked at all. It wasn't my concern.

Like the other ground-floor rooms, the windows in the study are full-height, with painted shutters so rarely used they now don't close. A partners' desk in the centre of the room meant my parents could work at the same time, although the only time they did so was when they were doing the VAT return, the stress of which invariably caused a row.

'Anna, ask your father to pass me the stapler,' Mum said one Saturday, when I'd pushed open the door to the study to see if they'd be much longer. I handed her the stapler myself and went out on my bike until it was all over.

Mostly my parents would take it in turns to stay late at the showroom, until I was old enough to join them at work after school, or to come home on my own.

My hand on the doorknob, I take a deep breath. I don't use this room. I don't go in there. I pretend it doesn't exist.

'You don't have to do this. All the important papers have been gone through.' It's a generously oblique reference to the long day Laura spent, patiently weeding out paperwork from the rest of my parents' belongings, to then spend another day on the phone on my behalf, changing the name on utility bills and cancelling dozens of subscriptions in my parents' names. My gratitude had been tinged with guilt. Who did this for Laura when Alicia died? I pictured a seventeen-year-old Laura in her newly acquired modern council house, sorting through her mother's paperwork, and my heart broke.

'It's time,' I say.

I want to know everything about my parents' lives. Everything I turned a blind eye to; everything I hoped wasn't true. I need to know it all. Who were my parents' friends? Who were their enemies?

Who killed them?

EIGHT

MURRAY

The archivist, Dennis Thompson, had been bordering on the large side when he and Murray had been on shift together. Now Dennis was as wide as he was tall, with a shiny pate and two sets of glasses perched above his eyebrows.

'Can't get on with varifocals.' He retrieved the reading pair and popped them on the bridge of his nose, then peered at the lids of the two files he had found for Murray. 'Tom Johnson. Caroline Johnson.'

The fact that the anonymous card had been delivered on the anniversary of Caroline Johnson's death suggested that was where suspicion lay, but since her death had been so inextricably linked with her husband's, Murray intended to start at the beginning.

'Those are the ones. Thanks.'

Dennis pushed an A4 book across the counter. On each page were neat columns recording signatures against every file removed from the archive, along with the date it was returned. Murray picked up the pen, then hesitated. He looked at his old crewmate.

'I don't suppose . . .'

'On the QT?'

'Please. I'll get them back before you know it.'

Sometimes, Murray concluded, as he left the archive room with the files, there were advantages to having been around as long as he had.

*

He wanted to look through the case file again on the bus home, but there were two response officers – their ties and epaulettes hidden beneath North Face fleeces – sitting directly behind him. They hadn't noticed him (it was funny how invisible you became once you'd retired) but Murray wasn't about to advertise his presence with illicitly obtained police files. Instead he looked out of the window, and wondered what Sarah would think about the Johnson case.

For most of his career Murray had taken his work home. In the early years of their marriage Sarah had struggled through a number of low-paid jobs. Each had required levels of punctuality, politeness and positivity that had proved impossible for Sarah to sustain, and each had triggered long periods of depression when they had ended prematurely. Eventually Sarah had given in to what Murray had suggested from the start: that she stay home and he bring home the bacon. It had been a relief for them both.

Murray had begun sharing snippets of his day with Sarah. He had been conscious of the confidentiality boundaries within which he worked, but he was mindful, too, that on days when Sarah felt unable to leave the house, this insight into the wider world was as important to her as it was interesting. To his surprise, he grew to rely on these exchanges as much as Sarah did, reaping the benefits of a fresh perspective, untarnished by police prejudice. He looked forward to telling her about Tom and Caroline Johnson.

The bus stopped at the end of Murray's street, a cul-de-sac of chalet bungalows built in the sixties and occupied by a mix of first-timers, families and pensioners. Several of the bungalows had been extended so much they were now rather grand two-storey detached houses, their back gardens decked for summer barbecues. With the exception of new carpets and a lick of paint every few years, Murray's house looked exactly the way it had looked when he and Sarah bought it in 1984, the year he finished his probationary period and was confirmed as a police officer.

Murray didn't get off the bus. Instead, he stayed on for another five stops, thanking the driver and walking the short distance to Highfield. Once a rather grand country home, the Grade II listed building was built in 1811 and had been used by the NHS since the early fifties. Surrounded by lovely gardens, the historic effect was marred somewhat by the surrounding Portakabins and cheap, flat-roofed buildings installed to house the growing department that was needed to support its patients. Patients like Sarah.

Murray was familiar with most parts of Highfield. There was a well-attended drop-in centre, with craft activities, a patient-run café and a peer support group. There were outpatient clinics, counselling services, and cookery classes for patients with eating disorders. There were wards for patients with various mental health problems, requiring varying levels of support, including a high-security ward on which Sarah had spent ten days in 2007, and which Murray could no longer pass without remembering the awful day he had pleaded with the doctors to section his wife.

Sarah had been upfront about her diagnosis the first time she and Murray had met; at the buffet lunch laid on after Murray's passing-out parade. Her older brother Karl had been part of the same intake, and although the two men hadn't been friends, Murray had been drawn to the vivacious girl standing with Karl's family. He'd wondered if she was Karl's girlfriend; had been relieved to discover she wasn't.

'You know I'm mental, right?' Sarah had thrown it down like a challenge. She'd been wearing enormous silver hooped earrings that swung when she laughed, and a luminous pink batwing jumper that hurt his eyes.

Murray hadn't laughed. Partly because political correctness

had been part of his make-up long before it had become part of police vocabulary, but mainly because he couldn't reconcile the term with the woman opposite him. She had so much energy she couldn't stay still, and her eyes sparkled as though they saw joy in everything. There was nothing 'mental' about Sarah.

'Borderline Personality Disorder.' She'd smiled that big smile again. 'It sounds worse than it is, I promise.'

BPD. Those three letters had bookended their relationship ever since. Murray had swiftly realised the sparkle appeared only on Sarah's better days, and that between times the pain and fear in those slate grey eyes would be unbearable.

Currently Sarah was a voluntary patient on a ward where Murray knew everyone by name. Visiting hours were restricted, but staff were understanding about Murray's shift patterns, and he signed his name in the book and waited in the family room while someone fetched Sarah.

Family rooms were different in every hospital and clinic. Sometimes you'd feel you were in a prison visiting centre, with stark walls and a uniformed member of staff watching over you. In other places they were more relaxed, with sofas and a TV, and staff dressed so casually you'd have to check for a name badge to make sure they weren't patients.

The family room at Highfield fell somewhere in between. It was divided into two sections. In the first, an arts and craft table boasted coloured paper and pots of felt-tip pens. Fiddly sticky pads were provided for children and their parents to embellish their homemade cards, without the safety risks presented by stolen rolls of Sellotape. The scissors were plastic-coated with rounded ends. In the second part of the room, where Murray took a seat, were sofas and low coffee tables scattered with magazines several months out of date.

Sarah put her arms around him and hugged him hard.

'How are you feeling?'

Sarah wrinkled her nose. 'There's a new girl in the room next

to me who bangs her head against the wall when she's stressed.'
She paused. 'She's stressed a lot.'

'Hard to sleep?'

Sarah nodded.

'Be quieter at home . . .' Murray saw the flicker of anxiety across Sarah's face. He didn't push it. It had been three weeks since Sarah had cut herself so badly she'd needed stitches in both wrists. A cry for help, the A&E sister had said, when it was discovered that Sarah had already called an ambulance; a bag in the hall containing the few things she'd need at Highfield.

'I could feel it happening again,' she'd said to Murray, when he'd broken every speed limit to get to the hospital.

It. An indefinable, overwhelming presence in their lives. *It* stopped Sarah going out. *It* meant she found it hard to make friends and even harder to keep them. *It* lay beneath the surface of Murray's and Sarah's lives. Always there, always waiting.

'Why didn't you phone Mr Chaudhury?' Murray had said.

'He wouldn't admit me.'

Murray had held her, trying to empathise but finding it impossible to relate to a logic that saw self-harming as the only route into a place of safety.

'I had an interesting day,' he said now.

Sarah's eyes lit up. She sat on the sofa cross-legged, with her back against the arm. Murray had never seen his wife sit properly on a sofa. She would lie on the floor, or sprawl with her head dangling off the edge of the seat and her legs stretched up so her toes touched the wall. Today Sarah was wearing a long grey linen dress, teamed with a bright orange hoodie with sleeves that she'd pulled over her hands so often they now stayed there of their own accord.

'A woman came in to report that her parents' suicides were, in fact, murders.'

'Do you believe her?' As usual, Sarah cut straight to the chase.

Murray hesitated. Did he? 'I honestly don't know.' He told

Sarah about Tom and Caroline Johnson: about their rucksacks filled with rocks, the witness reports, the chaplain's intervention. Finally, he told her about the anonymous anniversary card, and Anna Johnson's insistence that he re-open the investigations into her parents' deaths.

'Were either of the parents suicidal?'

'Not according to Anna Johnson. Caroline Johnson had no history of depression prior to her husband's death, and *his* suicide had come completely out of the blue.'

'Interesting.' There was a spark in Sarah's eyes, and Murray felt warmth spread through him. When Sarah was unwell her world shrank. She lost interest in anything outside of her own life, displaying a selfishness that was far removed from the woman she really was. Her interest in the Johnson job was a good sign – a great sign – and Murray was doubly glad he had decided to take a look at the case.

It hadn't troubled him that the subject matter might have been insensitive for a woman with a long history of self-harm; he had never tiptoed around Sarah in the way that so many of their friends had done.

They had been having coffee with a colleague of Murray's one time, when a discussion had begun on Radio 4 about suicide rates among young people. Alan had lunged across his kitchen to turn off the radio, leaving Murray and Sarah exchanging amused glances.

'I'm ill,' Sarah had said gently, when Alan had taken his seat again, and the kitchen was quiet. 'It doesn't mean we can't talk about mental health issues, or suicide.' Alan had looked to Murray for reassurance, and Murray had staunchly refused to make eye contact. Nothing was more likely to upset the tightrope on which Sarah lived than thinking she was being judged. Talked about.

'If anything, it makes me more interested than your average

lay-person,' Sarah had continued. 'And frankly,' she had given Alan a wicked grin, 'if anyone's an expert on suicide around here, it's me.'

People liked boxes, Murray had concluded. You were ill or you were well. Mad or sane. Sarah's problem was that she climbed in and out of a box, and people didn't know how to deal with that.

'Have you got the files with you?' Sarah looked around for his briefcase.

'I haven't looked at them myself yet.'

'Bring them tomorrow?'

'Sure.' He looked at his watch. 'I'd better go. Hope you get a bit more sleep tonight.'

She walked him to the door and hugged him goodbye, and Murray kept a smile on his face until he was safely out of sight. Sometimes it was easier to leave Sarah at Highfield when she was having a bad day. Easier to go home when she was curled up in a ball on her bed, because he knew she was in the best possible place. That she'd be safe; looked after. But when Sarah was calm – happy, even – every step away felt like a step in the wrong direction. How could Highfield, with its clinical smell and cell-like bedrooms, be better than their comfortable, cosy bungalow? How could Sarah feel safer in hospital than at home?

Later, when he'd cleared away his plate, and washed the pan he'd used for his omelette, Murray sat at the table and opened the Johnsons' files. He read through the call logs, the witness statements and the police reports. He looked at photographs of exhibits – of Tom Johnson's abandoned wallet, and his wife's handbag – and read the text messages sent by each of them prior to their deaths. He scrutinised the summing-up from each inquest, and the coroner's verdict of suicide.

Murray laid everything out on the kitchen table, along with

the evidence bag containing the anonymous card sent to Anna Johnson, which he placed in the middle, between her parents' files. After reading through the coroner's reports one more time, he put them at the back of the table and snapped open a brand-new notebook: as symbolic as it was practical. If Anna's mother had been murdered, Murray needed to approach this investigation as though it were fresh out of the box, and that meant starting from the beginning, with Tom Johnson's suicide.

Murray had become a detective in 1989, when files had still been written longhand, and cracking a crime had meant legwork, not cyber sleuthing. By 2012, when Murray had retired, the job had changed beyond all recognition, and among the feelings of loss as he handed in his warrant card was a barely acknowledged streak of relief. He had found it increasingly hard to get to grips with technology, and still preferred to write his statements with the engraved fountain pen that had been Sarah's present to him when he had won a place on CID.

For a second Murray felt his confidence waver. Who did he think he was, that he'd find something in these files that hadn't been seen before? He was sixty. Retired from the force and now working as a civilian. He'd spent the last five years checking driving licences and taking reports of lost property.

He fiddled with the fountain pen in his hand. Ran his finger over the writing. *DC Mackenzie.* Pulling his sleeve over his hand he buffed the silver until it shone. He wished Sarah were there.

Remember that post office robbery? he imagined her saying. *There were no leads. No forensics. No one had a clue. No one except you.*

They'd been close to filing the job, but Murray hadn't let it lie. He'd hit the streets, knocking on doors, shaking up the community. He'd tapped up his network of informants, and gradually a name had emerged. The lad had gone down for fourteen years.

That was a long time ago, a voice whispered in his head. Murray shook it away. He gripped his pen. The job might have changed, but criminals hadn't. Murray had been a good detective. One of the best. That hadn't changed.

NINE

Anna and Laura are picking through the life we left behind. I don't like it. I want to intervene – to stop them opening drawers and holding up notebooks and books and boxes of photographs.

The aftermath of a death is an unwanted gift to our loved ones. It is our children, our spouses, our friends who must tie up the loose ends and clear away the remnants of a sudden departure. I did it for my parents, at their house in Essex; you did the same for yours, here in Eastbourne. Now Anna's doing it for me. For the two of us.

I watch Laura pick up a ceramic pot that once held a succulent – dried earth clinging to the inside – and discard it. Two distinct piles are emerging on either side of the desk, and I wonder who is driving this efficiency. Anna? Or Laura? Did she make Anna sort through our belongings today? Is Laura pushing her unwittingly towards danger?

They're talking. Too distant for me to make out the words. My glimpse into this scene is narrow, obscured. It frustrates me because unless I know what's happening now, how can I influence what happens next?

Our granddaughter lies on a padded mat, beneath an arch from which hang brightly coloured animals. She kicks her legs and Anna smiles at her, and my breath catches for a second as I imagine being a mother who could walk through the door as though she'd never been away. A mother who hadn't missed a year of one life; the birth of a whole new one.

There are no decorations up, no twinkling lights on the

bannister or wreath on the door. It is four days until Christmas, and I wonder if they are waiting until Christmas Eve – forming new traditions as a family – or whether the absence of festive cheer is intentional. Whether Anna can't face the sight of tinsel and tawdry baubles.

Laura is looking through my diary. I see Anna glance at her; bite her bottom lip as if to stop herself from commenting. I know what she's thinking.

We'd been at Oak View for a year when the burglary happened. They didn't take a lot – there wasn't a lot to take – but they rifled through the whole house, leaving destruction in their wake. A messy search, the police called it. It was weeks before the house was back to normal, and months before I felt at ease again. There was nothing secret about our lives – not back then – but still I felt angry that someone knew so much about me, when I knew nothing about them.

That same feeling of anger returns as I watch Laura flick through the pages of my appointment diary. There's nothing of consequence in there, but the intrusion is unbearable. Stop it, I want to shout. Stop looking through my things, get out of my house!

Only it isn't my house any more. It's Anna's. And she laughs at something Laura says, and smiles a sad smile when Laura points something out that I'm not permitted to see. I am excluded. But Anna's laugh is short. Polite. Her smile doesn't reach her eyes. She doesn't want to be doing this.

Laura looks like her mother. I was at school with Alicia; the only person she told when, a week before her sixteenth birthday, she discovered she was pregnant. Skinny as a rake, she was showing before she was eight weeks gone, and out on her ear not long after, when the baggy jumpers she'd adopted did nothing to fool her mum.

When I left school two years later, my PA job just about covering an apartment with a lift and communal laundry, with enough left over for weekend chips and wine, Alicia was living on benefits in a high-rise in Battersea.

I took them on holiday. We spent three nights in a B&B in Derbyshire, sharing a double bed, with Laura in between.

'We should get a place together,' Alicia said, on the last day. 'We'd have the best time.'

How could I tell her that wasn't what I wanted from my life? That I'd been careful not to fall pregnant; that I loved my single life and my friends and my job? How could I tell her that I didn't want to live in a damp flat, and that – however much I liked spending time with her and Laura – I didn't want to live with someone else's baby?

'The best,' I agreed, and then I changed the subject.

I should have helped more.

Anna kneels on the carpet and pulls open the bottom drawer of the desk. It comes out with more force than she expects and she falls back, the drawer on her lap. I see Laura look up to check she's okay; watch Anna laugh at her own clumsiness. Laura goes back to the pile of my diaries, and Anna lifts the drawer to slot it back into the desk, but something stops her. She's seen something.

Anna sets the drawer to one side and reaches a hand into the base of the pedestal. I see her glance at Laura to check she isn't watching, and as Anna's eyes widen I know, as clearly as if I could see it, that her hand has closed around the smooth glass of a vodka bottle.

There's disappointment on her face.

I know that feeling, too.

She pulls out her hand, empty. Pushes the drawer back into the desk and leaves the bottle in its hiding place. She says nothing to Laura, and the feeling of exclusion disappears, thanks to this small complicity Anna isn't even aware of. Some secrets shouldn't be shared outside the family.

Others shouldn't be shared at all.

TEN

ANNA

I catch Laura looking at her watch. She's working her way through a stack of papers, heaping half of them onto a pile for the shredder. It's making me itch. Anything relating to work should be in the showroom, but what if she accidentally destroys something important? I'm a director of the business – albeit a somewhat passive one. I can't just throw paperwork away without checking what it's for.

The weight of my gaze makes Laura look up. 'All right?'

'You should get off. Mark'll be back soon.'

'I promised I'd stay till he got back.' She puts another sheaf of papers on the shredding pile.

'Blame me.' I haul myself to my feet and hold out a hand to help Laura up.

'We haven't finished sorting this lot.'

'We've done loads. It's practically finished.' It's a gross exaggeration. Laura's piles of 'things to keep' and 'things to throw' have merged, and I'm no longer sure whether I'm keeping a giant ball of rubber bands because I'm sentimental, or because they're useful, or because they've slid from one pile to the other.

'It's a mess!'

'That's easily solved.' I pick up Ella, usher Laura out of the room, and shut the study door. 'Ta da!'

'Anna! I thought we agreed that wasn't the way to deal with things?'

You agreed, I think, then immediately feel unfair. It was my idea to sort through my parents' study. Me who asked Laura to help. 'I'm not ignoring it because it's upsetting, though. I'm ignoring it because I don't want to tidy any more. Completely different.'

Laura narrows her eyes at me, unconvinced by my breezy tone. 'What are you going to do about the card?'

'You're probably right. Some sick joker with an axe to grind.'

'Right.' She's still not sure if she should leave me.

'I'm fine, I promise. I'll call you tomorrow.' I find her coat and wait patiently while she looks for her keys.

'If you're sure . . .'

'I am.' We hug, and as she walks to her car I stand at the door, one hand on Rita's collar to stop her running after phantom squirrels.

Laura's car gives a splutter, then cuts out. She grimaces. Tries again, revving hard to keep it from cutting out, and backs out of the driveway, waving from the open window.

When I can no longer hear the sound of her car, I return to the study. I survey the piles of papers, the birthday cards, the pens and paperclips and Post-it notes. There are no answers here, only memories.

Memories I want to keep.

I take the lid off a box of photographs and sift through them. On top are six or seven photos of Mum and Laura's mum, Alicia. In one they're in a sunny pub garden; in another a café, having a cream tea. In another the photo has been taken from an angle, as though the camera was propped up and slipping to one side. Mum and Alicia lie on their stomachs on a bed, Laura between them. She's perhaps two years old, which makes Mum and Alicia no more than eighteen. Just kids themselves.

There are dozens more photos in the box, but all – as far as I can tell – of Dad, the showroom, me as a baby.

I have lots of photos of Dad, but hardly any of Mum. Always

behind the lens, never in front of it – like so many women once they have a family. So intent on documenting their children's lives before they grow too old, it doesn't occur to them to document their own. That one day, their children will want to pore over photos of a time they were too young to remember.

In the short time between Mum going missing and her suicide being established, I gave the police the only clear photo I had of her, which lived in a silver frame on the mantelpiece in the siting room. They circulated it immediately, and when news of her death broke, the papers used the same photo to accompany the story. The police gave me back the framed picture, but every time I looked at it, I saw the headlines. Eventually I had to put it away.

Apart from their wedding photo, where she's hardly visible beneath the floppy hat that was all the rage at the time, there are no other photos of Mum on display. I put the ones of Mum and Alicia to one side so I can have a couple framed.

I open Mum's 2016 appointment diary. It's a fat A4 book, with each day over two pages: appointments on the left and space for notes on the opposite side. It's nothing fancy – a corporate gift from a car manufacturer – but I run my fingers over the gilt-embossed logo, and feel the weight of the pages as it falls open in my hands. The diary is filled with Mum's writing, and the words are illegible until I blink hard to stop them swimming. Every day is full. Meetings with suppliers. Repair visits booked for the photocopier, the coffee machine, the water cooler. On the right-hand side, that day's to-do list, with items neatly scored through when complete. *If you want something done, ask a busy person* – wasn't that what they said? Mum couldn't have fitted more into her life if she'd tried, yet I never heard her complain she had too much on her plate. When her own mother – a crotchety woman who rationed her affection like wartime sugar – was admitted to a hospice, Mum drove each day from Eastbourne to Essex, returning only once Granny was sleeping.

It was only afterwards Dad and I found out about the lump Mum had found in her own breast; the anxious wait she'd had for the all-clear.

'I didn't want to worry you,' was all she'd say.

The mix of work and home in the diary blindsides me. *Adele tickets for A's birthday?* is sandwiched between a reminder to call a Katie Clements back about a test drive, and the phone number for the local radio station. I press the heels of my palms into my eyes. I wish I'd looked through Mum and Dad's things earlier; I wish I'd known on my birthday what she'd thought of as a present.

I can't help myself – I turn to 21 December and look at the day she died. There are two appointments and a list of tasks left incomplete. Tucked into the back of the diary are a handful of business cards, leaflets and scribbled notes. The diary is a cross-section of Mum's life, as illuminating as an autobiography and as personal as a journal. I slip the photos inside and hug the book to my chest for a moment, and then I start to put everything back where it came from.

I replace the desk tidy, and with it the paperweight I made from clay and painted when I was in primary school. It used to live on the dresser in the kitchen, holding down the myriad classroom letters.

I run my finger over the superglued crack that divides it neatly in two, and I have a sudden, sharp memory of the sound it made when it hit the wall.

There were apologies.

Tears. Mine. Mum's.

'Good as new,' Dad said, once the glue had dried. But it wasn't, and nor was the patch of wall where he filled the dent and painted over it in a shade that didn't quite match what had gone before. I wouldn't talk to him for days.

I pull out the bottom drawer of the desk and retrieve the

68

bottle of vodka. It's empty. Most of them are. They're everywhere. At the back of the wardrobe; in the toilet cistern; wrapped in a towel in the depths of the airing cupboard. I find them, I pour away the contents, and I push the glass to the bottom of the recycling bin.

If there were bottles before I went to university, they were better hidden. Or I didn't notice them. I returned home to a life that had altered in my absence. Were my parents drinking more, or had I had my eyes opened to a world beyond the narrow scope of my childhood? After I found the first bottle there seemed to be hundreds – like learning a word and then seeing it everywhere.

An involuntary shiver tickles my spine. *Someone walking over your grave*, Mum used to say. It's dark outside. I catch a glimpse of something moving in the garden. My heart thumps, but when I look properly, it's my own pale face staring back at me, distorted by the old glass.

A noise outside makes me jump. *Pull yourself together, Anna*.

It's this room. It's full of memories, not all of them good. It's making me jumpy. I'm imagining things. A ghostly figure in the window, footsteps outside.

But wait: I *do* hear footsteps . . .

Slow and deliberate, as though the owner were trying not to be heard. A soft crunch of gravel underfoot.

There's someone outside.

There are no lights on upstairs, and none down here, save for the desk light in the study. From the outside the house will be in near darkness.

Could it be a burglar? This street is filled with high-value properties, crammed with antiques and paintings bought as much for investment as for show. As the business grew, my parents spent their money on beautiful things, many of which could be easily seen through the downstairs windows. Perhaps someone came by earlier, when Ella and I were at the police station, and decided to return under cover of darkness. Maybe – a hard knot of fear forms in my throat – maybe they've been observing for a while. All day I've been unable to lose the feeling I'm being watched, and now I wonder if my instincts have been correct.

As a child, I knew the code for the burglar alarm long before I could memorise our telephone number, but it hasn't been set since Mark moved in. He wasn't used to living in a house with an alarm. He'd set it off every time he came home, cursing in frustration as he fumbled with the keypad.

'Rita's enough of a deterrent, surely?' he said, after telling the alarm company that yes, it was *another* false alarm. I'd fallen out of the habit of setting it myself, and now that I was home all day with Ella, we had stopped using it entirely.

I consider setting it now, but I know I won't be able to fathom how to zone it in the dark, and the thought of being there, by the front door, as a burglar tries to get in, brings goosebumps to my arms.

I should take Ella upstairs. I can pull the chest of drawers in her room across the door. They can take what they want from down here – it doesn't matter. I assess the sitting room with an objective eye, wondering what they're after. The television, I suppose, and the obvious things like the silver punchbowl that once belonged to my great grandmother, and now holds African violets. On the mantelpiece are two porcelain birds I bought for my parents on their anniversary. They aren't valuable, but they look as though they could be. Should I take them with me? If I take the birds, what else should I take? So many memories in this house; so much I would grieve over. Impossible to take it all.

It's hard to work out exactly where the footsteps are. The quiet crunch of gravel gets louder, as though the prowler walked first to one side of the house, and is now returning to the other. I take up my mobile, lying next to the baby monitor. Should I call the police? A neighbour?

I pick up my mobile phone and scroll through the numbers

until I find Robert Drake's. I hesitate, not wanting to call him, but knowing it makes sense to do so. He's a surgeon, he'll be good in an emergency, and if he's still at home next door he can come out and take a look, or just turn on the outside lights and scare off whoever's out there . . .

His phone is switched off.

The crunch of footsteps on gravel gets louder, competing with the rush of blood singing in my ears. I hear a dragging noise. A ladder?

To the side of the house, between the gravelled front drive and the landscaped back garden, is a narrow strip of land with a shed and a log store. I hear a dull bang that could be the shed door. My heart accelerates. I think of the anonymous card, of my haste to take it to the police. Did I do the wrong thing? Was the card meant as a warning – that whatever happened to Mum could happen to me, too?

Maybe it isn't burglars outside.

Maybe whoever killed my mother wants me dead, too.

ELEVEN

MURRAY

Tom Johnson had been missing for fifteen hours when his wife, Caroline Johnson – at forty-eight, ten years Tom's junior – called the police. She hadn't seen Tom since they'd had what she called a 'stupid spat' as they'd left work the previous day.

'He said he was going to the pub,' her statement read. 'When he didn't come home I thought he'd gone to his brother's to sleep it off.' Their daughter Anna, who lived at home with them, had been away at a conference in London with the children's charity for whom she had worked since leaving university.

Tom Johnson hadn't turned up for work the next day.

Murray found the statement from Billy Johnson, Tom's brother and business partner, who had been unconcerned by Tom's absence.

'I assumed he had a hangover. He's a partner. What was I supposed to do? Give him a final warning?' Even in the dry black and white of a witness statement, Billy Johnson came across as defensive. It was a natural reaction for many people; a way of diffusing the guilt they felt at not seeming to have cared enough when it mattered.

The MisPer report had been completed by Uniform and graded as low-risk. Murray looked at the officer's name but didn't recognise it. None of the information at that stage had suggested that Tom Johnson had been vulnerable, but that wouldn't have stopped questions being asked when his suicide was reported; it wouldn't have stopped that officer questioning their own judgement. Would grading Tom as high-risk have changed anything? It was impossible to know. Nothing about Tom Johnson's disappearance had given rise to concern. He was a successful businessman, well known across the town. A family man with no history of depression.

The first text message had come at 9.30 a.m.

I'm sorry.

Ironically, Caroline Johnson had been relieved.

'I thought he was apologising for the row we'd had,' she said in her statement. 'He shouted at me – said a few things that had upset me. He had a temper, but he always said sorry afterwards. When the text came, I thought at least he's okay.'

He had a temper.

Murray underlined the words. How much of a temper had Tom Johnson had? Could he have argued with someone at the pub that night? Got into a fight? Enquiries at Tom's usual haunts had drawn a blank. Wherever he'd gone to drown his sorrows the night before he died, it hadn't been his local.

A request by the attending officer to trace Tom's phone had been refused, as at that stage there had been no evidence of a threat to life. Murray winced on behalf of the senior officer who'd made *that* call. It was a decision that had swiftly been reversed when Caroline had received a second text from her husband.

'I think he's going to kill himself . . .'

Murray listened to the recording of Caroline Johnson's 999 call. He closed his eyes, feeling her distress pulse through him as though it were his own. He heard her read out the message she had received from her husband; noted the calm response from the operator as she asked Caroline what was her husband's number and could she please keep that text message?

I can't do this any more. The world will be a better place without me in it.

He couldn't do what?

It was the sort of heat-of-the-moment comment anyone might make. It could mean nothing, or it could mean everything.

I can't do this any more.

Stay married? Have an affair? Lie?

What had Tom Johnson been doing that had led to such an outpouring of guilt?

There had been no further texts. Tom Johnson's mobile had rung out. Triangulation placed it near Beachy Head. ANPR cameras pinpointed the car he'd taken from work heading towards the same location and officers were despatched. Even though Murray knew the outcome of the job, he felt a pounding in his chest as he read through the pages of the log, imagining how it would have felt for the police officers involved in the race to save a life.

A call from a member of the public – Diane Brent-Taylor – reported seeing a man put rocks into a rucksack. It had struck her as an odd activity for a man in a suit, and she stood and watched as he made his way to the edge of the cliff. Horrified, she saw him remove his wallet and phone from his pocket, before taking a step forward and disappearing. Murray read the transcript of the call.

'The tide's high. There's nothing there. I can't see him.'

Coastal Rescue were in the water within minutes, but it was already too late. There was no sign of Tom Johnson.

Murray took a steadying breath. He wondered how Ralph Metcalfe, the coroner, coped with hearing stories about the dead day in, day out. He wondered whether he got used to it, or whether he went home and sank into a bottle of something to numb the senses.

Officers had scoured the area where Mrs Brent-Taylor had

described seeing Tom go over the edge. They had found his wallet and his mobile phone, the screen still showing the frantic messages from his wife.

Where are you?
Don't do this.
We need you . . .

Police had broken the news to Caroline Johnson in the kitchen of her home address, where she had been surrounded by family. A photocopied pocket notebook entry from PC Woodward listed the names, occupations and contact details of the friends and family who had gathered to support Caroline.

William (Billy) Johnson. Director at Johnson's Cars. Brother-in-law.

Robert Drake. Consultant surgeon, Royal Sussex. Neighbour.

Laura Barnes. Receptionist at Hard as Nails. Goddaughter.

Anna Johnson's details – *Regional Coordinator for Save the Children. Daughter* – had been recorded on a later page, suggesting she had arrived after PC Woodward had taken the initial roll call.

In the days following Tom Johnson's death, numerous enquiries had been carried out as CID officers had put together a file for the coroner. The content of Tom's smartphone had been extracted, including web searches made in the early hours of 18 May for: *Beachy Head suicide location* and *tide times Beachy Head.* Murray noted that high tide had occurred at 10.04 a.m., Diane Brent-Taylor's call coming in only a minute later. The water would have been around six metres deep at that point. Easily deep enough to swallow a man weighed down with rocks, the undertow dragging him out past the tideline. If his body was ever recovered, what would be left of him, nineteen months on? Would there be anything to say whether Tom Johnson was alone on the edge of the cliffs that morning?

The witness, Diane Brent-Taylor, hadn't seen anyone with Tom. She'd refused to give a statement or to attend an inquest. After several telephone conversations, during which Diane had been evasive to the point of obstruction, the police call handler had finally established that Diane had been on Beachy Head with a married man with whom she had been having an affair. The clandestine couple had been as anxious to keep their rendez-vous a secret as the police were to take a statement, and nothing could persuade Diane to commit her name to paper.

The timeline in Murray's notebook was complete. The investigation into Tom Johnson's death had been concluded within a fortnight, the file submitted and the CID officers assigned to other jobs. There had been a delay of several months while permission had been obtained to hold an inquest without a body, but as far as the investigation was concerned, the job was done. Suicide. Tragic, but not suspicious. End of story.

Except was it?

There were several CDs in the box file of CCTV footage seized during the immediate fear for Tom Johnson's welfare. They didn't appear to have been viewed, and Murray imagined the case had already reached its sad conclusion before the officers had had a chance to look at the hours of footage they potentially contained. Could the discs hold evidence of a crime so well hidden it was never even identified as one?

The brand-new Audi, taken by Tom from Johnson's Cars on the day he disappeared, had been given a cursory search, but with everything pointing towards suicide, not murder, no budget was allocated for forensic testing. Like the CCTV, though, evidence had been secured, and Murray wondered if there was any point in submitting the swabs and stray hairs seized from the car.

But what would that prove? There was no suspect with whom to compare evidence seized, and the car was a forecourt special; who knew how many test drives it had hosted?

More pertinently, how would Murray get a submission signed

off when he wasn't even supposed to be dealing with the job? So far nothing Murray had found suggested anything was amiss in the coroner's verdict of suicide.

Perhaps Caroline Johnson's file would yield more interest.

The police response to Anna Johnson's 999 call had been swift and extensive. The family's address was already flagged, and this time there was no question of grading Caroline Johnson as anything other than a high-risk vulnerable MisPer.

'My father's death hit her hard,' Anna Johnson's statement read. 'I had started working from home so I could keep an eye on her – I was really worried. She didn't eat, she was jumpy every time the phone rang, and some days she wouldn't even get out of bed.'

So far, so normal, Murray thought. Grief hit everyone in a different way, and bereavement by suicide carried an extra burden. Guilt – however misplaced – weighed heavy on the soul.

On 21 December Caroline Johnson had told her daughter she needed some air.

'She'd been distracted all day,' Anna had said. 'I kept catching her looking at me, and twice she told me she loved me. She was behaving oddly, but I put it down to the fact that we were both dreading our first Christmas without Dad.'

At lunchtime Caroline went to get milk.

'She took the car. I should have realised straight away some-thing was wrong – we always get milk from the shop at the end of the road. It's quicker to walk. As soon as I noticed the car had gone, I knew something awful was going to happen.'

The police were called at 3 p.m. A response officer who knew the family's history, and with too many Beachy Head jobs under his belt to be optimistic, had phoned the chaplaincy office. For years the charity had offered crisis intervention, proactive patrols and search teams, all aimed at reducing Beachy Head's annual death toll. An eager chaplain had confirmed that yes, he had indeed seen a woman matching that description, but that the officer could rest easy, she hadn't jumped.

Murray put down Anna Johnson's statement and found the entry on the call log where the update from the attending officer, PC 956 Gray, had been posted:

CHAPLAIN STATES HE HAD A LONG CONVERSATION ON EDGE OF CLIFF WITH AN ICI FEMALE IN HER FIFTIES. SUBJECT WAS IN A DISTRESSED STATE AND CARRYING RUCKSACK FILLED WITH STONES. SUBJECT STATED HER NAME WAS CAROLINE AND THAT SHE HAD RECENTLY LOST HER HUSBAND TO SUICIDE.

The chaplain had talked Caroline back from the edge.

'I waited while she took the stones out of her rucksack,' his statement read. 'We walked back to the car park. I told her God was always ready to listen. To forgive. That nothing was so bad God wouldn't help us through it.'

Murray admired those whose faith gave them such immense peace of mind. He wished he felt that depth of belief when he went into a church, but there were too many terrible things in the world for him to accept they were all part of God's grand plan.

Had even the chaplain's faith been shaken by what happened next? Had he sent up a prayer to help him come to terms with it?

Caroline's photo had been circulated, additional patrols sent to Beachy Head. Coastguard rescue worked in conjunction with the police, with the chaplaincy, as they were so often required to do. Volunteers and salaried officers working side by side. Different backgrounds, different training, but the same aim. To find Caroline Johnson alive.

Caroline's phone had been identified as being at or near Beachy Head, and just after 5 p.m., her handbag and mobile phone were found by a dog walker on the edge of the cliff. The tide had been at its highest at 4.33 p.m. that day.

A BMW, parked in the car park at Beachy Head with the keys in the ignition, was quickly traced back to Johnson's Cars, where Billy Johnson confirmed that the description given by the chaplain matched that of his sister-in-law, Caroline Johnson, a fellow director of Johnson's Cars, and the recent widow of Billy's brother, Tom Johnson.

With the exception of the suicidal texts – Caroline had sent none – it was a carbon copy of Tom Johnson's suicide, seven months previously. How must Anna have felt, to answer the door to another policeman with his hat in his hands? To sit in the kitchen with the same friends and family gathered around? Another investigation, another funeral, another inquest.

Murray put down the file and let out a slow sigh. How many times had Sarah tried to take her own life?

Too many to count.

The first had come a few weeks into their relationship, when Murray had gone to play squash with a colleague instead of seeing Sarah. He had returned home to find seven messages on his answerphone, each more desperate than the last.

Murray had panicked that time. And the next. Sometimes there were months between attempts; on other occasions Sarah would try several times a day to end her life. It would be these times that would prompt another stay at Highfield.

Gradually he had learned that what Sarah needed was for him to be calm. To be there. Not judging, not panicking. And so he would come home and hold her, and if she didn't need to go to hospital – as, more often than not, she didn't – Murray would bathe her arms and gently wrap gauze across the cuts, and reassure her he wasn't going anywhere. And only when Sarah was in bed – the lines on her forehead smoothed out by sleep – would Murray put his head in his hands and weep.

Murray rubbed his face. *Focus.* This job was supposed to fill some time. Distracting him from thinking about Sarah, not sending him down memory lanes he wished he'd never travelled.

He looked at his notebook, now filled with his neat handwriting. Nothing seemed out of place. So why would someone question Caroline's death? To stir up trouble? To upset Anna?

79

Suicide? Think again.

Something had transpired that day that wasn't in the police file. Something the investigating officers hadn't seen. It happened. Not often, but it happened. Sloppy detectives, or simply busy ones. Prioritising other cases; filing the dead ends when perhaps – just perhaps – there were more questions to ask. More answers to find.

Murray picked up the final sheaf of paperwork: miscellaneous documents in no apparent order – a photograph of Caroline Johnson, a copy of the contact list from her phone, and a copy of Tom Johnson's life assurance policy.

Murray looked at the latter. And looked again.

Tom Johnson had been worth a considerable amount of money.

Murray hadn't seen Anna's house, but he knew the street – a quiet, sought-after avenue with its own gated park – and properties there didn't come cheap. Murray assumed the house would have been jointly owned by the Johnsons, and would since have passed to their daughter, as would, he imagined, the pay-out from Tom's hefty life assurance policy. And that was before you factored in the family business, of which Anna now had joint control.

Whichever way you looked at it, Anna Johnson was an extremely wealthy woman.

TWELVE

ANNA

I fumble with my phone, finding *recent calls* and pressing Mark's number as I tiptoe into the hall towards the stairs, Ella in my arms. I silently beseech her not to make a sound.

And then three things happen.

The crunch of gravel beneath feet becomes the solid tap of shoes on steps.

The tinny ringing of Mark's phone at my ear is mirrored by a louder version coming from outside the house.

And the front door opens.

When Mark walks into the house, his ringing mobile still in his hand, he finds me standing in the hall, wild-eyed and high from the adrenalin coursing through my veins.

'You rang, m'lady?' He grins and taps his phone to end the call.

Slowly, I lower my own mobile from my ear, my heart-rate refusing to accept the danger has passed. I laugh awkwardly, relief making me as light-headed as fear did a moment ago.

'I heard someone walking around outside. I thought they wanted to get in.'

'Someone did. Me.' Mark comes forward to kiss me, Ella sandwiched between us. He drops a kiss on our daughter's forehead, then takes her from my arms.

'You were creeping about. Why didn't you come straight in?' My irritated tone is unfair, a by-product of the panic slowly dissipating through my bloodstream.

Mark tilts his head to one side and surveys me with more patience than my shortness merits. 'I was putting the bins out. It's collection day tomorrow.' He addresses Ella in a sing-song voice. 'Isn't it? Yes, it is!'

I squeeze my eyes closed for a beat. The dragging noise that might have been a ladder. The thud of the bin-store door. Noises so familiar I should have known instantly what they were. I follow Mark into the sitting room, where he turns on the lights and settles Ella in her beanbag chair.

'Where's Laura?'

'I sent her home.'

'She said she'd stay! I'd have come back earlier—'

'I don't need a babysitter. I'm fine.'

'Are you?' He takes each of my hands in his and holds my arms wide. I wriggle away from his inspection.

'Yes. No. Not really.'

'So where's this card?'

'The police have got it.' I show him the same photos I showed Laura, and watch him zoom in on the writing. He reads aloud.

'*Suicide? Think again.*'

'You see? My mother was murdered.'

'That's not what it says, though.'

'But that's the implication, isn't it?'

Mark looks at me thoughtfully. 'Alternatively, it was an accident.'

'An accident?' My incredulity is clear. 'Why not just say that then? Why the sinister message? The tacky card?'

Mark sits down with a long sigh that I think – I hope – is less about me and more about having spent the day in a stuffy classroom. 'Perhaps someone's trying to point the finger. Negligence rather than a deliberate act. Who's responsible for maintaining the cliff edges?'

I say nothing, and when he continues, his voice is softer.

'You see what I mean, though; it's ambiguous.'

82

'I suppose it is. Except Mum left her handbag and phone on the edge of the cliff, which would be a weird thing to happen accidentally as you fell . . .'

'Unless she'd put them down first. So she didn't drop them. She was looking over the edge, or trying to rescue a bird, and the edge crumbled, and—'

I sit down heavily next to Mark. 'Do you really think it was an accident?'

He twists around so we're facing each other. When he speaks, it's gentle, and he keeps his eyes trained on mine. 'No, sweetheart. I think your mum was desperately unhappy after your dad died. I think she was more unwell than anyone could have known. And,' he pauses, making sure I'm listening, 'I think she took her own life.'

Nothing he's saying is new to me, yet my heart drops back into my stomach and I realise how much I wanted his alternative narrative to be true. How ready I am to grab on to a lifeline that hasn't even been thrown.

'All I'm saying is that everything's open to interpretation. Including this card.' He puts my phone face down on the coffee table, the photos obscured. 'Whoever sent it wants to mess with your head. They're sick. They want a reaction. Don't give it to them.'

'The man at the police station put it in an evidence bag. He said they'd check for fingerprints.' *They're* taking it seriously, I want to add.

'Did you see a detective?'

'No, just the man who works on the front desk. He was a detective for most of his service, and when he retired he came back as a civilian.'

'That's dedication.'

'It is, isn't it? Imagine loving your job so much you don't want to leave it. Even after you've retired.'

'Or you're so institutionalised you can't imagine doing

anything else?' Mark yawns, his hand too late to catch it. From the front, his teeth are a perfect pearly white, but from this angle I can see the amalgam fillings in his upper molars.

'Oh. I hadn't looked at it that way.' I think of Murray Mackenzie with his careful concern and insightful comments, and whatever the reason, I'm glad he's still working for the police. 'Anyway, he was lovely.'

'Good. In the meantime, the best thing you can do is put it out of your mind.' He scoots to the corner of the sofa, his legs stretched out, and raises one arm in invitation. I slide into our well-worn position, snuggled under his left arm with his chin resting lightly on the top of my head. He smells of cold air and something I can't quite pinpoint . . .

'Have you been smoking?' I'm curious, that's all, but even I can hear the judgement that lies beneath the surface of my words.

'A couple of drags, after we finished. Sorry, do I stink?'

'No, I . . . I just didn't know you smoked.' Imagine not knowing your partner smokes . . . But I've never seen him with a cigarette. Never even heard him mention it.

'I quit years ago. Hypnotherapy. It's what made me go into counselling, actually. Have I not told you this story? Anyway, every few months I light one, have a few drags then stub it out. It reminds me I'm the one in control.' He grins. 'There's logic to it, I promise. And don't worry – I would never do it around Ella.'

I settle back into him. I tell myself it's exciting that we're still discovering things about each other – what we have in common; what sets us apart – but right now mystery isn't what I need in my life. I wish Mark and I knew each other inside out. That we'd been childhood sweethearts. I wish he'd known me before Mum and Dad died. I was a different person then. Curious. Amused. Amusing. Mark doesn't know that Anna. He knows bereaved Anna; pregnant Anna; Anna the mother. Sometimes, when Laura or Billy is around, I'll lose myself in a time before

84

Mum and Dad died, and I'll feel like the old me again. It doesn't happen often enough.

I change the subject. 'How was your course?'

'Lots of role-play.' I hear him grimace. He hates that sort of thing.

'You're later than I thought you'd be.'

'I dropped by the flat. I don't like leaving it empty.'

When Mark and I met he was living in Putney. He saw clients in a room of his seventh-floor apartment, and spent one day each week at a practice in Brighton – the same practice that distributed flyers around Eastbourne at the very moment I most needed it.

I told Laura about the pregnancy test before I broke the news to Mark.

'What am I going to do?'

'Have a baby, I guess.' Laura grinned. 'Isn't that how it usually works?'

We were sitting in a café in Brighton, opposite the nail bar where Laura used to work. She'd found a new job taking customer calls for an online shopping company, but I saw her looking at the girls laughing in the nail bar and wondered if she was missing the banter.

'I can't have a baby.' It didn't feel real. I didn't feel pregnant. If it wasn't for the half-dozen tests I'd done, and the absence of a period, I'd have sworn it was all a bad dream.

'There are other options.' Laura spoke softly, even though there was no one else within earshot.

I shook my head. Two lives lost were already too many.

'Well, then.' She held up her coffee mug in a mock toast. 'Congratulations, Mummy.'

I told Mark over dinner that night. I waited till the tables around us were full, protected by the company of strangers.

'I'm sorry,' I said, when I'd dropped my bombshell. There was a flicker of confusion on his face.

'Sorry? This is amazing! I mean . . . isn't it?' He scrutinised me. 'You don't think so?' He tried to be serious, but a slow grin was spreading across his face, and he looked around the restaurant as though expecting a round of applause from our oblivious dining companions.

'I . . . I wasn't sure.' But I put my hand on my still-flat stomach and thought that after the awfulness of the previous year, here was something good. Something miraculous.

'Okay, so it's maybe a little faster than we might have wanted—'

'Just a bit.' I could count the weeks we had been together on my fingers.

'—but it *is* what we wanted.' He looked for agreement and I nodded vehemently. It was. We'd even talked about it, surprising ourselves with our candour. Mark was thirty-nine when we met, bruised from a long-term relationship he'd thought was permanent, and resigned to the possibility that he might never have the family he wanted. I was only twenty-five, but painfully aware of how short life was. My parents' deaths had brought us together; this baby would provide the glue to keep us there.

Gradually Mark wound down his London-based business and scaled up his Brighton one, moving in with me and renting out the Putney flat. It seemed the perfect solution. The rent covered his mortgage, plus a little extra, and the tenants seemed happy to fix anything that went wrong. Or so we'd thought, until a call from environmental health informed us the upstairs neighbour had complained about a smell. By the time we got there the tenants had left with their deposit and a month's rent owing, leaving the place trashed too badly to rent out straight away. Mark was gradually putting things back together.

'How's it looking?'

'Grim. I've lined up someone to decorate but they're on another job till mid-January, so it'll be February before there's a chance of a deposit from new tenants.'

'It doesn't matter.'

'It does.'

We fall silent, neither looking for an argument. We don't need the rental income. Not now. We're not short of a bob or two, as Granddad Johnson would have said.

I'd hand back every penny if it meant one more day with my parents, but the bottom line is: their deaths left me solvent. Thanks to Granddad Johnson, the house has never been mortgaged, and a combination of Dad's savings and my parents' life assurance policies means that sitting in my bank account right now is a fraction over one million pounds.

'I'll sell the flat.'

'Why? This is bad luck, that's all. Switch agencies – find one that checks out references better.'

'Maybe we should sell both places.'

For a second I don't register what he's suggesting. Sell Oak View?

'It's a big house, and the garden's a lot to maintain, when neither of us knows what we're doing.'

'We'll get a gardener.'

'The Sycamore went on the market for eight fifty, and it's only four bedrooms.'

He's serious. 'I don't want to move, Mark.'

'We could buy somewhere together. Something that belongs to us both.'

'Oak View does belong to us both.'

Mark doesn't answer, but I know he doesn't agree. He moved in properly at the end of June, when I was four months pregnant and Mark hadn't spent a night at his flat in weeks.

'Make yourself at home,' I said cheerily, but the very fact that I'd said it reinforced my ownership. It was days before he stopped asking if he could make a cup of tea; weeks before he stopped sitting bolt upright on the sofa, like a visitor.

I wish he loved the house the way I do. With the exception

of my three years at uni, I have only ever lived here. All of my life is within these four walls.

'Just think about it.'

I know he thinks there are too many ghosts here. That sleeping in my parents' old bedroom is hard for me. Perhaps it's hard for him, too. 'Maybe.'

But I mean no. I don't want to move. Oak View is all I have left of my parents.

Ella wakes at six on the dot. Six a.m. used to be early, but when you've been through weeks of night-wakings, and resigned yourself to starting your day at five, 6 a.m. feels like a lie-in. Mark makes tea and I bring Ella into bed with us, and we have an hour as a family before Mark has his shower and Ella and I go down for breakfast.

Half an hour later Mark's still in the bathroom – I hear the clanging of the pipes and the rhythmic knocking that provide the musical accompaniment to our ensuite shower. Ella is dressed, but I'm still in my pyjamas, dancing around the kitchen to make her laugh.

The crunch of gravel outside makes me think of yesterday evening. As the morning light creeps into the kitchen I'm embarrassed by the way I worked myself into a state. I'm relieved Robert's phone was switched off, making Mark the only witness to my paranoia. Next time I'm alone at night I'll play loud music, turn on lights, walk through the house slamming doors. I won't cower in one room, creating a drama that doesn't need to exist.

I hear the metallic snap of the letterbox, the soft thud of letters dropping onto the mat beneath, and then the lightest of finger taps that tells me the postman has left something in the porch.

When Ella was five weeks old, and full of colic, the postman delivered a textbook Mark had ordered. It had taken me a full hour to settle her and she had finally dropped off to sleep when the postman banged the door knocker with such force the light fittings rattled. I wrenched open the door in a sleep-deprived, post-natal rage, giving the poor man both barrels, and then some. Afterwards, when my fury had burned itself out and my cries no longer rivalled Ella's, the postman suggested he might simply leave further packages outside the door, with no danger of disturbing us. It appeared I was not the only house on his round at which this was the preferred modus operandi.

I wait until his footsteps leave our drive, not wanting to greet him in my pyjamas, and still mortified by my tears that day, then I pad into the hall and collect the post. Circulars, more bills, an official-looking letter in a buff envelope for Mark. I take the key from its hook beneath the windowsill and unlock the front door. It sticks a little, and I pull hard to open it.

But it isn't the force of opening the door that makes me take a step back, or the icy cold sucked instantly into the warm hall. It isn't the parcel that rests on the pile of logs to one side of the porch.

It's the blood smeared across the threshold, and the pile of entrails on the top step.

THIRTEEN

They say money is the root of all evil.

The cause of all crime.

There are others like me – other people wandering around in this half-existence – and they're all here because of money.

They didn't have any; they had too much.

They wanted someone else's; someone wanted theirs.

And the result?

A life, taken.

But it won't end there.

FOURTEEN

ANNA

The rabbit is on the top step, its stomach cut neatly open in one continuous, careful slice. A gelatinous mass of flesh and guts oozes from within. Glassy eyeballs stare out at the street, above a gaping mouth exposing sharp white teeth.

I open my mouth to scream, but there's no air in my lungs and I take a step back instead, clutching at the coat stand to the side of the front door. I feel the prickle of my milk letting down, the need to feed my baby an instinctive reaction to danger.

I find air.

'Mark!' The word explodes from me bullet-fast. 'Mark! Mark!' I keep shouting, unable to tear my eyes away from the bloody mess on our threshold. A morning frost has coated the rabbit and its blood in glistening silver, and the effect serves only to make the spectacle more macabre, like a gothic Christmas decoration. 'Mark!'

He comes downstairs at something between a walk and a run, stubbing his toe on the bottom step and swearing loudly. 'What the— Jesus . . .' He's wearing nothing but a towel, and he shivers involuntarily as he stands in the open doorway, staring at the step. Droplets of water cling to the sparse hair on his chest.

'Who would have done such a horrible thing?' I'm crying now, in that post-shock relief that comes with realising you're safe.

Mark looks at me, confused. 'Who? Don't you mean what?

A fox, presumably. Good job it's so cold or it'd be stinking.'

'You think an animal did this?'

'A whole park across the road, and it chooses our doorstep. I'll get some clothes on, then I'll get rid of it.'

Something doesn't make sense. I try to work out what, but it slips away from me. 'Why didn't the fox eat it? Look at all that meat and,' I swallow the nausea that threatens my gullet, 'the guts. Why kill it then not eat it?'

'That's what they do, isn't it? Urban foxes feed from the bins. They kill for fun. If they get into a hen coop they'll slaughter the whole flock, but they won't eat a damned one.'

I know he's right. Years ago my father decided to keep geese, penned in a run at the bottom of the garden. I can't have been older than five or six, but I remember pulling on my wellies and running to collect the eggs and throw grain onto the muddy grass. Despite the geese's Christmas fate, my mother named them all, calling them individually as she rounded them up at nightfall. Her favourite – and by default, therefore, mine – was a sprightly bird with grey-tipped feathers she called Piper. While the others would hiss and flap their wings if you got too close, Piper would let my mother feed her by hand. Her docility was her undoing. The fox – so bold he didn't wait for darkness – was deterred by the bad-tempered siblings, but clamped his jaws around poor Piper's neck, leaving her decapitated body for my mother and me to find that evening.

'Filthy animals,' Mark says. 'You can see where the fox hunt brigade's coming from, can't you?'

I can't. I've never seen a fox in the countryside, but I've seen plenty in town, trotting down the centre of the street, as bold as you like. They're so beautiful I can't imagine terrorising them in punishment for their own instincts as hunters.

As I stare at the mutilated rabbit, I pinpoint what's been troubling me. I speak slowly, the thoughts solidifying along with the words.

'There's too much blood.'

There's a pool of it beneath the lifeless rabbit, and more on the three steps down to the drive. Gentle amusement shows on Mark's face as he takes in my announcement.

'I remember dissecting frogs in fourth-form biology, but we never did a rabbit. How much blood *should* there be?'

The sarcasm irritates me. Why isn't he seeing what I'm seeing?

I try to stay calm. 'Let's suppose a fox did it. And let's suppose there's enough blood in a tiny wild rabbit to produce this mess in front of us. Did it wipe its paws on the other steps?'

Mark laughs, but I'm not joking.

'Did it use its tail to paint smears of blood?'

Because that's what it looks like; like someone has taken a paintbrush, dipped it into the rabbit and covered our steps with irregular daubs of blood. It looks, I realise with sudden clarity, like a crime scene.

Mark becomes serious. He puts a strong arm around me and uses his free hand to close the door, then he turns me to face him. 'Tell me. Tell me who did this.'

'I don't know who did it. But they did it because I went to the police. They did it because they know something about Mum's death, and they want to stop me finding out about it.' Voicing my theory does nothing to make it sound less fantastical.

Mark is impassive, although I detect a hint of concern. 'Sweetheart, this doesn't make sense.'

'You think this is normal? An anonymous card yesterday, and now this?'

'Okay, let's think this through. Suppose the card wasn't someone being spiteful—'

'It wasn't.'

'What did they want to achieve by questioning your mother's death?' He doesn't wait for me to answer. 'And what do they want to achieve by scaring you with dead animals on the door-step?'

I can see his point. It feels disjointed. Why push me towards the police, then warn me off?

He takes my silence as defeat.

'It was a fox, sweetheart.' Mark moves forward and kisses my forehead. 'I promise. Why don't I take Ella while you have a nice bath? I haven't got a client till eleven today.'

I let Mark lead me upstairs and run me a bath, putting in some of the ludicrously expensive bath salts he bought me when Ella was born, which I've never had time to use. I soak beneath the bubbles, thinking about foxes, rabbits, blood. Wondering if I'm paranoid.

I picture the anonymous card; imagine the sender's hand sliding it into the envelope, putting it in the postbox. Did that same person cut open a rabbit with surgical precision? Smear blood across the steps of my house?

My pulse won't slow down. It beats a staccato rhythm in my temple and I sink lower in the bath, letting the hum of the water fill my ears instead. Someone wants to frighten me.

I wonder if the two acts are really that disjointed after all? I saw the anonymous card as a call to action, a direction to look into my mother's death. But what if it wasn't an instruction, but a warning?

Think again.

A warning that Mum's death wasn't as it seemed; that someone out there meant my family harm. Still does.

I close my eyes and see blood, so much blood. Already my memory is playing tricks on me. How big was the rabbit? Was there really that much blood?

Photographs.

The thought occurs suddenly, and I sit up, sloshing water over the side of the bath. I'll take pictures and then I can take them to Murray Mackenzie at the police station and see if he thinks it could have been a fox.

A tiny voice asks if I'm doing this to convince Mark or to

convince the police. I bat it away, pull the plug and hop out, drying myself with such haste my clothes stick to my damp skin.

I find my phone and rush downstairs, but Mark has already cleared away the dead rabbit and washed the steps with bleach. When I open the front door there's nothing there at all. It's as if it never happened.

FIFTEEN

MURRAY

Winter sun filtered through the bedroom curtains as Murray got dressed. He tucked the duvet underneath the pillows and smoothed out the wrinkles before arranging the cushions the way Sarah liked. Opening the curtains, he noted the thick grey clouds rolling in from the north, and put a V-necked sweater over his shirt.

Later, once the dishwasher was on and he'd pushed the Hoover around, and the first load of laundry was hanging on the line, Murray sat at the kitchen table with a cup of tea and a chocolate biscuit. It was half past nine. The hours stretched out in front of him. He remembered a time when a morning off was full of promise, full of expectation.

He drummed his fingers on the table. He would go and see Sarah. Spend the morning with her – perhaps he could persuade her to go to the café, or to take a walk around the grounds – and go on to work from there.

He was buzzed in by Jo Dawkins, Sarah's key worker, who had worked at Highfield for the last ten years.

'I'm sorry, love. She's having a bad day.'

A bad day meant Sarah didn't want to see him. Ordinarily, Murray would go straight home, accepting that everyone had times when they wanted to be alone. Today he felt different. He missed Sarah. He wanted to talk about the Johnson job.

'Would you try again? Tell her I won't stay long.'

'I'll see what I can do.' Jo left him in reception, the hall of the original country house. It had been clumsily converted, long before listed buildings had become something to protect. Thick fire doors, all with key-code access, led off to wards and offices, and ugly woodchip paper covered both walls and ceiling.

When Jo returned, it was clear from her face nothing had changed.

'Did she give any reason?'

BPD. That was the reason.

Jo hesitated. 'Um, not really.'

'She did, didn't she? Come on, Jo, you know I can take it.'

The nurse looked him square on, assessing him. 'Okay. She thinks you should be' – she lifted her hands and made repeated quote marks in the air, disassociating herself from what was to follow – '"fucking other people and not wasting your life loving a loony".'

Murray blushed. His wife ordering him to leave her (and then attempting suicide at the prospect) had been a common theme throughout their marriage, but that didn't make it any less awkward to hear via a third party.

'Would you tell her' – he raised his hands to mirror Jo's quote marks – 'that "loving a loony" is exactly what I like best?'

Murray sat in the car park of Highfield, leaning back against the headrest. He should have known better than to have tried to surprise Sarah. She was unpredictable at the best of times, but predictably so in the mornings. He would try again on his way home from work.

So now what?

He had two hours before his shift started, and no desire to go back to an empty house and watch the minutes tick by. The fridge was full, the garden tidy and the house clean. Murray considered his options.

'Yes,' he said aloud, as he was inclined to do. 'Why not?' His time was his own; he could do what he wanted with it.

He headed out of town across the Downs, pressing his foot hard against the floor for a burst of speed you never got on buses. A shortage of parking at the police station meant public transport was often more convenient for work, but Murray enjoyed driving, and he put on the radio and hummed along to a track he only half knew. The threatened rain hadn't yet materialised, but the clouds hung low above the hills, and when the sea hove into view it was flecked with angry white tips.

The car park was near-empty, save a half-dozen cars, and Murray found eighty pence among the loose change he kept in the otherwise redundant ashtray, and popped the ticket on the dash. A large sign next to the pay-and-display machine gave the contact number for the Samaritans, and as Murray walked towards the coastal path he passed a series of further signs.

It helps to talk.

You are not alone.

Could a sign make a difference? Might a person, hell-bent on suicide, stop to take in a message meant for them?

You are not alone.

For every person who fell to their death off Beachy Head, there were a dozen more who didn't. A dozen more who lost their nerve, had a change of heart, encountered one of the volunteers who patrolled the cliffs, and reluctantly agreed to join them for a cup of tea instead of carrying out their plan.

It didn't end there, though, did it? An intervention was a comma, not a full stop. All the tea, all the conversation, all the support in the world might not change what happened the next day. Or the day after that.

Murray thought of the poor chaplain who'd found Caroline Johnson on the cliff edge, her rucksack weighed down with stones. How must he have felt to learn that the woman he'd talked down from suicide had gone straight back to the same spot and jumped anyway?

Had she been with someone that day? Had the chaplain been

so focused on saving Caroline's life that he had neglected to see a figure in the shadows, keeping well back?

Was Anna's mother pushed? Perhaps not physically, but could someone have forced Caroline into taking her own life?

The headland rose above Murray, each stride taking him higher above sea level. Local folklore suggested malignant ley lines converged at Beachy Head, drawing those susceptible to such things to their death. Murray held no truck with magic and mystery, but it was hard to ignore the power of the place. The expanse of grass ended abruptly in bright white cliffs, the contrast muted by the mist that swirled around the lighthouse below. As the clouds shifted Murray caught glimpses of grey sea, and he felt a rush of vertigo, stepping backwards even though he was twelve feet or more from the crumbling edges.

Caroline had come here to die. That much had been clear from the chaplain's testimony. Yet the implication in the anonymous anniversary card was clear: her suicide was not as it seemed.

Murray pictured Caroline Johnson standing where he now stood. Had she *wanted* to die? Or been *willing* to die? There was a subtle, but important, distinction. Willing to die so that someone else would be spared? Her daughter? Perhaps Anna herself was the key to all this. Could Caroline Johnson have taken her own life because someone threatened to hurt her daughter if she didn't?

Far from clearing his head, Beachy Head was sending him around in circles.

In the centre of a well-trodden patch of grass was a stone plinth topped with a slate slab. Murray read the engraving, his lips moving silently.

Mightier than the thunders of many waters,
mightier than the waves of the sea,
the Lord on high is mighty!

99

Beneath the psalm, a final reminder: *God is always greater than all of our troubles.*

Murray felt something well up inside him. He turned abruptly from the plinth, looked one last time at where the cliffs gave way to oblivion, and then marched back towards the car park, angry he had let it get to him. He had come for research purposes, he told himself, not to get maudlin. He had come to see where Anna Johnson's parents had died. To fix the scene in his mind, thinking it might have changed since he was last there.

It hadn't.

It had been one of the patrol volunteers who had found Sarah. She'd been sitting on the edge of the cliff, her feet dangling into oblivion. She hadn't wanted to kill herself, she'd told the chaplain; she just didn't want to be in the world any more. There was a difference, she'd insisted. Murray had understood that. He wouldn't change his wife for the world, but he wished so much he could change the world for his wife.

Murray had picked up the call, left work and driven to the pub at Beachy Head, where Sarah was sitting with a woman whose dog collar was all but hidden beneath her waterproofs. The landlord was a quiet, thoughtful man, experienced in the difference between a stiff drink and Dutch courage, quick to call the police if the latter looked as though it would end badly. He had retired discreetly to the other end of the pub, while Sarah had cried on Murray's shoulder.

Beachy Head hadn't changed. It never would. It was – would always be – a beautiful, haunting, agonising place. At once uplifting and destroying.

Murray parked the car in the street behind the police station, checked the time and took out his access card. A pair of response officers were jogging down the corridor, nodding their thanks as Murray swung open the door for them, before getting into a marked car parked in the back yard. Within seconds they were out of the gate, wheels spinning as they rounded the corner. Murray stood until the sound of the siren had all but disappeared, a barely-there smile on his face. There was nothing like a blue-light run for getting the blood pumping.

The Criminal Investigation Department – or CID – was at the end of a long corridor. In Murray's day, there had been five or six small offices on each side, but by the time he'd retired most of the internal walls had been demolished to create open-plan workspaces. Officers were expected to 'hot-desk' now, Murray knew, and he was grateful the concept hadn't been mooted while he was still on the department. How could you solve a jigsaw puzzle when you had to keep packing away the pieces?

Detective Sergeant James Kennedy looked up as Murray entered, his face showing genuine warmth. He shook Murray's hand vigorously. 'How the devil are you? Still on the front desk? Lower Meads nick, isn't it?'

'That's the one.'

'Rather you than me.' James shuddered. 'Soon as I get my pension I'm out of here. You won't catch me back under the cosh. Working Christmas, instead of watching the kids open their stockings? It's a mug's game, right?'

James Kennedy was in his early thirties. He'd arrived on CID two months before Murray's leaving do, and now there he was: leading a team, and no doubt one of the most experienced detectives in the office. He might think his retirement – still years in the future – would never involve a uniform, but wait till he got there, Murray thought. Thirty years left a gap that was hard to fill.

James took in Murray's civvies. 'In early? You're keen.'

'I was just passing. Thought I'd pop in and see how things were.'

There was a moment's hesitation while the stark reality of

Murray's empty life hung in the air between them, before James rallied.

'Well, I'm glad you did, it's good to see you. I'll put the kettle on.'

As James clattered about in the corner of the office, where a kettle and tea tray on top of a fridge formed a makeshift kitchen, Murray looked at the ongoing cases on the whiteboard.

'I see Owen Healey's still outstanding?'

James put two mugs of tea on the desk, the bags still bobbing about in them. Murray fished his out and dropped it in the bin by his feet.

'He always used to run with the Matthews lads when they were kids – lived on the estate behind Wood Green. They're still thick as the proverbial.'

There was an awkward pause. 'Oh. Ha! Right. We'd better check that out, then. Good job you swung by!' James clapped Murray on the shoulder with enforced joviality, and Murray wished he hadn't said anything. He might be retired but he still worked for the police. He still heard things; still knew things. He didn't need to be humoured. People always did, though. Not only because he was old, but because—

'How's Sarah?'

There it was. The head, cocked to one side. The 'thank God it's you and not me' look in his eyes. James's wife was at home, looking after their two children. She wasn't in a mental health unit for the hundredth time. James wouldn't be rushing home from work because his wife was kneeling in the kitchen with her head in the oven. Murray checked himself. No one knew what went on behind closed doors.

'She's fine. Should be home soon.'

Murray had no idea if that was true. He had long given up asking, instead seeing Sarah's frequent stays at Highfield – whether voluntary or not – as a chance for him to gather his strength to have her back home. Respite.

'Actually, while I'm here, I was going to ask you about a job.'

James looked relieved to be back on more familiar territory. 'All ears, mate.'

'Your team dealt with a couple of suicides at Beachy Head in May and December last year. Tom and Caroline Johnson. Husband and wife. She killed herself at the same spot he did.'

James stared at his desk, drumming his fingers as he tried to place the job. 'Johnson's Cars, right?'

'That's it. Do you remember much about them?'

'They were identical. Copycat suicides. In fact, we were a bit worried it might spark a load more – the papers really went to town on it – but, touch wood, it's been quiet on that front. The last jumper was a couple of weeks ago. Got blown into the cliffs on his way down.' James winced.

'Anything else strike you as odd?' Murray was keen to stay on track.

'About the Johnsons? In what way? People topping themselves at Beachy Head is hardly unusual. I seem to remember the coroner's reports being fairly cut and dried.'

'They were. I just thought . . . You know how you have a feeling about a job, sometimes? Something not right – as though the truth is hiding in plain sight, but you can't quite get hold of it.'

'Sure.' James was nodding politely, but there was no spark of recognition. His generation of detectives didn't work on feelings. They worked on facts. Forensics. It wasn't their fault – the courts didn't go a bundle on intuition, either. Murray did. In his experience, if something smelled like a fish and tasted like a fish, it was almost certainly a fish. Even if it didn't look like one.

'But you didn't feel like that about these jobs?'

'Pretty standard stuff, mate. They were in and out of the office within a couple of weeks each time.' He leaned forward and lowered his voice, even though there was no one else in the office. 'Not exactly taxing stuff for CID, am I right?'

Murray smiled politely. He supposed an open-and-shut suicide didn't present much of a challenge to a team of hungry detectives with an array of rapes and robberies on their desks. It had been different for Murray. His motivation had been people, not crimes. Victims, witnesses, even offenders – they'd all fascinated him. He had felt – still felt – compelled to investigate the mysteries in their lives. How he wished he had been sitting at James's desk when the Johnson suicides had come in.

Murray stirred himself. 'I'd better get off.'

'Things to do, people to see, right?' James clapped him on the shoulder again. 'Why the interest in the Johnsons?'

That was the point at which Murray should show him Anna Johnson's anonymous card. The point at which he should officially hand over the job to CID and go back to his front desk job.

Murray looked at the list of jobs on the whiteboard, at the piles of ongoing files on each detective's desk. Would James prioritise this one? A job with no clear answers, handed to him by a retired cop?

'No reason,' Murray said, before he'd properly thought it through. 'Idle curiosity. I saw the name on an old briefing sheet. I bought a car from them a few years ago.'

'Right. Cool.' James's eyes flicked to his screen.

'I'll let you get on. Have a good Christmas.'

Anna Johnson was vulnerable. In a little over a year she'd lost both her parents and had a baby. She felt threatened and confused, and if this job was going to be investigated then it needed to be done properly, not given a cursory glance before being filed again.

'Great to see you, mate. Keep up the good work!' James half stood as Murray left the office. He was back in his seat before the older man had reached the door, the Johnson case already forgotten.

Murray would quietly investigate Caroline Johnson's death, and the moment he had concrete evidence of foul play, he'd come back to DS Kennedy.

Until then, he was on his own.

SIXTEEN

ANNA

'It just seems a bit over the top, that's all I'm saying.'

'Not to me.' We stand in the open doorway, Ella in her car seat between us. Mark looks at his watch, even though he only just checked the time. 'You don't have to come. You can drop me at the police station and go on to work, if you'd rather.'

'Don't be silly, of course I'll come.'

'Silly? I'd hardly call a dead rabbit—'

'I didn't mean the rabbit! Christ, Anna! I meant: "Don't be silly, I'm not going to leave you to go to the police on your own".' Mark exhales noisily and stands squarely facing me. 'I'm on your side, you know.'

'I know. I'm sorry.'

There's a shout from next door. 'Morning!'

Robert Drake is standing outside his house, his hands on the railings between our driveways.

'Bit early, isn't it?' Mark slips easily into Jovial Neighbour mode, going down the steps to greet Robert through the railings.

'First one off for six years – I'm going to milk it.'

'I don't blame you. Six years!'

I watch them shake hands through the railings.

'Still on for Christmas drinks at mine?'

'Absolutely,' Mark says, with far more enthusiasm than I'd be able to muster. Robert holds a party every year. He cancelled it last year, out of respect for my parents, but the invitation for this year's dropped through the door a couple of weeks ago. Presumably my mourning period is over. 'What can we bring?'

'Just yourselves. Unless you want soft drinks. Not many of those around. Ha!'

Dad and Billy used to play golf with Robert from time to time, but Mum never joined them. She said Robert was *smug*. I look at him now – at his expensive shirt and his confident stance – and think she was right. Robert Drake has the innate arrogance of someone so on top of their professional game that they adopt the same position in their private life.

Fuck off, Robert.

The voice in my head is so clear I think for a moment I've said it out loud. I imagine Mark's face, and Robert's, and stifle a snort of laughter that erupts from nowhere. I think perhaps I'm going mad, the way I think my mum did after Dad died. Laughing at things that weren't funny, crying at things that weren't sad. My world feels tipped upside down and this man next door, with his cheery Christmas greetings and his jokes about soft drinks, feels not just insignificant but inappropriate after the events of the last twenty-four hours.

My mother was murdered, I want to tell him. *Now someone's threatening me.*

I don't, of course. But it occurs to me that Robert, with his penchant for wandering outside to chat to the neighbours, might have seen something useful. I join Mark by the railings.

'Did you see anyone outside our house this morning?'

Robert stops short, his festive cheer dimmed by the intensity of my stare. 'Not that I recall.' He's a tall man, but not broad, like Mark. He stoops slightly, and I imagine him leaning over the operating table, scalpel in hand. I shiver. Imagine that same hand slicing open a rabbit . . .

'Were you outside the house late last night?'

The abruptness of my question is followed by an awkward pause.

Robert looks at Mark, even though it's me who asked the question. 'Should I have been?'

'Someone put a rabbit on our doormat,' Mark explains. 'There was blood all over the steps. We wondered if you might have seen anything.'

'Good God. A rabbit? What a peculiar . . . But why?'

I examine his face, looking for any sign that he's faking. 'You didn't see anyone?' Even as I ask, I'm not sure what answer I'm expecting. *Yes, I watched someone put a mutilated rabbit outside your house, but didn't think to ask what the hell they were doing. Or: Yes, I put it there as a joke. Ha ha. An early Christmas present.*

'I wasn't back till late last night . . . Both your cars were in the driveway, but there were no lights on. And I'm afraid I had a lie-in this morning. Off till New Year. I know: lucky bugger, eh?'

This is stupid. Robert Drake is the sort of person who starts Neighbourhood Watch schemes and reports cold callers. If he had seen someone putting a rabbit on our step, he'd have told us. As for putting it there himself . . . the man's a doctor, not a psychopath.

I turn to Mark. 'We should get going.'

'Sure.' He picks up Ella's car seat and takes it to his car, strapping it in with no sense of urgency. I sit in the back next to her.

I don't think Mark is taking this seriously. My parents were murdered. How much more proof does he want? The anonymous card. A dead rabbit. These aren't normal events.

He stands for a while outside the closed car door, then moves away. I hear the crunch of gravel underfoot. I stroke Ella's cheek with one outstretched finger and wait for Mark to lock the front door. I have a sudden memory of waiting in the car for my parents, sitting in the back like this, while Dad tapped the steering wheel and Mum rushed back to the house for something she'd forgotten.

'I wish you could meet them,' I say to Ella.

When I left university I desperately wanted a place of my own. I'd had a taste of independence – seen a world outside of Eastbourne – and I liked it. But the charity sector is built for job satisfaction, not salary goals, and the property ladder remained stubbornly out of my grasp. I moved back home, and never left.

Dad was fond of reminding me I didn't know how good I had it.

'Kicked out at sixteen to learn the trade, I was. You'd never have caught my old man doing laundry for Bill and me past our teens.'

I was fairly confident that Granddad Johnson had never been near a washing machine in his life, his wife having been the sort of woman who revelled in home-making and shooed intruders from the kitchen.

'I worked twelve-hour days for years. By the time I was your age I had a flat in Soho and a wallet full of fifties.'

I exchanged a conspiratorial grin with Mum. Neither of us pointed out that it had been Granddad who had lined up the apprenticeship at a friend's garage, and Granny who had sent food parcels up with the trade platers. Not to mention the fact that in 1983 it was still possible to buy a flat in London for fifty grand. I changed the subject before he claimed he'd been sent up chimneys as a schoolboy.

I was never academic, but I'd inherited my parents' work ethic. I admired them both for the hours they put in to making the family business a success, and did my best to emulate them.

'Find a job you love,' Dad was fond of saying, 'and you'll never do a day's work in your life.'

The trouble was, I didn't know what I wanted to do. I got a place at Warwick to do sociology, scraped a 2:2 and left with no clearer idea. The first step on my career path was an accidental one. I took a job with Save the Children, collected a red body-warmer and clipboard, and traipsed the streets, knocking on doors. Some people were kind, others less so, but I soon discovered I did have a little of my parents' charm, after all. I recruited more monthly donors that first month than the rest of the team put together. A temporary promotion to regional supervisor ended when a position became vacant for the national post, and I slid into a desk that felt a world away from the exam halls of an undiagnosed dyslexic teen who would never amount to anything. 'Chip off the old block,' Dad said.

I worked closely with the fundraising team, thought up innovative ideas for raising awareness, and looked after my three-hundred-strong team of door-knockers across the country. I defended them fiercely from middle-class complaints about 'chugging', and praised each and every one of my staff for the contribution they made to children around the globe. I loved the job I'd found. But it wasn't well paid. Living at home was the only option.

Besides, uncool though it might have been to admit it, I liked living at home. Not for the clean washing or the home-cooked meals, or my dad's infamous wine cellar, but because my parents were genuinely good company. They made me laugh. They were interested and interesting. We chatted late into the night about plans, politics, people. We discussed our problems. There were no secrets. Or so they pretended.

I think of the vodka bottle beneath my parents' desk; the others secreted around the house. Of the kitchen table littered with empty wine bottles, yet always spotless by the time I got up in the morning.

Towards the end of my first term at Warwick I spent the weekend with Sam, a friend from halls, at her parents' house. The absence of wine at dinner felt strange, like they'd dished up a meal without knives or forks. A few weeks later I asked Sam if her parents minded her drinking.

110

'Why would they?'

'Aren't they teetotal?'

Sam laughed. 'Teetotal? You should see Mum on the sherries at Christmas.'

My cheeks burned. 'I thought . . . They didn't drink when I came to stay.'

She shrugged. 'Can't say I noticed. Sometimes they drink, sometimes they don't. Like most people, I guess.'

'I guess so.'

Most people didn't drink every evening. Most people didn't fix a gin and tonic when they got home from work, saying it was 'six o'clock somewhere, right?'

Most people.

'All set?' Mark gets into the car and puts on his seatbelt. He looks at me in the rearview mirror, then twists around to see me properly. He clears his throat, a subconscious habit I recognise from our early meetings. It's a form of punctuation. A full stop between what's been said and what he's about to say. A way of saying: 'Listen to me now: this is important.'

'After we've been to the police . . .' He hesitates.

'Yes?'

'We could make an appointment for you to see someone.'

I raise an eyebrow. *See someone.* The middle-class euphemism for *go find a shrink – you're going nuts.* 'I don't need to see another counsellor.'

'Anniversaries can do funny things.'

'Hilarious,' I joke, but Mark doesn't smile. He turns back around and starts the car.

'Think about it at least.'

There's nothing to think about. It's the police I need, not a shrink.

But as we pull out of the drive I take a sharp breath and lean across Ella to put a hand on the window. Maybe I do need a shrink. For a second, that woman walking . . . It isn't Mum,

111

of course, but I'm shocked by the intensity of my disappointment, by the very fact that a part of me thought it might be. Yesterday, on the anniversary of her death, I felt her presence so strongly that today I'm conjuring up ghosts where none exist.

And yet I have the strangest feeling . . .

Who says ghosts don't exist?

Doctors? Psychiatrists?

Mark?

Maybe it's possible to summon the dead. Maybe it's possible they return of their own accord. Maybe – just maybe – my mother has a message for me.

I share none of this with Mark. But I stare out of the window as we drive to the station, willing myself to see ghosts, to see some sort of sign.

If Mum's trying to tell me what really happened the day she died, I'm listening.

SEVENTEEN

I've been here too long. The longer I stay, the more likely it is that someone will see me.

But I have to do this now – it could be my only chance.

Mark straps the baby into the back of the car, and Anna slides into the adjacent seat. Mark closes the car door. He stands for a second with his palms flat on the roof of the car. Like that, he's concealed from Anna, but I can see the anxiety on his face. Is he worried about Anna? The baby? Or something else?

He walks back to the side of the house, where Robert is lingering, pretending to move some pots about. I feel panic building inside me, even though he can't touch me, can't even see me. The two men talk in low tones through the railings, and I wonder if Anna can hear the same snippets I do.

'. . . still grieving . . . very difficult . . . a touch of post-natal depression . . .'

I wait.

They drive away. Robert abandons his plant pots and goes back inside.

And then it's time.

A single breath later I'm through the locked door and standing in the hall. Instantly I'm overwhelmed with sensation, assaulted by memories I never imagined would have lingered.

Painting the skirting boards, kneeling awkwardly over my growing bump. Piling duvets on the stairs for a pint-sized Anna to sledge down, you egging her on, me with my fingers over my eyes.

Playing happy families. Hiding how we really felt.

How easily life changes. How easily happiness disintegrates. The drinking. The shouting. The fights.

I kept it from Anna. I could at least do that for her.

I check myself. The time for being maudlin is long gone; too late now to dwell on the past.

I move quickly and silently through the house, my touch feather-light. I leave no mess, no prints. No trace. I want to see the papers Anna put to one side. My diary. The photographs that only tell a story when you know the way it ends. I look for the key that will tell everyone why I had to die.

I find nothing.

In the study, I work my way efficiently through the drawers. I ignore the stab of nostalgia that pierces deeper with each trinket and notebook I pick up. You can't take it with you, that's what they say. I remember an old school project of Anna's on the 'grave goods' selected by ancient Egyptians, designed to smooth the deceased's passage to the afterlife. Anna spent weeks on a painting of a sarcophagus, surrounded by carefully drawn images of her own precious belongings. Her iPod. Salt and vinegar crisps – six packets. Portraits she'd drawn of you and me. A favourite scarf, in case she got cold. I smile at the memory and consider what I would have taken, had it been possible; what would have made my afterlife more bearable.

There is no key. Not in any of the bags dotted about downstairs, or in the drawer of the dresser in the hall where everything accumulates when it doesn't have a home.

What has Anna done with it?

EIGHTEEN

MURRAY

'I found my mother's diary from last year.' Anna handed him a thick A4 diary. 'I thought it might help piece together her movements.' They were sitting in the kitchenette behind the front desk at Lower Meads police station, where Murray had first spoken to Anna Johnson. Anna's partner, Mark, was with her, and together they had reported one of the strangest occurrences Murray had ever been asked to investigate.

Mark Hemmings had thick dark hair and glasses that were currently pushed up on his forehead. He was sitting back in his chair with one ankle on the knee of his other leg. His right arm rested on the back of Anna's chair.

Anna Johnson took up half the space of her partner. She sat on the edge of her seat, leaning forwards with her legs crossed and her hands clasped together as though she were in church.

There were various leaflets and business cards filed within the pages of the diary, and as Murray opened the front cover, a photograph fell out.

Anna reached for it. 'Sorry, I put it there so it didn't get creased. I was going to get it framed.'

'Your mother?'

'There, in the yellow dress. And that's her friend Alicia. She died of an asthma attack when she was thirty-three. Her daughter Laura is Mum's goddaughter.'

Murray remembered the pocket notebook entry from the

115

attending officer. *Laura Barnes. Goddaughter.* The women – girls, really – in the photo were laughing outside a pub, their arms entangled so they looked like extensions of each other. In the background of the photo was a table of young men, one of whom was looking across at Alicia and Caroline admiringly. Murray could make out a wagon and horses on the swinging sign outside the building behind them.

'Funny place for a holiday – about as far as you can get from the sea – but Mum said they had the best time.'

'Lovely photo. You never met Anna's parents, Mr Hemmings?'

'Sadly not. They'd both passed away before we met. In fact, it was because of them we met at all.' Instinctively both Mark and Anna looked at their daughter, who, Murray supposed, would not have existed without the tragedy that had befallen the family.

'I'll speak to a Crime Scene Investigator about the rabbit, but without examining it—'

'I'm sorry. We didn't think.' Anna shot a look at her partner.

'I'll just leave it there next time, shall I?' Mark said. He spoke mildly, but with an undertone that suggested this was a conversation already had at least once. 'Let the flies have a really good go at it?'

'It can't be helped. I've submitted the anniversary card to forensics. They'll check for fingerprints and DNA, and try to enhance the postmark so we have a better idea of where it came from. And I'll take a look through this diary, thank you.' Murray passed the photo back to Anna, but she didn't put it in her bag. She held it in both hands, staring at the image as though she could bring it to life.

'I keep thinking I see her.' She looked up. Mark moved his arm from the back of her chair to her shoulders. His lips were pressed tightly together as Anna tried to explain. 'At least . . . not *see* her exactly. But *feel* her. I think . . . I think she might be trying to tell me something. Does that sound mad?'

Mark spoke softly, as much to Murray as to Anna. 'It's very common for people who are grieving to imagine they see their loved ones. It's a manifestation of emotion; you want to see them so badly you think—'

'What if I'm not imagining it?'

There was an awkward pause. Murray felt as though he were intruding, and wondered if he should fabricate a reason to leave the couple alone. Before he could move, Anna turned to him.

'What do you think? Do you believe in ghosts? In an afterlife?'

Police officers were, by nature, a cynical breed. Throughout his service Murray had kept his thoughts on ghosts to himself, avoiding the ribbing that would inevitably have ensued. Even now, he didn't commit. One's belief or otherwise in the supernatural was a personal matter – like religion or politics – and not one to be debated in a side room of a police station.

'I'm open to it.' There were more things in heaven and earth, Shakespeare had said, than anyone could ever imagine, but that didn't make Murray's job any easier. He couldn't go to CID with a report that Anna Johnson was being haunted by a murdered relative. He leaned forward. 'Do you get a sense of what she might be trying to tell you?' Murray ignored the almost tangible disparagement that was emanating from Mark Hemmings.

'I'm sorry. It's just a . . . feeling.'

It was going to take more than a feeling to convince CID that Tom and Caroline Johnson had been murdered.

Nisha Kaur had been a Crime Scene Investigator back when they were called Scenes of Crime Officers.

'Same shit, different job title,' she'd say cheerfully. 'Give it another ten years and some bright spark upstairs will be rebranding us all SOCOs again.'

Not that Nish would be there in ten years' time. She had been new in post when Murray was a young detective, joining the force with a BTEC in photography, a strong stomach, and the

117

enviable ability to get on with everyone. Thirty years later she was Principal CSI, responsible for the force forensic team, and counting down to her own retirement.

'Pet photography,' she said, when Murray asked her plans. She laughed at the surprise on his face. 'The uniform's better, there's less blood, and have you tried being depressed when there's a kitten in the room? I can pick and choose my jobs – no more arsey punters for me – and work my own hours. All very low-key. More of a hobby than a job.' They were sitting in the closed canteen, where a triptych of vending machines served the weekend workers.

'Sounds like a good plan.' Privately Murray doubted Nish could do anything on a low-key basis. Within eighteen months of retirement she'd be working flat out again. 'What are you doing over Christmas?'

'On call. You?'

'Nothing special. Quiet one. You know.'

'Is Sarah . . . ?' Nish didn't do the head tilt.

'At Highfield. Voluntarily, this time. She's fine.' It sounded insincere, even to Murray. You'd have thought he would have found Sarah's admissions easier as time went by, but the last few occasions had drained him more than ever before. He was getting older, he supposed; finding stress harder to handle.

'What did you want to see me about?' Nish, perceptive as ever, changing tack.

'How much blood is there in a rabbit?'

It was a measure of the variety of Nish's job, and the breadth of her experience, that the question provoked no surprise.

'A couple of hundred millilitres, if that. A small glassful,' she added, seeing Murray's blank look.

'Enough to cover three steps?'

Nish scratched her chin. 'You're going to have to give me a bit more to go on.'

Murray didn't mention the suicides at first. He recounted the report that Anna and Mark had made, and how Anna had been convinced the rabbit hadn't been placed there by an animal.

'I'd say she could be right.'

Murray leaned forward in anticipation, and Nish held up a warning finger. 'This is totally off the record and entirely hypothetical, understood? Without photos, and without examining the scene, it's impossible for me to make a professional judgement.'

'But?'

'Blood – in the quantity we're talking about – doesn't pour out of a prone rabbit. It seeps. And it coagulates. So, although a hundred and fifty mill tipped on the floor would make a hell of a mess – ever dropped a glass of wine? – the same amount oozing from a rabbit would congeal long before it dripped onto the step below. Most of it would be caught in the fur.'

'Right. So, someone deliberately tipped blood on the other steps to make a more impressive crime scene?'

'Sounds like it. The bigger question is why?' Nish eyed Murray, her head tilted slightly to one side. 'There's more to this than you're telling me, isn't there.'

It wasn't a question.

'There were two suicides at Beachy Head last year. Tom and Caroline Johnson – they owned the car showroom on the corner of Main Street.'

Nish snapped her fingers. 'Left a black Audi in the car park, right? Rocks in his rucksack.'

'You're good. That was Tom Johnson. His wife, Caroline, died seven months later – exactly a year ago. Same place, identical method. Anna Johnson is their daughter.' He passed Nish a plastic evidence bag containing the anonymous anniversary card, together with a photograph of the pieced-together card.

'Suicide?' Nish read aloud. 'Think again.' She looked up. 'Very dramatic. The suggestion being that she was murdered?'

'That's certainly how Anna Johnson interpreted it. This

119

morning she opened the door to find the rabbit smeared across their top step.'

'Beats dog shit through the letterbox.'

'What do you think?'

'Other than the fact that it's a waste of a nice rabbit pie? I think it's fishy. What do CID say?'

'Not a lot.'

Nish had known Murray a long time. 'Oh, Murray . . .'

'I'm doing the background work, that's all. You know what CID are like nowadays. Stretched to buggery. I'll package it up for the DI as soon as there's something concrete to go on. Fingerprints, for example.' He gave Nish a winning smile and pushed the exhibit bag closer to her.

Nish pushed it back. 'Not without a budget code, I'm afraid.'

'Couldn't you put it through on the original job?'

'You know I'm not supposed to do that.'

'She lost both her parents, Nish. She's a new mother, desperately trying to hold it all together without mum there to give her moral support.'

'You're going soft in your old age.'

'Whereas you're still hard as nails, of course. What was it you were saying about kittens?' He pushed the evidence bag back across the table.

This time, she took it.

NINETEEN

The rocking chair was a wedding present from my parents. It has a high back and smooth curved arms exactly the right height for sleepy night-time feeds. It arrived with a red ribbon, two soft cushions, and a note that said 'for the nursery'.

I spent hours in this chair. You never got up – men didn't, in those days – and I was afraid to turn on the light in case it kept Anna awake, so I rocked back and forth in the dark, willing her to sleep.

When Anna moved out of the nursery I brought the rocking chair downstairs, where it divided its time between the kitchen and the sitting room. But now it is back here, in Anna's nursery.

In our granddaughter's nursery.

The room is large. Extravagant for a baby, especially one currently sleeping in her parents' bedroom, judging by the Moses basket on Anna's side of the bed. Above the white cot is a string of pink and white bunting, with the name Ella picked out in pale green.

Adjacent to the cot is a chest of drawers and, on the opposite wall, a matching wardrobe and a changing table with gingham-lined baskets filled with nappies and talcum powder.

I mean only to peek inside – I think it's unlikely I'll find the key here – but my feet find their way across the soft grey carpet to the rocking chair. My rocking chair.

Back and forth, back and forth. The light low. The view across the rooftops the same as it's been for twenty-six years. Anna in my arms.

They called it the baby blues, then. It felt more than that. I was overwhelmed. Frightened. I wanted to call Alicia – the only one of my friends who might have understood – but I couldn't bring myself to pick up the phone. I had everything she didn't: a husband, a big house, money. What right did I have to cry?

I've stayed here too long. I need to get on. I need to get out.

Downstairs I check the kitchen, automatically straightening the tea towel hanging on the Aga. There's a pile of magazines on the table, and a scattering of post dumped in the empty fruit bowl on the island. I don't find the key I'm looking for.

There's a scuffle of paws from the utility room.

Rita.

My breath catches in my throat and although I don't make a sound, I hear her whine. She can sense I'm here.

I pause, my fingers resting lightly on the door handle. Surely being seen by a dog isn't the same as being seen by humans? Rita whines again. She knows I'm here – walking away would be cruel.

A quick hello and then I'll leave. Where's the harm in that? She can't tell anyone she's seen a ghost.

The door is barely open an inch when it's forced open by a barrel of fur moving so fast it tumbles over itself and twice rolls along the tiled floor before standing again.

Rita!

She jumps backwards, her hackles up and her tail wagging as though she doesn't know how she should be feeling. She barks once. Twice. Jumps forward and then back. I remember her growling at shadows in the hedgerows on our evening walks, and wonder what she saw then that I dismissed as nothing.

I drop to my knees and hold out a hand. She knows my smell, but my appearance is confusing her.

'Good girl, Rita.'

The sob in my voice catches me unawares. Rita's ears prick up in recognition, and the ridge of bristling fur along her spine

122

subsides. Her tail is a blur, taking her back end with it. Another whine.

'Yes, it's me, Rita. There's a good girl. Come on.'

She needs no further invitation. Satisfied that, contrary to first impressions, her mistress is indeed in her kitchen, she throws herself at me, licking furiously at my face and leaning so heavily against me I have to put out a hand to steady myself.

I sit with her, my quest forgotten as I bury my face in her fur. I feel the advent of tears and I swallow hard and refuse to let them fall. When Rita arrived from Cyprus she'd been in a rescue centre for eight months. She was affectionate and gentle, but had such acute separation anxiety that even leaving the room was an ordeal. The first time we went out she howled so loudly we could still hear her at the end of the street, and I had to turn back and leave you to go on alone.

Gradually Rita realised she was here for keeps. That if we went out we'd be back with treats for being such a brave girl. She still greeted us on our return with excitement and relief, but the howling ceased, and she settled into a calm and happy dog.

Guilt seeps through me as I imagine how she must have felt the day I didn't come home. Did she wait by the front door? Run the length of the hall and back, whining to see me? Did Anna stroke her? Reassure her I'd be back soon? All the while wondering herself what had happened. Worrying as much as Rita. More.

Rita suddenly sits up, nose in the air and ears alert. I freeze. She's heard something. Sure enough, a second later, I hear it too. The crunch of gravel. Voices.

A key in the lock.

TWENTY

ANNA

Mark insists on coming with us into the house, instead of dropping us at the kerb.

'So, you *are* worried?' I say, as he carries Ella's car seat indoors. 'Now that you know it wasn't a fox that left that rabbit.' There's a chill in the hall, and I turn up the thermostat until I hear the heating kick in.

'He actually said they couldn't be certain either way.'

'Without photos, you mean?'

'Without *forensics.*' He gives me a look and I bite back a further retort. Bickering won't help. 'But yes, I'm worried,' he says, and his tone is serious. I feel childishly vindicated, but Mark isn't done. 'I'm worried about *you.*' He shuts the front door. 'What you said at the police station . . . about feeling your mother's presence . . .' He doesn't finish, and I don't help him out. 'It's a perfectly normal part of the grieving process, but it could be a sign you're not coping. And then there's Ella, and all the hormones involved in becoming a mother . . .'

I wait for several beats. 'You think I'm going mad.'

'No. I don't think that.'

'What if I *like* feeling as though Mum's still here?'

Mark nods thoughtfully and rubs a forefinger across his lips, his thumb beneath his chin. His listening face. It makes me feel like a patient, not a partner. A case study, not the mother of his child.

'What if I *want* to see ghosts? Sorry – what if I want to have *post-bereavement hallucinatory experiences*?' The correction is sarcastic, and I see hurt in Mark's eyes, but I'm past the point where I can calm myself down.

'I'll see you later.' He doesn't kiss me goodbye and I don't blame him. He shuts the door and I hear the jangle of his keys as he double-locks it behind him. I wonder fleetingly if he thinks he's keeping the danger out, or shutting it in.

'Your mother is an idiot, Ella,' I tell her. She blinks at me. Why did I have to be so unpleasant? Mark's worried, that's all. Personally and professionally. Wasn't it precisely his compassion that attracted me to him? Now I'm seeing that same trait as a flaw.

I shiver. Bend down to feel the radiator. It's warming up but it's still so cold in here. I laugh out loud – all the ghostly clichés are coming out now – but it's unconvincing, even to me, because it isn't just the temperature that makes me feel as though someone else is in the room.

It's my mother's perfume.

Addict, by Dior. Vanilla and jasmine. So faint I think I'm imagining it. I *am* imagining it. Because even as I stand at the foot of the stairs, my eyes closed, I realise that I can't smell it at all.

'Come on, you.' I unbuckle Ella from the car seat. Talking aloud to her quells the churning feeling in my stomach, as though a thousand butterflies were caught in a net.

Despite the Aga, the kitchen is icy, too. There's a smell of fresh, cold air; a drift of jasmine I make myself ignore. Rita whines from the utility room. I open the door and go to fuss her, but she ignores me and runs into the kitchen, where she chases her nose in circles along the floor. Around and around she runs, and it makes me smile in spite of myself.

'Silly dog!' I say to Ella. 'Isn't she a silly dog?'

I find a piece of marrowbone, and reluctantly Rita leaves her imaginary rabbit chase and takes it to her bed by the Aga, where she gnaws contentedly.

Post-bereavement hallucinatory experiences. Such a clinical way to describe something so magical. So inexplicable.

'Some people claim to have had entire conversations with their loved ones,' Mark said at the police station. 'It's often part of a disordered grieving process known as pathological grief, but occasionally it can be a symptom of something more serious.'

Symptoms. Processes. Conditions.

Names for things we don't understand, because we're frightened of what they might mean. What they might do to us.

Entire conversations . . .

I'd give anything to hear my parents' voices again. I have a few videos: birthday speeches; summer holiday antics; a film from my graduation, snippets recorded throughout the day, then stitched together. My parents are the wrong side of the camera – they kept it proudly trained on me – but the microphone picked up every whispered word as they sat in their front-row seats in the Butterworth Hall at Warwick Arts Centre.

'Our little girl . . .'

'I can't believe it.'

'Look at that one in the jeans – you'd think he'd have put a proper pair of trousers on.'

'You can talk – you look like you've been gardening in those.'

'How stupid of me – I thought today was about Anna! If I'd known it was a fashion parade for parents . . .'

They took me for lunch at Tailors, where Dad became prouder – and louder – with each course, and Mum wiped tears away as she shared my mediocre degree result with another stranger. By dessert I was desperate to leave, but I couldn't steal this moment from them. I was their only child. The first Johnson to go to university. They deserved a celebration.

I've played the films so often I know every word by heart, but it isn't the same. It could never be the same.

I close my eyes. Tip up my head. On impulse, I hold out my arms, palms uppermost, thinking how if anyone looks in the window right now, I will never live this down. But if I can *feel* Mum, if I can smell her perfume . . .

'Mum? Dad?' My voice sounds small and tinny in the empty kitchen. 'If you can hear me . . .'

There's a whistle of wind from outside, a rustle from the trees in the garden. Rita whines, a faint, high-pitched cry that fades into nothing.

When I was eleven Laura showed me how to make a Ouija board, explaining how we could summon the dead with nothing more than some strategically lit candles and a board on which we had carefully marked the letters of the alphabet. She swore me to secrecy, and we waited until the next time Laura babysat to set everything up.

Laura turned the lights low. She took a CD from her bag and played a track I didn't recognise, by an old-fashioned singer I'd never heard of.

'Ready?'

Our forefingers on the small piece of wood in the centre of the board, we waited. And waited. I stifled the giggles. Laura's eyes were closed, her face screwed up in concentration. I was getting bored. I'd expected a fun night in with Laura, scaring each other with ghost stories, the way my friends and I did at sleepovers.

I pushed the marker.

Laura's eyes snapped open. I mirrored her look of shock.

'Did you feel that?'

I nodded furiously. She narrowed her eyes at me.

'Did you move it? Swear you didn't move it.'

'I swear.'

Laura closed her eyes again. 'Is there someone there?'

Gently, I pushed the marker across the board. *Yes.*

And then I wished I hadn't. Because Laura's face crumpled

like paper, and tears pushed their way from beneath her eyelids and clung to her lashes.

'Mum?'

I wanted to cry too. I couldn't tell Laura I'd been messing around, but I couldn't carry on with a game she wasn't playing. Her fingers trembled, but the marker didn't move. It was an age before she took away her hands.

'Shall we play something else instead?'

'Are you okay?' I was tentative, but Laura had already blinked away the beginnings of tears. She blew out the candles, whisked me into a game of Monopoly.

Years later I confessed. We were sharing a bottle of wine, and I had a sudden memory of crouching over our homemade Ouija board, a sudden need to clear my conscience.

'I know,' she said, when I'd unburdened my soul.

'You know?'

'Well, I guessed. You were a crap liar when you were eleven.' She grinned and aimed a punch at my shoulder, then took in my face. 'Don't tell me it's been eating you up all this time?'

It hadn't, but I was relieved to discover it hadn't been weighing on *her* mind, either.

Now, my skin prickles, the hairs on the back of my neck stand on end, one by one. I catch a trace of jasmine in my nostrils.

And then . . .

Nothing.

I open my eyes and drop my arms to my side, because this is absurd. Ridiculous. My parents are dead, and I can no more summon them from my kitchen than I can spread wings and fly.

There are no messages. No hauntings. No afterlife.

Mark's right. It's all in my head.

TWENTY-ONE

MURRAY

'I take it the husband doesn't believe in ghosts,' Sarah said. They were sitting on the black leather sofa of Highfield's family room, where Murray had joined Sarah for the forty-five minutes permitted for his evening meal break.

'Partner. No, he says they're post-bereavement hallucinatory experiences.'

'Casper will be devastated.'

The door to the family room opened and a young girl came in. She was so thin her head seemed disproportionately large, and a criss-cross of fine scars covered her arms from wrist to shoulder. She didn't acknowledge Murray or Sarah, just picked up a magazine from the coffee table and took it back out of the room.

'According to Mark Hemmings, up to sixty per cent of bereaved people report seeing or hearing a loved one after death, or sense their presence in some other way.'

'So, what's the difference between that and a ghost?' Sarah was flicking through the pages of Caroline Johnson's diary. They ate early at Highfield, like kids fed their tea at five o'clock, and so Sarah had sat cross-legged on the sofa and looked through the case papers while Murray ate his sandwiches.

'Beats me.'

'I shall haunt you, when I'm gone.'

'Don't.'

'Why not? I would have thought you'd be glad to see me.'

'I didn't mean that. I meant . . . Oh, never mind.' Don't talk about dying, he'd meant. He looked out of the window. The sky was clear and sprinkled with stars, and Murray had a sudden memory of lying in the park when he and Sarah first got together, pointing out the constellations they knew, and making up names for the ones they didn't.

'That's the Plough.'

'And there's the Porcupine.'

'Idiot.'

'Idiot yourself.'

They had made love on the damp grass, only moving when their empty stomachs reminded them they hadn't eaten since lunchtime.

'Fancy a walk?' Murray said now. 'Once around the block?'

Instantly the spark in Sarah's eyes was replaced with anxiety. She drew up her knees to her chest, hugging them close, her fingers gripping Caroline's diary like they were glued to it.

It was new, this fear of being outside. Not agoraphobia – not according to her consultant – just another small piece of the anxiety mosaic that was Murray's beautiful, funny, intensely complex wife.

'No problem.' He waved an arm, dismissing the idea and, with it, the hope that Sarah was ready to come home. Small steps, he thought. It was Friday. Christmas wasn't till Monday. There was plenty of time to get her home. 'Anything leap out at you?' He indicated the diary. Slowly, now that he wasn't suggesting she leave the premises, Sarah's muscles began to unwind. She opened the book, looking for a particular date.

'Did the daughter say anything about a planning objection?'

'Not that I recall.'

Sarah showed him the page, a month before Caroline had died, on which a reference number had been noted, beneath the reminder *planning objection*. 'People get very het up about planning permission.'

'Het up enough to kill someone?'

'Nowt so queer as folk.'

Murray brought up the Eastbourne planning portal on his phone and peered at the reference on the diary, tapping it in with his forefinger. 'It's an application for an extension.' He found the applicant's name. 'Mr Robert Drake.' Murray remembered the list of friends and relatives who had consoled Caroline Johnson the day of her husband's death. 'He lives next door to Anna Johnson.' Murray scanned the summary. 'It was rejected. Although it looks like he's trying again now – there's a linked appeal.'

'You see. There's your motive, Poirot.'

'There were thirty-four objections. I'd better check they haven't all been bumped off.'

Sarah raised an eyebrow. 'Go on, take the piss out of my theories . . . What's your money on, Detective?'

Murray wasn't a betting man. There were enough variables in life without seeking out more, and the picture around the Johnson investigation was far from clear.

Suicide? Think again.

'Caroline Johnson's suicide was a carbon copy of her husband's,' he said, as much to himself as to Sarah. 'The similarities added weight to the coroner's verdict, not least because of details from Tom Johnson's death that had never been released to the press.'

The *Gazette* had run an obituary following Tom's death. The family had been well known locally, the business handed down through three generations. They had referred to the personal effects left on the cliff top, the car abandoned in the car park, but not to the rucksack Tom had filled with rocks. The only people privy to that piece of information had been the family, and the woman who witnessed Tom's suicide: Diane Brent-Taylor.

Murray thought about the anonymous card sent to Anna, the rabbit on their doorstep. He thought about the convenience of a suicide at high tide, leaving no bodies to spill their secrets on the slab. Both Tom and Caroline had researched tide times, but why would it matter to either of them if their bodies were found? It all seemed too convenient. Too . . . staged.

Sarah took in her husband's thoughtful expression. 'What is it?'

'I've got no evidence . . .'

'Instinct first, evidence later. Isn't that what you used to say?'

Murray laughed. He had worked on that basis for most of his career, and it hadn't let him down yet. He was a long way from knowing exactly how Tom and Caroline Johnson had died, but all his instincts pointed one way.

'You think she was murdered, don't you?'

Slowly, Murray nodded. 'I think they both were.'

Sarah looked thoughtful. She returned to Caroline's diary, flicking through the bundle of loose flyers and business cards tucked into the back of the book. She picked one up and held it in front of her.

'I thought you said Mark Hemmings hadn't met the Johnsons.'

'He didn't; they'd died before he and Anna met.'

'Not according to this.'

Murray took the flyer Sarah was holding up. *Mark Hemmings, Dip.ST, DipSTTS, MA (Psych), UKCP (Accredited), MBACP.* He turned it over. In handwriting he recognised from the many lists in Caroline Johnson's diary was a note. *2.30 p.m., Wednesday 16 November.*

Sarah turned to the relevant page of Caroline's diary, on which the same appointment was noted. She looked at Murray. 'He's lying.'

TWENTY-TWO

ANNA

At six the doorbell rings. I open the door to find Uncle Billy standing there, a bottle of wine in hand. I stare at him blankly.

'You hadn't forgotten, had you?'

'Of course not! I was miles away. Lovely to see you.' I pull him into a hug to hide my lie. 'Sorry for storming out yesterday.'

He shrugs off my apology. 'Heat of the moment. Think nothing of it. Now, where's my gorgeous great-niece?'

We head for the kitchen and I give Ella to Billy, who holds her awkwardly, as though he's guessing the weight of a marrow at the county show. She keeps reaching for his nose, which makes him laugh, and the pair of them look so sweet I pick up my phone and take a quick snap. There's a text from Mark.

Running late, sorry x

I fire off a quick reply.

No worries. Billy here for supper x

Great.

I put my phone away and smile brightly at Uncle Billy. 'Mark'll be home soon. He's really looking forward to seeing you!'

Billy's smile doesn't quite reach his eyes. 'Great.'

I pour myself a large glass of wine. Pregnancy and breastfeeding have broken the drinking habits created by my parents, but tonight I think I'm going to need this.

Dad loved telling the story of how – aged six and learning to read a clock – I was tested by friends of my parents who were over for drinks.

'What time is it, Anna?'

'Wine o'clock,' I chimed. I don't remember it; can't even be sure it wasn't just one of Dad's stories, although it has the ring of truth about it.

It's past seven when Mark gets home, full of apologies and carrying a huge bunch of Stargazer lilies.

'Sorry,' he says as he hands them to me, and I know he's not talking about being late.

'Me too,' I say softly.

'Good to see you.' Mark pumps Billy's hand enthusiastically. I hover beside them, my cheeks aching from the force of my smile.

'You too. Looking after this one, I hope.'

'Billy, I'm quite capable of looking after myself.'

Mark winks at me. *Let it go.* 'I'm doing my best, Bill. How's business?'

'Never better.'

As Billy walks ahead of us, into the sitting room, Mark shoots me a confused look. I shake my head.

Since Dad died, profits have plummeted, and Billy's struggling. Dad's half of the business passed first to Mum and then to me, but I haven't even begun to make sense of it. I told myself maternity leave was the perfect time to sit down and go through everything – to learn how the business works – but I underestimated the demands of a tiny baby. I'm lucky if I get time to read the back of a cereal packet. All I know is the headline figures, and they don't look good.

Now isn't the time to call Billy out. I leave Mark fixing drinks and retreat to the kitchen. When I return, the two men are sitting in silence. I wrack my brains to think of something Mark and Billy have in common, besides me.

'Oh! Tell Billy about Ella dancing.' I prod Mark, who looks perplexed. 'When you put Guns 'n' Roses on?' I pause, but he's still not with me. 'And we turned around and she was waving and kicking her legs and it was in time with the music, and she looked like she was dancing.'

'Right! Yes. Well, that's it, really. Like she was dancing.'

Billy laughs politely. This is excruciating. It's a relief when the doorbell rings. Mark jumps up, but I get there first. 'It's like Piccadilly Circus in here tonight!' I say brightly.

I have never been so relieved to see anyone as I am to see Laura.

'I just dropped by to see how you were, after yesterday.' She surveys me. 'Are you all right? You look a bit manic.' I drag her inside and into the kitchen, shutting the door.

'You have to stay for supper.'

'I can't, I have plans.'

'Laura, please! You have to save me. I love Billy dearly, and I love Mark – obviously – but I'm fast coming to the conclusion that they can't be in the same place at the same time.'

'Are they arguing again?'

'No, but it's only a matter of time.'

Laura laughs. 'It'll cost you.'

I hold up the bottle of wine in one hand, an empty glass in the other.

'Done.'

Sure enough, when we walk into the sitting room, the men are in full flow.

'There was no such thing as mental health in my day. Therapists, counsellors, mumbo jumbo claptrap. You just got on with it.'

'Which is probably why we're seeing such a huge fallout from it now.'

'Do you think World War Two pilots called in sick with stress? With depression?'

'I think we're only now starting to understand the—'

'Bloody snowflakes.'

I cut in. 'Look who I found!' I present Laura as though she's just jumped out of a cake. 'Now it's a proper dinner party.'

'Laura! You with us for Christmas, love?'

'Not this year. I've got a boozy lunch booked with some mates. Four Bridget Joneses and as much Prosecco as we can handle.' She grimaces, but I know she's looking forward to it. She slides onto the sofa next to Billy. 'Talk cars to me. Mine's on its last legs and I don't know what to replace it with.'

'I've got a three-year-old Skoda I could do a good price on.'

Laura wrinkles her nose. 'That wasn't quite the look I was going for.'

'There's an MX-5 that might be more up your street, although it depends on your budget. Tell you what – try a few out for size. Take the Skoda for a day or two, and anything else you fancy, and see how they drive.'

With the conversation safely steered away from the value, or otherwise, of Mark's job, I return to the kitchen.

Wine blunts the barbed edges of Billy's and Mark's comments, and by the time we've finished eating, I finally relax.

'I see your neighbour's going for planning permission again.' Billy is mellow, no longer looking to point-score over Mark. I'm grateful to them both.

'He's made a few changes since he was knocked back. It's a bit less *Grand Designs* now.'

'It was the light Caroline was worried about.' Laura points to the window, where the outside light illuminates the patio and the fence between our garden and Robert's. 'It'll completely overshadow your garden. You should put in an objection.'

'I wouldn't want to fall out with Robert.' He might be irritating, but he was very kind when Mum and Dad died, and I don't want to cause any awkwardness.

'The system's there for a reason,' Laura says. 'It doesn't have to get personal. You just fill out a form and say why you oppose the plans.'

Mark frowns. 'Maybe we should, Anna. A big extension will make it very dark in here. That could really affect the market value.'

'But we're not selling,' I say.

I don't care about next-door's extension. Mum had an argument with Robert over it when he first applied. Dad had only been gone a month, and Mum's responses to everyday situations were – understandably – a little erratic. When the corner shop ran out of bread she launched into a verbal tirade that had the poor girl behind the counter shaking. I led Mum away and put her to bed. The girl from the shop was very sympathetic when I went back to apologise. Everyone was. Robert, too. Mum became obsessed by his planning application. She latched on to it like it was a life raft, reading up on conservation areas and listed buildings, and gathering support from other residents in the street. I don't even know how much she really cared about the extension. It was another project for her to get her teeth into, like the fundraising appeal for the Cypriot dog rescue charity, or the Brexit rallies she'd tagged along on. When Mum found a project, she stuck with it. I couldn't have cared less if Robert had been building a football stadium in his back garden. We were dealing with our grief in different ways.

'We're not selling now, but eventually . . .'

'Not ever!' I push my chair back with unnecessary force.

The silence that ensues would be uncomfortable, were it not for Ella, snoozing in her bouncy chair, who screws up her face and grunts out a loud and exceptionally noxious fart. Everybody laughs. The moment passes.

'We should put her to bed, I suppose,' Mark says, making no move to do so.

'Leave her. I don't think it matters where you sleep when you're two months old.'

'Two months already!' Billy says.

'I know. It goes so fast.'

'About time you made an honest woman of Anna, isn't it, Mark?'

I start clearing the plates.

'It's not for want of trying.'

'There's no rush, Uncle Billy. We've got a baby together – that's more of a commitment than a wedding ring.'

'I tell you what,' Billy says. 'I reckon a big wedding's just what this family needs, after everything that's happened.' His lips are stained purple from the red wine. 'I'll pay for it.'

'We don't want your money, Bill.'

Laura sees my face and jumps in. 'You'd best get yourself on Tinder, Billy, if you're that desperate for a wedding. We'll be your bridesmaids, won't we, Anna?'

I shoot her a grateful glance.

'Nice idea, but I don't think there's much of a market for overweight car salesmen past their prime.'

'Oh, come on, Uncle Billy – you're quite the eligible bachelor. Nice house, good business, own teeth . . . They are your own teeth, aren't they?'

I leave them laughing, and start stacking the dishwasher.

The first time Mark proposed was the night I told him I was pregnant. I said no. He didn't have to do that.

'It's not about having to – I want to. I want to be with you. Don't you want to be with me?'

I skirted the question. I did – of course I did – but I wanted him to want me for my sake, not for our baby's.

He asked twice while I was pregnant, and again just after Ella was born. I almost said yes that time, lying in a post-birth glow, filled with drugs and the euphoria of having created the tiny life that lay sleeping in my arms.

'Soon,' I promised.

Like most women, I've imagined my wedding. The identity of the groom has changed over the years – from six-year-old Joey Matthews when I was in primary school, through a series of unsuitable boyfriends, to a couple of almost suitable ones – but the congregation has remained constant. Friends. Billy. Laura.

Mum and Dad.

When I think about marrying Mark, all I can think about is who won't be there to see it.

It's late by the time Billy and Laura leave. I walk out with them and wave them off, glad of the cold air to clear my wine-filled head. I wrap my arms around myself and stand on the pavement, looking back at the house. I think about Mark's suggestion that we sell up and start afresh, and even though I know he's right, the very thought of leaving Oak View hurts.

I glance next door. There are lights on downstairs and one on what I assume must be the middle landing. The pink planning notice Billy saw is fixed to the gate with plastic cable ties, tiny print explaining the process for lodging a complaint. I suppose there'll be a consultation period, an address for people to write to, should they object to the plans.

I can't help but feel there are more important fights to have than whether Robert Drake's extension will block light to our kitchen. Unlike my parents, who seemed at times to thrive on confrontation, the idea of entering into a dispute with a neighbour fills me with dread. Perhaps it's being an only child, with no sibling warfare to toughen me up, but the hint of an argument is more likely to push me to tears than fire me up for retaliation.

I'm just walking back to the house when there's a loud crash, and the sound of breaking glass. The night air is disorientating; I can't tell where it came from. As I open the front door I catch a glimpse of Mark, running upstairs. Seconds later he calls out. I run up the stairs.

'What is it? What's happened?'

There's a gust of cold air in Ella's nursery, and the open curtains blow into the room, the glass behind them shattered. I let out a cry.

Mark points at her cot. It's covered in shards of glass that glint in the glow from the overhead light, and in the centre of the mattress is a brick. An elastic band holds a sheet of paper in place.

Gingerly, Mark picks up the brick.

'Fingerprints!' I remember.

He holds the paper by a single corner, and twists his head to read the typed message.

No police. Stop before you get hurt.

TWENTY-THREE

MURRAY

Anna Johnson looked tired. Dark circles ringed her eyes, and although she smiled politely when she opened the door, she had none of the determination Murray had seen in her the previous day. She showed him through to the kitchen, where Mark Hemmings was clearing the table from breakfast.

Murray found the dynamic interesting. Despite Anna's obvious strength, when the couple were together she seemed to let Mark take charge. Murray wondered if this was by choice, or by design. Was it Mark who called the shots in this relationship? Had he really lied about not knowing Caroline Johnson?

'I'm sorry – am I interrupting?'

'Not at all. We're a bit late getting going today, after last night.'

'Last night?' There were several wine glasses upturned on the draining board. Murray smiled, wanting to diffuse the tension he didn't fully understand. 'Ah – a good time had by all?' He looked at Anna and then Mark, and his smile faded. Anna was glaring at him, her mouth open.

'A good time? What the—'

Mark crossed the room and put an arm around Anna. 'It's okay.' He addressed Murray. 'Someone threw a brick through our daughter's window, with a note wrapped around it. It could have killed her.'

Murray got out his notebook. 'What time was this?'

'Around midnight,' Anna said. 'We were—'

Mark interrupted. 'Do we have to go through this again? We were up till two a.m. giving statements.'

It was then that Murray noticed the paperwork on the kitchen table. The card with contact details for the Police Enquiry Centre; the Victim Support leaflet with the phone number ringed in biro. He put away his notebook.

'No, of course not. I'll check in with the officers who attended, and make sure they've got all the information they need.'

Mark's eyes narrowed. 'They asked if we had a crime number.'

Somewhere in the pit of Murray's stomach, he felt a familiar sensation.

'From the other job – the anniversary card.'

When Murray had been a probationer, he had cuffed a job that had come back to bite him. The sergeant – a sharp Glaswegian – had hauled Murray into the office to ask why nothing had been done about 'what seems to me to be an open-and-shut case, laddie,' then promptly assigned Murray to traffic duties. He had stood in the rain, water dripping off his helmet, and felt sick to his stomach. Three weeks into the job and he'd already been told off. Was that it? Would his skipper write him off as a bad lot?

It wasn't, and the skipper didn't. But that might have been because, from that moment, Murray vowed to treat every victim with the consideration they deserved, and to play everything by the book.

He hadn't played this one by the book.

'Not to worry,' he said, as brightly as he could manage. 'I'll sort all that out, back at the station.'

'Why don't we have a crime number?' Anna said. She picked up the baby from her bouncy chair and walked towards Murray. 'You are investigating it properly, aren't you?'

Metaphorical hand on metaphorical heart, Murray nodded. 'I assure you, I am.' Better than if I'd passed it straight to CID, he thought. Nevertheless, the knot of anxiety in his stomach

142

remained, and he wondered if, even now, someone back at the police station was asking why Murray Mackenzie, a retired police officer now working on Lower Meads front desk, was investigating a possible double homicide.

'I wanted to check something, actually,' Murray said. He reached into his inside pocket for the leaflet Sarah had found in Caroline Johnson's diary, keeping it inside his hand for the time being. 'Mr Hemmings, you never met Anna's parents?'

'That's right. I told you that yesterday. It was because of their deaths that Anna came to see me in the first place.'

'Right. So, when you met Anna, that was the first you'd heard of her . . .' Murray searched for the right word, acknowledging his clumsiness with a sympathetic smile in Anna's direction. 'Her situation?'

'Yes.' There was a touch of impatience in Mark's reply.

Impatience? Or something else? Something he was trying to hide? Murray produced the flyer.

'Is this yours, Mr Hemmings?'

'Yes. I'm not sure I'm following . . .'

Murray handed him the flyer, turning it over as he did so. Curious, Anna moved to see the writing, clearly visible on the reverse. There was a single, sharp inhalation, followed by a look of complete confusion.

'That's Mum's writing.'

Murray spoke gently. 'It was found in your mother's diary.'

Mark's mouth was working, but nothing was coming out. He brandished the flyer. 'And . . . what? I don't know why she had it.'

'It seems she had an appointment with you, Mr Hemmings.'

'An appointment? Mark, what's going on? Was Mum . . . a patient of yours?' Anna took a step back, unconsciously distancing herself from the leaflet, from the father of her child.

'No! Christ, Anna! I told you, I don't know why my leaflet was with her things.'

'Right. Well, I just wanted to double-check.' Murray held out his hand for the flyer. The younger man hesitated, then dropped it into Murray's open palm with such deliberate lack of direction that Murray was forced to catch it before it fluttered to the floor. Murray smiled politely. 'I'll leave you to it, then.'

Light the blue touchpaper and stand well back, Murray thought as he left the house. Mark Hemmings had some explaining to do.

TWENTY-FOUR

ANNA

'You'd think he'd have known about last night, wouldn't you?' Mark starts clearing the table again, transferring our cereal bowls from table to dishwasher. 'The left hand doesn't know what the right hand's doing – it's ridiculous.' He bends to stack the dishes, rearranging what's already there from last night. It crosses my mind that he's deliberately taking his time, deliberately avoiding looking at me.

'Did you know my mum?'

'What?' He drops our spoons into the rack. One, two.

'Mark, look at me!'

He straightens slowly, picks up a tea towel and wipes his hands, then folds it and places it on the counter. Then he looks at me. 'I never met your mum, Anna.'

If Mark and I had been together for a decade – if we'd met as teenagers, grown up together – I'd know if he was lying. If we'd been through the challenges other couples go through – ups and downs, break-ups and make-ups – I'd know if he was lying.

If I knew him better . . .

His face is unreadable, his eyes unflinchingly on mine.

'She made an appointment with you.'

'Lots of people make appointments with me, Anna. *You* made an appointment with me. We leaflet-drop the whole of Eastbourne, for Christ's sake.' He breaks his gaze, turns back to the dishwasher, even though there's nothing left on the side.

145

'But you don't remember speaking to her?'

'No. Look, some people book with me direct, others go through Janice. The chances are, I never had any contact with her.'

Janice sits on reception in the lobby of the office block that houses Mark's Brighton practice, along with a dozen other small businesses that don't need – or can't afford – their own building, their own staff. She manages their diaries, welcomes their clients and answers the phone, matching her greeting to whichever line is flashing on her phone.

Serenity Beauty, can I help you?

Brighton Interiors, can I help you?

'The point is, she never kept the appointment.'

'How do you know?' The words don't sound like mine. They're harsh and accusatory. Mark makes a sound like air escaping from a tyre: exasperated, irritated. It's the first time we've argued. Properly, like this, snapping at each other, turning away to roll eyes at an invisible audience as though trying to summon support.

'I'd have remembered.'

'You didn't remember she'd booked an appointment.'

There's a beat before he answers.

'It'll be on the system. Janice updates it when they arrive.'

'So, you can check?'

'I can check.'

I hand him his mobile.

He lets out a short, humourless laugh. 'You want me to do it now?'

I wonder if this is what it's like when you think your husband's cheating, if this is what you turn into. I have become the sort of woman I've always despised: a folded-arm, pursed-lips harridan demanding on-the-spot answers from a man who has never once given me cause to distrust him.

But his leaflet was in my mother's diary.

He scrolls through his contacts, taps the entry for the practice. I hear Janice's sing-song tones on the other end of the phone and know what she's saying, even though I can't hear the words.

Holistic Health, can I help you?

'Janice, it's me. Would you mind checking something on the system? Wednesday sixteenth of November last year. Two-thirty p.m. Caroline Johnson.'

The bravado I felt a moment ago morphs into uncertainty. If Mark were lying he wouldn't check right now, in front of me. He'd say he needed to look it up at work, or that the records didn't hold that level of detail. He's not lying. I know he isn't.

'And she didn't re-book?'

I busy myself picking up Rita's toys and dropping them into the basket.

'Thanks, Janice. How are the next couple of days looking? Any cancellations?' He listens, then laughs. 'No chance of Christmas Eve off, then!'

He says goodbye and finishes the call.

Now it's my turn to avoid his gaze. I pick up a toy pheasant from which Rita has extracted the stuffing. 'I'm sorry.'

'She was marked as a no-show. She didn't make another appointment.' He crosses the kitchen and comes to stand in front of me, gently hooking his forefinger under my chin and lifting it until I'm looking at him. 'I never met her, Anna. I wish I had.'

And I believe him. Because why would he lie?

TWENTY-FIVE

MURRAY

'Can we go inside now?'

Murray squeezed Sarah's hand. 'Let's do one more.' They were walking around Highfield, close enough for Sarah to trail a hand along the brickwork, anchoring herself to the building.

'Okay.'

Murray heard her breath quicken. She tried to speed up – to get it over with – but he kept the measured pace they had followed for the previous two laps of the building. He did his best to distract her.

'Tom Johnson's will left the house to his wife, along with his share of the business, and all his assets except for a hundred grand, which he left to Anna. His life assurance pay-out went to Caroline.'

'Even though it was suicide?'

'Even though.' Murray now knew far more about life assurance and suicide than he had ever needed to know. Most companies had a 'suicide clause' in their policies that meant no pay-out if the policy had been taken out within twelve months of the policy-holder's suicide. It was to stop people committing suicide to escape debt, the helpful woman from Aviva had explained to Murray when he'd rung. Tom Johnson's policy had been in place for years; the pay-out to his wife made as soon as the death certificate had been issued.

'What about Caroline's will?'

Sarah's trailing hand still followed the line of the wall, but now Murray saw air between her fingers and the brickwork. He kept talking. 'A small sum to her goddaughter, a ten-grand legacy to a Cypriot animal rescue charity, and the rest to Anna.'

'So, Anna ended up with the lot. You're sure she didn't bump them both off?' Her hand dropped to her side.

'And send herself an anonymous note?'

Sarah was thinking. 'Maybe the card was from someone who knows she killed them. Anna panics, brings the card to the police station because that's what a normal, non-murderous person would do. It's a double bluff.'

Murray grinned. Sarah was far more creative than any detective he'd ever worked with.

'Any fingerprints?'

'Several. Nish is working her way through them now.' Tom Johnson's car had been dusted for prints after his death, and elimination sets taken from his daughter and the staff at Johnson's Cars. The anonymous card carried full prints from both Anna Johnson and from her uncle, Billy, who had ripped it into pieces before Anna could stop him, and several partials which could have come from anywhere – including the shop where the card had been bought. None of the prints had triggered a hit on the Police National Computer.

At the mention of their friend's name, Sarah had brightened. Her hand relaxed a little in Murray's. 'How is Nish?'

'She's well. She asked after you. Suggested we have dinner together, when you're up to it.'

'Maybe.'

Maybe was okay. Maybe was better than no. Tomorrow was Christmas Eve, and Sarah's consultant, Mr Chaudhury, had decided Sarah should be discharged. Sarah had other ideas.

'I'm not well,' she'd said, worrying at her frayed sleeves.

People who proclaimed themselves to be champions of mental health issues were fond of comparing them to physical ailments.

'If Sarah had broken her leg we'd all understand that it needed fixing,' Murray's line manager had said, when Murray had apologised for taking time off to support his wife. The diversity box had been duly ticked.

Only it wasn't like a broken bloody leg. A broken leg could be fixed. X-rays, a plaster cast, perhaps a metal splint. A few weeks on crutches. Resting, physio. And then – what? The odd twinge, perhaps, but fixed. Better. Sure, it might break more easily next time you came off a bike, or took the stairs awkwardly and tripped, but it wouldn't snap spontaneously. It wouldn't freeze in horror at the prospect of answering the door, or crumble into pieces if someone whispered out of earshot.

Borderline Personality Disorder was nothing like a broken leg.

No, Sarah wasn't well. But she never would be.

'Sarah, Borderline Personality Disorder is not something we are going to cure.' Chaudhury's Oxbridge accent was undercut by a Birmingham twang. 'You know that. You know more about your condition than anyone. But you are managing it well, and you will continue to do that at home.'

'I want to stay here.' Sarah's face had creased into tears. She looked more like a homesick child than a fifty-eight-year-old woman. 'I don't like it at home. I'm safe here.'

Murray had pasted a smile to his face to hide the right hook he'd felt to his stomach. Mr Chaudhury had been firm.

'You'll be safe at home. Because for the last few days it hasn't been us keeping you safe.' He had paused and leaned forward, pointing steepled fingers towards Sarah. 'It's been you. You'll continue with daily sessions, then we'll move towards weekly visits. Small steps. The main priority is to get you back home with your husband.'

Murray had waited for the left hook. But Sarah nodded meekly, and reluctantly agreed that tomorrow she would go home. And then she had surprised Murray by agreeing to go for a walk.

Murray stopped. 'There. That's three.'

Sarah looked taken aback to see the main door again, their three laps of the building complete.

'I'll pick you up tomorrow morning. Okay?'

She frowned. 'It's group in the morning.'

'Lunchtime, then.'

'Okay.'

Murray kissed her and began walking down the path to the car park. Halfway down he turned to wave, but she'd already scuttled inside.

Murray spent the next hour tidying the already spotless house, in preparation for Sarah's homecoming. He changed the sheets in their bedroom, and made up the spare bed too, putting fresh flowers in both rooms, just in case she wanted to be alone. When the place was pristine, he got in his car and drove into work.

The fact that Diane Brent-Taylor – the witness who had called the police to report Tom's suicide – had not attended the inquest was troubling Murray. Brent-Taylor had claimed she had been on Beachy Head that morning with a lover, and that she couldn't take the risk of her husband finding out where she'd been. CID had tried several times to persuade her, but to no avail. They had no address details for her – just a mobile phone number – and when that had been disconnected, they had given up. This was a suicide investigation, after all. Not a murder. Not then.

Murray wasn't going to give up.

There were plenty of Taylors and lots of Brents on the Police National Computer and the Electoral Register, but no Diane Brent-Taylors. Neither did Murray have any joy on open source systems – Facebook, Twitter, LinkedIn – although he would be the first to admit he was hardly an expert in the field. His expertise lay in lateral thinking. He drummed his fingers on the desk, and then started his search again, this time putting a fresh sheet of paper to the side of his keyboard. There was, no doubt, a system that would do this job for him in a fraction of the time, but pen and paper had never failed Murray yet. Besides, taking this to Force Intelligence would prompt questions he didn't yet want to answer.

On the left-hand side of his paper he jotted down the home addresses of everyone with the surname Brent in a twenty-five-mile radius of Eastbourne. If he had to widen the search, he would, but for now he was working on the basis that the witness had been local. Next, Murray began a new list of all the addresses occupied by people with the surname Taylor.

It was half an hour before he got a match.

Bingo.

24 Burlington Close, Newhaven. Occupied by a Mr Gareth Taylor, and a Mrs Diane Brent.

Murray looked up with a broad smile on his face. The only person around to see it was John, Murray's dour colleague who had been confused to see Murray arrive in work an hour previously.

'I thought you were on leave till the New Year?'

'I've got a few bits to fill in on my PDR.'

John's confusion had grown. No one voluntarily worked on their Personal Development Record unless they were going for a new job or prepping for promotion boards. As for doing it in your own time . . .

Now John looked at Murray with complete bafflement. 'I've never seen anyone look so happy to do their PDR.'

'Just taking pride in my work, John.' Murray whistled as he made his way out of the station.

Twenty-four Burlington Close was a quiet cul-de-sac off Southwich Avenue in Newhaven, halfway between Eastbourne and Brighton. Murray waited a moment before ringing the door-bell, taking in the carefully tended flowerpots around the front door, and the 'no cold callers' sign in the frosted window. A shadow moved towards him as he reached for the white plastic bell, and he realised Mrs Brent-Taylor must have seen him pull

152

up on the drive, and been waiting in the hall. She opened the door before the chime had died away. A dog barked from somewhere in the house.

Murray introduced himself. 'I'm investigating a case I think you might have had some involvement in. May I come in?'

Mrs Brent-Taylor narrowed her eyes. 'I have to pack for my daughter's. It's her turn to do Christmas.'

'It won't take long.'

She stepped back from the open door. 'I can only give you half an hour.'

As welcomes went, Murray had had worse. He smiled and thrust out his hand in a way that made it impossible for Mrs Brent-Taylor not to take it. She glanced around as if the neighbours might already be passing judgement.

'You'd better come in.'

The hall was dark and narrow. There was an umbrella stand and two pairs of shoes on the floor, and an organised pinboard on which Murray could see a variety of leaflets and reminders. Something caught his eye as he passed the board, but he was ushered on into the depths of the house.

He was momentarily confused to be directed up a flight of stairs, but his bearings became clear as he reached the top to find a large open-plan living space and floor-to-ceiling windows with a stunning view of the sea.

'Wow.'

Diane Brent-Taylor appeared at the top of the stairs a full minute after Murray. She seemed mollified by his compliment, the corners of her mouth curling slightly in what seemed to pass for a smile. 'I'm very fortunate.'

'Have you lived here long?'

'It'll be twenty years in March. If I move now it'll be into a bungalow.' She gestured to a mustard-coloured sofa, and took the chair next to it. She sank into it with an audible exhalation.

Murray hesitated. He had finessed his line of questioning on the way here, starting with the identity of Mrs Brent-Taylor's lover. After all, it was entirely possible that Brent-Taylor had refused to give a statement not just to hide her extramarital activity, but because she – or her lover – had been involved in Tom Johnson's death. Could Diane Brent-Taylor have been protecting someone?

But now he felt entirely wrong-footed.

Mrs Brent-Taylor was in her late seventies. Possibly even in her eighties. She wore the sort of trousers his mother would have described as 'slacks', teamed with a busily patterned blouse in colours significantly more cheerful than its wearer. Her blue-tinged hair was set in rigid waves, close to her head, and her nails were painted a pale coral.

It was, of course, possible that Mrs Brent-Taylor had a lover. But given the time it had taken her to climb the stairs, and the walking stick he had glimpsed propped up behind her armchair, Murray felt it was unlikely she had been gallivanting around Beachy Head with him.

'Um, is your husband home?'

'I'm widowed.'

'I'm so sorry. Was it recent?'

'Five years last September. May I ask what this is about?

It was becoming increasingly clear that either Murray had the wrong house or . . . There was only one way to find out. 'Mrs Brent-Taylor, do the names Tom and Caroline Johnson mean anything to you?'

She frowned. 'Should they?'

'Tom Johnson died at Beachy Head on the eighteenth of May last year. His wife Caroline died in the same spot on the twenty-first of December.'

'Suicide?' She took Murray's silence as agreement. 'How dreadful.'

'Tom Johnson's death was reported to police by a witness giving your name.'

'Giving *my* name?'

'Diane Brent-Taylor.'

'Well, it wasn't me. I mean, I've been to Beachy Head, obviously – I've lived in or around the area all my life – but I've never seen anyone jump off. Thank God.' She muttered this last to herself.

What were the chances of there being two Diane Brent-Taylors in the Eastbourne area?

'It's an unusual name.'

'It isn't properly double-barrelled, you know,' Mrs Brent-Taylor said defensively, as though this exonerated her. 'My husband liked the sound of them together. He thought it went down well on the golf course.'

'Right.' Murray steeled himself. It was already clear that today's excursion had been a wild-goose chase, but he wouldn't be doing his job properly if he didn't dot all the 'i's and cross all the 't's. 'So, just to clarify, you definitely didn't call 999 on the eighteenth of May 2016 to report seeing a man throw himself off the cliffs at Beachy Head.'

Mrs Brent-Taylor narrowed her eyes. 'I may be getting on a bit, young man, but I still have my full faculties.' Murray just managed to stop himself thanking her for the misplaced compliment.

'One final thing – and I apologise if this seems a little impertinent – is it at all possible that on the eighteenth of May last year you might have been on Beachy Head with someone else's husband?'

Within seconds Murray found himself standing outside 24 Burlington Close, with the door slammed firmly in his face. Really, he thought, Diane Brent-Taylor moved quite quickly when she wanted to.

TWENTY-SIX

ANNA

Running feet make a pleasing sound on wet tarmac. My trainers feel strange after what must be a year at the bottom of the under-stairs cupboard, and my leggings cut into the soft flesh around my waist, but it feels good to be moving. Out of the habit, I have forgotten my headphones, but the rhythmic sound of my own breathing is hypnotic. Reassuring.

Mark's mum, Joan, has come for Christmas, and as soon as she arrived, early this morning, she and Mark practically press-ganged me into letting her take Ella out.

'It'll give her a chance to get to know me.'

'A little break will do you good, sweetheart.'

'And don't you dare do housework. You're to put your feet up and read a magazine.'

'Go back to bed, if you want to.'

Reluctantly I packed Ella's bag with nappies and expressed milk, issued Joan with a list of instructions I knew she'd ignore, and walked around my house, looking for ghosts.

The house was too quiet, the ghosts all in my head. I drove myself mad sniffing the air for jasmine; screwing shut my eyes in an effort to better hear voices that weren't there. There was no way I'd sleep, or even settle for a few minutes with a magazine, so I went upstairs to put on my running things. The landing was darker than normal, the piece of board over the nursery window blocking out the light.

156

I run past a parade of shops, colourful lights strung like bunting across the street.

Tomorrow is Christmas Day. I wish I could go to sleep tonight and wake up on Boxing Day. Last year Mum had been dead for four days. Christmas didn't happen; no one even pretended to try. This year the weight of expectation sits heavily on my shoulders. Ella's first stocking, her first time on Santa's knee. Our first Christmas as a family. We are making memories, but every one is bittersweet.

'Do you have to work today?' I asked Mark this morning.

'Sorry. Christmas is a difficult time for a lot of people.'

Yes, I wanted to say. Me.

My lungs are burning and I haven't run more than a mile. The year before last I did the Great South Run; now I can't imagine making it to the beach without collapsing.

The high street is thronged with harassed shoppers buying last-minute presents. I run into the road to skirt the queue at the butcher's, customers snaking down the road for their turkeys and chipolatas.

I haven't been paying attention to my route, but as I turn the corner I see Johnson's Cars at the end of the road. My pace falters. I put one hand on the stitch in my side.

On Christmas Eve Mum and Dad would always shut up shop at lunchtime. They'd lock the doors and gather the staff, and I'd fill sticky glasses with sweet mulled wine, while Billy and Dad handed out the bonus cheques, and 'I Wish It Could Be Christmas Every Day' piped through the speakers.

I could turn back. Take the side street on the left and double back towards home. Put Mum and Dad, and the police investigation, and the smashed nursery window, out of my mind for a few more hours.

I could.

I don't.

'Run, Annie, run!'

Billy is walking across the forecourt. He's pumping his arms as though he's sprinting, and I laugh because he looks ridiculous and he doesn't care. He comes to a halt a few feet away from me and does half a dozen star jumps before stopping abruptly.

'Hope the lads don't put that on YouTube.' He wipes the back of his hand across his forehead. 'Christ, I haven't done that since the Green Goddess was on the box.'

'Maybe you should. YouTube?' I stretch, feeling my hamstring burn as I push down on my extended leg.

'CCTV.' Billy gestures vaguely up and around us. 'Used to be dummies, but the insurance company insists on real ones now. And trackers on the cars, after . . .' He breaks off, reddening. After two partners in the business made off with brand-new cars, abandoning them in the public car park at Beachy Head.

'Billy, someone threw a brick through the nursery window last night, just after you left.'

'A brick?' A couple browsing the forecourt look up, and he lowers his voice. 'Christ alive . . . Is Ella okay?'

'She was still downstairs with us. She sleeps with us at the moment anyway, but we could have been changing her, or put her down for a nap, or . . . It doesn't bear thinking about. The police came straight away.'

'Do they think they'll be able to find out who did it?'

'You know what they're like. "We'll do our best, Miss Johnson."'

Billy made a dismissive sound.

'I'm scared, Billy. I think Mum and Dad were murdered, and I think whoever killed them wants to stop us finding out more. I don't know what to do.' My voice cracks and he opens his arms and wraps me in a bear hug.

'Annie, sweetheart, you're getting yourself in a state.'

I pull away. 'Do you blame me?'

'The police looked into your mum and dad's deaths – they said they were suicides.'

'They were wrong.'

We look at each other for a second. Billy nods slowly.

'Then I hope they know what they're doing this time.'

I point to a black Porsche Boxster in pride of place on the forecourt. 'Nice wheels.'

'Picked it up yesterday. Wrong weather for it, of course – probably won't shift till the spring – but I'm hoping it'll pull in the punters.' There's a worried look in his eyes.

'How bad is it, Uncle Billy?'

He says nothing for the longest time, and when he eventually speaks, he keeps his eyes trained on the Porsche. 'Bad.'

'The money Dad left you—'

'Gone.' Billy gives a bitter laugh. 'It paid off the overdraft, but it didn't touch the loan.'

'What loan?'

Silence again.

'Billy, what loan?'

This time he looks at me. 'Your dad took out a business loan. Trade had been slow for a while, but we were doing okay. You have to ride the rough with the smooth in this game. But Tom wanted to do the place up. Get the lads using iPads instead of carrying clipboards; smarten up the forecourt. We had a row about it. Next thing I know, the money's in the account. He went ahead and did it anyway.'

'Oh, Billy . . .'

'We fell behind with the repayments, and then . . .' He stops, but I hear the rest of his story in my head. *Then your dad topped himself, and left me with the debt.*

For the first time in nineteen months, Dad's suicide starts to make sense. 'Why haven't you told me this before?'

Billy doesn't answer.

'How much is the loan? I'll pay it off.'

159

'I'm not taking your money, Annie.'

'It's Dad's money! It's right that you have it.'

Billy turns so he's standing square on to me. He puts his hands on either side of my shoulders and holds me firmly. 'First rule of business, Annie: keep the company money separate from your own money.'

'But I'm a director! If I want to bail out the business—'

'It's not how it works. A company needs to stand on its own two feet, and if it can't . . . well, then it shouldn't be in business.' He cuts across my attempts to argue. 'Now, how about a test drive?' He points at the Boxster. Our conversation is over.

I learned to drive in a Ford Escort ('Start with something sensible, Anna'), but once I got my licence, the sky was the limit. In exchange for valeting every weekend, I'd borrow cars from the forecourt, knowing I risked the wrath of both my parents and Uncle Billy if I didn't bring them back in mint condition. I never developed the same speed gene as my mother, but I learned how to handle fast cars.

'You're on.'

The wet roads mean the Boxster's a little tail-happy on bends, and I head out of town so I can open her up. I grin at Billy, enjoying the freedom of a car with no baby seat in the back. A car with no back seats at all. I catch a worried look on his face.

'I'm only doing sixty-two.'

Then I understand it's not the speed Billy's concerned about, but the sign for Beachy Head. I hadn't been thinking about where we were going; I'd been enjoying the feel of a responsive engine, of a steering wheel that twitched like a live thing beneath my hands.

'I'm sorry. It wasn't intentional.'

Billy hasn't been to Beachy Head since Mum and Dad died. On test drives he takes people the other way, towards Bexhill and Hastings. I glance to the side and see his face, pale and crumpled, reflected in the nearside mirror. I take my foot off the accelerator, but I don't turn around.

'Why don't we take a walk? Pay our respects.'

'Oh Annie, love, I don't know . . .'

'Please, Uncle Billy. I don't want to go on my own.'

There's a heavy silence, then he agrees.

I drive to the car park where Mum and Dad left their cars. I don't need to look for ghosts here; they're all around us. The paths they trod, the signs they passed.

I last came on Mum's birthday, feeling closer to her up here than in the corner of the churchyard where two small plaques mark my parents' lives. The cliffs look the same, but the questions in my head have changed. No longer 'why' but 'who'. Who was Mum with that day? What was Dad doing up here?

Suicide? Think again.

'Okay?'

Billy nods tightly.

I lock the car and take his arm. He relaxes a little, and we walk towards the headland. Focus on the good times, I think.

'Remember that time you and Dad dressed as the Krankies for the summer party?'

Billy laughs. 'We argued over who got to be Wee Jimmy. And I won, because I was the short arse, only then—'

'Then the two of you got pissed and fought about it all over again.' We burst out laughing at the memory of Wee Jimmy and Dad rolling around the showroom floor. Dad and Uncle Billy fought in the way only brothers fight: fast and furious, and over as soon as it began.

We fall into a companionable silence as we walk, interspersed with occasional snorts of laughter as Billy recalls the night of the Krankies all over again. He squeezes my arm.

'Thank you for making me come. It was about time I faced up to it.'

We're standing on the cliff top now, safely back from the edge.

Neither of us have proper coats on and the rain is coming from all directions, soaking through my running jacket. Out at sea a small boat with red sails cuts through grey choppy water. I think of Mum, standing where we are now. Was she scared? Or was she here with someone she trusted? Someone she thought was a friend. A lover, even – although the thought sickens me. Is it possible my mother had been having an affair?

'Do you think she knew?'

Billy doesn't say anything.

'When she came up here. Do you think she knew she was going to die?'

'Anna, don't.' Billy starts walking back towards the car park.

I run to catch up. 'Don't you want to know what really happened?'

'No. Give me the keys – I'll drive back.' The rain has pasted Billy's hair to his head. He holds out his hands, but I stand still, defiant, the keys between us.

'Don't you see: if Mum and Dad were killed, it changes everything. It means they didn't leave us; they didn't give up on life. The police will look for their murderer. They'll find answers for us, Billy!'

We stare at each other, and then to my horror I see Billy is crying. His mouth works without words, like the TV on mute, and then he turns up the sound and I wish with all my being I'd driven towards Hastings instead.

'I don't want answers, Annie. I don't want to think about how they died. I want to think about the way they lived. I want to remember the good times and the funny times, and the nights in the pub.' His voice gets gradually louder until he's shouting at me, the wind whipping the words straight at me. The tears have stopped, but I've never seen Billy like this before. I've never seen him out of control. His fists are tightly balled and he shifts from one foot to another like he's spoiling for a fight.

'Mum was murdered! Surely you want to know who did it?'

162

'It won't change anything. It won't bring her back.'

'But we'll have justice. Someone will pay for what they did.'

Billy turns and walks away. I run after him, pulling him back by the shoulder. 'I just want answers, Uncle Billy. I loved her so much.'

He stops walking, but he won't look at me, and in his face is a mixture of grief and anger and something else, something confusing. Understanding comes a split second before he speaks, so quietly the wind almost takes it away without me hearing it. Almost, but not quite.

'So did I.'

We sit in the car park, watching the rain on the windscreen. Every now and then a strong gust of wind rocks the car, and I'm glad we came down from the cliffs when we did.

'I remember the first time I saw her,' Billy says, and it should feel awkward but it doesn't because he's not really here. He's not sitting in a Porsche Boxster at Beachy Head with his niece. He's somewhere else entirely. Remembering. 'Tom and I were living in London. Tom had done some big deal at work and we'd gone to Amnesia to celebrate. VIP passes, the lot. It was a big night. Tom drank champagne all night; spent the whole time on the sofa with a string of girls. I think he thought he was Peter Stringfellow.' Billy gives me a sidelong glance. He flushes, and I worry he's going to clam up, but he keeps talking.

'It was 1989. Your mum was there with a friend. They didn't give a second glance to the VIP area – they were on the dance floor all night. She was stunning, your mum. Every now and then some guy would come up to them and make a move, but they weren't interested. Girls' night out, Caroline said later.'

'You spoke to her?'

'Not then. But I gave her my number. I'd been plucking up the courage all night, then suddenly it was last orders and everyone was leaving, and I thought I'd missed my chance.'

I've almost forgotten that he's talking about my mother. I'm

163

captivated by the expression on Billy's face; I've never seen him like this before.

'Then there she was. In the queue for the cloakroom. And I thought: if I don't do it now . . . So, I did. I asked if she would take my number. Give me a call. Only I didn't have a pen, and she laughed and said was I the sort of bloke who would forget his wallet, too, and her friend found an eye-liner pencil and I wrote my number on Caroline's arm.'

I can see it so clearly. Mum in her eighties finery – big hair and neon leggings – Uncle Billy gauche and sweating with nerves. Mum would have been twenty-one, which would have made Billy twenty-eight, Dad three years older.

'Did she call you?'

Billy nodded. 'We went out for a drink. Had dinner a few days later. I took her to see Simply Red at the Albert Hall, then . . .' He stopped.

'What happened?'

'I introduced her to Tom.'

We sit in silence for a while, and I think about poor Uncle Billy, and wonder how I feel about my parents breaking his heart.

'I saw it straight away. She'd had a laugh with me, but . . . I went to get the drinks, and when I came back I stood in the doorway and watched them.'

'Oh Billy, they didn't—'

'No, nothing like that. Not for ages. Not till they'd both talked to me, and apologised, and said they never meant to hurt me. But they had this *connection* . . . I already knew I'd lost her.'

'But then you all worked together. How could you bear it?'

Billy gives a rueful laugh. 'What was I supposed to do – lose Tom, too? By the time your granddad got ill and Tom and I took over the business, you were on your way and it was water under the bridge.' He shakes himself and turns to me with his trademark jollity. Except that I know it's an act, and I wonder how many other times I've been fooled.

I wonder if Mum and Dad were fooled.

'I love you, Uncle Billy.'

'I love you too, sweetheart. Now, let's get you back to that baby of yours, shall we?'

We drive back sedately, Billy cornering the Boxster like he's in a Toyota Yaris. He drops me off outside Oak View.

'One more sleep!' he says, the way he used to when I was a kid. 'I'll see you first thing in the morning.'

'We'll have a great Christmas.' I mean it. Billy didn't let his past dictate his future, and I can't either. Mum and Dad are gone, and whatever the circumstances of their deaths, nothing's going to change that.

Joan isn't due back with Ella for another hour. Ignoring the damp seeping through my running clothes, I put on an apron and make two batches of mince pies. I fill the slow cooker with red wine, orange slices and spices, pour in a generous slug of brandy and turn the heat on low. The doorbell rings, and I rinse my hands and look for a towel. It rings again.

'All right, I'm coming!'

Rita barks, just once, and I put my hand on her collar, half to chastise, half in reassurance. She lets out a series of miniature growls like a revving engine, but doesn't bark again. Her wagging tail tells me there's nothing amiss.

Our front door is painted white, with a stained-glass panel across the top half that catches the afternoon sun and throws colours onto the tiled floor. When visitors arrive, their silhouettes stretch out across the floor, interrupting the rainbow. As a child, I would tiptoe around the edges of the hall when I answered the door. Stepping through someone's shadow felt like walking on a grave.

The winter sun is low, and the visitor's outline stretches thin like the reflection in a carnival mirror, their head almost touching the base of the bannister. A child again, I skirt the wall towards the door. Rita has no such qualms. She bounds across the shadow, her claws skittering, and comes to a skidding halt by the front door.

I turn the key. Open the door.

And then the world falls silent and all I can hear is the blood pounding in my head. I see a car pass in the street but it makes no noise because the drumming in my ears beats faster and faster, and I put out my hand to steady myself but it isn't enough and my knees are buckling beneath me, and it can't be – it can't be.

But there on the step. Somehow different. And yet the same.

There on the step, undeniably alive, is my mother.

PART TWO

TWENTY-SEVEN

ANNA

I have lost the power of speech. I have lost the power of thought. A thousand questions race around my head and I wonder if perhaps I've gone mad. If I'm imagining that my mother – my dead mother – is standing on my top step.

Her hair – long, and kept ash-blonde for as long as I can remember it – has been dyed black, the length cropped harshly to above her chin. She wears unflattering wire-framed glasses and a shapeless, baggy dress unlike anything I've ever seen her in.

'Mum?' I whisper it, afraid that speaking out loud will break whatever spell has been cast, and that my mother – this odd new version of my mother – will vanish as quickly as she appeared.

She opens her mouth, but it seems I'm not the only one lost for words. I see the tears build above her lower lashes, and as they fall I feel wetness on my own cheeks.

'Mum?' Louder, this time, but still hesitant. I don't know what's happening, but I don't want to question it. My mother has come back to me. I've been given a second chance. Pressure builds in my chest and it seems impossible my ribs can contain the thumping coming from my heart. I let go of Rita, because I can't breathe and I need my arms free; I need to put my hands on my face, to feel that I'm real because this can't be happening.

It can't be happening.

Rita springs forward and jumps at Mum, licking her hands and weaving between her legs, whining and wagging her tail furiously. My mother, whose frozen stance has until now mirrored mine, bends to fuss her, and the familiar movement releases an involuntary gasp from within me, as though I'm emerging from water.

'You're—' I drag each word out into the world as if using them for the first time. 'Actually here?'

She straightens. Takes a breath. Her tears have stopped, but there's such anxiety in her eyes it's as though she's the one mourning me. Life is moving like sand beneath my feet and I don't know what's real and what's not any more. I'm seized by paranoia. Has the last year been a nightmare? Could it have been me who died? It feels that way. My head spins with a light-headedness that makes me sway, and my mother steps forward, one hand outstretched in concern.

I step back, confusion making me frightened, and she takes her hand away, hurt in her eyes. I've started to cry noisily, and she glances over her shoulder towards the road. Every movement she makes is achingly familiar. Every movement makes this harder to understand because it means this isn't my imagination. I haven't conjured a vision of my mother; I haven't gone mad. She isn't a ghost. She's actually here. Living. Breathing.

'What's happening? I don't understand.'

'Can I come in?' My mother's voice, low and calm, is the voice of my childhood. Of bedtime stories and post-night-terror reassurance. She calls the dog, who has tired of running circles around her, and is sniffing the gravel at the bottom of the steps. Rita obeys instantly, trotting inside. My mother takes another cautious glance around. Hesitates on the threshold; waiting to be asked.

I have imagined this moment every day for the last year.

I have dreamed about it. Fantasised about it. Coming home and finding my parents going about their business as though nothing had happened. As though the whole thing had been a terrible dream.

I've imagined getting a call from the police to tell me my father was swept out to sea. That he was rescued by a fishing boat; lost his memory. That my mother survived her fall. That they were coming back to me.

In my dreams, I throw myself at my parents. We cling to each other fiercely; hugging, touching. Making sure. And then we talk, words tumbling over each other. Interrupting, crying, apologising, promising. In my dreams there is noise and happiness and sheer joy.

My mother and I stand silently in the doorway.

The grandfather clock whirrs in the prelude to the hour. Rita, who has never liked the sound, disappears to the kitchen, having presumably satisfied herself that her mistress is here. Is real.

The chimes ring out. When my father brought home this clock, bought at auction the year I started secondary school, the three of us looked at each other as it rang the hour.

'We'll never sleep through that!' my mother said, half laughing, half appalled. Even the ticking was intrusive, echoing each passing second in the empty hall. But sleep we did, and before too long I only noticed the clock when the mechanism had stopped, and the absence of *tick-tock*, *tick-tock* made the house feel empty.

Now we look at each other, my mother and I, as each hour echoes into the space between us. Only when it has stopped, and the final peal has faded, does she speak.

'I know this is a shock.'

Was there ever more of an understatement?

'We've got a lot to talk about.'

I find my voice. 'You didn't die.' There are so many questions, but this one – the fundamental truth – is the one with which I am struggling the most. She didn't die. She isn't a ghost.

She shakes her head. 'We didn't die.'

We. I hold my breath. 'Dad?'

A beat. 'Darling, there's a lot you have to know.'

Slowly, I make my brain compute what I'm hearing. My father is alive. My parents didn't die at Beachy Head.

'So, it was an accident?'

I knew it. Was certain of it. My parents would never try to kill themselves.

But . . . an accident. Not murder; an accident.

Two accidents?

A ticker tape runs through my head as I apply this new narrative to the scenes I never have understood. Two accidents. Eyewitnesses mistaken. Falls, not jumps.

Identical falls?

The tape stops.

A sigh from my mother. Resigned. Tired. She fidgets, pushing one black strand of hair behind her ears in a gesture futile now that it is so short. She nods towards the kitchen.

'Can I come in?'

But the ticker tape has jammed. It twists into knots in my head because what I'm imagining doesn't make sense. It doesn't add up.

'Dad sent you a text.'

The longest of pauses.

'Yes.' She holds my gaze. 'Please – can we sit down inside? It's complicated.'

But suddenly it seems simple. And the shifting sands beneath my feet grow still, and the tilted world starts to spin again. There's only one explanation.

'You faked your deaths.'

I observe my calmness as though standing in the wings; congratulate myself on my presence of mind. Yet even as I say it – even as I know without any shred of doubt that I'm right – I pray that I'm wrong. Because it's preposterous. Because it's illegal. Immoral. But more than that, because it's cruel. Because their leaving me broke my heart, and has continued to chip away at it every day since, and to know that my parents did that deliberately will shatter it completely.

My mother's face screws up like paper. Tears splash onto the stone step.

A single word.

'Yes.'

The hand I move could belong to someone else. I touch the edge of the door, lightly, with two fingers.

And I slam it hard in her face.

TWENTY-EIGHT

MURRAY

The second floor of the police station was deserted. Most of the back-office staff didn't work weekends, and those who did were already on leave. Only the superintendent's office was occupied, with the boss himself on a call, and his PA typing a report without a single glance at her fingers.

She had tinsel in her hair and was wearing bauble earrings that flashed distractingly. 'The super needs case papers typing up,' she had explained, when Murray had wondered what she was doing at work on a Sunday morning, and Christmas Eve, to boot. 'He wants everything shipshape before the break.'

'Doing something nice tomorrow?' she said now.

'Just a quiet one at home.' There was a pause. 'You?' he added, when it became clear she was waiting for the question.

'Off to Mum and Dad's.' She stopped typing and leaned her folded arms on the desk. 'We all still have stockings, even though my brother's twenty-four. We open those first, then we have smoked salmon and scrambled eggs with Buck's Fizz.' Murray smiled and nodded as she took him through the traditions of her family Christmas. He wondered how long his bollocking was going to last.

The office door opened.

'Murray! Sorry to keep you waiting.'

'No problem.' Murray omitted the 'sir'. Not only because he was a civilian now, and no longer bound by rank, but because when Leo Griffiths had been a probationer, and Murray his tutor constable, the younger man had been a grade-A turd.

There were two easy chairs in Leo's office, but the superintendent sat at his desk, and so Murray took the wooden chair across from him. An expanse of polished wood lay between them, on which Leo pushed around the paperclips that justified his salary.

Leo laced his fingers together and leaned back in his chair. 'I'm a little confused.' He wasn't, of course, but the superintendent liked to show his workings-out, which tended to draw out the process somewhat. 'Night-turn attended an incident just before midnight last night, where they spoke to a Mr Mark Hemmings and his partner, Miss Anna Johnson.'

Ah, so it was indeed about the Johnson case.

'A brick was thrown through a bedroom window. It had a threatening note wrapped around it.'

'So I heard. A few of the houses in that street have their own security cameras. It would be worth—'

'All in hand, thank you,' Leo interrupted smoothly. 'I'm more concerned about the fact that Miss Johnson reported the incident as part of an ongoing series.' He paused for dramatic effect. 'An ongoing series being investigated by . . . you.'

Murray said nothing. You could tie yourself up in knots, saying something for the sake of it. Filling gaps. Ask a question, Leo. Then I'll answer it.

The pause went on for ever.

'And what I'm confused about, Murray, is that I was under the impression you were a Station Duty Officer. A *civilian* Station Duty Officer. And that you retired from CID – and indeed from the police service – several years ago.'

No comment.

A hint of annoyance had crept into Leo's voice. He was having to work far harder than he was used to. 'Murray, are you investigating a crime series involving two historic suicides?'

'I'm not, no.' They were murders, not suicides.

'Then what, exactly, *have* you been doing?'

'Anna Johnson came in to the front counter on Thursday to discuss some concerns she had over her parents' sudden deaths, both of which occurred last year. I spent some time answering her questions.' Murray gave Leo a benign smile. 'One of the objectives in my PDR is to deliver a high level of customer service. Sir.'

Leo narrowed his eyes. 'Night-turn said she'd received a malicious communication.'

'An anonymous card, delivered on the anniversary of her mother's death.'

'There's nothing on the system. Why didn't you generate a crime report?'

'What offence would that have been?' Murray asked politely. 'There was no threat in the card. No abuse. It was upsetting, of course, but it wasn't illegal.' There was a long pause while Leo digested this information.

'A brick through a window—'

'Is a criminal act,' interrupted Murray smoothly, 'and I'm sure the attending officers will do an excellent job investigating it.'

'Miss Johnson seems to think her mother's suicide was, in fact, murder.'

'So I understand.' Murray gave a polite smile. 'Of course, it was the CID team here who looked at the case last year.'

Leo looked at Murray, assessing whether the insinuation had been intentional. If he told Murray off for not taking the job to CID, there was an implicit criticism that the original investigation had been mishandled.

Murray waited.

'Write up your involvement so far, and pass everything up to CID for them to take a proper look at. Understood?'

'Perfectly.' Murray stood, not waiting to be dismissed. 'Merry Christmas.'

'Indeed. And Murray?'

'Yes?'

'Stick to your own job.'

Murray hadn't lied to the superintendent yet, and he wasn't going to start now. 'Don't worry, Leo.' He gave the boss a cheery smile. 'I won't do anything I'm not qualified to do.'

Downstairs, Murray found an empty report-writing room and closed the door before logging on to the computer. He had given back his force laptop when he retired, and there were a few more checks he wanted to do before he went home for Christmas. If Leo Griffiths had the nous to look at Murray's intranet activity, it could be easily explained away as essential information required for the write-up he would have to put together for CID.

He looked up Oak View on the Command and Control system that logged every call made to police. This basic check would have been done by the original investigating officers, but there were no printouts in the archived file, and Murray wanted to be thorough. He was looking for break-ins, harassment, suspicious activity connected to Oak View or the Johnsons. Anything that might suggest Tom and Caroline had been targeted prior to their deaths.

Oak View appeared several times over the years since computerised records had been kept. Twice, a silent 999 call had been made from the address. Each time, control room had called back and been given the same explanation.

OCCUPANT APOLOGISES. TODDLER WAS PLAYING WITH PHONE.

Murray checked the date on the log. 10 February 2001. Toddler? Anna Johnson would have been ten. Too old to be making accidental phone calls. Had there been a toddler in the house, or were the silent 999 calls a deliberate cry for help?

In 2008 control room had received a call from a neighbour, Robert Drake, who reported hearing a disturbance next door. Murray looked through the log.

CALLER STATES HE CAN HEAR SHOUTING. SOUND OF BROKEN GLASS. POSSIBLE DOMESTIC. UNITS DESPATCHED.

No crime had been recorded.

ALL QUIET ON ARRIVAL. DETAILS TAKEN. BOTH OCCU-
PANTS DENY ANY DOMESTIC INCIDENT.

Caroline Johnson had appeared 'emotional', Murray noted,
but there was scant detail in the brief log, and without tracking
down the attending officers – and hoping they could recall an
incident that occurred more than a decade ago – that was all
he had to go on.

It was enough. Murray was starting to build up a picture of
the Johnsons, and it wasn't the one their daughter had portrayed.
Perhaps Tom's brother, Billy Johnson, would throw more light
on proceedings. Murray looked at his watch. Bloody Leo Griffiths
and his posturing. He'd be late to collect Sarah if he didn't go
now. She'd be emotionally fraught enough as it was today; even
the tiniest change of plans could knock her off-kilter.

'I'll come with you.'

Murray had made it just in time, only for Sarah to immediately
ask after the Johnson case, and insist on accompanying him to
see Billy.

'It'll keep till after Christmas.' Murray put the car in gear and
drove slowly out of Highfield. It felt good to have Sarah in the
car. To know he wasn't going home to an empty house.

'It's fine, honestly. It's practically on our way home, anyway.'

Murray stole a glance at his wife. Even in the car she didn't
sit properly. One foot was tucked beneath the knee of her other
leg. She held the seatbelt away from her neck with one hand,
her elbow resting on the bottom of the window.

'If you're sure?'

'I'm sure.'

Johnson's Cars had been given a facelift since Murray had bought
his Volvo. There was still the same motley collection of part-
exchange bangers parked around the back, but most of the

178

forecourt was filled with gleaming Jags, Audis and BMWs, the most expensive angled on ramps that made the cars look like they were about to make a break for it.

'Ten minutes,' he said.

'No rush.' Sarah took off her seatbelt and opened her book. Murray pocketed the keys, automatically scanning the inside of the car for anything that might present a risk. She's been discharged, he reminded himself as he walked away. Relax.

He looked back as he crossed the forecourt, but Sarah was engrossed in her book. Clean-shaven sales reps circled like sharks, two homing in on him from opposite directions, both with an eye on their commission. A gangly lad with a shock of ginger hair reached him first, his colleague peeling off towards a sharply dressed couple, wandering hand in hand along a line of convertibles. A far safer bet, Murray thought.

'Billy Johnson?'

'In the office.' The ginger lad jerked his head towards the showroom. 'But perhaps I can assist.' His smile was all tooth and no sincerity. He cocked his head on one side, making a show of appraising Murray. Considering. 'Volvo man, am I right?'

Considering Murray had just got out of precisely such a car, this insight was less impressive than it might have been. He kept walking.

'Through here, is it?'

Ginger shrugged, his shiny smile vanishing with his chances of a sale. 'Yeah. Shaneen on the desk'll get him for you.'

Shaneen had a face two degrees darker than her neck, and lips so glossy Murray could see his reflection in them. She was standing behind a large curved reception desk, tinsel taped to the side, setting out glasses on a tray for a Christmas Eve tipple. She smiled as he approached.

'Welcome to Johnson's Cars, how may I help you?' she rattled off, so fast Murray had to pause for a second to process what he'd heard.

'I'd like to see Billy Johnson, please. I'm from Sussex Police.'

'I'll see if he's free.' She teetered on pointed-toe heels that couldn't possibly be the same shape as her feet, click-clacking across the polished floor to her boss's office. Tinted glass meant Murray couldn't see inside it, and he looked out of the vast showroom windows instead, wishing he'd been able to park the Volvo a little closer. The angle meant he couldn't see Sarah. He glanced at his watch. He'd already taken three of the ten minutes he'd promised he'd be.

'Come through, Mr . . .' Shaneen appeared in the doorway, tailing off as she realised she'd forgotten to ask Murray's name.

'Mackenzie. Murray Mackenzie.' He smiled at the receptionist as she passed him, and walked into an impressive office housing two large desks. Billy Johnson stood up. His forehead glistened, and when he shook Murray's hand it was warm and clammy. He didn't smile, and he didn't offer Murray a seat.

'CID, eh?'

Murray didn't set him straight.

'To what do we owe the pleasure? Our last break-in was six months ago, so that's a piss-poor response time, even by your standards.' The smile implied a joke the words lacked.

Billy Johnson was generous of stomach. Portly, rather than fat, and not unattractive with it, Murray supposed, although what did he know? He wore a well-cut suit, highly polished shoes, and a bright yellow tie that matched the stripes on his wide-collared shirt. The defensiveness was undoubtedly due to stress, not aggression, but nevertheless Murray stayed within striking distance of the door.

'If it's about the VAT—'

'It isn't.'

Billy relaxed a little.

'I'm making enquiries about the deaths of your brother and his wife.'

'You the officer our Annie's been dealing with?'

180

'You're her uncle, I believe?'

Even through Billy's distress, his affection for Anna was evident. His eyes softened, and he nodded repeatedly, as though the action reinforced the fact. 'Such a lovely girl. This has all been very hard for her.'

'For all of you,' proffered Murray.

'Yes, yes, of course. But for Annie . . .' He pulled a large white handkerchief from his pocket and wiped at his brow. 'I'm sorry – it's been a rather emotional morning. Please, sit down.' He sank down into a leather swivel chair. 'She's convinced herself Tom and Caroline were murdered.'

Murray paused. 'I think she's right.'

'Christ.'

Through the window behind Billy, Murray caught sight of a familiar figure meandering through the rows of cars. Sarah. Twenty yards behind her, walking as swiftly as it was possible to walk without running, was Ginger.

'Were you close to Tom, Mr Johnson?' Murray spoke quickly, half an eye on the forecourt.

Billy frowned. 'We were brothers.'

'You got on well?'

He seemed irritated by the question. 'We were brothers. We had each other's backs, but we got each other's backs up too. You know what I mean?'

'Business partners, too, I understand.'

Billy nodded. 'Dad had dementia and couldn't run the business any more, so Tom and I took over in 1991. Family,' he added, as though that explained everything. There was an open chequebook in front of him, next to a pile of envelopes and a printed list. He shuffled the envelopes together needlessly; nodded to the cheque-book. 'Christmas bonuses. Smaller than normal, but that's life.'

'How did you get on with Caroline?'

A crimson flush crept over the man's neck. 'She ran the desk. Tom looked after that side of things. I managed the sales team.'

Murray noted that Billy hadn't answered his question. He didn't push it. He wasn't supposed to be there at all; the last thing Murray needed was another complaint to Leo Griffiths. He tried another tack.

'Did they have a good relationship?'

Billy looked out of the window, as though deciding whether or not to impart whatever was in his head. Ginger was steering Sarah towards a Defender with a 'POA' sign dangling from the rearview mirror. Murray hoped she was okay. Hoped Ginger wouldn't say anything to set her off.

Billy turned back to Murray. 'He didn't treat her right. He was my brother, and I loved him, but he wasn't good enough for her.'

Murray waited. There was obviously a story behind this.

'He liked a drink. Well, we all do, but . . .' Billy shook his head. 'This isn't right. Speaking ill of the dead. It isn't right.'

'Are you suggesting Tom had a problem with alcohol, Mr Johnson?'

There was a long pause before Billy spoke. He looked out of the window. 'Caroline tried to cover for him, but I'm not stupid. Even if Tom thought I was.' This last was said bitterly, muttered more to himself than to Murray.

Behind him, Murray saw Ginger open the driver's door of the Defender. Sarah settled herself behind the wheel and adjusted the seat. Ginger would have her out on a test drive if Murray didn't leave soon. He stood up.

'You've been very helpful, Mr Johnson. Thank you.'

Murray felt bad leaving the man slumped at his desk, visibly distressed by the memories Murray had forced him to confront. But his priority was Sarah.

She was walking towards him as he got to the forecourt. Ginger was standing by the Defender, hands thrust miserably in his pockets.

'Are you okay?' Murray said, when Sarah reached him. She

182

seemed perfectly content, and he breathed a sigh of relief that Ginger hadn't upset her.

'Right as rain.' She had a wicked grin on her face and Murray glanced again at Ginger, who looked as though someone had just told him Christmas had been cancelled.

'What happened to him?'

'I told him I was interested in the latest model.'

'Right . . .'

'That I wanted something very high-spec, with lots of extras, and that I was looking to take something away today.'

'Okay . . .'

Sarah grinned again. 'And then I said maybe I'd stick to my bike.'

TWENTY-NINE

ANNA

My mother rings the bell instantly, then again without dropping her hand, and again and again and again. Rita runs into the hall, skids on the tiles, then jumps at the door. She looks back at me, then up at the silhouette of my mother, framed inside the stained-glass panel. She whines, confused.

My chest feels tight, my face numb. I can't do this. My hands shake uncontrollably, and as the doorbell rings again panic builds inside me.

'Anna!'

I turn around. Make my feet move. I walk slowly towards the foot of the stairs.

'We have to talk about this. I need you to understand. Anna!'

Her voice is quiet, but she is pleading, desperate. I stand, one hand on the bannister, one foot on the step. My parents are alive. Isn't this everything I've wanted for the last year? Grandparents for Ella, in-laws for Mark. My mum and dad. Family.

'Anna, I won't leave until you understand. I had no choice!'

And all at once I'm decided. I take the stairs two at a time, running from the hall, from the begging. From the excuses my mother is trying to give for the inexcusable.

No choice?

I had no choice. No choice but to grieve for my parents. No choice but to see the police pore over our lives; to sit in a coroner's court while their deaths were dissected; to organise a

184

memorial service and phone their friends to hear the same platitudes over and over. I had no choice but to go through pregnancy, labour, the early weeks of anxious motherhood, without my mother's guidance.

I had no choice.

They did.

My parents chose to deceive me, not only when they disappeared, but on every single day since.

The doorbell rings again, again, again. My mother keeps her finger pressed, and the bell rings, shrill and insistent, through the spine of the house.

I clamp my hands over my ears and curl into a tight ball on my bed, but still I hear it. I sit up. Stand. Pace the length of the bedroom.

I go into the ensuite and turn on the shower, sitting on the edge of the bath while the room fills with steam and the mirror mists over. Then I strip off my running clothes and step in, pulling the door shut and cranking the temperature till it's so hot it hurts. Beneath the shower I can't hear the bell. I tip up my head, letting the water fill my ears, my nose, my mouth, until it feels as though I'm drowning. I give in to the tears that started when I saw my mother, and froze the second I understood she'd chosen to stay away. I cry with a physicality I have never before experienced, doubled over with the sobs that force their way from the pit of my stomach.

When I have sobbed so hard I feel too weak to stand, I sit and wrap my arms around my knees, the water running off my bent head and pooling in my lap. I cry until I am exhausted. Until the water runs to ice and my flesh is goosebumped.

When I switch off the shower, my limbs stiff and cold, I listen. Silence.

She's gone.

The sharp stab of grief takes me by surprise. I chastise myself for the chink of weakness it suggests. I have lived without my parents for over a year. I have survived. I will survive. There is

185

nothing they could say now that would win my forgiveness. It is too late.

I find comfort in the softness of an old pair of jogging bottoms and a faded sweatshirt I steal from Mark's side of the wardrobe. Thick cashmere socks. I rough-dry my hair with a towel and twist it into a loose bun.

Just as I am beginning to feel, if not better, then more together, the doorbell rings.

I freeze. Wait a full minute.

It rings again.

The single-mindedness I used to admire – envy, almost – in my mother now taunts me. She's not going to give up. I could stay here all day, and she will wait and ring and shout. White-hot rage cracks through the veneer of calmness I had convinced myself was real, and I storm from my bedroom and down the stairs. How dare she?

A whole year.

It rattles around my head like a ball bearing in a pinball machine, firing shots indiscriminately. For a whole year she has lied to me. To everyone.

I arrive in the hall so fast, and with so little control, that my socks slip from under me and I crash onto my back; the breath knocked from me with such velocity that when I pick myself up I feel as sore as if I'd fallen from the top of the stairs.

The doorbell rings again. Rita's nowhere to be seen. Even the dog has stopped hoping I'll answer the door, but when my mother sets her mind to something, she doesn't rest.

A whole year.

If someone had told me, six months ago – this morning, even – that I would one day tell my mother to leave me alone, I'd have thought them insane. But that is exactly what I'm going to do. The past can't be undone; you can't lie to someone and then bowl back into their lives and expect to be forgiven. Some lies are too big for that.

A whole year of lies.

I fling open the door.

'There you are! I thought you must be upstairs. You'll have to bring the pram up for me, dear. I don't like doing it with the baby inside, in case it topples.' Joan looks at me curiously. 'Are you all right, dear? You look like you've seen a ghost.'

THIRTY

MURRAY

Sarah was mopping the kitchen floor. This was not a reflection on Murray's own efforts the previous day, but an indication of Sarah's rising anxiety. The change had been sudden, like the sun disappearing behind a cloud. Murray had tried to hang on to the feeling of contentment he'd had as they'd driven home from Johnson's Cars, laughing about Ginger's thwarted sale, but – like trying to recall thirty-degree heat in the depths of winter – it had eluded him.

Murray wasn't sure what the trigger had been. Sometimes there wasn't one.

'Sit down and have a cup of tea.'

'I want to do the windows first.'

'It's Christmas Eve.'

'So?'

Murray looked through the *Radio Times* for something to distract them both. *It's a Wonderful Life* was probably not ideal. '*The Snowman*'s on in a minute.'

'There's a surprise.' She dumped the mop in the bucket. 'I bet even Aled Jones is sick of that one.'

Murray would have riffed on it, but Sarah's brow was knitted into a deep V as she looked under the sink for window cleaner and a cloth, so he let it go without comment. Murray was good at reading the signs, at taking his lead from someone else, and mirroring their reaction back to them. He'd done it for years

188

with criminals, long before non-verbal communication became something you had to be taught in a classroom. He'd done it for years at home.

It was tiring, though, and not for the first time Murray wished he and Sarah had children to dilute the ripples of her condition. He had wanted them – desperately – but Sarah had been too frightened.

'What if they take after me?'

He had deliberately misunderstood. 'Then they'll be the luckiest kids in the world.'

'What if they inherit my head? My fucked-up, bastard, shitty head?' She had started crying, and Murray had wrapped her up in his arms so she couldn't see that his own eyes were leaking too.

'Or my nose?' he said gently. There was a hiccough of laughter from the folds of his jumper, and then she'd pulled away.

'What if I hurt them?'

'You wouldn't. You've only ever hurt yourself.'

Murray's reassurances had fallen on deaf ears. Sarah became terrified of falling pregnant – refusing to be intimate with Murray. She spiralled into a paranoiac episode involving weeks of pointless pregnancy tests, in the unlikely event that Eastbourne had been selected as the location of the next Immaculate Conception. Eventually their GP had agreed to refer Sarah for sterilisation, for the sake of her mental health.

Which meant it was just Murray and Sarah. They could have spent Christmas with Sarah's brother and his family, but Sarah's recent admission meant that no plans had been made. Murray wished he hadn't already got the tree down from the loft, or that he'd had the foresight not to buy a pre-decorated one. At least that would have given them something to do.

Something other than cleaning.

Sarah was kneeling on the draining board to do the kitchen window, and Murray was looking for another cloth – he may as well make himself useful – when he heard the sound of singing from outside the front door.

'We three Kings of Orient are / One in a taxi, one in a car / One on a scooter, blowing his hooter . . .' The singing stopped and was replaced by raucous laughter.

'What on earth . . .'

Sarah was curious enough to put down the Windolene and come with Murray to the front door.

'Happy Christmas!' Nish's partner Gill thrust a bottle of wine at Murray.

'And welcome home!' Nish handed Sarah a gift bag with a large beribboned tag. 'You don't get anything,' she said to Murray, 'cos you're a miserable old codger.' She grinned. 'Aren't you going to invite us in? Proper carol singers get mince pies and mulled wine.'

'Mince pies I think we can do,' Murray said, opening the door wide. Sarah was clutching the gift bag with both hands, her eyes startled.

'I was just . . .' She looked towards the kitchen, as though planning her escape.

Murray felt his heart sink. He held her gaze and wondered how to make her understand that he needed this. Friends over on Christmas Eve. Mince pies. Carols. Normality.

Sarah hesitated, then gave a tentative smile. 'I was just getting everything ready for Christmas. Come on in!'

Murray found the Waitrose mince pies he'd been keeping for the next day, and glasses for the wine Nish and Gill had brought. He found a CD of King's College carols, and then Nish found one of top ten Christmas hits. Sarah opened her present, and hugged everyone for the impromptu party, and Murray thought Nish and Gill could never know what a perfect gift they'd given him.

'A little bird tells me you were in the Lion's den this morning . . .' Nish said.

That hadn't taken long.

'The Lion?' Gill was topping up everyone's glasses. Sarah held hers out, and Murray tried not to let his face reflect his thoughts. A bit of alcohol made Sarah buoyant. Happy. A lot had the opposite effect.

'Superintendent Leo Griffiths,' Nish explained. 'Fond of roaring.'

'Would the little bird who told you that have had flashing bauble earrings and tinsel in her hair?'

'No idea – she texted me. I take it your plan to single-handedly solve Eastbourne's historic murders has been thwarted?'

Murray took a sip of his wine. 'If anything, I'm even more determined to get to the bottom of what happened to the Johnsons, especially now things have escalated.'

Nish nodded. 'The brick's gone for further analysis. No fingerprints, I'm afraid – it's a bugger of a surface, and whoever wrapped the paper around it was forensically aware enough to wear gloves. But I *can* tell you that the note wrapped around the brick was printed on different paper to the one used for the card. *And* it was produced on a different printer.'

Sarah put down her glass. 'They came from different people?'

'Not necessarily, but it's possible.'

'That makes sense.' Sarah looked at Murray. 'Doesn't it? One person prompting Anna to dig into the past; the other warning her off.'

'Maybe.' Like Nish, Murray was reluctant to commit, but he was fast coming to the same conclusion himself: they weren't dealing with one person, but two. The anniversary card came from someone who knew the truth about what had happened to Caroline Johnson, and wanted Anna to ask questions. Last night's note was a different matter. An instruction. A threat.

No police. Stop before you get hurt.

'Why send a warning, unless you're the murderer?'

Murray couldn't fault Sarah's logic.

Whoever threw that brick through the window of Anna's house was responsible for Tom's and Caroline's deaths, and it looked as though they weren't finished with the Johnsons yet. Murray needed to unravel this case before Anna – or her baby – got hurt.

THIRTY-ONE

ANNA

Mark and Joan talk, but it's as though I'm under water. Every now and then one of them shoots me a concerned look, before offering me tea, or wine, or *why don't you have a little sleep?*

I don't need to sleep. I need to understand what the hell is going on.

Where have my parents been for the last year? How did they fake their suicides so convincingly that no one suspected a thing? And – most importantly – why did they do it?

It doesn't make sense. I've found no evidence of debts, no suggestion that my parents moved large amounts of money out of their accounts before they disappeared. When the wills were read, everything – more or less – came to me. Dad borrowed money for the business, but it was only after he died – and Billy fell apart – that the business started struggling. My parents weren't bankrupt – they can't have done this for financial reasons.

My head is spinning.

'We need to talk,' I say, when Joan's out of the room.

'We do.' Mark's face is serious. 'After Christmas, once Mum's gone home, let's get a babysitter and go out for dinner. Have a proper talk about everything. I was thinking: the counsellor doesn't have to be someone I know, if that's what's bothering you – I can get a recommendation.'

'No, but—'

Joan comes back in. She's holding a game of Scrabble. 'I wasn't sure if you had a set, so I brought mine. Shall we have a game now?' She looks at me with her head cocked to one side. 'How are you doing, love? I know it's hard for you.'

'I'm okay.' Lying by omission; passing off my peculiar mood as a symptom of grief. Another Christmas without my parents. *Poor Anna. She misses them so much.*

I shuffle Scrabble letters around on the little tray in front of me, unable to see the patterns in even the simplest of words. What am I going to do? Should I call the police? I think of lovely, kind Murray Mackenzie and feel a fresh wave of shame. He believed me. The only person who admitted there was something not quite right. The only person who agreed my parents might have been murdered.

And all the time it was a lie.

'Jukebox!' Joan says. 'Seventy-seven.'

'Two words, surely?'

'Definitely one.'

I tune out from their good-natured argument.

At various times over the last nineteen months, grief has been overtaken by another emotion.

Anger.

'It's completely normal to feel angry when a loved one dies,' Mark said, during my first counselling session. 'Particularly when we feel the person who died made an active choice to leave us.'

An active choice.

My hand – holding a letter E I picked from the pile in the middle of the table – starts to shake violently. I drop the letter onto the rack and push my hands into my lap, squeezing them between my knees. I have spent the last year actively 'working through' – to use Mark's vocabulary – my anger over my parents' suicides. Turns out it was entirely justified.

Every second I hold on to this secret is making me more nauseous. More anxious. I wish Joan wasn't here. It's only the

194

third time I've ever met her; how can I throw this at her? And on Christmas Eve . . .

Mark puts down a single tile. 'Ex.'

'Nine,' Joan says.

'I think you'll find that's a double word score . . .'

'Oops! My mistake. Eighteen.'

'Watch her, honey. She's a terrible cheat.'

'Don't listen to him, Anna.'

Hey, guess what, guys. My parents aren't dead after all – they were just pretending!

It doesn't feel real.

The thought takes hold. What if it isn't?

For the last two days I've imagined my mother's presence so strongly I even smelled her perfume; saw her in the park. What if I've conjured her up? What if the conversation I had on the doorstep was one of the post-bereavement hallucinations Mark was so insistent I was experiencing?

I'm going mad. Mark was right. I need to see someone.

But it seemed so real.

I don't know what to believe any more.

Just after eleven, we get ready for midnight mass. The hall is a muddle of coats and umbrellas and Ella's buggy, and I think about all the people I'll see at the church, all the people who will wish me well, and tell me they're thinking of me, and say how hard it must be without Tom and Caroline.

And I can't. I just can't.

We're standing in the doorway, half in, half out. Laura pulls up in the street – no room on the drive with Joan's car squeezed alongside mine and Mark's – and jumps out, wrapping a scarf around her neck. She walks towards us.

'Happy Christmas Eve!'

There are introductions – Mum, this is Laura, Laura, this is Joan – and all the time my heart is thumping fit to burst, and

I stare at the floor in case what's in my head is written across my face.

'How are you doing, lovely?' Laura squeezes my shoulder. Solidarity, not sympathy. She thinks she knows what I'm going through. How I feel. Guilt gnaws at my insides. Laura's mother died. Mine lied.

'I'm not feeling too good, actually.'

There's a flurry of concern.

'You do look a bit peaky.'

'Do you think it was something you ate?'

'Such a hard time – it's understandable.'

I cut in. 'I think I might stay here. If you don't mind.'

'We'll all stay,' Mark says. He makes light of it, even though I know he and his family have never missed a Christmas Eve service. 'I never have enough breath for that Gloria one, anyway.'

'No, you go. Ella and I will have an early night.'

'If you're sure, dear?' Joan is practically down the driveway. 'I'm sure.'

'I'll stay and look after her.' Laura comes up the steps, concern in her eyes.

'I'm fine.' I don't mean to snap. I half smile, in apology. 'Sorry. Headache. I mean, I'd rather be on my own.'

They exchange glances. I see Mark weighing up whether it's safe to leave me; whether I'm safe to be left. 'Call if you change your mind. I'll come back for you.'

'Feel better soon,' Laura says. A proper hug, this time; her hair tickling my cheek. 'Happy Christmas.'

'Have a lovely time.' I close the door and press my back against it. My pretence at illness was only half a lie. My head aches and my limbs are stiff from tension.

I unzip Ella from her padded snowsuit and lift her from the pram, then take her into the sitting room to feed her.

Ella's eyes are just starting to drop when I hear a noise from the kitchen. Rita jumps up. I exhale slowly, trying to slow my heart, which is hammering against my chest, then take Ella off my breast and rearrange my top.

Cautiously, with one hand on Rita's collar, I walk across the hall. From inside the kitchen I hear the scrape of a chair on tiles.

I open the door.

The faint scent of jasmine gives me the warning I need not to scream.

My mother sits at the table. Her hands are folded neatly in her lap, two fingers twisting the fabric of the same cheap woollen dress she had on earlier. She's wearing her coat, even though the heat from the Aga makes it far too warm in here for outside clothes, and it's jarring to see her sitting like a visitor in the kitchen that was once hers.

She's alone. I feel a rush of anger that my father hasn't had the courage to face me himself; that he's sent Mum ahead to soften the blow. My father. So confident in business. Full of banter with the customers. Almost cocky with the reps, who would hang on his every word, thirsty for the nuggets of wisdom they hoped would one day lead to a showroom with their own name above the door. Yet he doesn't have the balls to face his own daughter. To own what he's done.

My mother says nothing. I wonder if she, too, has lost her nerve, then I realise she is transfixed by Ella.

I speak to break the spell. 'How did you get in?'

A pause. 'I kept a key to the back door.'

The penny drops. 'Yesterday, in the kitchen. I smelled your perfume.'

She nods. 'I lost track of time. You almost caught me.'

'I thought I was losing my mind!' The shout startles Ella, and I make myself calm down, for her sake.

'I'm sorry.'

'What were you doing here?'

Mum closes her eyes. She looks tired, and so much older than before . . . *before she died*, my head still wants to say.

'I came to see you. I was going to tell you everything. But you weren't alone – I panicked.'

I wonder how many times she's used her key, slipping in and out of the house like a ghost. The thought makes me shiver. I shift Ella from one hip to the other. 'Where have you been?'

'I rented a flat up north. It's' – she grimaces – 'basic.'

I think of the uneasy feeling I've had over the last few days. 'How long have you been back?'

'I came down on Thursday.'

Thursday. Twenty-first of December. The anniversary of her . . . not her death. She didn't die. I repeat this fact to myself, trying to make sense of it.

'I've been staying at the Hope since then.' She flushes slightly.

The Hope is a church-funded hostel near the seafront. They run the food bank, collect donations of clothing and toiletries, and offer temporary accommodation to women in need, in exchange for domestic chores. She sees my face.

'It's not that bad.'

I think of the five-star hotels my parents enjoyed, and imagine my mother on her knees cleaning loos in return for a bed in a dormitory of down-on-their-luck women.

Mum's looking at Ella. 'She's beautiful.'

I wrap protective arms around my daughter, as though by hiding her from view I can shield her from her grandmother's lies, but Ella arches her back and fights my embrace. She twists to see this stranger in our kitchen, this thin, ill-kempt woman who stares at her with filmy eyes I will not acknowledge.

I will not.

And yet my chest aches with a heaviness that has nothing to do with what my parents did, and everything to do with the pain I see on my mother's face. The love. A love so tangible it arcs between us; so tangible I'm convinced Ella feels it. She reaches out a pudgy hand towards her grandmother.

A whole year, I remind myself.

Fraud. Conspiracy. Lies.

'Could I hold her?'

The audacity takes my breath away.

'Please, Anna. Just once. She's my granddaughter.'

There's so much I could say. That my mother relinquished any familial rights the night she faked her own death. That a year of lies means she doesn't deserve the reward of Ella's chubby hand in hers, of the talcum-powdered scent of a freshly washed head. That she chose to be dead, and as far as my daughter is concerned that is how she will remain.

Instead I walk towards my mother and hand her my baby.

Because it's now or never.

Once the police know what she's done they'll take her away. A trial. Prison. The media circus. She had the police out searching for Dad, when all the time she knew he was fine. She claimed his assurance money. *Theft, fraud, wasting police time . . .* My head spins with the crimes they've committed, and with the fresh-found fear that I am now an accessory to them.

My parents brought this on themselves.

But I'm not a part of it. And neither is Ella.

My daughter shouldn't be punished for other people's actions. The least I can give her is a cuddle with a grandmother she's never going to know.

My mother takes her as gently as if she were made of glass. With the ease of experience, she nestles her into the crook of her arm and runs her gaze across every detail.

I stand inches away, fingers twitching at my sides. Where is my father? Why has Mum come back now? Why come back at all? A hundred questions run through my head, and I can't bear it any more. I snatch Ella back, so swiftly she lets out a cry of surprise. I shush her in my arms, pressing her against my chest when she tries to turn back towards her grandmother, who sighs softly – not in admonishment, but something more akin to contentment. As though her granddaughter were all that mattered.

199

For a second my mother and I lock eyes; we agree on that one thing, at least.

'You need to leave. Now.' It's more abrupt than I intended, but I no longer trust myself to stick to the script. Seeing my daughter in my mother's arms is softening my heart. I feel myself wavering.

She lied to me.

I have to do the right thing. I have to tell Mark, the police.

But she's my mother . . .

'Ten minutes. I want to tell you something, and if you still feel the same then—'

'There's nothing you can tell me that—'

'Please. Just ten minutes.'

Silence. I hear the grandfather clock in the hall, the call of an owl from the garden. Then I sit.

'Five.'

She looks at me and nods. She takes a deep breath and lets it slowly out. 'Your father and I haven't been happy together for many years.'

The words fall into place as though I've been waiting for them. 'You couldn't split up, like normal people?'

Lots of my friends had divorced parents. Two houses, two holidays, two sets of presents . . . No one wants their parents to separate, but even a child can learn to understand it's not the end of the world. I would have coped.

'It wasn't as simple as that.'

I remember hiding in my bedroom once, my iPod turned up to drown out the argument going on downstairs. Wondering if this was it; if they were going to get divorced. Then, in the morning, going downstairs to find everything calm. Dad drinking his coffee. Mum humming as she put more toast on the table. They pretended everything was fine. And so I did, too.

'Please, Anna, let me explain.'

200

I will listen. And then, when Mark gets back, I will tell him. To hell with what Joan thinks. I'll phone the police, too. Because once everyone knows, I can distance myself from this insane scheme cooked up by my parents as a preferable alternative to divorce.

'You found a vodka bottle under the desk in the study.'

She's been watching me.

And I thought I was going mad. Seeing ghosts.

'Did you find others?' Her voice is calm. She stares at the table in front of her.

'They were Dad's, weren't they?'

Her eyes snap to mine. She searches my face, and I wonder if she resents me for not acknowledging this sooner, for leaving her to shoulder the burden alone.

'Why did he hide them? It was no secret he liked a drink.'

Mum's eyes close briefly. 'There's a difference between liking a drink and needing a drink.' She hesitates. 'He was clever about it, like many alcoholics are. Careful to hide it from you; from Billy.'

'Uncle Billy didn't know?'

Mum gives a humourless laugh. 'The cleaner found a bottle of vodka stashed in the bin under Dad's desk. She brought it to Billy in case it had been thrown away by mistake. I panicked. Told Billy it was mine. Said I'd bought the wrong sort and no one would have drunk it so I'd thrown it away. He didn't believe me, but he didn't push it. Didn't want to, I suppose.' She stops and looks at me, and there are tears in her eyes. 'I wish you'd told me you knew Dad drank. You shouldn't have had to cope with that on your own.'

I shrug, an obtuse teen again. I don't want to share confidences with her. Not now. The truth is, I'd never have said anything. I hated that I knew. I wanted to exist in my happy bubble, pretending everything was perfect, and never listening to the myriad signs that told me they weren't.

'Well.' Another deep breath. 'When he was drunk – and only when he was drunk' – she rushes to make this clear to me, as though it makes a difference; as though any of this makes a bloody difference to what they've done – 'he hit me.'

My world spins on its axis.

'He never meant it – he was always so sorry. So ashamed of what he'd done.'

Like that makes it all right.

How can she be so calm? So matter-of-fact? I picture my father – laughing, teasing – and try to reframe my memories. I think of the arguments that would end abruptly when I came home; the shift in atmosphere I took pains to ignore. I think of my smashed paperweight; of the stashed bottles around the house. I had seen my dad as a loveable rogue. A loud, jovial, generous man. Fond of a drink, occasionally crass, but ultimately good. Kind.

How could I have got it so wrong?

I open my mouth to speak, but she stops me. 'Please, let me finish. If I don't get it out now, I don't know if I can bear to do it at all.' She waits, and I give the tiniest of nods. 'There's so much you don't know, Anna – and I don't want you to know it. I can spare you that, at least. Suffice to say, I was scared of him. Very, very scared.' She stares out of the window. The garden light is on, and the shadows around the patio flicker as a bird flies across its beam.

'Tom messed up at work. He took out a business loan without telling Billy, and they couldn't make the repayments. The business started going downhill – oh, I know Billy will have told you it was fine, but that's your uncle for you. Tom was mortified – three generations, and he'd put them into debt. He came up with a mad plan. He wanted to fake his own death. He'd disappear, I'd claim the life assurance, and then in a year or so he'd turn up at a hospital and pretend he had amnesia.'

'And you went along with it? I can't even—'

'I thought it was the answer to my prayers.' She gives a shallow laugh. 'At last I'd be free. I knew there'd be repercussions when he turned up, but all I could think about was not being frightened any more.'

I look at the clock. How long does midnight mass last?

'So you went along with it. Dad disappeared.' I want to know about how he made it look like suicide, but the detail can wait till I know how this ends. 'You were safe. And then you . . .'

You left me too, I want to say, but I don't. I'm keeping emotion out of this; treating it like a case study at work. An awful, shocking story that happened to someone else.

'Only I wasn't safe,' she says. 'I was stupid to think I would have been. He kept calling me. He even came to the house, once. He wanted money for a fake passport. Documentation. Rent. He said the life assurance was his; that I'd stolen it. He'd changed his mind about faking amnesia; said it wouldn't work. He wanted the money so he could start a new life. He said he'd hurt me if I didn't pay up. I started giving him small amounts of money, but he wanted more and more.' She leans forward and pushes her hands towards me. I stare at them, but make no move to take them. 'That money was for your future – it's what you would have inherited when we died. I wanted you to have it. It wasn't fair of him to take it.'

I feel numb. I'm still trying to equate this version of my father with the man I thought he was.

'You have no idea what he's capable of, Anna,' she says. 'Or how frightened I was. Your father died to pay off his debts. I died to escape him.'

'So why come back?' My words are full of bitterness. 'You got what you wanted. You got your freedom. Why come back at all?'

She leaves a silence that makes me shiver even before the answer lands.

'Because he found me.'

THIRTY-TWO

I have a temper. Hasn't everyone?

I'm no more or less out of control than you are; no more likely to lash out than you. It's all about the triggers.

We all have one. Just because you haven't found yours yet doesn't mean it isn't there. Better that you know about it, otherwise one day someone else will press your button, and the red mist will descend.

Know your trigger and you can control it. At least, that's the theory.

Mine's alcohol.

I'm not your stereotypical drunk. You won't find me asleep in doorways with piss down my trousers and a can of Tennent's Extra in one hand. I won't roll down the street, shouting at strangers. Getting into fights.

I'm what they call a functioning alcoholic.

Smart suits. Never a hair out of place. Schmoozing customers, giving them the patter. Smiling at the staff. A drink at lunchtime? Why not – that was a great sale!

Money makes it easier. Look at the races, look at the pretty young things in their posh hats tottering along with a bottle of champagne in each hand. It's fun, right? But swap the posh hats for filthy beanies, and the bubbly for cooking brandy, and you'd cross the street to stay out of their way.

Money means silver hip flasks at a school sports day, when paper-bag-concealed whiskey would cause an outcry. Money means you can drink Bloody Marys on a Sunday morning, G&Ts

after work, Pimm's whenever there's a glimpse of sun, and nobody gives you a second glance.

I had my pick-me-ups, of course. You can't drink Bloody Marys when you're wrapping up a test drive, but you can sip from a water bottle of vodka. You can take a swig from something stashed among the plant pots, in your desk, under the stairs.

When I started drinking, I drank for fun.

Later I drank because I couldn't stop.

Somewhere in the middle, I'd lost my way.

That baby trapped me. You wanted marriage, domesticity, family trips to the zoo. I wanted my old life. I missed London. I missed noisy nights in bars, picking up a one-night stand and not caring if the bed was cold when I woke up. I missed taking home a pay cheque without worrying whether the business could afford it. I missed my freedom.

It made me bitter. Resentful. Angry. All of which I could handle – sober.

My trigger is alcohol.

Alcohol makes me lose control. It makes me numb to the consequences of my actions. It makes my fists fly.

I know a lot about functioning alcoholics. I know a lot about anger, now.

I knew a lot then, too.

Except how to stop.

THIRTY-THREE

ANNA

Mum takes a piece of paper from her pocket and unfolds it. It's a black and white photocopy of the inside of a card.

Suicide? Think again.

The card I was sent.

I think of how hard that day was; how I woke up with grief tugging at my heart, and how every minute had felt like an hour. I think of the kick in the stomach as I slid out the card to see the *Happy Anniversary* message, and the nausea as I read the message inside.

On Mum's photocopy, beneath the printed message, and scrawled in red marker pen, is another line.

I could tell her everything . . .

'Dad sent it?'

She nods slowly. Reluctantly.

'But why?'

'To show me I couldn't get away that easily? That he could still control me, even from the grave?' Tears roll down her cheeks. 'I thought I'd been so clever. I went somewhere we'd never been together – somewhere I haven't been for years. I rented a horrible flat because it was the only place the landlord didn't ask for references. I cleaned loos for cash in hand, I didn't go online, I didn't make any contact with anyone, even though I wanted to – Anna, I wanted to so much! And he still found me.'

It's too much to take in.

'You're going to have to start at the beginning. I don't understand how Dad managed it – there was a witness . . . She saw
him jump.'

She doesn't speak, but her eyes say it all.

My head reels. 'You made the 999 call. Diane Brent-Taylor.
That was you.' I might have been the first in the family to go
to university, but that didn't make me any cleverer than the
generations before. I always knew Mum was smart – too smart
to be working on reception at Johnson's Cars – but the devi-
ousness . . . It's hard to take in.

'He planned it for weeks. Talked about nothing else. He made
me practise, over and over, and every time I messed up he hurt
me. He gave me a mobile to make the call; made me hold it
into the wind as I spoke, so my voice would be distorted. He'd
thought of everything.'

'You should have gone to the police.'

Her smile is sad. 'Easy to say now. When someone has you
under their control like that, it's . . . it's hard.'

I think of my job, of the children around the globe everyone
works fiercely to protect. So many of them are abused, cowed,
coerced. So many could tell a teacher, a friend. Yet so few do.

'I kept thinking he'd never actually do it. That it was fantasy.
Then one day he woke up and said: "Today. I'm doing it today.
While Anna's away."'

I remember that morning. 'Enjoy yourself,' he said. I was
running late, rifling through my bag for my keys with a piece
of toast in my free hand. Dad was sitting at the island, reading
the *Daily Mail* and drinking strong black coffee. It took two
cups to get him out of bed; three before he managed conversation; a fourth when he reached work, to get him firing on all
cylinders.

'Work hard, but play hard, too.' He'd winked. And that was
that. He hadn't hugged me, hadn't told me he loved me, or given
me sage advice I would cherish later. Just *work hard, play hard.*

In the months after his death I decided I was glad of the lack of ceremony. It meant he hadn't been planning to kill himself, I decided. If he'd known it was the last time he was going to see me, it would have felt different.

But he did know. He just didn't care.

'That day was horrendous,' Mum said. 'He picked fights with everyone. Billy, the reps, me. I thought it was an act – that he wanted to make his suicide convincing – but I wonder if it was nerves. I said it wasn't too late for him to change his mind – that we'd find a way to pay the money we owed – but you know your dad. He was always stubborn.'

Do I know my dad? I don't think I do any more.

'When work finished we went our separate ways. He took an Audi from work, told Bill he wanted to see how it drove. That was the last time I saw him.'

I can't sit still any more. I walk to the window and stare into the garden, at the big bay tree in the pot, and the roses Mum trained along the fence between our garden and Robert's. I glance upwards to Robert's house and think of his planned extension, and my irrational thought that he had something to do with the rabbit on our front step.

I pull the curtains. 'What happened then?'

'The agreement was that I'd hear nothing till ten a.m. He'd researched the tide times; he knew that at high tide, if a body is weighed down, it can be dragged out along the sea bed. That it might never be found.' She shudders. 'But at nine-thirty he sent a text to say he was sorry.' She screws up her face and I see she's trying not to cry. 'And I didn't know if he was sorry for what he was making me do, or for all the times he'd hurt me, or if it was just another part of his plan.'

I cross the kitchen again and put the kettle on the Aga, then change my mind and take it back off. I get out two glasses and the bottle of whiskey reserved for hot toddies, and pour myself a finger of rich, amber liquid. I look at Mum and hold up the bottle, but she shakes her head. I sip mine, and hold it in my mouth until it burns.

'At ten the second text came: *I can't do this any more.* I started to believe he was really going to kill himself. I decided that I had to go through with it. That no one could prove I knew anything about his plan. I did what he'd told me to do. I replied to his message, then I called the police. I called you.'

A sudden flash of anger. 'Have you any idea how terrifying that call was?' I don't remember the drive home; I only remember the blind panic that Dad wouldn't be found. That we'd be too late. 'You should have told me!'

'We'd committed a crime!' Mum stands up.

As she walks towards me I take a step back. I don't mean to – my feet move of their own accord – but it makes her stop short, hurt in her eyes.

'We could have gone to prison – we still might! I didn't want to ruin your life as well as my own.'

We fall silent. I take another sip of whiskey. It's after midnight. Mark and Joan will be home soon.

'We held a memorial service for you,' I say quietly. 'Laura organised it all. Billy made a speech.' I think of the young chaplain who cried at the inquest. Who found me afterwards and took my hands, and told me he was sorry his actions hadn't been enough to save my mother from herself.

A thought strikes me. 'Someone put a brick through the nursery window last night.'

'A brick?' She looks at Ella in horror.

'She's fine. She was downstairs with Mark. There was a note with the brick, telling us not to go to the police. To stop before we got hurt.'

I look at Mum, who has covered her mouth with her hands, her fingers splayed around her eyes. 'No. No, no, no.'

Fear courses through me. 'Did Dad do it?'

Silence.

I stand up. 'You need to leave.'

'Anna, please—'

'Mark will be back soon.'

'There's so much we need to talk about.' She follows me out to the hall, trying to talk to me, but I won't listen. I can't listen to any more. I open the door, check the street is empty, then push her out into the cold, and for the second time today, I slam the door on my mother.

I lean my back against the stained-glass panel. I wonder if she'll knock and ring, as she did this morning. There's a moment's pause, then I hear her footsteps on the steps, on the gravel. Silence.

My mind whirs. My father was a violent man. So cruel to Mum that she faked her own death to escape him.

And now he's coming after me.

THIRTY-FOUR

MURRAY

When Murray woke up on Christmas morning, Sarah's side of the bed was cold. He felt the familiar clutch of panic as he searched the house for her. The back door was unlocked, and Murray cursed himself for leaving the key out, but when he tore it open and ran out into the garden, he found Sarah sitting quietly on the bench.

She was barefoot, dew from the bench soaking into the cotton robe she wore over her nightdress. Her thin arms encircled the knees drawn up to her chest, a mug of tea warming her hands, which were black with soil.

Ignoring the damp, Murray sat on the bench beside her. The garden was narrow, a once well-tended vegetable patch at the end, with a greenhouse, and a neat rectangle of lawn between two beds raised with railway sleepers. Closer to the house, where he and Sarah sat, was a square patio lined with pots. Murray watered them on the rare occasions the British weather failed to deliver rain, but didn't know what to cut back and what to leave, and gradually the colour had disappeared from the patio.

'Look.'

Murray had followed Sarah's gaze to the largest pot, in which a willow obelisk was embedded. There had been something growing, Murray remembered, with pale pink flowers as thin as tissue paper, before it had dried and withered, nothing more than a collection of dry sticks clinging to the willow. The sticks

211

were on the ground now, the earth cleared of weeds and freshly turned.

'That looks a lot tidier.'

'Yes, but look.'

Murray looked. Beside one corner of the obelisk, where the willow sunk into the earth, was the tiniest shoot of light green. Murray felt a glimmer of hope as Sarah slipped her hand into his.

'Happy Christmas.'

Dinner was turkey crown and all the trimmings.

'You sit there,' Sarah said, pushing Murray into the sofa. 'Relax.'

It was hard to relax when he could hear Sarah swearing as several things came to the boil at once, just as something else proved to be 'fuck, that's hot'. After a while Murray poked his head around the door.

'Need a hand?'

'All under control.'

There were pans everywhere, including several on the floor and one balanced precariously on the windowsill.

'It's still just the two of us, right?'

'We'll have leftovers tomorrow.'

And for the next three weeks, Murray thought.

'Oh crap, I've burned the bread sauce.'

'I hate bread sauce.' Murray undid Sarah's apron. He pushed her gently towards a chair. 'Sit there. Relax.'

As he stirred the gravy he felt Sarah's eyes on him. He turned around.

She chewed at a piece of skin at the side of her fingernail. 'Tell me the truth: is it easier when I'm at Highfield?'

Murray had never lied to her. 'Easier? Yes. As enjoyable? Nowhere near.'

Sarah digested his answer. 'I wonder if he's after her money.'

It was a while before Murray caught up. 'Mark Hemmings?'

'Anna thinks Mark never met her parents, but *we* know Caroline had an appointment with him. We also know that together, Caroline and Tom were worth a fuck-load of money.' Sarah poured herself a small serving of wine, and stood to top up Murray's glass. 'Caroline goes to see Mark when she's distraught over the death of her husband. She discloses that she's worth somewhere in the region of a million pounds. Mark bumps her off and moves in on the daughter. Boom.'

Murray looked sceptical. 'I suppose it's marginally more convincing than your theory that Caroline was murdered for lodging a planning objection against the neighbour.'

'I haven't ruled that one out completely. But I think the money's more likely.'

'Mark and Anna aren't married. He wouldn't automatically inherit.'

'Yet,' Sarah said darkly. 'Bet he's working on it. And once he's got his hands on her money and the house . . .' She drew a single finger across her throat, making a melodramatic gargling sound as she did so.

Murray laughed at Sarah's macabre mime as he started to dish up, covering the burned bits of potato with gravy, but the thought that Anna Johnson might be in danger sent a shiver down his spine. 'As soon as the bank holiday's over, I'll see what the High Tech Crime Unit can do on the number used to make the Diane Brent-Taylor call. I'd put money on the fact that whoever put the brick through Anna Johnson's window also made that call, and whoever made that call knows how Tom Johnson died.' He put a plate, piled high with food, in front of Sarah, and sat opposite her.

'It'll be someone close to the family, though, mark my words,' Sarah said, picking up her knife and fork. 'It always is.'

Not for the first time, Murray thought she was probably right. But who?

213

THIRTY-FIVE

ANNA

I haven't held Ella all evening. She's been passed around like a parcel, seemingly enjoying the attention, and offering no resistance to the arms of friendly strangers. Robert's Christmas Day drinks party is the last place I want to be right now, but it has at least provided a respite from the scrutiny of Mark and his mother, whose sympathy for me on Christmas Eve had waned by lunchtime today. I was doing my best – opening a stocking for Ella I'd filled only hours before, sipping a weak Bellini at breakfast – but every conversation was an effort. Every word felt like a lie.

'She could make a bit of an effort. It's Ella's first Christmas, after all.'

It was somewhere around three, and Mark and Joan were washing up after lunch. I paused on the stairs and dug my socked toes into the carpet. Not eavesdropping, just . . . listening.

'She's grieving, Mum.'

'I grieved when your father died, but I didn't give up, did I? I put on my face, and my apron, and carried on looking after you all.'

Mark said something I didn't catch, and I carried on down the stairs and into the hall, deliberately stepping on the loose board I always made sure to avoid. The voices in the kitchen stopped abruptly, and by the time I came into the kitchen they were washing up in silence.

'There she is! Here's Mummy!' Joan was falsely bright. 'Did you have a nice nap, dear?'

I hadn't napped. How could I have done? But I had seized the invitation to do so, as an escape from Mark's cloying concern and Joan's increasing irritation that I wasn't the life and soul of the party. I had lain on the bed, staring at the ceiling, my mind racing.

It is still racing. Where is Mum now? Did she spend Christmas at the Hope? Is she safe? Why do I even care? The thought of Ella being in the nursery when that brick came through the window is horrific. My mother brought this to our door as surely as if she'd thrown the brick herself.

How can I forgive her for that?

And why, knowing what my father has done, is there a part of me that still wants to see him?

For the last twenty-four hours I've replayed the narrative of my childhood with the filter provided by the knowledge that my father was not the man I thought he was. My life is collapsing into foundations that were built on lies.

Faking your death isn't something you enter into lightly. Mum must have been desperate.

She needs me.

I can't forgive her.

I need her.

Around and around in circles.

Robert's drawing room is full of our neighbours. There are a handful of children here, although most of the residents are older than us, their offspring grown and with their own families. I know everyone in the room, except the couple by the fireplace who must be the new occupants of Sycamore – I saw the removal van there last week.

Mark is engrossed in an animated discussion about alternative therapies with Ann and Andrew Booth from two doors down, and Joan has found a comfortable spot on a sofa and isn't moving. I am walking slowly from room to room. There are pockets of people in the kitchen, the hall and the drawing room, and I drift from one to the other, with a plate of food in one hand, and a drink in the other, as though I'm en route to my seat. No one stops me. I don't want to stand in a corner and make people feel they have to come and check I'm okay. I don't want to talk.

Everyone tonight has offered their condolences, even though everyone did just that at my parents' memorial service. I grow hot as I remember the tears that were shed, the speeches made, the kindness of near strangers who took time out of their week to write a card, make a casserole, send flowers.

What would they say if they knew?

Each well-meaning, heartfelt platitude makes me sick with guilt, and so I keep moving from room to room, avoiding eye contact, never stopping. I move past Robert, who is holding court with the elderly sisters who live in the corner house. Not technically our street, but they make amazing sausage rolls, which ensure them invitations to any communal celebration.

'. . . sympathetically designed. I'd be happy to show you the plans.' One by one, he's gaining support for his extension. He hasn't won over Mark yet, but I have no doubt he will.

'I would, of course, be happy to compensate you for the inconvenience,' Robert had said, when he came over to show us the plans, which involve temporarily removing the boundary between our properties, and digging up the disused septic tank and sewerage system. 'I'll ensure that any planting disturbed is replaced, and a brand-new lawn installed when everything's finished.'

'I'm just a little concerned about the light,' Mark had replied, again.

He'd have got on well with Mum. He could have joined her campaign to stop back-garden development, listened to her arguments about environmental impacts and the integrity of historic buildings. For a second I see the two of them plotting over the kitchen table, and I have to swallow hard to stop myself from crying. Mark would like Mum – I know he would. And she'd like him; she'd like anyone who looked after me the way he does.

I have a sudden picture of Murray Mackenzie with Mark's business flyer, of my mother's handwriting on the reverse. I shake it away.

They never met. Mark says they didn't, and he has no reason to lie. I trust him.

I trust him, but I can't tell him about Mum. The second I do, he'll make me call the police. There are no grey areas for Mark; he's straight down the line. I used to like that in him. I still like it; it's just . . . complicated now. I wander back to the kitchen. A neighbour from several doors away catches my eye from the opposite side of the room, and without thinking I smile. I look away, but it's too late; he makes a beeline for me, his wife following in his wake.

'I said to Margaret we must catch you before we go, didn't I, Margaret?'

'Hi Don. Hello Margaret.'

Having reached me, Don takes a deliberate step back in order to look me up and down, like an absent uncle. I wonder if he's about to comment on how much I've grown, but instead he sighs.

'Spitting image of her, you are. Isn't she, Margaret?'

'Oh yes. Two peas in a pod.'

I force a smile. I do not want to be like my mother.

'How are you?'

'I'm fine, thank you.'

Don looks positively disappointed. 'It must be hard, though.'

'Christmas,' Margaret chimes in, in case I've forgotten what day it is.

Despite spending the last nineteen months grieving, I am

suddenly paralysed with uncertainty. Should I be crying? What do they expect from me?

'I'm fine,' I repeat.

'It still doesn't feel real,' Don says. 'I mean, both of them – such a shame.'

'Terrible shame,' Margaret echoes. They're talking to each other now – my presence irrelevant – and I have the uncomfortable feeling of having been sought out as a catalyst for their entertainment. For the ghoulish pleasure derived from talking about those less fortunate. I scan the kitchen to see who is holding Ella, so I can manufacture a breastfeeding-related exit.

'I thought I saw her in the park yesterday.'

I freeze.

'Funny how your mind plays tricks on you.' Margaret gives a little trill of laughter. She looks around – a storyteller in full flow – and her laughter stops abruptly as her eyes reach mine. She rearranges her face into something approximating sympathy. 'I mean, when I looked properly, it was nothing like Caroline. Older, black hair – very different. Clothes she wouldn't have been seen dead in—' Too late, she realises her faux pas.

'Will you excuse me?' I say. 'The baby . . .' I don't even bother finishing my sentence. I retrieve Ella from another neighbour's arms and find Mark in the study with Robert, looking at the extension plans.

'I'm going to take Ella home. She's tired. All the excitement!' I smile at Robert. 'Thanks for a lovely party.'

'I'll come with you. Mum'll be wanting her bed, too. We're all done here, I think?'

The men shake hands and I wonder what they've been discussing, but I'm already on my way to find Joan. As always, it takes ages to leave, as we say goodbye and Merry Christmas to people we see in the street or the park most days anyway.

'See you on Sunday!' someone calls out as we leave.

I wait till we're out of earshot. 'Sunday?'

218

'I invited the neighbours over for New Year's Eve.'

'A party?'

He sees my face. 'No! Not a party. Just a few drinks to see in the New Year.'

'A party.'

'Maybe a little party. Oh, come on! We'd never get a babysitter on New Year's Eve. This way we get to stay home, but still have fun. Win-win. Text Laura – see if she's already made plans. Bill too, of course.'

It's days away, I tell myself. I have more pressing things to worry about.

'I've told Robert we'll support his planning application,' Mark says, when Ella's in her Moses basket and Mark and I are getting ready for bed.

'What changed your mind?'

He grins through a mouthful of toothpaste. 'Thirty grand.'

'Thirty grand? It's not going to cost thirty grand to replace the lawn and stick some plants back in.'

Mark spits and swills water around the basin. 'If that's what it's worth to him, I'm not going to argue.' He wipes his mouth, leaving a white smear on the hand towel. 'Now I don't have to worry about the flat being empty for a while.'

'You didn't have to worry anyway – I told you.'

He gives me a minty kiss and heads for bed.

I stare in the mirror. My skin is still free from lines, but the bones over which it stretches are undeniably my mother's.

Margaret thinks she saw Mum in the park yesterday. She doesn't know it, but she probably did. It's only a matter of time before someone really does recognise her; before someone calls the police.

I could stop all of this, right now, by telling the truth.

So why haven't I? I've known for more than twenty-four hours that my parents are alive; that my father faked his death to escape debt, and my mother faked hers to get away from my father. She betrayed me. Lied to me. Why aren't I calling the police?

My face stares back at me from the mirror, the answer written in my eyes.

Because she's my mother, and she's in danger.

THIRTY-SIX

'A baby?' I said. 'But we took precautions!'

'The pill's only ninety-eight per cent reliable.'

I didn't believe it. Said so.

'See for yourself.'

The thin blue line was unwavering. So was I.

I didn't want a baby.

There were options, of course, but I was made to feel like a monster for even suggesting it.

'How could you?'

'It's a collection of cells.'

'It's a baby. Our baby.'

Our parents were delighted. They met each other over an awkward afternoon tea and discovered they got on famously. It was time we settled down – they'd been respectively worried about our 'wild ways', suspicious of our London lifestyles. How wonderful we'd found each other; what a miracle this baby was!

It had all been taken out of my hands.

A shotgun wedding. A new house ('Much more family-friendly than that dreadful flat'), a new job ('So much less cut-throat than the City'), a move to the fucking sea ('The air's so much cleaner!') . . .

I'd never felt so trapped in my life.

Yet it was impossible not to love Anna when she arrived. She was bright and beautiful and filled with curiosity. But it was impossible, too, not to resent her. There was a whole life out there, waiting for me, and instead of running at it with both hands I was standing still with a baby in my arms. I fantasised about leaving. Told myself an absent parent was better than one who didn't want to be there. But I didn't leave. I did what I'd always done when life was hard.

I drank.

THIRTY-SEVEN

MURRAY

Boxing Day was always an anti-climax. When Murray had been in uniform, Boxing Day had meant one domestic after another, as hangovers were assuaged with more booze, familial tension exploding after twenty-four hours reined in for Christmas.

For someone like Sarah, who felt everything so keenly, the comedown was even worse. It was midday before she appeared downstairs, and then only to take the tea Murray made her and retreat back to bed. Murray tidied the kitchen, made himself some lunch, and wondered what to do. He didn't want to leave Sarah alone when she was like this, but the house was beginning to close in on him.

He got out the Johnson file and spread it on the kitchen table. Tom Johnson had made several Google searches relating to suicide, Beachy Head and tide times. All had been made between midnight on 17 May and nine the following morning. Perfectly plausible for a man contemplating suicide – which was presumably what the investigating officers had decided – but in the context of the picture Murray had now built up, the searches were too careful. Too convenient. They had clearly been made by whoever had murdered the Johnsons and engineered the fake suicides.

Who would have had access to Tom's phone? It was an impossible question, without knowing where the man had been the morning prior to his death. CID had made attempts to retrace his steps, but once the Audi had been picked up on the ANPR camera sited near Beachy Head, nothing more had been done. There had been no need.

Where had Tom been overnight? Who had he been with that morning? Murray covered three pages of his notebook with possible lines of enquiry, frustrated by the holiday period, which meant no one was at work for him to speak to.

It was early evening when Murray put a hand on the mound of tangled duvet and suggested that Sarah might feel better if she had a shower and got dressed. The air in the bedroom was stale, and the cup of tea he'd pressed into Sarah's hand had gone untouched, a shiny film across the surface.

'I just want to go back to Highfield.'

'You're seeing Mr Chaudhury on Friday.'

Sarah was crying, burying herself beneath the duvet so her words were muffled. 'I don't want to be here. I want to be at Highfield.'

'Shall I bring the duvet downstairs? We can veg out on the sofa and watch black and white movies.'

'Go away!'

Had Sarah been visible, Murray would have hidden the hurt on his face beneath the smile of a supportive husband. And indeed he put a hand where he imagined Sarah's shoulder was, and began to form the words he needed. The words *she* needed. Only he suddenly felt overwhelmingly, bone-crushingly tired. None of it made a difference. Whatever he said, whatever he did, it wouldn't help Sarah. Nothing could help Sarah.

He stood up and left the room, closing the bedroom door behind him. He stood on the landing and looked across the street, where houses were adorned with Christmas lights, and inside families were playing board games and arguing over the remote.

'Snap out of it, Mackenzie,' he muttered.

Downstairs he put two slices of cheese on toast under the

grill. He would ring Anna Johnson. To hell with public holidays. The woman was mourning her parents; she'd had a brick through her window. These were hardly normal times. She'd been desperate for him to re-open the investigation, and – mindful of his bollocking from Leo Griffiths – Murray knew CID would soon be taking the lead. It was time to tell Anna Johnson what he knew.

He turned the grill low and picked up the phone.

'Hello?'

'Hello. It's Murray Mackenzie. From the police,' he added, when Anna didn't speak.

'Right. Actually, it's not a great time—'

'I'm sorry to disturb you on Boxing Day. I just wanted to tell you that I think you're right. There's more to your parents' deaths than meets the eye.' It came out in a rush, as much for Murray's own benefit as Anna's. A little of the tightness eased from his chest. He imagined Anna's hand at her throat; perhaps even tears of relief that finally someone had listened to her. He waited. There was the tiniest sound on the other end of the line and then silence.

Murray rang back.

'I think the line dropped out. I thought we might meet tomorrow, perhaps. If you're free? I can fill you in on what I've found out, and we can discuss—'

'No!'

It was Murray's turn to fall silent. He wasn't even sure if this sudden, loud command had been directed at him, or at someone in Anna's house. Her partner? A dog? The baby?

'I've changed my mind.' There was a tremor in Anna's voice, but she pressed on, getting louder as though she was having to force the words out. 'I need to move on. Accept what happened. Accept the verdicts.'

'That's what I'm saying, though, Anna. I think you're right. I think your parents were murdered.'

Anna made a sound of frustration. 'You're not listening to me. Look, I'm sorry I wasted your time, but I don't want this. I don't want you digging up the past. I don't want you doing anything.' The timbre of her voice changed and Murray realised she was crying. 'Please just drop it!'

This time the click at the end of the line was louder. Anna Johnson had hung up.

The tightness in Murray's chest returned, and he swallowed the ridiculous urge to cry. He stood without moving, the phone in his hand, and it was only when the smoke alarm pierced through the still air that he realised his supper was burning.

THIRTY-EIGHT

ANNA

On Wednesday, the day after Boxing Day, Joan goes home. There are parcels of leftovers and promises to go up and see her, and several assertions that it's been lovely to spend time as a family, but eventually she is in her car and we're standing in the driveway, waving her off.

It is that curious time between Christmas and New Year, when you have to look on the calendar to check the date, and every day seems to be a bank holiday. Mark takes out the recycling, and I lie with Ella on the floor of the sitting room. She is enthralled by the crinkly pages of a black and white book we gave her for Christmas, and I turn them over for her, one by one, repeating the names of the animals on each page. Dog. Cat. Sheep.

It has been three days since Mum came back. I promised myself that, after Christmas – after Joan left – I would tell Mark, and we would go to the police together.

And now Christmas is over.

I wonder if my failure to come clean is a criminal act, and whether such an offence becomes progressively serious over time. Is twenty-four hours acceptable, but seventy-two a matter for the courts? Is there mitigation for whatever offence this is I'm committing? I mentally tick off the reasons I'm keeping this secret.

I'm scared. Of the newspaper headlines, the doorstepping from

227

the press, the looks from the neighbours. The internet means there's no such thing as tomorrow's chip papers; Ella will deal with the aftermath of this for ever.

There's a more immediate, more urgent fear, too. Fear of my father. I have heard from Mum what he's capable of; glimpsed enough of it myself to take it seriously. If I go to the police with everything I know, I need them to move fast: to arrest Dad and make sure he can't hurt us. But what if they can't find him? What might he do to us?

I worry about what Mark will say. What he'll do. He loves me, but our relationship is still new, still fragile. What if this is too much? I try to imagine what I'd do if the tables were turned, but the thought of sensible, strait, Joan faking her own death is too ludicrous to consider. But I'd stay, wouldn't I? I'd never leave Mark because of something his parents did. Still, I worry. For all the time Mark and I have been together, my grief has been as present as another person in our lives. Mark has worked around it, made allowances. If we take that away . . . I finally pinpoint what I'm scared of. That without the grief that brought us together, we might start to pull apart.

I turn the page for Ella. She grabs a corner in a tightly clenched fist and brings it to her mouth. There's another reason I haven't been to the police.

Mum.

I can't condone what she's done, but I can understand why she left. I wish with all my heart she had done it differently, but going to the police won't change that. The choice I make now will either send her to prison or keep her out of it.

I can't put my own mother in jail.

In the last few days I've watched Joan with Ella, and seen the joy of a relationship that crosses generations. We've bathed Ella, walked through the park and taken it in turns to push the pram. I want to do those things with my own mother. I want Ella to know both her grandmothers.

228

My mum has come back, and I want so much to keep her in my life.

I need to clear my head. I find Mark.

'I'm going to take Ella for a walk.'

'Good idea. If you can wait five minutes I'll come with you.'

I hesitate. 'Would you mind if we went on our own? What with Joan here, and the party at Robert's, I feel like I've not had a second to myself.'

His face tells me he's weighing up my request. Do I need time out because I want some peace and quiet, or because I'm cracking up?

Despite how I feel inside, evidently I don't look like I'm a danger to myself – or to Ella – because he smiles. 'Sure. See you later.'

I walk to town. The wind – hardly noticeable inland – picks up, and whips along the seafront. I stop to clip the plastic cover across the front of the pram. The shingle is dark and shiny from overnight rain, and it's quiet, with most of the shops still closed for the holidays, but there are people out walking on the beach and the esplanade. Everyone seems in a good mood – filled with festive cheer and the joy of an extra day off work – but perhaps it only feels like that because of the turmoil in my own head. Everyone has troubles, I remind myself, although I think it's unlikely anyone else is wrestling with parents who have come back from the dead right now.

I don't mean to go to the Hope, although I suspect it was inevitable. My feet find their way there, and I don't fight it.

It's an unprepossessing house, rubble-rendered in grey, and wider than it is tall. I ring the bell.

The woman who comes to the door is still and gentle. She stands like a ballerina, with her feet in first position, and her hands together at her waist.

'I was wondering if I could see Caroline . . .' I hesitate, deciding not to use her surname. 'She's staying with you.'

'Wait here, please.' She smiles and closes the door again, gently but firmly.

I wonder if bad people come here. Abusive husbands, wanting their wives back home. I doubt this woman smiles then. I wonder if Dad's looked for Mum here. I look around. Has he been watching me? He must have done, to know that I went to the police. I start to shake, my fingers gripping the handle of Ella's pram.

'I'm afraid there's no one of that name here.' She's back so quickly I wonder if she went at all, or whether she simply stood behind the door for a moment. Perhaps this is a stock answer, delivered regardless of whether the owner of the name is in residence.

It's only when the door closes again that I realise my mistake. Mum wouldn't use her real name – first or last – not when she's supposed to be dead. I walk away, wondering if I should go back and describe her; wondering if it is a good thing I didn't find her here. If it's meant to be this way.

'Anna!' I turn around. Mum is stepping out of the door, wearing the same clothes she wore on Christmas Eve. She pulls the hood of her coat over her head. 'Sister Mary said someone was looking for Caroline.'

'She's a nun?'

'She's amazing. Fiercely protective – she'd have said no, whatever name you'd given.'

'I did wonder. I'm sorry – I didn't think.'

'It doesn't matter.' We've fallen into step, walking back towards the seafront. 'Angela.'

I look at her, momentarily confused.

'The name I use now. It's Angela.'

'Right.'

We walk on in silence. I didn't go to the Hope with a prepared speech or plan. I feel awkward. Tongue-tied. I take my hands off the pram handle and move to the side and, wordlessly, Mum takes over, and it's so easy – so *right* – that I could cry.

I can't send her to prison. I want her – need her – in my life. In Ella's life.

There are more people on the pier. Children race up and down, letting off steam after days cooped up inside. I see Mum pull her hood tighter and keep her head down low. We should have walked somewhere quieter – what if we see someone we know?

The helter-skelter is covered over; the coconut shy boarded up for winter. We walk to the end and look out at the sea. Grey waves throw themselves against the legs of the pier.

We are both trying to think of something to say.

Mum goes first. 'How was your Christmas?'

It's so ridiculously mundane, I feel laughter welling up inside me. I catch Mum's eye, and she starts to laugh too, and suddenly we're crying and laughing and her arms are wrapped tightly around me. Her smell is achingly familiar. How many embraces have I had from my mother? Not enough. It could never be enough.

When our sobs have subsided, we sit on a bench and pull Ella's pram close.

'Are you going to tell the police?' Mum speaks quietly.

'I don't know.'

She says nothing for a while. When she speaks, it comes out in a rush. 'Give me a few days. Till the New Year. Let me spend some time with Ella – let me get to know her. Don't decide until then. Please.'

It's easy to say yes. To delay my decision. We sit in silence, watching the sea.

Mum puts her arm through mine. 'Tell me about your pregnancy.'

I smile. It seems like a lifetime ago. 'I had awful morning sickness.'

'Runs in the family, I'm afraid. I was sick as a dog with you. And the heartburn . . .'

'Horrendous! I was swigging Gaviscon from the bottle by the end.'

231

'Any cravings?'

'Carrot sticks dipped in chocolate spread.' The look on her face makes me laugh. 'Don't knock it till you try it.' There's a warm glow inside me, despite the wind that whistles across the pier. When the women in our NCT group moaned about the unwanted advice from their mothers, I thought how much I longed for pearls of wisdom from my own. How I wouldn't care how much she interfered; how I'd value every visit, every call, every offer of help.

'All I wanted when I was pregnant with you was olives. Couldn't get enough of them. Dad said you'd come out looking like one.'

My laugh dies on my lips, and Mum quickly changes the subject.

'And Mark – is he good to you?'

'He's a great dad.'

Mum looks at me curiously. I haven't answered the question. I'm not sure I can. Is he good to me? He's kind and thoughtful. He listens, he helps out around the house. Yes, he's good to me.

'I'm very lucky,' I tell her. Mark didn't have to stick by me when I fell pregnant. Lots of men wouldn't have done.

'I'd love to meet him.'

I'm about to say how wonderful that would be if only she could, when I see her face. She's deadly serious. 'You can't be . . . It isn't possible.'

'Isn't it? We could tell him I'm a distant cousin. That we lost touch, or fell out, or . . .' She trails off, giving up on the idea.

In the choppy water below the pier I see a flash of movement. An arm. A head. Someone's in the water. I'm half standing when I realise they're swimming, not drowning. I shiver on their behalf; sink back down onto the bench.

My self-imposed deadline gives me four days left with Mum before I either tell the police, or let Mum disappear to somewhere she won't be recognised. Either way, I have four days before I have to say goodbye to my mother for the second time.

Four days to have what I've longed for since Ella was born. Family. Mark and Ella and Mum and me.

I wonder.

She looks nothing like the few photos Mark has seen. She's thinner, older, her hair is jet black and cut in a way that changes the shape of her face.

Could we?

'And you're sure you've never met him?'

She raises her eyebrows at my abrupt questioning. 'You know I haven't.'

'The police found one of Mark's leaflets in your diary.' I try to keep my tone neutral, but it still sounds like an accusation. 'You made an appointment with him.'

I take in her furrowed brow, the movement of her jaw as she worries at the inside of her lower lip. She stares at the wooden planks beneath our feet, at the swimmer, who cuts cleanly through the waves.

'Oh!' She turns back to me, relief showing on her face now that she has solved the mystery. 'Counselling services. Brighton.'

'Yes. You made an appointment with him.'

'That was Mark? Your Mark? God, how extraordinary.' She picks at a loose piece of skin around a fingernail. 'It came through the door after your dad left. You know what I was like – I was in pieces. I couldn't sleep; I was jumping at the slightest thing. I had no one to turn to, not really. I needed to tell someone – get it off my chest – so I booked the appointment.'

'But you didn't keep it.'

She shakes her head. 'I thought whatever I said would be in confidence. Like confession, I suppose. But when I looked through the small print it said that discretion couldn't be guaranteed if the client's life was at risk, or if they disclosed a crime.'

'Right.' I wonder if Mark has ever betrayed a client's confidence by going to the police, and if he'd ever tell me if he had.

'So, I didn't go.'

'He doesn't remember.'

'He must deal with a lot of people.' She takes my hands, rubs them with her thumbs. 'Let me be part of a family again, Anna. Please.'

A beat.

'He'll know it's you.'

'He won't. People believe what they want to believe,' Mum says. 'They believe what you tell them. Trust me.'

I do.

THIRTY-NINE

True story: more people die over Christmas than at any other time.

The cold weather gets them. Hospital resources fail them. Loneliness sends them reaching for the pills, a knife, a rope.

Or they fall into a fist.

I threw my first punch on 25 December 1996.

Merry Christmas.

Anna was five. Sitting by the tree in a sea of wrapping paper, clutching a Buzz Lightyear with undisguised delight.

'They've sold out everywhere, you know,' Bill said, with more than a touch of smugness. 'You wouldn't believe what I had to do to get hold of that one.'

Next to Anna, discarded on the floor, was a Barbie. It had hair that grew, eyeshadow that changed colour. Articulated bloody ankles. A Barbie I'd worked for, chosen, paid for. She'd looked at it once – saw how the hair could grow longer with the little wheel at the back – then she'd dropped it on the floor. I don't think she picked it up again all Christmas.

I poured my first drink then. Felt judgemental eyes on me as I knocked it back, so I poured another, just because. I sat. And I seethed.

You messed up Christmas lunch. Overcooked the turkey, undercooked the sprouts. You'd had a drink yourself. You thought it was funny. I didn't.

You tried to make Bill stay. Didn't want to be on your own with me. When he insisted, you walked him to the door and pulled him into the sort of embrace you never gave me any more. I drank more. Seethed more.

'Shall we ask Alicia to join us next Christmas?' you said. 'Awful to think of her and Laura in that horrible flat.'

I said yes, but I wasn't so sure. If I was honest I couldn't imagine Alicia here, in our house. She was different to us. She spoke differently; dressed differently. She belonged in her world, not in ours.

We'd kept our own presents till last. Anna was in bed, and the turkey wrapped in foil (although it couldn't have got any drier), and you made us sit on the floor like we were five ourselves.

'You first.' I handed you a present. I'd paid for it to be wrapped, but you pulled off the ribbon without looking at it and I thought next time I wouldn't bother.

'I love it.'

I knew you would. The camera had caught Anna just as the swing hit its highest point. She was laughing, her legs swinging and her hair flying. The frame was silver. Expensive. It was a good present.

'Now you.' You put it in my hands. You were nervous. 'You're so hard to buy for!'

Carefully, I peeled back the sticky tape, slid the package out of the red and white paper. Jewellery? Gloves?

It was a CD.

Easy Listening: A compilation of the world's greatest hits. Just relaaaaaax . . .

In the corner of the case was a sticky patch where you'd scraped off the label.

It was as though someone had stolen two decades from me. Marched me into C&A and dressed me in beige trousers, with an elasticated waistband. I thought of my life before you; before Anna. Of the parties, the coke, the lays, the fun.

And now, what was my life?

An easy listening CD.

You'd think it would have happened quickly, but for me it was the reverse. Time slowed down. I felt my fingers curl into a fist; felt my nails in the soft flesh of my palm. I felt the shiver of tension run from wrist to shoulder, pause at the top and then run back again. Building, building, building, building.

The bruise ran from your temple to your throat.

'I'm sorry,' I said. I was. I was ashamed. A little frightened – although I'd never have admitted it – of what I was capable of.

'Forget it.'

I didn't, of course, and nor did you. But we pretended we had.

Until the next time.

It scared me enough to make me stop drinking for a while. But I wasn't an alcoholic, remember? That's what I told myself. So, there was no need to go cold turkey. A cool beer here, a glass of wine there . . . It wasn't long before I needed the sun over the yardarm long before six o'clock.

You never know what goes on behind closed doors. Out of every ten of your friends, two of them are in violent relationships. Two. How many friends did we have? We can't have been the only ones.

I found it reassuring, in a way. We weren't unusual.

We kept it a secret, of course. If we hadn't, it might not have gone on for so long. But no one's proud of a failed marriage. No one's proud of being a victim.

You didn't say anything, and neither did I.

I'd like to say I was out of control. After all, I only ever hit you when I was drunk; surely that absolved me of some responsibility?

You never called me out on it, but you knew – and I knew – that I must have had at least a modicum of control. I never lashed out when Anna was in the room, or even – once she was old enough to understand the nuances of an adult relationship – when she was at home. It was as though her presence was a calming influence; a reminder of how a rational person behaves.

That, and I was too ashamed to let her see me that way.

Each time it happened I told you I was sorry. Each time I said it had 'just happened', that I hadn't planned it, hadn't been able to stop myself. I hate myself now, for the lies I told then. I knew exactly what I was doing. And after that first time, however drunk I was – however angry I was – I never again hit you where the bruise would show.

FORTY

MURRAY

The High Tech Crime Unit was a mile from the nearest police station, in the middle of an industrial estate. Marked cars and uniformed officers were strictly forbidden, and nothing about Unit 12 suggested that inside the grey concrete box were dozens of IT specialists taking apart laptops, analysing hard-drives and extracting the worst kind of pornography from encrypted files.

Today the car park was empty, save for one car. Murray pressed the buzzer and looked up at the camera.

'What, no Santa hat?' came the disembodied voice, followed by a harsh buzzing noise and a loud click as the door released.

Sean Dowling had the sort of personality that entered a room a second before he did. Broad-shouldered and stocky, he still played rugby every Saturday, despite pushing sixty, and today sported a deep purple bruise across the bridge of his nose. He shook Murray's hand vigorously.

'Could have used you against Park House the other week.'

Murray laughed. 'Long since retired, mate. I don't know where you get the stamina.'

'Keeps me young.' Sean grinned. He held open the door. 'Good Christmas?'

'Quiet. Sorry to drag you in over the holidays.'

'Are you joking? Tracy's mum's staying – I was halfway out the door before you put the phone down.'

They caught up as they walked, promising to get together for

239

a beer, and wondering aloud why they'd left it so long. It was so easy, Murray thought, when you were working on a case. So easy to socialise, to make new friends and stay in touch with old ones. By returning to a civilian job after retiring, he had hoped this element of the job he loved so much would have survived unharmed, but as more of Murray's peers had retired, so the after-work beers had petered out. Murray doubted any of the officers at Lower Meads even knew their front-counter civvy had once been one of Sussex's most respected detectives.

Sean led Murray to the corner of a large open-plan room. Air-conditioning units – installed for the benefit of the myriad computers, rather than their users – rattled at either end of the room, and the floor-to-ceiling windows were obscured by blinds, preventing curious passers-by from looking inside.

Only Sean's workstation was in use, a dark green parka hung over his chair. On the desk were three storage boxes, each filled with clear exhibit bags, their red plastic seals protruding at all angles. Beneath his desk were another two boxes, both full. In each bag was a mobile phone.

'We've got a bit of a backlog.'

'No kidding.'

Sean pulled up a second chair and flipped open a large black project book. At the top of the page was the mobile number of the caller who had given the name Diane Brent-Taylor.

'The SIM card was pay-as-you-go, so we'll need to work on the handset itself. It was active for six months after the incident, although no calls were made.' Sean spun his pen like a baton through his fingers.

'Is there any way of finding out where the handset is now?'

'Not unless your witness – or whoever has it now – turns it on.' An over-enthusiastic twirl sent the pen flying across the room, where it skittered under a filing cabinet. Absentmindedly, Sean reached for another pen and began the same well-practised movement. Murray wondered how many pens there were under the cabinet. 'Now, what we could do is extract the call data and find the IMEI—'

'In English?'

Sean grinned. 'Every device has a fifteen-digit unique number: the IMEI. It's like a fingerprint for mobiles. If we can trace your witness call back to the handset, we can work back from that to the point of purchase.'

And from that, Murray thought, he might stand a chance of tracing the caller, particularly if they used a bank card to make the transaction. 'How soon could you get me a result?'

'You know I'm always happy to do a mate a favour, but . . .' Sean looked at the rammed storage boxes in front of them and rubbed his face, forgetting his bruise and wincing at the oversight. 'What's the big deal with this job, anyway?'

'No big deal.' Murray spoke more casually than he felt. 'The daughter came in to report some concerns over the verdict, and I'm looking into it for her.'

'In your own time? I hope she appreciates it.'

Murray looked at the desk. He was trying not to dwell on his phone call to Anna. He had caught her at a bad time, that was all. It was bound to be distressing; it was only natural she'd have doubts. Once he had hard evidence that something suspicious had happened to her parents, she'd be grateful he had pressed on regardless. Nevertheless, the sharp click as she hung up the phone still echoed in his ears.

Sean sighed, mistaking Murray's expression for disappointment in him. 'Look, I'll see what I can do.'

'I appreciate it.'

'More importantly, get your diary out, and let's get that beer sorted. You know it'll never happen otherwise.' Sean opened a calendar on his laptop, firing off dates then instantly realising they were already booked. Murray patiently turned the pages of his National Trust pocket diary until Sean found a window, then he borrowed a pen and wrote on the pristine page.

He hummed along to the radio as he drove away from the industrial unit, the winter sun low in his eyes. With any luck, Sean would get back to him later today. The holidays were providing a legitimate reason for Murray's delay in writing up the job for CID, and if he could get a result on the phone before he did so, he might be able to hand it over with a suspect attached.

Besides getting the phone looked into, there was something nagging him about his visit to Diane Brent-Taylor's house. It wasn't Diane herself – Murray prided himself on being a good judge of character, and if the twin-set-and-pearls pensioner was a murderer, he'd eat his trilby.

But there was definitely something.

Something he'd seen on the noticeboard by the front door. A leaflet? A card? It was infuriating not being able to remember, and as Diane had been packing to go away the day Murray had visited her, there was nothing he could do to jog his memory.

At home, he paused with his key in the lock, feeling the familiar anxiety fill his chest. The pause represented the last few seconds where life was under control; where he knew which way was up. On the other side of the door anything could be waiting. Over the years Murray had perfected a neutral greeting while he waited to see how Sarah was – what she expected from him – but he had never stopped needing those three seconds between the two halves of his world.

'I'm home.'

She was downstairs, which was an improvement. The curtains were still drawn, and as Murray pulled them open, Sarah winced and covered her eyes with her hands.

'How are you feeling?'

'Tired.'

Sarah had slept for twelve hours, but she looked as though she'd pulled an all-nighter. Heavy circles ringed her eyes, and her skin was grey and dull.

'I'll make you something to eat.'

'I'm not hungry.'

'Cup of tea?'

'I don't want one.'

Gently, Murray tried to take the duvet to shake it out, but Sarah clung on to it and buried herself deeper into the sofa. The television was on mute, playing a kids' cartoon featuring animals in a zoo.

Murray stood for a while. Should he make something anyway? Sarah sometimes changed her mind once the food was actually in front of her. Just as often, though, she didn't. Just as often, Murray ate it, or tipped it away, or covered it with cling film in the hope she might fancy something later. Murray looked at the pile of duvet, at his wife, who had manoeuvred herself as far from him as it was possible to get without actually leaving the sofa.

'I'll just be through here, then. If you need anything.'

There was no sign that Sarah had heard him.

Murray brought in an empty recycling box from the garden. Methodically, he opened each drawer in the kitchen, removing the sharp knives, the scissors, the blades from the food processor. He took the kitchen foil from the cupboard and carefully pulled out the strip of serrated metal from its cardboard housing. He collected the caustic cleaning products from under the sink and the over-the-counter medicines from the dresser drawer. It had been a while since he had felt the need to do this, and he didn't want to think about why it felt necessary now. Instead he mentally walked through his visit to Diane Brent-Taylor, in the hope he would remember what it was that had caught his eye on her noticeboard.

The front door had been white UPVC, the external doormat a mix of coir and rubber. Inside, the hall floor was laminate, and deep red walls had made the already gloomy downstairs even darker. The noticeboard had been on the left, above a shelf with a motley collection of items. What had been there? A hair-brush. A postcard. Keys. He visualised each section of the shelf until the items took shape, a grown-up version of the memory game he had played as a child.

Murray put everything in the recycling box and took it down to the bottom of the garden. He opened the shed and began burying the box beneath dusty decorating sheets.

As he did so, his thoughts returned to the board. What was on it? More postcards – at least three. One with Table Mountain on it (he remembered it because Cape Town was on his list of dream destinations). A leaflet for a beauty salon. A list of tele-phone numbers. Had he recognised a name on that list? Was that what had been nagging him?

'What are you doing?'

Murray hadn't seen Sarah come into the garden, and the voice directly behind him made him clumsy. He collected himself before turning around. Sarah was shivering, her lips tinged blue after just a few seconds out of the warmth. Her feet were bare and her arms wrapped around herself, each hand tucked beneath the sleeve of the opposite arm. Her fingers moved rhythmically, and Murray knew she was scratching at skin already red raw from the same action.

He touched his hands on both of her upper arms, and the movement ceased.

'I *am* hungry.'

'I'll make you something.'

Murray led her back up the garden, found her slippers and sat her in the kitchen. Sarah said nothing as he made her a sandwich with a blunt knife that tore at the bread, but she ate ravenously, and Murray counted that as a win.

'I've been working on the Johnson job.' He searched for a spark of interest in Sarah's eyes, but found none. Murray's heart sank. She had taken his litmus test, and the results reinforced what Murray already knew: that Sarah was heading into another

244

difficult period. He felt as though he was flailing in deep water, halfway across the channel with no support boat. 'Not that there's much point now,' he added, and he couldn't have said whether he was talking about Anna's change of heart, or the fact that the investigation was no longer the lifeline it had seemed to be for him and for Sarah.

Sarah stopped eating. Deep lines furrowed her forehead as she looked at him.

'Anna Johnson doesn't want an investigation,' Murray said slowly, pretending he hadn't seen her react; pretending he was talking to himself. He stared at a spot just to the right of Sarah's plate. 'So I don't see why I should spend my spare time—'

'Why doesn't she want an investigation?'

'I don't know. She told me to drop it. She was angry. She hung up.'

'Angry? Or scared?'

Murray looked at Sarah.

'Because if she's scared it might sound like she's angry. Like she doesn't want you to carry on.'

'She was certainly very clear about that,' Murray said, remembering the way Anna had slammed down the phone. 'She doesn't want my help.'

Sarah was thoughtful. 'She might not want it.' She picked at her sandwich, then pushed it away and looked at Murray. 'But maybe she needs it.'

FORTY-ONE

ANNA

The phone echoes in the hall. It rarely rings – we both use our mobiles – and when it does it is usually a double-glazing cold call or a PPI phishing trip. Mark makes to stand up, but I leap to my feet. It's been two days since I put the phone down on Murray Mackenzie, and I've been on edge ever since, waiting for him to call back.

'I'll get it.' I haven't told Mark about it. What could I say? Having dismissed the anniversary card as nothing more than a sick practical joke, the brick through the window was a threat he couldn't ignore. Every day he's been on the phone to the investigating officers.

'Apparently they're "doing everything they can",' he said, after the last time. 'Which doesn't seem to be a lot.'

'Can they get fingerprints?' The police have my parents' DNA and prints. They took them from personal effects at home and at work, in the hope that – if a body surfaced – they would be able to identify them. I wondered if Dad knew that, if he'd have been careless with his mark. What will happen if they find his prints? They'll know he's not dead; they'll realise Mum isn't, either. The two of them are inextricably bound; if one goes to prison, the other surely will, too.

Is that what I want?

'Nothing on the note, and apparently brick's a bad surface for prints.'

The relief I feel takes me by surprise.

'They're waiting for DNA results on the elastic band.' He shrugged, already writing off any hope of a conclusion. In the meantime, the nursery window's been repaired, and an order placed for front and back security lights.

'Hello?' I say.

The phone line is quiet.

'Hello?' Fear pools in my stomach.

Silence. No, not quite silence. A rustle. Breathing.

Dad?

I don't say it. I can't. Not only because Mark is listening, but because I'm worried my voice will betray me. That the anger that fills my heart and head for what Dad did to Mum – to me – will be overshadowed the second I start speaking. That the fear and hatred that has descended in the last week will be cancelled out by twenty-six years of love.

Twenty-six years of lies, I remind myself, steeling my heart and closing my mind to the memories that assault me: Dad, calling to say he'll be late; to wish me a happy birthday, when he and Billy were away with work; to remind me to revise; to see if we need anything; to ask me to record *Planet Earth*.

I press refresh on the images; see instead what I now know to be the truth. Dad, throwing my homemade paperweight against the wall in a fit of rage; relying on booze to get through the day; stashing bottles around the house; hitting Mum.

I can't put the phone down. I stand, feet frozen to the spot, receiver clamped to my ear. Desperate for him to speak, yet terrified of what he'd say.

He says nothing.

There's a quiet click, and the line goes dead.

'No one there,' I say when I return to the sitting room, in answer to Mark's enquiring look.

'That's a bit concerning. We should let the police know. They might be able to trace the call.'

247

Could they? Do I want them to? I can't think straight. If the police arrest Dad, we will be safe. Mum will be safe. His fake suicide will be uncovered, and he'll go to prison. Mum'll be in trouble too, but surely domestic abuse is mitigation enough? Women have been acquitted of more in similar circumstances.

But.

Maybe Dad used a call box. Maybe there's CCTV. Maybe the police will trace the call; see the images. They'll know that Dad is still alive, but he won't be safely behind bars. Maybe he won't ever be behind bars. Mum's faked suicide will be uncovered, and Dad'll still be out there. Still free. Still a threat.

'It was one of those call centres,' I say. 'I could hear the other operators in the background.'

It seems once you start lying, it's easy to carry on.

It's eight o'clock when the text message comes. The television is showing a re-run of some early classic with Richard Briers that neither of us is watching. We're both looking at our phones, scrolling through mindless Facebook updates, tapping 'like' on every other one. My phone is on silent, the message appearing on my screen from a number I've saved under 'Angela'.

Now?

My heart beats furiously. I glance at Mark, but he's paying no attention. I tap a reply.

I'm not sure about this.

Please, Anna. I don't know how much longer I can risk staying here.

I tap another message. Delete it; tap another; delete that too.

How could I have even entertained the idea of bringing Mum here, introducing her to Mark? She's supposed to be dead. Okay,

248

so her hair's different; she's thinner; she looks older than she is. But she's still my mother.

He'll know.

I'm sorry – I can't do this.

I type out the message, but as I tap 'send' the doorbell rings out, confident and clear. I look up, eyes wide in panic. Mark's already on his feet, and I scramble to follow him into the hall, where it's clear from the shape of the stained-glass silhouette that it's her.

He opens the door.

If she's nervous, she's hiding it well.

She looks him in the eye. 'You must be Mark.'

There's a fraction of a pause before he responds. I move to stand next to him, although I'm convinced he'll be able to hear my heart thudding, and as he waits politely for an explanation, I know I have no alternative but to continue the charade.

'Angela! Mark, this is Mum's second cousin. We bumped into each other yesterday and she said she'd love to meet you and Ella, so . . .' I tail off. The story Mum and I concocted as we walked along the seafront seems ludicrous now, the lies we're feeding Mark making me sick to the stomach.

But my lies are to protect him. I can't have Mark implicated in my parents' crimes. I won't.

He steps back with the broad smile of a man who is used to guests dropping in unannounced. I wonder if Mum sees – as I do – the concern behind this cheery façade. Concern because I've never mentioned a cousin before? Or because his emotionally unstable partner has apparently once again forgotten to tell him she invited someone over? For once I hope it's the latter.

I scour his face for signs of suspicion, for a flicker of recognition.

Nothing.

It's only now that I realise how uneasy I've been about Mum's handwriting on Mark's flyer; that I needed this confirmation, despite the reassurance from both sides.

'Hi, I'm Mark.' He extends a hand, then shakes his head and laughs at his formality, stepping forward instead to pull Mum into a warm embrace. 'It's great to meet you.'

I breathe out.

'Caroline and I had a stupid falling-out,' Mum says, when we're installed in the sitting room, glasses of wine in hand. 'I can't even remember what it was about now, but we didn't speak for years and . . .' She breaks off, and I think she's dried up, but she swallows hard. 'And now it's too late.'

Mark rests an elbow on the arm of the sofa. His thumb on the base of his chin, he rubs his forefinger lightly along his top lip. Listening. Considering. Does he think it odd that 'Angela' should suddenly turn up in Eastbourne, a year after my mother's death? My eyes flick between Mark and Mum. She meets my gaze for a split second, then drops her eyes away. Looks for a tissue.

'We can't change the past,' Mark says gently. 'We can only change the way we feel about it, and the way it affects our future.'

'You're right.' She blows her nose and tucks the tissue up her sleeve in such a familiar gesture it's a moment before I can breathe again. Rita is sitting as close to Mum as it is possible to get, leaning so heavily that if Mum moved her legs, the dog would topple over.

'You're honoured,' Mark says. 'She's usually wary of strangers.'

I daren't catch Mum's eye.

'It's lovely to meet someone from Anna's side. I know Bill, of course, and Caroline's goddaughter, Laura, who's practically family.' He gives me a sidelong glance, winking to neutralise whatever's coming next. 'Another one for the top table.'

'You're getting married?'

'No,' I say, and laugh because that's what Mark's doing. I shift in my seat.

'Maybe you can persuade her, Angela – I'm not having much luck.' It's a throwaway comment, meant as a joke.

'But you're so young, Anna!'

'I'm twenty-six.' As if she didn't know that. Hadn't carried me for nine months when she was younger than I am now.

'You shouldn't rush into anything.'

There's an uncomfortable silence. Mark coughs.

'Are you married, Angela?'

'Separated.' She glances at me. 'It didn't work out.'

Another awkward pause follows, while Mum and I think about the way that separation came about, and Mark thinks about . . . what? The face of a good counsellor gives nothing away.

'How long are you planning on being in Eastbourne?' I ask.

'Not long. Till New Year's Day, that's all. Enough time to see the people who matter, and avoid those who don't.' She laughs.

Mark grins. 'Where are you staying?'

A red flush colours Mum's cheeks. 'At the Hope.' Mark's face is impassive, but Mum's embarrassment intensifies. 'Things are a bit tight and . . . anyway, it's only for a few nights. It's fine.'

'Why don't you stay with us?' He looks at me for confirmation, even though the offer's already been made. 'We've got plenty of room, and it would be lovely for Ella to spend time with you.'

'Oh, I couldn't—'

'We insist. Don't we?'

I daren't look at Mum to see if the alarm in her eyes mirrors my own. She thought she was safe. She thought Dad would never track her down. If he knows she's here . . .

'Of course,' I hear myself saying. Because what explanation could I possibly give for saying no?

'In fact, you'd be doing me a favour. I've got some appointments I can't cancel, and it would be great to know I'm not leaving the girls on their own.'

251

He means me. He's worried I'm having some kind of break-down. He's not that far off the truth.

'Well, if you're sure . . .'

'We're sure.' Mark speaks for us both.

'Then I'd love to. Thank you.'

Mark turns to me. 'Maybe Laura could come over. Do you know Laura, Angela?'

Her face is white, despite the pasted-on smile. 'I . . . I don't think we've met.'

I make my smile match theirs. Tell myself it's all going to be fine. Mark will be at work. I can tell him Laura's got yet another new job, or that she's away with friends. As long as I can keep Mum indoors, out of sight, there's no reason why anyone should suspect a thing.

And Dad?

My pulse picks up.

I try telling myself he won't want to come here, where people might recognise him. Mum was hiding out up north – that's where he found her. He'll be looking for her there.

Except . . .

Suicide? Think again.

He sent the card. He threw the brick. He knows what Mum did. He knew I'd been to the police. Somehow, he can see exactly what's happening in this house. If he doesn't already know Mum's at Oak View, I have no doubt he soon will.

My pulse quickens. Did Dad ring the house because he thinks Mum's here? Was he hoping she'd pick up? Give him the confirmation he needs?

If Mum had only gone to the police when Dad first mentioned his absurd scheme, none of this would ever have happened. Mum wouldn't have felt the only way to escape was a fake suicide, and I wouldn't be here now, harbouring a criminal. She should never have done it.

She should never have helped him disappear.

FORTY-TWO

I would have done it unaided, if it had been possible.

It wasn't.

The practicalities alone made it too hard for one person. One car to leave at Beachy Head, another to drive us back. Witnesses to fabricate, tracks to cover, evidence to destroy. Even with two of us, it was a struggle.

We could have asked Anna for help. We could have told her everything, promised her the world if she'd lie for us. But I didn't want to involve her; didn't want to make a mess of her life, the way I'd made a mess of my own.

Now she's up to her neck in it anyway.

She's frightened. I don't like it, but there's no other way. My lies are unravelling, and unless the police back off, everything we did is going to be splashed across the papers, and I'll be heading for a prison cell – if they can find me.

I thought I had no choice but to involve someone else.

I wish I'd tried harder.

If I'd done it alone, I wouldn't have had to put my trust in another person. I wouldn't have had to lie awake at night, wondering if secrets were being spilled.

If I'd done it alone, I could have kept the money.

FORTY-THREE

MURRAY

Murray woke to the sound of the radio. He opened his eyes and rolled onto his back, blinking at the ceiling until the grit had cleared and he was properly awake. Sarah had fallen asleep on the sofa the previous evening, and although he had known she wouldn't make it upstairs, he was still disappointed to see that her half of the bed was untouched.

The radio was loud. Someone was washing their car, or doing their garden, with little thought for whether anyone else in the street wanted to listen to Chris Evans. Murray swung his legs out of bed.

The spare room was empty, too, the duvet still downstairs on the sofa. Sarah had an appointment at Highfield today. Murray would try and speak to Mr Chaudhury alone. Tell him how Sarah had been over the last day or two.

He was halfway down the stairs when he realised the radio was coming from inside the house. In the sitting room, the curtains were drawn and Sarah's duvet was neatly folded on the sofa. From the kitchen, Chris Evans laughed at his own joke.

'Tosser. Play some music.'

Murray's soul lifted. If Sarah was swearing at radio presenters, she was listening to what they were saying. Listening meant stepping out of her own world into someone else's. Something she hadn't been doing yesterday, or the day before that.

'No tossers on Radio Four.' He joined her in the kitchen. She was still wearing yesterday's clothes, and a faint smell of sweat clung to her. Her grey hair was greasy, and her skin still dull and tired. But she was awake. Upright. Making scrambled eggs.

'What about Nick Robinson?'

'I like Nick Robinson.'

'He's a tosser, though.'

'He's a Tory. It's not the same thing.' Murray stood next to the hob and turned Sarah to face him. 'Well, not always. How's today shaping up?'

She hesitated, as though she didn't want to commit, then nodded slowly. 'Today feels like it might be okay.' Tentatively, she smiled at him, and he moved forward to kiss her.

'Why don't I take over here, and you can go and have a quick shower?'

'Do I stink?'

'You're a tiny bit fragrant.' Murray grinned as Sarah opened her mouth to object, before rolling her eyes good-naturedly and heading for the bathroom.

Murray was finishing a call when Sarah emerged. He put his mobile in his pocket and took out the two plates from the oven, where they had been keeping warm.

'I don't suppose you feel up to a shopping trip, do you?'

Sarah's face pinched, her lips tightening, even as she tried to be supportive. 'It'll be busy.'

Murray generally avoided shops between Christmas and New Year, and judging from the adverts on TV, the sales were already in full swing. 'Yes.'

'Do you mind if I stay here?' She saw Murray's face and lifted her chin. 'I don't need babysitting, if that's what you're thinking. I'm not going to top myself.'

Murray tried not to react to the casual reminder of all the times she had indeed attempted suicide. 'I wasn't thinking that.' But he had been. Of course he had been. 'I'll do it another time.'

'What do you need?'

'Sean from High Tech Crime emailed. The handset used for the 999 call reporting Tom Johnson's suicide was bought at Fones4All in Brighton.'

'Do you think they'll have a record of who bought it?'

'That's what I'm hoping.'

'Go!' Sarah waved a fully loaded fork in the air. 'Just think: you could have this all wrapped up before CID even know it's happened.'

Murray laughed, although the same thought had crossed his mind. Not that he could make an arrest, of course, but he could line everything up, and then . . . Then what? Look into another cold case? Interfere with someone else's investigation?

When Murray's thirty years had been up, he hadn't been ready to retire. He hadn't been ready to leave his police family, to step away from the satisfaction that comes from doing a job that makes a difference. But he couldn't stay for ever. At some point he would have to step down, and was he really going to wait until he was old or infirm before he did so? Until he was too decrepit to enjoy the last few years of his life?

Murray looked at Sarah and, in that instant, he knew exactly what he was going to do once the Johnson case was concluded. He was going to retire. Properly, this time.

Sarah had good days and bad days. Murray didn't want to miss any more of the good ones.

'Are you sure you'll be okay?'

'I'll be okay.'

'I'll ring you every half-hour.'

'Go.'

Murray went.

In the mobile phone shop, a giant sign suspended from the ceiling advertised the latest Bluetooth speaker, and shoppers pored over stands, perplexed looks on their faces as they tried to establish the differences between models. Murray walked straight through the middle of the shop and stood next to a rack displaying the latest – and most expensive – iPhone, knowing this to be the most effective way of summoning assistance. Sure enough, within seconds a lad barely old enough to leave school appeared at his side. His pale blue suit was too wide at the shoulders, the trousers creasing into shallow folds above his trainers. His shiny gold name badge read 'Dylan'.

'Nice, aren't they?' He nodded towards the iPhone stand. 'Five-point-five-inch screen, wireless charging, OLED display, fully waterproof.'

Murray was momentarily distracted by the only feature that mattered to someone who had twice let his – far less expensive, but nevertheless vital – phone fall out of his back pocket into the loo. He made himself focus, showing Dylan his police ID.

'Could I speak to the manager, please?'

'That's me.'

Murray turned his 'oh!' of surprise into one of enthusiasm. 'Great! Right. Well, I'm investigating a purchase made in this store at some point prior to the eighteenth of May 2016.' He looked up, where two prominent cameras pointed at the queue of customers. Another two cameras focused on the entrance to the shop. 'How long do you retain CCTV footage?'

'Three months. Some of your lot came in a couple of weeks ago, with a load of stolen phones. We could prove they were taken from here, but they were nicked six months ago so there was no CCTV.'

'Pity. Can you trace this purchase on the tills, to see how the suspect paid?'

Dylan did little to conceal his lack of enthusiasm for this task. 'We're very busy.' He looked at the tills. 'It's the Christmas holidays,' he added, as if this might be news to Murray.

Murray leaned forward, doing his best impression of a TV

257

cop. 'It's in connection with a murder enquiry. You find me this transaction, Dylan, and we could crack the whole case.'

Dylan's eyes widened. He straightened his tightly knotted tie, glancing around as though there was a risk the murderer might be standing right beside them. 'You'd better come through to my office.'

Dylan's 'office' was a cupboard into which someone had shoehorned an Ikea desk and a broken swivel chair, its back leaning drunkenly to one side. Several certificates for employee of the month were pinned to a noticeboard above the computer.

Dylan magnanimously offered Murray the chair, perching on a stock box half the height, and reached to enter his password on a grubby keyboard. Murray politely looked away. On the wall was a photograph of six men and two women, all smartly dressed and grinning enthusiastically for the camera. Dylan was second from the left, wearing the same light blue suit he had on today. The cardboard mount read 'Fones4All Manager Course 2017'.

'What's the IMEI?'

Murray read out the fifteen-digit serial code that Sean had given to him.

'Cash.' With one word, Dylan brought Murray's investigation to a devastating halt. He looked anxiously at Murray. 'Does that mean we can't catch the perp?'

Murray allowed himself a wry smile at the youngster's jargon, gleaned directly from American cop shows. He shrugged. 'Not this way, I'm afraid.'

Dylan looked as though he'd been dealt a personal blow. He sighed, then stared at Murray, his mouth slightly open as something occurred to him. 'Unless . . .' He turned back to the screen and tapped deftly on the keyboard, then reached for the mouse and scrolled through the screen. Murray watched, his mind on Sean, and whether there was anything else the tech team could do to trace the transaction. Without the identity of the caller, he had little to go on.

'Yes!' Dylan gave an entirely unselfconscious air punch, then swiped his open palm through the air towards Murray. 'Go us!' he prompted, and Murray raised his own and high-fived Fones4All's most enthusiastic manager.

'Loyalty card,' Dylan explained, grinning so wildly Murray could see his fillings. 'Every manager is judged on how many sign-ups they get in store each month – the winner gets a Samsung Galaxy S8. I've won three times because I give the prize to the person in my team who flogged the most loyalty cards.'

'That's nice of you.'

'Shit phones, Samsungs. Anyway, my team are competitive, right? Don't let anyone walk away without signing up. And your perp' – he jabbed at the screen – 'was no exception.'

'We've got a name?'

'And an address.' Dylan presented the information with the flourish of a magician confident of applause.

'So, who is it?' Murray leaned forward to read the screen. Dylan got there first.

'Anna Johnson.'

He must have misheard. Anna Johnson?

Murray read the details for himself: *Anna Johnson, Oak View, Cleveland Avenue, Eastbourne.*

'Is that our murderer, then?'

Murray opened his mouth, about to say that no, that wasn't their man, that was the victim's daughter; but however helpful Dylan had been, he was still a member of the public and as such would need to be kept in the dark a little longer.

'Could you print this off for me? You've been very helpful.' He made a mental note to write to Dylan's boss when all this was over. Perhaps they'd send him something other than a Samsung Galaxy S8.

The printout seemed to burn in his pocket as he made his way, faster this time, through the shopping centre and out towards The Lanes.

259

Anna Johnson?

Anna Johnson bought the phone used to make the witness call confirming her father's suicide.

Murray was getting more and more confused. Nothing about this case added up.

Had Tom Johnson borrowed his daughter's phone for some reason? Sean's digging had confirmed that the fake witness call purporting to be from Diane Brent-Taylor was the first time the handset had been used. Was it credible that Anna had bought the phone for an innocent reason, and that Tom had taken it that same day, hours before his death?

Murray walked back to his car, oblivious to the crowds now.

If Tom Johnson didn't go to Beachy Head to commit suicide, why did he go there? To meet someone? Someone who was secretly planning to kill him?

Murray played out scenarios in his head as he drove home. A clandestine affair uncovered by a jealous husband; a struggle that resulted in Tom going over the cliff edge. Had the killer used the phone Tom had borrowed from his daughter to make false calls to the police? The lover? Why choose Diane Brent-Taylor as an alias?

Murray shook his head impatiently. The killer wouldn't have had a spare SIM card unless Tom's murder was pre-meditated. And if it was pre-meditated, the murderer would have acquired their own burner phone, not happened upon a spare one in his victim's pocket. None of it made sense. It was all so . . . Murray struggled to pinpoint the word.

Staged. That was it.

It didn't feel real.

If he took the witness call out of the equation, what did he have? A missing person. A suicidal text from Tom's phone, which anyone could have written. Hardly evidence of murder.

Hardly evidence of suicide . . .

And Caroline's death: was that any more substantial? Everything pointed towards suicide, but no one had seen her.

The chaplain – poor man – had guided her back to safety. Who was to say she hadn't stayed there? A dog walker had found her bag and phone on the cliff edge, conveniently in the spot where the chaplain had found a distressed Caroline. Circumstantial evidence, sure, but hardly conclusive. And like her husband's disappearance, somehow too staged. Real deaths were messy. There were loose ends, pieces that didn't fit. The Johnson suicides were far too tidy.

By the time Murray pulled up on his driveway, he was certain.

There was no witness to Tom's death. There was no murder. There were no suicides.

Tom and Caroline Johnson were still alive.

And Anna Johnson knew it.

FORTY-FOUR

ANNA

It is strange to see Mum back in Oak View. Strange and wonderful. She's nervous, but whether it's due to fear of detection by Mark or by Dad, I couldn't say. Either way, she jumps at the slightest sound from outside, and offers little contribution to the conversation unless asked directly. Rita shadows her wherever she goes, and I wonder how she will be affected when Mum leaves again.

Because that's the deal. Three more days as a family – albeit a family filled with secrets – and then it's over.

'You don't have to go.' We're in the garden, my words turning to mist as they leave my mouth. It's dry today, but so cold it hurts my face. Ella is in her bouncy chair in the kitchen, facing the window so I can keep an eye on her.

'I do.' Mum begged to come out into her beloved garden. It's overlooked only on one side – the high hedges on the other two sides protecting us from curious glances – but even so my heart is in my mouth. Mum's tackling her roses – not the expert pruning that will need doing in spring, but cutting them by a third, so the winter winds don't snap the stems. I have neglected the garden – Mum's pride and joy – and the roses are leggy and unbalanced. 'Someone will see me, if I stay. It's too big a risk.'

She glances continually at Robert's house, the only place from which we can be seen, despite the fact we saw him drive away this morning, loaded with late Christmas presents for relatives up north. Mum is wearing Mark's gardening coat, a woolly hat pulled low over her ears.

'You should have cut these buddleias back last month. And the bay tree needs fleecing.' She shakes her head at the fence between our garden and Robert's, at the climbing roses and the sprawl of clematis I should have cut back after it flowered.

It's looking better already, although I hear Mum tut from time to time, and suspect my lack of attention has left some plants too far gone to save.

'There's a book in the kitchen – it tells you what needs doing each month.'

'I'll look at it, I promise.' A lump forms in my throat. She's serious about leaving. About not coming back.

I read somewhere that the first year of loss is the hardest. The first Christmas, the first anniversary. A full set of seasons to endure alone, before a new year brings fresh hope. It's true it was hard. I wanted to tell my parents about Ella, to share pregnancy stories with my mother and send Mark and my dad to the pub to wet the baby's head. I wanted to cry for no reason, while Mum folded tiny babygros and told me everyone got the baby blues.

The first year was hard, but I know there are harder times ahead. The finality of death is unarguable, but my parents are not dead. How will I come to terms with that? My mother will leave me of her own free will, because she is too scared to be here where my father will find her; too scared to be where she may be recognised, and her crimes exposed. I will no longer be an orphan, yet I will still be without parents, and the grief that I feel is every bit as raw as if I were truly bereaved.

'Robert's paying for the garden to be landscaped, once his building work has been done. Will the plants against the fence survive being moved?' Too late, I realise I shouldn't have mentioned the extension.

'Have you lodged an objection? You must. It'll make the

kitchen incredibly dark, and you'll have no privacy on the patio.'
She begins to list the reasons why Robert's extension is a trav-
esty, her voice an octave higher than it was, and I want to ask
why she cares when she has made it clear she won't come back
here again. But then I think of the way she is carefully tending
roses she won't see bloom. We are programmed to care long
after we need to.

I make vaguely supportive noises and don't mention the money
Mark negotiated in compensation for the inconvenience of
building works.

'Help me move this.' Mum has finished fleecing the bay tree.
It stands in a vast terracotta pot on top of a manhole cover. 'It
needs to be somewhere more sheltered.' She tugs at the pot, but
it doesn't even shift an inch. I walk over to help her. Robert's
builders will move it when they dig up the sewers for his foundations, but I don't want to set Mum off again. Together, we
drag the pot across the patio to the opposite side of the garden.

'There. That's a good morning's work.'

I tuck my arm through Mum's and she squeezes hard, locking
me in place.

'Don't go.' I have managed without crying, up to now, but
my voice cracks and I know it's a losing battle.

'I have to.'

'Can we come and see you? Ella and me? If you won't come
here, can we visit you?'

A moment of silence tells me the answer isn't one I want to
hear.

'It wouldn't be safe.'

'I wouldn't tell a soul.'

'You'd slip up.'

'I wouldn't!' I pull my arm away, hot tears of frustration
stinging my eyes.

Mum looks at me and sighs. 'If the police find out Tom and
I are really alive, and that you knew it – that you concealed our

crimes, *harboured* me – you'll be arrested. You could go to prison.'

'I don't care!'

Mum speaks slowly and quietly, her gaze locked on mine. 'Tom isn't going to let this lie, Anna. In his mind, I've double-crossed him. Made a fool of him. He won't rest until he knows where I am, and it's you he'll use to find me.' She waits, letting her words sink in.

The tears come, falling silently down cheeks numb with cold. For as long as I know where Mum is, I'm at risk. Mark and Ella, too. I look back at the house, to where Ella has fallen asleep in her bouncy chair. I can't let her suffer.

'It's the only way.'

I make myself nod. It's the only way. But it's a hard way. For all of us.

FORTY-FIVE

MURRAY

'Do you think she was involved from the start?' Nish scratched at a mark on the knee of her jeans. She was sitting at Murray's kitchen table, a mug of tea beside the pile of paperwork Murray had accumulated.

'Her statement says she was at a conference the night Tom went missing.' Murray made quote marks in the air. 'The organisers confirm she was there for registration, but can't say if or when she left.'

'So, her alibi's shaky.'

'She didn't fake their deaths.'

Nish and Murray looked at Sarah, who – up until now – had been silent, listening to the two colleagues go over the case.

'What makes you so certain?' Nish asked.

'Because she asked you to re-open the case. It doesn't make sense.'

Nish picked up her mug to drink, and then put it down again as a theory took shape. 'Unless someone sent her the card to let her know they were on to her. And her husband saw it, so she brought it to us because that's what an innocent person would do.'

'He was at work. He didn't see it till later.'

Nish flapped a hand at Murray, as though the point were immaterial. 'Or the postman. A neighbour. The point is, the police report was a double bluff.'

Murray shook his head. 'I don't buy it. It's a massive risk.'

'When did she tell you to back off?' Sarah said.

'Boxing Day.' Murray looked at Nish, who hadn't been privy to this piece of the puzzle. 'She hung up on me. Twice.'

'Then she found out some time between the twenty-first and the twenty-sixth.' Sarah shrugged. 'S'obvious.'

Murray grinned. 'Thanks, Columbo.'

'So, what now?' Nish said.

'I need hard evidence. A phone purchase isn't enough – especially when, as it stands, Anna Johnson was miles away from Eastbourne at the time of the offence. I can't start claiming two dead people are alive, or storming down to Cleveland Avenue to arrest Anna, without proof the Johnsons are alive and well, and that she knew about it.'

'We need to think logically,' Sarah said. 'Why do people fake their own deaths?'

Nish laughed. 'Do a Reggie Perrin, you mean? You make it sound like it happens all the time.'

'There was the canoe man,' Murray said. 'That was an insurance job. And that politician in the seventies – what was his name? Stone something.'

'Stonehouse. Left his clothes on a beach in Miami and ran off with his mistress.' Years of watching daytime quiz shows had made Sarah an expert in trivia.

'Sex and money, then.' Nish shrugged. 'Same as most crimes.'

If only one of the Johnsons had disappeared, Murray might have placed more importance on the former, but as Caroline had followed in Tom's footsteps, it was unlikely that Tom had run off to be with a lover.

'Tom Johnson was worth a lot of money,' Murray reminded her.

'So, Caroline stayed to claim the life assurance, then joined Tom in Monaco? Rio de Janeiro?' Nish looked between Murray and Sarah.

'She claimed the life assurance all right, but she left Anna the lot. If she's living the high life somewhere, she's doing it on someone else's dime.'

'Either they wanted to escape for some other reason,' Sarah said, 'and Anna's reward was the money, or the three of them agreed to split the cash, and she's just sitting tight till the dust has settled.'

Murray stood up. This was pointless – they were going around in circles. 'I think it's about time I paid Anna Johnson another visit, don't you?'

FORTY-SIX

ANNA

We stand and survey the garden: the piles of leaves, ready for the bonfire; the neatly fleeced bay tree; the lopped roses.

'It doesn't look much now, but you'll really see the benefits come spring.'

'I wish you were going to be here to see it.'

She puts an arm around me. 'Why don't you put the kettle on? I think we deserve a cuppa, after all that.'

I leave her standing in the garden, and it's only when I've kicked off my wellies, and the door is closed, and the kettle is whistling on the Aga, that I look out and see that she's crying. Her lips are moving. She's talking to her plants; saying goodbye to her garden.

I'll look after it, I tell her silently.

I let the tea brew, and give Mum the solitude she so clearly needs. I wonder if she will go back up north, or if she'll find somewhere new to settle. I hope she has a garden again, one day.

I fish out the teabags, drop them into the sink, and pick up the mugs awkwardly in one hand, leaving the other free to open the door.

I'm halfway across the kitchen when the doorbell rings.

I stop. Look through the glass doors at Mum, who shows no sign of having heard the door. I put the mugs down, slopping the contents onto the table. A dark stain seeps into the stripped pine.

The doorbell rings again, longer this time, the caller's finger pressed hard against the buzzer. Rita barks.

Go away.

It's fine, I tell myself. Whoever it is can't know anyone's home, and you can't see into the garden without walking down the side of the house. I keep an eye on Mum, to make sure she stays out of sight. She bends down and pulls out a weed from between two paving stones.

The bell rings again. And then I hear footsteps, the crunch of gravel.

Whoever it is, they're walking around the house.

I run to the hall, tripping over in my haste to get there, and yank open the door. 'Hello?' Louder. 'Hello?' I'm about to run outside in my socks, when the crunch of footsteps comes back towards me, and a man appears from the side of the house.

It's the police.

My chest tightens, and I can't think what to do with my hands. I clasp them together – my thumbnail digging into the palm of the opposite hand – then pull them apart and thrust them into my pockets. I feel acutely aware of my face; I try to keep my expression neutral but can't remember how that might look.

Murray Mackenzie smiles. 'Ah, you're home. I wasn't sure.'

'I was in the garden.'

He takes in my mud-spattered jeans, the knee-length woollen socks that fit under my boots. 'May I come in?'

'It's not a good time.'

'I won't stay long.'

'Ella's about to go down for a nap.'

'Just a moment.'

Throughout our brief exchange he has been walking towards me, and now he's on the bottom step, the middle, the top . . .

'Thank you.'

It isn't that he forces his way into the house, more that I can't think of a way to refuse him. Blood sings in my ears, and the tightness in my chest makes my breath come fast and shallow. I feel like I'm drowning.

Rita pushes past me and onto the drive, where she squats for a pee, then sniffs at the marks left by unseen cats. I call her. The lure of the cat is stronger, and selective deafness takes hold.

'Rita – get here now!'

'Through here?' Murray's on his way into the kitchen before I can stop him. There is no way he won't see Mum. The back wall of the kitchen is an almost unbroken sheet of glass.

'Rita!' There are cars in the road – I can't leave her. 'Rita!' Finally she lifts her head and looks at me. And then, after a pause long enough to make it clear that the decision to come inside is hers, she trots back into the house. I push the door hard, leaving it to slam on its own while I run after Murray Mackenzie. I hear a sharp sound – an exclamation.

Not now. Not like this. I wonder if he will arrest her himself, or whether he will wait here for uniformed officers to arrive. I wonder if he'll let me say goodbye. If he'll take me, too.

'You have been busy.'

I move to stand next to him. Our neat pile of leaves and prunings is the only evidence that anyone has been in the garden. A finch flies across the patio to the fence, where Mum has replenished the bird feeder. It hangs upside down, pecking at the ball of peanut butter and seeds. Aside from the birds, the garden is empty.

Murray walks away from the window. He leans against the breakfast bar and I keep my gaze steadily on him, not daring to glance again at the garden. This man is too perceptive. Too shrewd.

'What was it you wanted to speak to me about?'

'I wondered how many mobile phones you had.'

The question takes me off guard. 'Um . . . just the one.' I slip my iPhone out of my back pocket and hold it up in evidence.

'No others?'

'No. I had a second phone for work, but I handed that back when I went on maternity leave.'

'Do you remember what the brand was?'

'Nokia, I think. What's all this about?'

His smile is polite but guarded. 'Just tying up some loose ends from the investigation into your parents' deaths.'

I go to the sink and start washing my hands, scrubbing at the dirt under my fingernails. 'I told you I'd changed my mind. I don't think they were murdered. I told you to drop it.'

'Yet you were so adamant . . .'

The tap runs hotter, burning my fingers until I can hardly bear to hold them under the water. 'I wasn't thinking straight.' I scrub harder. 'I've just had a baby.' I add *using my daughter as an excuse* to my mental list of things to feel guilty about.

There's a noise from outside. Something falling over. A rake; a spade; the wheelbarrow. I turn around, leaving the tap running. Murray isn't looking outside. He's looking at me.

'Is your partner at home?'

'He's at work. It's just me.'

'I wonder . . .' Murray breaks off. His face softens, losing the sharpness that makes me so uneasy. 'I wonder if there's anything you want to talk about.'

The pause stretches interminably.

My voice is a whisper. 'No. Nothing.'

He gives a brief nod, and if I didn't know he was a police officer, I might have thought that he looked rather sorry for me. Just disappointed, perhaps, not to have found what he was looking for.

'I'll be in touch.'

I walk him to the door, standing with one hand on Rita's collar while he crosses the road and gets into an immaculately polished Volvo. I watch him drive away.

Rita pulls away, complaining, and I realise I'm shaking, holding her collar too tight for comfort. I drop to my knees and give her a fuss.

Mum's waiting in the kitchen, her face ashen. 'Who was that?'

'The police.' Articulating it makes it even more frightening, even more real.

'What did he want?' Her voice is as high-pitched as mine, her face as drawn.

'He knows.'

FORTY-SEVEN

MURRAY

Nish was still talking to Sarah when Murray returned home.

'That didn't take long.'

'She wasn't exactly hospitable.' Murray was trying to pinpoint exactly what had been wrong with the scene at Oak View. Anna had been jumpy, certainly, but there had been something else.

'Did you ask her outright?'

Murray shook his head. 'At this stage, we don't know whether she's only recently found out her parents are alive, or if she's known from the start. If she's guilty of conspiracy, she needs to be interviewed under caution by a warranted officer, not questioned in her kitchen by a has-been.'

Nish stood up. 'Much as I'd like to stay, Gill will be sending out a search party if I don't get back soon – we're supposed to be going out later. Let me know if you turn anything up, won't you?'

Murray walked her to the door, joining her outside as she found her car keys in the depths of her bag.

'Sarah seems to be doing well.'

'You know what it's like: two steps forward, one step back. Sometimes the other way around. But yes, today's a good day.'

He watched Nish drive away, raising a hand as she turned the corner.

Back inside, Sarah had spread out Caroline Johnson's bank statements. They had been examined at the time of Caroline's apparent suicide, a summary note on file concluding they held nothing of interest. There had been no large payments or transfers immediately prior to Caroline's apparent suicide, no activity abroad that might hint at a pre-planned hideaway. Sarah moved her finger down the rows of figures, and Murray settled on the sofa with Caroline's diary.

He marked with Post-it notes the period in the diary between Tom's disappearance and Caroline's. Did the pair meet up? Make arrangements? Murray scoured the pages for coded reminders, but found only appointments, lists of things to do, and scribbled reminders to *buy milk* or *call solicitor*.

'A hundred quid's a lot to take out of a cashpoint, don't you think?'

Murray looked up. Sarah was running a neon pink highlighter across a statement. She lifted the pen, moved it a couple of inches lower, and carefully highlighted a second line.

'Not for some people.'

'Every week, though.'

Interesting. 'Housekeeping money?' It was a bit old-fashioned, but some people still budgeted that way, Murray supposed.

'Her spending's more erratic than that. Look, she uses her card all the time – Sainsbury's, Co-op, the petrol station – and takes out cash with no obvious pattern. Twenty quid here, thirty quid there. But on top of that, every seven days in August, she took out a hundred quid.'

Murray's pulse quickened. It could be nothing. Then again, it could be something . . .

'What about the next month?'

Sarah found September's statement. There, too, among ad hoc cash withdrawals and card payments, were weekly withdrawals – this time for a hundred and fifty pounds.

'How about October?'

'A hundred and fifty again . . . No, wait – it goes up halfway through the month. Two hundred quid.' Sarah rifled through the papers in front of her. 'And now three hundred. From mid-November, right up to the day before she disappeared.' She dragged the nib of the highlighter across the last few lines, and handed the sheaf of statements to Murray. 'She was paying someone.'

'Or paying them *off*.'

'Anna?'

Murray shook his head. He was thinking about the 999 calls that had been made from Oak View; the pocket notebook entry describing Caroline Johnson as 'emotional', following the report of a domestic from the next-door neighbour, Robert Drake.

The Johnson's marriage had been a tempestuous one. Possibly even a violent one.

Ever since Murray had realised the Johnsons had faked their deaths, he had been looking at Caroline as a suspect. But was she also a victim?

'I think Caroline was being blackmailed.'

'By Tom? Because she'd cashed in his life assurance?'

Murray didn't answer. He was still trying to work through the possibilities. If Tom had been blackmailing Caroline, and she had been paying up, that meant she'd been scared.

Scared enough to fake her own death to get away?

Murray picked up her diary. He had already been through it several times, but back then he had been looking for leads on why Caroline had been at Beachy Head, not where she'd gone afterwards. He scoured the leaflets and scraps of paper tucked into the back, hoping he'd find a receipt, a train timetable, a scribbled note with an address. There was nothing.

'Where would you go, if you wanted to disappear?'

Sarah thought. 'Somewhere I knew, but where no one knew me. Somewhere I felt safe. Maybe a place I knew from way back.'

Murray's mobile rang.

'Hi, Sean. What can I do for you?'

'It's more what I can do for you. I've had the results back on a reverse IMEI search on that handset of yours.'

'Which tells us what, exactly?'

Sean laughed. 'When you brought me the job, I checked the networks to see what handset that SIM card had been used in, right?'

'Right. And you traced it back to Fones4All, in Brighton.'

'Okay, so the same thing can happen in reverse, it just takes a bit longer. I asked the networks to tell me if that handset has appeared on their systems at any point since the witness call from Beachy Head.' He paused. 'And it has.'

Murray felt a surge of excitement.

'What is it?' Sarah mouthed, but he couldn't answer – he was listening to Sean.

'The offender put a new pay-as-you-go SIM card in it, and it popped up on Vodafone back in the spring.'

'I don't suppose—'

'I know what calls were made? Come on, Murray, you know me better than that. You got a pen? Couple of mobiles, and a landline that might just give you a location for your man . . .'

Or woman, Murray thought. He wrote down the numbers, trying not to be distracted by Sarah, who was flapping her arms at him, demanding to know what had got him so excited. 'Thanks Sean, I owe you one.'

'You owe me more than one, mate.'

The call finished, and Murray grinned at Sarah, filling her in on what the High Tech Crime officer had told him. He spun his notebook around, until the list of phone numbers faced Sarah, and marked an asterisk beside the only landline.

'Do you want to do the honours?'

Then it was Murray's turn to wait, while Sarah spoke to an inaudible voice on the other end of the phone. When she'd finished, he held up his hands.

'Well?'

Sarah put on a posh voice. 'Our Lady's Preparatory.'

'A private school?' What did a prep school have to do with Tom and Caroline Johnson? Murray wondered if they were heading up a blind alley. The fake witness call, allegedly from Diane Brent-Taylor, had been made last May, ten months before the mobile had been used again with a different SIM card. It could have passed through any number of hands in the meantime. 'Where's the school?'

'Derbyshire.'

Murray thought for a moment. He turned over the diary in his hands, remembering the photos that had fallen out from between the pages when Anna Johnson had handed it to him: a youthful Caroline, on holiday with an old school friend.

Mum said they had the best time.

They had been in a pub garden, a wagon and horses on the sign above them.

About as far as you can get from the sea.

He opened Safari on his phone and Googled 'wagon and horses pubs UK'. Christ, there were pages of them. He tried a different tack, looking up 'furthest point in UK from the sea'.

Coton in the Elms, Derbyshire.

Murray had never heard of it. But a final Google search – 'wagon and horses Derbyshire' – gave him what he wanted. Tarted up since the photo, and with a new sign and hanging baskets, but undeniably the same pub that Caroline and her friend had visited all those years ago.

Luxury B&B . . . best breakfast in the Peak District . . . free Wi-Fi . . .

Murray looked at Sarah. 'Fancy a holiday?'

FORTY-EIGHT

I grew up with sand in my socks and salt on my skin, and the knowledge that, when I was old enough to decide where I lived, it would be miles away from the ocean.

It was one of the few things we had in common.

'I don't understand why people obsess over living near the sea,' you said, when I told you where I was from. 'I'm a city-dweller, through and through.'

So was I. Escaped the first chance I had. I loved London. Busy, noisy, anonymous. Enough bars that being kicked out of one didn't matter. Enough jobs that losing one meant finding another the next day. Enough beds that sliding out of one never left me lonely.

If I hadn't met you, I'd still be there. Maybe you would be too.

If it hadn't been for Anna we wouldn't be together.

We'd have parted ways after a few weeks, on to pastures new. Different arms, different bars.

I remember the first morning at Oak View. You were still sleeping, your hair messed up and your lips a fraction apart. I lay on my back and I fought the urge to leave. To tiptoe down the stairs with my shoes in my hand and get the hell out of there.

Then I thought of our unborn child. Of the stomach I'd once run my fingers over and now couldn't bear to even touch. Taut as a drum. Big as a beach ball. Anchoring me to this bed. To this life. To you.

Twenty-five years of marriage. It would be wrong to say I was unhappy for all that time; equally wrong to suggest that I was happy. We co-existed, both trapped in a marriage that convention wouldn't let us leave.

We should have been braver. More honest with each other. If one of us had left, we both would have had the lives we wanted.

If one of us had left, no one would have blood on their hands.

FORTY-NINE

MURRAY

'What will you do if we find her?' Sarah was navigating, the sat nav on her phone sending them up the M40 past Oxford. She tapped the screen. 'Off at junction three.'

'Arrest her,' Murray said, then remembered he wasn't a warranted officer any more. He would have to call in reinforcements.

'Even though you think she was forced into it?'

'That might mitigate the offences, but it doesn't negate them. She's still committed fraud, not to mention wasting police time.'

'Do you think they're together?'

'Your guess is as good as mine.'

Before they'd set off, Murray had called the Wagon and Horses and made enquiries about Tom and Caroline Johnson. Their descriptions hadn't rung any bells with the landlady, and so coming up themselves had felt like the only option. Would he have done the same, had he still been a detective? He might have wanted to – a jolly on the DCI's budget was always a perk – but there would have been more efficient ways of finding out if the Johnsons were in Coton in the Elms. He would have put in a request to Derbyshire Constabulary; asked officers to make enquiries; checked their intelligence systems. All of which was possible when you were a warranted officer, and none of which could be easily achieved by a retired DC, who had already had his knuckles rapped by the superintendent.

'It's nice to get away,' Sarah said. She was gazing out of the window as though she was seeing rolling hills or ocean views, not a motorway service station on the approach to Birmingham. She grinned at Murray. 'Like Thelma and Louise, but with less hair.'

Murray rubbed a hand over his head. 'Are you saying I'm going bald?'

'Not at all. You're just follicularly challenged. You need to stay in the left-hand lane here.'

'Maybe we should do this more often.'

'Track down dead people who aren't really dead?'

Murray grinned. 'Take road trips.' Sarah was scared of flying, and in the forty years they had been together, they had only been abroad once, to France, where Sarah had had a panic attack on the ferry, hemmed in by cars waiting for their turn to drive off. 'There are so many beautiful places to see in this country.'

'I'd like that.'

Another reason to retire properly, Murray thought. If he was at home all the time they could take off whenever they wanted to. Whenever Sarah felt up to it. Maybe they could buy a motorhome, so she never had to worry about other people. Just the two of them, parked up in a pretty campsite somewhere. He would see this job through – he'd never yet given up on a case, and he wasn't going to start now – and then he would hand in his notice. He was ready to go now, and for the first time in a long while he looked to the future without misgivings.

Coton in the Elms was a pretty village a few miles south of Burton upon Trent. According to the pile of pamphlets in their room – a nicely finished double on the first floor of the Wagon and Horses – there was plenty to do within a short drive, but little in the village itself. Murray couldn't imagine it had been the most scintillating of destinations for two young women, although he supposed if you lived in inner-city London, the contrast of fresh air and beautiful countryside was a holiday in itself. In the photograph, Caroline and Alicia had looked as though they hadn't had a care in the world.

In the recently refurbished bar, the landlady was putting up decorations for the following night's New Year's Eve party.

'It was lucky you only wanted one night. We're packed out tomorrow. Pass us that Blu Tack, will you, duck?'

Sarah obliged. 'Are there many places to rent in the village?'

'Holiday cottages, you mean?'

'Something more permanent, really. Flats, perhaps. Cash in hand, no questions asked – that sort of thing.'

The landlady looked over her glasses at Sarah. She narrowed her eyes.

'It's not for us.' Murray grinned. He'd worked with a few detectives whose questioning skills lacked refinement, but Sarah beat them hands down.

'Oh! No, it's not for us. We're looking for some people.'

'The couple you mentioned on the phone?'

Murray nodded. 'It's possible they're in the area. If they are, they'd want to stay out of the spotlight.'

The landlady gave a snort of laughter that wobbled her ladder. 'In Coton? Everyone knows everyone's business here. If your pair were here, I'd know about it.' She took another piece of Blu Tack from Sarah, and stuck a bunch of silver balloons onto a fake beam. 'Speak to Shifty, tonight. He might be able to help.'

'Who?'

'Simon Shiftworth. Shifty suits him better, though. You'll see why. People who can't get a council flat get one of Shifty's. He'll be in around nine – always is.'

Sarah looked at Murray. 'It's a date.'

They ate in the village's other pub, the Black Horse, in order to ask the landlord if he knew of any incomers to the village. He didn't. Murray was surprised to discover he wasn't overly bothered by their lack of progress. In fact, if the entire trip proved to be fruitless, he didn't care. Sarah was looking happier than he'd seen her in months. She had polished off steak and chips, and a treacle tart, along with two glasses of wine, and the pair of them had laughed in a way Murray didn't think they'd laughed since they first got together. A change was as good as a rest, they said, and Murray could feel his own spirits lifting, as surely as if he'd spent a week in a health spa.

'If Shifty's not here, we can just go to bed,' Sarah said, as they walked back to the Wagon and Horses.

'It's still early, I'm not . . .' Murray caught Sarah's wink. 'Oh. Good plan.' He hoped Shifty would decide to have a quiet one at home. But as they headed to the bar to get a nightcap to take upstairs, the landlady jerked her head towards the snug.

'In there. You can't miss him.'

Murray and Sarah exchanged a glance.

'We'll have to see him.'

'But . . .' It had been a very long time since Murray had had an early night.

Sarah suppressed a laugh at his obvious frustration. 'We've come all this way.'

They had. And with any luck, their chat with Shifty wouldn't take long. Plenty of time for an early night.

The landlady had been right; there was no missing Shifty.

In his sixties, he had greasy yellowed hair pasted across a bald head, and thick-rimmed glasses so smeared it was a wonder he could see through them. A cold sore wept in the corner of his mouth. He wore pale blue jeans, black trainers with white socks, and a leather jacket, cracked at the creases of each elbow.

'He looks like a public service announcement for paedophiles,' whispered Sarah.

Murray shot her a look, but Shifty showed no sign of having heard. He looked up as they approached.

'Caz says you're looking for someone.'

'Two people. Tom and Caroline Johnson.'

'Never heard of them,' Shifty said, too fast for it to mean anything, either way. He looked Murray up and down. 'Not police, are you?'

'No,' Murray said, with a clear conscience.

Shifty drained his pint glass and set it down deliberately in front of him.

Murray knew the score. 'Can I get you a drink?'

'I thought you'd never ask. I'll have a pint of Black Hole.'

Murray caught the landlady's eye. 'A pint of Black—'

'And a whiskey chaser,' Shifty added.

'Right.'

'And a couple lined up for later. I'm feeling thirsty.'

'I tell you what.' Murray opened his wallet. 'Why don't I give you this?' He pulled out two twenty-pound notes and laid them on the bar. From his pocket he took out photographs of Tom and Caroline Johnson, given to the police after each was reported missing. 'And you tell me if you've rented a flat to this couple.'

Shifty pocketed the cash. 'Why do you want to know?'

Because they're pretending to be dead.

If Shifty had half the nous he appeared to have, he'd tell them nothing and get on the phone to the *Daily Mail*.

'They owe us money,' Sarah said.

Inspired. Murray wanted to applaud. Shifty was nodding, no doubt reflecting on his own experiences of absent debtors.

'Never seen this bloke.' He jabbed at the photograph of Tom Johnson. 'But the bird,' he jabbed at Caroline, 'she's in one of my bedsits in Swad. Different hair, but definitely her. Goes by the name Angela Grange.'

Murray could have kissed him. He knew it! Fake suicides. This was huge. He wanted to spin Sarah around, buy champagne, tell the whole pub what they'd discovered.

'Great,' he said.

285

'At least, she was . . .'

So close.

'She scarpered, owing me a month's rent.'

'Take it out of her deposit,' Sarah suggested helpfully.

Murray tried to keep a straight face and failed.

Shifty looked at her as though she had suggested he wash his hair. 'What deposit? People rent from me because there *are* no deposits. No contracts. No questions.'

'No carpets,' Caz contributed, from behind the bar.

'Fuck off,' Shifty said mildly.

'Could we take a look around the bedsit?' Nothing ventured, Murray thought. A regular landlord would tell him where to go. Shifty, on the other hand . . .

'No skin off mine. Meet you there tomorrow morning.' He looked at the full pint and the tumbler of whiskey in front of him. 'Better make it after lunch.'

The address Shifty had written down for them was in Swadlincote, five miles from Coton in the Elms, and with none of the latter village's charm. An array of charity shops and boarded-up premises graced the town's high street, and a motley collection of youths outside Somerfield suggested employment opportunities were limited.

Murray and Sarah found Potters Road and parked outside the block of flats Shifty had described. The building was red brick. Several windows had been covered with metal grilles, which had in turn been covered with graffiti. A large yellow penis was sprayed across the front door.

'Nice place,' Sarah said. 'We should move here.'

'Lovely outlook,' Murray agreed. A cairn of mattresses filled the scrubby garden at the front of the property. In the centre, a charred circle showed where someone had tried to set fire to them.

Sarah nodded towards an oncoming car – the only one in the deserted street. 'Do you think that's him?'

There was nothing low-key about Shifty's car: a white Lexus with lowered suspension and out of proportion wheels. Blue LEDs glowed from behind a silver mesh grille, and a giant spoiler weighed down the rear end.

'Classy.'

Murray got out. 'Maybe you should wait in the car.'

'Not a chance.' Sarah hopped out and waited for Shifty to emerge from behind the tinted windows of the Lexus. The man was a walking cliché; Murray was surprised he hadn't seen a gold medallion glinting between his shirt buttons.

No time was wasted on good mornings. Shifty gave them a curt nod and strode past towards the penis-adorned entrance.

The bedsit where Angela Grange – aka Caroline Johnson – had spent the last twelve months was depressing. It was clean – cleaner, Murray suspected, than when Caroline had moved in, judging by the filth in the communal stairwell – but the paint was peeling from the walls, and with all the windows shut fast, condensation glistened on every wall. Murray nodded at the extra bolts on the inside of the front door.

'Standard around here, are they?'

'She did that. Someone had the frighteners on her.'

'Did she say that?'

'She didn't have to. She was jumpy as fuck. None of my business.' Shifty was wandering around the room, checking for damage. He pulled open a drawer and picked up a black bra, turning to Murray with a leer. 'Thirty-six C, if you're asking.'

Murray wasn't. But if Shifty was going to poke around, so was he.

Someone had the frighteners on her . . .

Tom. It had to be. And if Caroline had skipped town, did that mean he'd found this flat? Murray was finding it hard to keep up. This investigation had morphed from a double suicide, to a possible double murder, to a fake suicide and now . . . what?

Was Caroline still on the run, or had Tom caught up with her?

287

Was Murray now looking at an abduction?

It would be the perfect crime. After all, who's going to look for a dead woman?

There wasn't much in the flat. Some clothes, a tin of soup in the cupboard, milk in the fridge Murray wouldn't risk opening. The bin stank of rotting food, but Murray took the lid off regardless. A clutch of bluebottles flew into his face. He picked up a wooden spoon from the draining board and poked around in the rubbish. His mind was working overtime. What if Caroline hadn't faked her own death for financial reasons, but because she was scared? Tom had been blackmailing her, asking for more and more money, until Caroline felt the only avenue open to her was to disappear. After all, it had worked for her husband.

Murray's attention was caught by a sheaf of paperwork buried beneath a pile of used teabags. Something about the layout – the logo – was familiar, and when he pulled it out he knew exactly what it was. The question was, why did Caroline have it?

As he read through the document, pieces of the puzzle began to drop into place. He didn't have the whole answer – not yet – but everything was beginning to make sense. Fake suicides were driven by money, yes. Sex, too. But there was another reason why people wanted to disappear, and it looked as though Murray had just found it.

FIFTY

ANNA

Mum is packing. She doesn't have much – the small bag she took with her to the Hope, and a few bits I've persuaded her to take from her own wardrobe at Oak View. I sit on her bed, wanting to beg her to stay, but knowing it's pointless to try. She won't stay. She can't stay. The police will be back, and next time they won't let me off so lightly. It's going to be hard enough convincing them I know nothing about my parents' crimes, without worrying about whether Mum is well hidden enough.

'Won't you at least stay for the party?' Mark said, when she announced at breakfast she would leave today. 'See in the New Year with us?'

'I'm not really one for parties,' she said easily.

She loves parties. At least, the old Mum loved parties. I'm not sure about this one. My mother has changed – and I don't just mean the weight loss and the dyed hair. She's anxious. Subdued. Constantly watchful. She's been broken, and now my grief is two-fold. I am mourning not only a mother, but the woman she used to be.

I make one final attempt to keep her.

'If we told the police everything—'

'Anna, no!'

'They might understand why you did what you did.'

'And they might not.'

I fall silent.

'I'll go to prison. You might too. You'll tell them you've only known since Christmas Eve that I'm alive, but do you think they'll believe that? When it looks as though Tom and I planned this together? When the house is in your name now?'

'That's my problem.'

'And when you're arrested it'll be Mark's and Ella's. Do you want that little girl growing up without a mother?'

I don't. Of course I don't. But I don't want to be without one either.

Mum zips up her bag. 'There. Done.' She tries for a smile that convinces neither of us. I reach for her bag, but she shakes her head. 'I can manage. In fact . . .' She breaks off.

'What is it?'

'You'll think me ridiculous.'

'Try me.'

'Could I say goodbye to the house? Just a few minutes . . .'

I pull her to me, hugging her so tightly I feel the very bones of her. 'Of course you can. It's your house, Mum.'

Gently, she breaks away; smiles sadly. 'It's *your* house. Yours, Mark's and Ella's. And I want you to fill it with happy memories, do you understand?'

I nod, blinking hard. 'Mark and I will take Ella around the park. Give you a bit of time to say your goodbyes.'

I don't think her ridiculous at all. A home is far more than just a house, far more than bricks and mortar. It's why I wouldn't countenance Mark's suggestion that we sell up; why I didn't want to challenge Robert's *Grand Designs* extension. This is where I live. I'm happy here. I don't want anything to change that.

In the park Mark pushes Ella's pram, and I tuck my hand into the crook of his arm.

'You haven't had a call from the police, have you?'

I look at him sharply. 'What do you mean? Why would I have had a call from the police?'

Mark laughs. 'Relax. I don't think the FBI have caught up with you *just* yet. The guy from CID said he'd ring today to let us know if they'd managed to get any DNA from the rubber band. I've had nothing on my mobile, and I thought they might have tried the house phone.'

'Oh. No, nothing.' The pram's wheels leave puddle tracks on the path. 'Actually, I've been thinking about that and I . . . I think we should drop it.'

'Drop it?' Mark stops short, and I walk into the pram handle. 'Anna, we can't drop it. It's serious.'

'The note said no police. If we drop it, they'll stop.'

'You don't know that.'

I do. I take my arm from Mark's and begin walking again, pushing the pram away from him. He runs to catch up.

'Please, Mark. I just want to forget about it. Start the New Year off on a positive note.' Mark is a big believer in fresh starts. New chapters. Clean pages. Perhaps all counsellors are.

'For the record, I think it's the wrong thing to do—'

'I want to move on from what happened to my parents. For Ella's sake.' I look down at her, as much to hide my face as to reinforce my point, feeling guilty for using her as emotional collateral.

He nods. 'I'll tell them we're dropping it.'

'Thank you.' My relief, at least, is genuine. I stop again, this time to kiss him.

'You're crying.'

I wipe my eyes. 'It's all a bit much, I think. Christmas, New Year, the police . . .' *Mum.* I get as close to the truth as I dare. 'I'm really going to miss Angela.'

'Did you spend much time together when you were younger? You never talk about her; I didn't realise you knew her that well.'

The lump in my throat hardens, and my chin wobbles as I try my hardest to stop myself from sobbing. 'That's the thing about family,' I manage. 'Even if you've never met before, you feel as though you've always been together.'

Mark puts one arm around me, and we walk slowly back to Oak View, where twinkly lights around the porch mark the start of New Year's Eve, and the beginning of the end of this terrible, wonderful, extraordinary year.

Mum's in the garden. I slide open the glass door and she jumps, panic on her face until she sees that it's me. She's not wearing a coat, and her lips are tinged with blue.

'You'll catch your death,' I say, with a wry smile she doesn't return.

'I was saying goodbye to the roses.'

'I'll look after them, I promise.'

'And make sure you put in an objection to—'

'Mum.'

She stops, mid-sentence. Her shoulders sag.

'It's time to go.'

Inside, Mark's opened a bottle of champagne.

'An early New Year.'

We clink glasses and I fight back tears. Mum holds Ella, and they look so alike I try to fix the moment in my memory, but it hurts so much. If this is what it's like to lose someone slowly, I would pray for a sudden death every time. A sharp break to my heart, instead of the slow splintering I feel right now in my chest, like cracks crazing across a frozen lake.

Mark makes a speech. About family, and re-connecting; about New Years and new starts – this last with a wink in my direction. I try to catch Mum's eye, but she's listening intently.

'I hope the year brings health, wealth and happiness to us all.' He raises his glass. 'A very happy New Year to you, Angela; to my beautiful Ella; and to Anna, who I am hopeful might this year say yes.'

I smile fiercely. He will ask me tonight. At midnight, perhaps, when my mother is on a train to heaven knows where, and I'm grieving on my own. He will ask me, and I will say yes.

And then I smell something. An acrid burning, like melting plastic, teasing my nostrils and catching the back of my throat.

'Is there something in the oven?'

Mark is a second behind, but quick to catch up. He moves swiftly to the door and into the hall.

'Jesus!'

Mum and I follow. The smell in the hall is even worse, and below the ceiling hangs a mushroom of black smoke. Mark is stamping on the doormat – black fragments of burned paper fly out from beneath his feet.

'Oh my God! Mark!' I scream, even though it's obvious that whatever flames there were have been extinguished, the cloud of smoke already dissipating.

'It's okay. It's okay.' Mark's trying to stay in control, but his voice is a notch higher than normal, and he's still stamping on the doormat. It's the rubber surround I could smell, I realise. Whatever was put through the letterbox has disappeared; would probably have burned itself out even without Mark's input. Paper kindling designed to frighten us.

I point to the front door. Sweat trickles down the small of my back.

Someone has written on the outside of the stained-glass panels on the upper section of the door. I see the block capitals, distorted by the different thicknesses of glass.

Mark opens the door. The letters are written in thick black marker pen.

FOUND YOU.

FIFTY-ONE

MURRAY

It was dark before they hit the motorway. Murray had made one phone call after another once they'd left the bedsit, and when it was obvious he wasn't going to be free to drive any time soon, he had handed the keys to Sarah.

'I'm not insured.'

'You'll be covered under mine.' Murray mentally crossed his fingers and hoped he was right.

'I can't remember the last time I drove.'

'It's like riding a bike.'

He shut his eyes as they joined the M42, Sarah pulling out in front of a ten-tonne truck amid a cacophony of horns. She settled into the middle lane at a steady seventy miles per hour, ignoring the cars that flashed her from behind to move over, her knuckles white on the steering wheel.

Murray hadn't been able to get hold of anyone at Eastbourne borough planning office, and he didn't have the authority to call someone out. Before he found someone who did, he needed to get his facts right. He smoothed out the papers he'd found in the bin of the bedsit. It was a printout of Robert Drake's planning application, crumpled and stained, but still readable.

There had been many occasions over Murray's thirty-year career when a gut feeling had provided the key to an otherwise frustrating investigation. He might be a few years out of date with the latest legislation and procedure, but instinct never retired. Drake had something to do with his neighbours' disappearances, Murray was sure of it.

Murray skimmed over the objections, interested not in the content, but in the details of the complainants. Next, he worked his way through the supporting documents. He scanned the elevation drawings, and compared the proposed footprint with the existing one. It was a huge extension; Murray wasn't surprised by the number of objections.

He looked at the next page, reading through the long list of building materials, techniques and suggested methodology for the extension. He couldn't have explained what he was looking for, only that he felt certain the key to this case lay with Robert Drake.

He found it buried in a paragraph halfway down the final page.

Murray looked up, almost surprised to find himself still in the car. In his head he'd been in the CID office, amid the hustle and bustle of a dozen live cases, the good-natured ribbing between colleagues, and the fallout from office politics.

There was no time to ponder on how life had changed. No time to do anything other than finally call in the job he'd been sitting on since Anna Johnson first walked into Lower Meads police station.

'Hello?' Detective Sergeant James Kennedy did not sound like a man on duty. He sounded, in fact, like a man who had the good fortune to be off for a couple of days after a Christmas on call, and was settling down with a beer, his wife and his kids, for a quiet New Year's Eve in. Murray was about to change all that.

'James, it's Murray Mackenzie.'

A brief pause, before James feigned enthusiasm. Murray imagined him glancing at his wife, shaking his head to indicate that *no, it's nothing important.*

'Remember I mentioned the Johnson suicides when I swung by last week?' Whether James did or didn't, Murray didn't wait to find out. 'Turns out they weren't suicides.' Murray felt the familiar buzz of a job gaining momentum; heard his voice assume the energy of younger years.

'What?'

Murray had his attention now. 'Tom and Caroline Johnson didn't kill themselves. The suicides were faked.'

'How do you—?'

It didn't matter that Murray was going to get another bollocking from Leo Griffiths. What did he care? He was going to resign anyway. He took another glance at Sarah, her knuckles still white on the steering wheel, and decided it might be better if he did the driving in the new motorhome.

'On the twenty-first of December – the anniversary of Caroline Johnson's death – the Johnsons' daughter, Anna, received an anonymous note suggesting the suicides weren't straightforward. I've been looking into them since then.' Intercepting James, he kept on talking. 'I should have handed it over, but I wanted to give you something more concrete to go on.' And I didn't think you'd take it seriously, he wanted to add, but didn't. Neither did he add that the case had given him a focus; that it had given him and Sarah a distraction from their own lives.

'And now you have?' Murray heard a door being closed, the background sounds of James's children fading away.

'The witness call on the nines, saying Tom Johnson had gone over the cliff, was a fake. It was made on a mobile phone bought by the Johnsons the day Tom allegedly died.'

'Hang on, I'm making notes.' There was no hesitation now, no question lingering in James's voice about the validity of Murray's claims. There was no pulling rank, no insistence that Murray go through proper channels.

'No one saw Caroline jump. The chaplain was a credible witness because he really *did* see Caroline on the edge of the cliff, appearing as though she was going to jump.'

Murray remembered the young chaplain's statement, his angst that he hadn't been able to save Caroline Johnson. When all this was over Murray would find the poor chap and tell him what had really happened. Give him some peace of mind.

'There's a planning application in with Eastbourne Borough Council,' Murray went on. If James was surprised by this apparent change of tack, he didn't show it. 'I can't get hold of anyone in the office. We need access to the back end of the planning portal and the IP addresses of everyone who lodged an objection to an extension proposed for the house next door to the Johnsons'.'

'What are we looking for?'

'Confirmation. One of those objections will be from an IP address in or near Swadlincote, Derbyshire, from a woman using the name Angela Grange.' Murray was certain of it. Caroline had been just as determined to stop that extension as Robert Drake had been to push it through. If she didn't regret that already, she soon would.

'I'll put in a call.'

'The anonymous note Anna received was intended to flush Caroline out, and it did just that. She left Derbyshire on the twenty-first of December. It doesn't take a genius to guess where she went.'

'The family home?'

'Bingo. And if we don't get there soon, someone's going to get hurt.'

'Why will . . . ?' James broke off. When he spoke again it was more urgent, more serious, as though he already knew the answer to his question. 'Murray, where's Tom Johnson?'

Murray was as sure as he could be, but he still hesitated. Within seconds of putting down the phone, James would be picking it up again. Requesting resources, calling officers in from home, CSI, detectives, warrants, a method of entry team – the full major incident machine.

What if Murray was wrong?

'He's there too.'

FIFTY-TWO

ANNA

Mum and I look at each other, horror freezing our faces into identical masks.

'He knows you're here.' It's out before I can stop it.

Mark looks between us. 'Who does? What's going on?'

Neither of us answers. I doubt either of us knows how.

'I'm calling the police.'

'No!' In unison.

I glance outside. Is he there? Watching us? Seeing our reaction? I shut the front door, pulling across the chain with fingers that shake so much I drop it twice. Buying myself time.

Mark picks up the phone.

'Please don't.'

I should never have gone to the police station when the anniversary card arrived; it only made things worse.

'Why on earth not? Anna, someone just tried to set fire to the house!'

Because my mum will go to prison. Because I'll be arrested for hiding her.

'First a brick through the window, now this . . .' His fingers hover over the keys. He stares at me, reading my expression, then looks between me and my mother. 'There's something I don't know, isn't there?'

My dad isn't dead. He sent the anniversary card because he knew my mum wasn't either, but when he realised I'd gone to

298

the police, he tried to stop me. He put a dead rabbit on our doorstep. He threw a brick through our daughter's bedroom window. He's unstable, and he's dangerous, and he's watching the house.

'Because . . .' I look at Mum. I have to tell him. I never wanted to drag him into this mess, but I can't lie to him any more – it isn't fair. I do my best to convey this to Mum, who steps forward, one hand in front of her, as though she can physically stop the words leaving my mouth.

'I haven't been honest with you about why I'm in Eastbourne.' She speaks quickly, before I've even managed to formulate the explanation Mark is long overdue. She holds my gaze. *Please.*

It's all too much. Helping Mum pack; preparing to lose her for the second time; Murray Mackenzie stopping just short of accusing me of conspiracy.

Now this.

It feels as though my nerve-endings are outside my body, each revelation a series of electric shocks.

'Then you better explain. Now.' Mark moves the phone from one hand to the other and back again, a call to the police just seconds away. The coldness in his eyes makes me shiver, even though I know it is only worry putting it there. I take Ella from Mum, for the reassurance of her weight in my arms, the feeling of a warm body against mine.

Mum glances at me. She shakes her head almost imperceptibly. *Don't.*

I keep quiet.

'I'm running away,' she says. 'My marriage broke down last year, and I've been hiding from my husband ever since.'

I keep my eyes trained on Mark. There's no sign that he doesn't believe Mum, and why wouldn't he? It's the truth.

'Just before Christmas he found out where I was living. I didn't know where to go. I thought if I laid low for a bit . . .'

'You should have told us, Angela.' The words are admonishing, but Mark's tone is soft. Many of his patients have come from – or are still in – abusive relationships. Perhaps some are abusers themselves; I've never asked, and Mark would never say. 'If there was a chance he could follow you here – that you might put us at risk, too – you should have told us.'

'I know. I'm sorry.'

'I suppose it was him who put the brick through the window?'

'I bought a train ticket online. He must have looked at my emails; it's the only way he would have known where I was headed. Caroline was the only Eastbourne address in my contacts.'

Mark looks at the phone in his hand, then back at the door, where the letters show back to front. 'We need to tell the police.'

'No!' Mum and I, together.

'Yes.'

'You don't know what he's like. Who you're dealing with.'

Mark looks at me. 'Have you met him?'

I nod. 'He . . . he's dangerous. If we report him to the police we can't stay here, not when he knows we're here. He could do anything.' I'm still shaking. I rock Ella from side to side, more to expel some of the adrenalin coursing through my veins than to soothe her. Mark paces the hall, tapping the phone against his thigh as he walks.

'I'll go.' Mum has her bag in her hand. 'It's me he wants. I should never have come here – it's not fair to involve you.' She takes a step towards the door and I grab her arm.

'You can't go!'

'I was leaving anyway. You knew that.' She takes my hand off her arm and gives it a gentle squeeze.

'It's different now. He knows where you are. He'll hurt you.'

'And if I stay, he'll hurt you.'

It's Mark who breaks the ensuing silence. 'You both need to go.' He's decisive, rummaging in the dresser drawer for a set of keys he hands to me. 'Go to my flat. I'll wait here and call the police.'

'What flat? No, I can't involve you both in this. I need to go.' Mum tries to open the door, but Mark's quicker than her. He puts one hand flat against the door.

'You've already involved us, Angela. And much as I sympathise with your situation, my priority is keeping Anna and our daughter safe, which means getting them the hell away from this house, until your ex is safely behind bars.'

'He's right,' I say. 'Mark's flat's in London – no one will know we're there.' Ella squirms in my arms, awake and hungry for a feed.

Mum's face is pale. She's searching for an argument but there are none to be had. This is the best way forward. Once we're safely out of Eastbourne, Mark can call the police, and I'll convince Mum that we have to come clean. There's no other way.

'I don't want Anna and the baby with me,' Mum says. 'It's not safe.'

'Given that your ex has just tried to set fire to our house, it's hardly safe for them here.' Mark holds out the keys. 'Go.'

'Listen to him.' I put a hand on Mum's arm. 'Take us.' All I can think about is getting far away from Eastbourne. From Dad. From Murray Mackenzie and questions that circle around the truth.

She sighs, relenting. 'I'll drive. You sit with Ella – we don't want to have to stop.' She looks at Mark. 'Be careful, won't you? He's dangerous.'

'Call me when you're at the flat. And don't let anyone in except me. Understood?'

Mum grips the steering wheel, her eyes intent on the road. I'm in the back, Ella strapped into her seat beside me, sucking furiously on the knuckle of my thumb, in lieu of the breast she wants. It won't be long before she starts crying for milk. Perhaps we can pull over once we're safely away from Eastbourne.

'Dad doesn't even know Mark's flat exists,' I repeat, when I see Mum check the rearview mirror for the hundredth time since we left. 'It's okay.'

'It's not okay.' She's close to tears. 'Nothing's going to be okay.'

I feel my own eyes stinging. I need her to be strong. I need her strong so that *I* can be strong. That's the way it's always been.

I remember falling over as a child, feeling the searing pain in my skinned knee.

'Upsy-daisy!' Mum would sing, pulling me to my feet. I'd read her face and see her smile, and without actively thinking whether it hurt more or less, I would feel the pain of my skinned knee slipping away.

'The police were always going to find out, Mum.'

In the mirror, her face is ashen.

'It's Dad they'll go for. They'll go easy on you – they'll see you were forced into it. You probably won't even go to prison; you'll get a suspended sentence . . .'

She's not listening. She's scanning the street, looking for something – looking for Dad? – and suddenly she slams on the brakes and I shoot forward, the lap strap in the middle seat of my car doing little to hold me back.

'Get out.'

'What?' We're on the outskirts of Eastbourne.

'There's a bus stop, just there. Or you can ring Mark to come and pick you up.' Her foot rests on the clutch; her hand on the brake. She's crying now. 'It was never meant to be like this, Anna. I never meant anyone to get hurt. I never meant for you to be involved.'

I don't move. 'I'm not leaving you.'

'Please, Anna – it's for your own good.'

'We're in this together.'

She waits a full ten seconds. Then, with a sound that is midway between a cry and a moan, she releases the handbrake and carries on driving.

'I'm sorry.'

'I know you are.' All those years of mopping up my tears and sticking plasters on my knees, and now I am the strong one. It's Mum who needs me. I wonder if this metamorphosis has taken place only because of the extraordinary circumstances in which we find ourselves, or whether this is the natural progression of women as they move from daughter to mother.

We drive in silence, except for Ella, who has progressed from fractious squawks to full-blown wails.

'Can we stop again?'

'We can't.' Mum's checking the rearview mirror again. And again.

'Just for five minutes. She won't stop if I don't feed her.'

Mum's eyes flick from the mirror to the road and back. She's seen something.

'What is it?'

'There's a black Mitsubishi behind us.' She presses hard on the accelerator and the burst of speed pushes me against my seat. 'It's following us.'

FIFTY-THREE

When you spend your life selling cars, you learn how to handle them.

Foot hard against the floor. Sixty. Sixty-five. Seventy. Seventy-five . . .

A sharp corner. One, then the other. We've both taken it too wide. I see the terrified look of the oncoming driver, the jerk of his hands as he swerves from our path.

Into the next bend, tapping the brakes but using the gears. Changing down, down, down. Spinning the wheel and then flooring the accelerator till it feels as though the back end of the car is going faster than the front.

The gap narrows.

My pulse races so fast I can hear it above the roar of the engine, and I lean forward as though the movement will make a difference.

Cat and mouse.

Who will win?

Driving fast means thinking fast. Reacting fast. Not skills that an alcoholic has – even a high-functioning one – and it's just another reason among many that I'm glad I quit drinking.

It was easy, in the end. No AA meetings, no therapy, no intervention from well-meaning friends.

Just you.

The look in your eyes when you fell to the floor that night. It meant nothing at the time; it was just another fight. Another punch, another kick. It was only afterwards, when I remembered your face – saw the disappointment, the pain, the *fear* – that I finally understood what the drink had made me do to you.

No. What I'd done to you.

I'm sorry. It's not enough, and it's too late, but I'm sorry.

I've slowed down. I need to focus. I grip the steering wheel; force my foot back down.

How did it come to this?

I want to rewind; undo my mistakes. I've messed up. Spent our entire marriage thinking about me, and now look at us.

What am I doing?

I can't stop. I'm in too deep.

Anna.

She's there – in the back seat. Ducking down, trying to stay hidden. I catch a glimpse as she peers up to look out of the back window. Trying to see without being seen.

Failing.

I never wanted to hurt her.

It's too late.

FIFTY-FOUR

ANNA

I twist in my seat. Behind us is a brand-new Mitsubishi Shogun, a steady hundred yards away, but gaining. The windows are tinted – I can't see the driver.

'Is it him? Is it Dad?'

I've never seen my mother like this. Shaking with barely controlled fear. 'You should have got out. I tried to make you get out.' She looks again in the mirror, then yanks the wheel to the right to avoid a discarded piece of bumper lying in the road. My stomach lurches.

'Concentrate on driving.'

'Keep down – he might not have seen you. I don't want him knowing you're with me.'

I respond automatically to my mother's instructions, the way I always have, unclipping my seatbelt, pulling my legs to one side and leaning over Ella's car seat. Mum pulls a sharp left and I brace myself against the car door, sliding across the top of Ella's seat. She lets out a cry of alarm and I try to soothe her, but my heart feels like it might seize up, and my 'shhh, shhh' is more hysterical than her own wails. The backs of my knees are wet with sweat, my palms hot and clammy.

'It's still following!' Gradually, my mother's air of control is disappearing, cracking to reveal the same blind panic I feel surging inside me. 'And getting closer!'

Ella's cries intensify, each scream building in volume and pitch

306

as she tunes in to her grandmother's hysteria. I have one hand planted on the inside of the door, the other on the back of the driver's seat. Within the semi-circle of my arms is Ella, screaming inches from my ear. The sound finds my left eardrum and departs with a ringing that offers no let-up as she draws breath for another cry. I pull my phone from my pocket; swipe to unlock it. There is no option left but to call the police.

'Drive faster!'

Another lurch to the left, swiftly followed by a right turn that loosens my grip around Ella's car seat and sends me into a painful heap on the floor on the opposite side of the car. My phone shoots under the passenger seat and out of arm's reach. Mum floors the accelerator and I crawl back up to wrap my arms around Ella's seat. I move my head up, not wanting to see him, my father, but unable to stop myself from looking.

Mum screams at me. 'Stay down!'

Ella stops crying, jolted into silence, then draws breath and screams again.

In the rearview mirror I see tears stream down Mum's face, and like a child who only cries when she sees her mother's mask slip, I lose it too. This is it. We're going to die. I wonder if Dad will ram the car, or push us off the road. If he wants to kill us, or keep us alive. I brace myself for impact.

'Anna.' Mum's voice is urgent. 'In my bag . . . When I knew I'd been found, I was so scared I . . .'

Another sharp turn. Squealing brakes.

'I never planned to use it – it was insurance. In case . . .' She stumbles. 'In case he caught up with me.'

Still half lying across the back seat, my feet braced against the passenger seat and the door, I open the bag by my feet, root around in the clothes I saw her packing just an hour or so ago. It feels like a lifetime.

I snatch back my hand.

My mother has a gun.

She turns the wheel like she's at the dodgems. My head slams against the car door. Ella screams. I swallow, tasting vomit in the back of my throat.

'A gun?' I'm not touching it.

'I got it from the man I rented a flat from.' The effort of keeping the car on the road forces her words out as though each follows a full stop. 'It's loaded. Take it. Protect yourself. Protect Ella.'

There's a squeal of brakes as she takes a bend too fast. The car spins out – skids left, then right – before she takes back control. I close my eyes. Hear the gearstick, the pedals, the engine.

A sharp left. The top of my head jammed against the door, the handle of Ella's car seat pressed into my chest.

The car slides to a juddering stop.

And there's silence.

I hear my mother's breathing, tense and ragged. I move my face until my lips are touching my daughter's, and swear silently to her I will die before I let her come to harm.

I will die.

Would I use the gun? Slowly, I reach for it. I feel the weight of the grip in my hand, but I don't lift it.

Protect yourself. Protect Ella.

Would I kill my own father, to save my daughter? To save myself?

I would.

I screw my eyes shut, listening for a car door. For the sound of Dad's voice.

We wait.

'We've lost him.'

I hear my mother's words, but they don't register. My body is still rigid, my nerve-endings still jangling.

'That last bend.' She's out of breath. 'We turned off before he

308

rounded the corner. He didn't see.' She bursts into noisy tears. 'He didn't see us turn off.'

Slowly I sit up and look around. We are on a farm track, half a mile or so away from where a parting between hedges shows where the road is. There are no other cars.

I unclip the fastenings on Ella's seat and pull her to me, kissing the top of her head and holding her so tightly she wriggles to be let free. I lift my T-shirt and unclip my bra, and she feeds thirstily. We relax into each other and I realise my body has been craving this as much as hers has.

'A gun?' It doesn't sound real. 'A fucking *gun*?' I pick up the bag and place it on the front seat next to her. It was less than three feet from Ella's head. I don't let myself think what might have happened if it had gone off; if I'd picked up the bag the wrong way, stepped on it . . .

Mum says nothing. Her hands are still gripping the steering wheel. If she's having some kind of breakdown, I need to get her into the passenger seat. I wonder if we should abandon the plan and drive to a police station. Whatever we do, we need to go soon; we're sitting ducks here, in open countryside. Dad'll realise we turned off; he'll double back.

'I told you. It was insurance. I don't even know how the bloody thing works.'

I pull Ella gently off my breast and feel under the seats for my phone. There's a text from Mark.

No sign of the ex yet. Have texted everyone to cancel the party. Police are on their way. They need Angela's date of birth and address. Call me!

I avoid answering.

Black Shogun followed us but we managed to lose him. Will call when we get to the flat. Love you x

A deep breath heads off the tears. 'Let's go. We should use the back roads till we hit the motorway.' I strap Ella back in, and put on my own seatbelt. We drive – more carefully now, although with no less urgency – on winding B roads within spitting distance of the A23. The twists and turns – and the frequency with which I turn around to check on the cars behind us – make me nauseous, and the journey seems to go on for ever.

We don't talk. I try, twice, but Mum's in no fit state to make plans. I just need her to get us to Mark's flat in one piece.

I feel better once we're on the M23. The motorway is busy; we are one of thousands of cars on their way to London. The chances of my father finding us here are tiny, and if he did, what would he do, with so many witnesses? So many cameras? I catch my mother's eye and give her a small smile. She doesn't return it, and I feel my anxiety well up in response. I scan the surrounding cars for the Shogun.

We join the M25. I look into the cars either side of us. Most are packed with families heading home after Christmas, or to friends for New Year, the seats piled high with presents and spare duvets. A couple in a beat-up Astra are singing enthusiastically, and I picture the CD of classic hits in the car stereo.

My phone rings; an unfamiliar number on the screen.

'Miss Johnson?'

Murray Mackenzie. I curse myself for answering; contemplate hanging up and blaming a bad line.

'I've got something to tell you. Something . . . unexpected. Is someone with you?'

I glance at my mother. 'Yes, I'm in the car. My . . . a friend's driving, it's okay.' In the rearview mirror my mother looks quizzical and I shake my head to tell her it's nothing to worry about. She moves into the fast lane, seeking speed again now we're so close to safety.

Murray Mackenzie seems to be struggling to find the right words. He starts several sentences, none of them making sense.

'What on earth has happened?' I say eventually. My mother's eyes watch me in the mirror, flicking between me and the road. Anxious on my behalf.

'I'm sorry to break this to you over the phone,' Murray says, 'but I wanted to let you know as soon as possible. Officers are at your house now. I'm afraid they've found a body.'

I put my hand to my mouth to stifle a cry. *Mark.*

We should never have gone. We should never have left him to face my father.

Murray Mackenzie is still going. He's talking about fingerprints and deterioration and DNA and a tentative ID and—

I interrupt, unable to process what I think I heard. 'Sorry, what did you say?'

'We can't be certain, but early indications suggest the body is your father. I'm so sorry.'

The relief I feel that we're safe is instantly tempered by the knowledge that the only person at Oak View when we left was Mark.

I'll wait here and call the police.

What if Dad showed up before the police arrived? Mark's strong; he can take care of himself. Did he attack my father? Defend himself?

'How did he die?'

I try to work out how long since the Shogun was behind us. Why would Dad go back to Oak View, when he knew we wouldn't be there? Even if he doubled back straight away, how could he have got there so quickly? In the rearview mirror, my mother is frowning. Hearing half a conversation, even more confused than I am.

'We'll have to wait for the post-mortem to be certain, but I'm afraid there's little doubt he was murdered. I'm so sorry.'

I feel hot, the nausea returning. Has Mark killed my dad?

Self-defence. It would have been self-defence. He can't go to prison for that, can he?

There's something pulling at the corners of my mind, like a

child tugging my hand and telling me to *look* . . . I wonder if my mother is following this; if, in spite of herself, she feels a tug of sorrow at the death of a man she presumably once loved. But in the rearview mirror her eyes are cold. Whatever was once between my parents died a long time ago.

Murray is talking, and I'm thinking, and my mother is staring at me in the rearview mirror, and there's something about the look in her eyes . . .

'. . . in the septic tank for at least twelve months, probably longer,' Murray is saying.

In the septic tank.

This has nothing to do with Mark.

I picture the narrow, well-like hole in the garden of Oak View; the bay tree in the heavy pot. I remember Mum's insistence that we move the pot away; think of her obsession over Robert Drake's extension. The extension that required digging up the disused tank.

She knew. She knew he was there.

My chest is too tight. Each breath is smaller than the last. My eyes are locked on my mother's, and although the phone is by my ear, I can't hear what Murray is saying. I can't speak. Because I realise there's only one reason she would know Dad was in the septic tank.

Because she put him there.

PART THREE

FIFTY-FIVE

ANNA

My mother's eyes flick between me and the motorway. I remain frozen, the phone clamped to my ear. Murray Mackenzie is still talking, but I'm not taking anything in. Mum moves into the fast lane again and we overtake the same couple in the beat-up Astra. Still happy, still singing.

'Miss Johnson? Anna?'

I'm too scared to answer. I'm wondering if there's any chance my mother might not have heard what Murray had to say – might not have guessed from my expression what I've heard – but the look in my mother's eyes tells me it's all over.

'Give me the phone.' Her voice shakes.

I do nothing. Tell him, a voice inside screams. *Tell him you're on the M25 in a Volkswagen Polo. They have cameras, motorway patrols, response officers. They'll get to you.*

But my mother speeds up. Cuts back into lane sharply and without warning, the car behind pressing violently on the horn. The volume of traffic that earlier felt comforting now feels terrifying; every car is a potential collision target. Ella's car seat, once so robust, now appears flimsy and insecure. I tighten the seatbelt around it; pull on my own. Murray's no longer talking. Either the line's dropped out or he's ended the call; assumed I've hung up on him again.

'Who was that in the Mitsubishi?'

Nothing.

315

'Who was that chasing us?' I scream it, and she takes a breath but ignores my question.

'Give me the phone, Anna.'

She's as terrified as I am. Her knuckles are white with fear, not anger; her voice shakes with panic, not rage. The knowledge should make me feel safer – stronger – but it doesn't.

Because she's in the driving seat.

I give her the phone.

FIFTY-SIX

It was an accident. That's what you have to understand. I never meant for it to happen.

I didn't hate you. I didn't love you, but I didn't hate you either, and I don't think you hated me. I think we were young and I was pregnant, and we did what our parents expected us to do, and then we were stuck with each other, like a lot of people in relationships.

It's taken a while for me to understand that.

For all of our marriage I was either drinking, or recovering from drinking, or thinking about drinking. Rarely enough to be drunk; rarely so little to be sober. On and on, for so many years that no one who had never seen me sober would ever know that I wasn't.

I blamed you for cutting short my freedom, never seeing that what I had in London wasn't freedom at all. It was just as much a cage, in its own way, as marriage was: a never-ending cycle of working, boozing, clubbing, looking for a one-night stand, slipping away in the early hours.

I thought you trapped me. I never realised you were actually saving me.

I fought it. And I went on fighting it for twenty-five years.

On the night you died I was halfway down a bottle of wine, with three G&Ts under my belt. With Anna away I didn't have to hide anything – I'd long since stopped pretending in front of you.

Not that I'd ever have admitted I had a problem. They say

that's the first step. I hadn't taken it – not then. Not till afterwards.

'Don't you think you've had enough?' You'd had a drink, too. Otherwise you'd never have dared. We were in the kitchen, Rita curled up in her bed. The house felt empty without Anna, and I knew I was drinking more because of it. Not just because I could, but because it felt strange. Unbalanced. The way it did when she was at university. Then, I had a glimpse of how life would be when she moved out for good, and I didn't like it. Our marriage was built around our daughter; who were we without her? The thought unsettled me.

'Actually, I think I'll have another one.' I didn't even want it. I poured the rest of the wine into a glass meant to be more empty than full. I held the empty bottle upside down by its neck. Taunting you. 'Cheers.' A dribble of red wine ran down my sleeve.

You looked at me like you were seeing me for the first time. Shook your head, like I'd asked you a question. 'I can't do this any more, Caroline.'

I don't think you'd planned it. It was just one of those things you say. But I asked what you meant, and it made you think, and I saw the moment the decision made itself in your mind. The decisive nod, the firmness in your lips. Yes, you were thinking, this is what I want. This is what's going to happen.

'I don't want to be married to you any more.'

Like I said: my trigger is alcohol.

I was drunk the first time I hit you, and I was drunk the last time. It's not an excuse – it's a reason. Did it make a difference to you that I was sorry afterwards? Did you know that I meant what I said, that each time I vowed to myself it would be the last? Sometimes the apologies came late; sometimes they came right away, when the sudden release of pent-up anger sobered me as surely as if I'd slept it off.

318

When the police came, you lied with me. Nothing to see here. After the 999 calls, we said it was a mistake. A child, messing with the phone.

You stopped saying you forgave me. You stopped saying anything at all; just pretended it hadn't happened. When I hurled Anna's clay paperweight at you, and it ricocheted off you and broke against the wall, you picked up the pieces and glued them back together. And you let Anna think you'd broken it.

'She loves you,' you said. 'I can't bear to think of her knowing the truth.'

That should have stopped me. It didn't.

If I hadn't been drinking that last night, I might have got upset rather than angry. I might even have nodded, thought: You're right – this isn't working. I might have realised that neither of us was happy, and maybe it was time to call it quits.

I didn't do that.

Before the words were even out of your mouth, my arm was moving. Hard. Fast. Unthinking. The bottle smashed against your head.

I stood in the kitchen, the neck of the bottle still in my hand, and a carpet of green glass at my feet. And you. Lying on your side. A glossy pool of blood beneath your head, from where you'd hit the granite worktop on your way to meet the tiles.

Dead.

FIFTY-SEVEN

MURRAY

Murray pressed redial, but Anna Johnson's phone went straight to voicemail.

'I don't want the daughter knowing anything till we've got a positive ident,' DS Kennedy had said when he'd called to say that Murray had been right, there was a body in the septic tank, and early indications suggested it was Tom Johnson.

Murray had considered what to do. The detective sergeant was right, of course. It couldn't possibly be anyone other than Tom Johnson in the septic tank, but until the body had been recovered and identified, information should be on a strictly need-to-know basis.

But surely Anna *did* need to know? And at the earliest opportunity. It had been Anna who had insisted the police look again at her mother's suicide; Anna who had been abandoned when her parents disappeared within months of each other. She deserved to know that there was a very high probability her father had been murdered, and his body hidden in his own septic tank.

As Murray scrolled through his phone for her number, he ignored the voice in his head that said he was calling as much for his own benefit as for hers. You carried on digging after she told you to stop, the voice said. Now you want to show her you were right to have done that.

Only Anna had hung up on him again. And now her phone

was switched off. She was in shock, of course. People did strange things at times of crisis. But even so, Murray had a horrible feeling he had done the wrong thing by calling her.

Sarah pulled up on the driveway. Murray was feeling deflated; not just from Anna's reaction, but from suddenly having nothing to do on the investigation in which he had been so heavily invested. He recognised the feeling from his time as a uniformed response officer, when the rush of picking up a juicy job was swiftly followed by the anti-climax of handing it over to CID. Never knowing what the suspect had said in interview; sometimes not even knowing who had been charged, or what sentence they'd received. Seeing someone else get the pat on the back, when you were the one who'd torn your trousers in a rugby tackle, who'd pulled out a child from a drink-drive wreckage.

'You should go.' Sarah was resting one hand lightly on the gearstick, looking totally at home behind the wheel now. It had been a long time since Murray had been a passenger, and when his battery had died, and he could no longer make calls, he had rested his head against the seat and watched his wife's confidence grow by the mile. It occurred to him that his efforts to protect Sarah's comfort zone over the years might sometimes have been better spent helping her climb out of it.

Murray got out of the car. 'James is there. It's his job now.'

'It's your job, too.'

Was it? If Murray went inside and put on his slippers, stuck something on the TV, the police world would keep turning. James had the scene under control; officers were out looking for Caroline Johnson. What could Murray do?

And yet there were loose ends that were frustrating him. How had Caroline managed to get Tom – by no means a small man, the case files confirmed – into the septic tank? Had someone helped her? Who had sent the anniversary card that suggested Caroline Johnson hadn't really jumped?

'Go.' Sarah pressed the car keys into his hand.

'We were going to see in the New Year together.'

'There'll be other New Years. Go!'

Murray went.

In Cleveland Avenue, police tape surrounded Oak View. Music was playing from a neighbour's house, and party-goers – already half-cut – stood with their drinks by the gated park, and gawped at the comings and goings. Murray ducked under the blue and white tape.

'Excuse me, can you tell me what's going on?' the man called out to Murray from behind the railings that separated Oak View's driveway from the one next door. He wore faded red chinos and a cream blazer with an open-neck shirt. He was holding a glass of champagne.

'And you are?'

'Robert Drake. I live next door. Well, here, actually.'

'Ready to ring in the New Year, I see.' Murray motioned to the champagne.

'It's supposed to be Mark and Anna's party. But I just sort of . . .' he searched for the term, 'inherited it!' He laughed, pleased with himself, then stopped, suddenly serious. 'Where are they? Mark texted everyone. Said he and Anna had to go to London, and the party was off. Next thing the whole street's cordoned off.' His eyes filled with alarm. 'Good God. He hasn't murdered her, has he?'

'Not that I'm aware of. Now, if you'll excuse me . . .' Murray walked away. So that was Robert Drake. Murray should have thanked him, really. If it hadn't been for his more-money-than-sense extension plans, Tom Johnson's body might never have been discovered.

How must Caroline have felt, when she realised the building works would mean digging up the septic tank? Assuming she killed Tom the day of his supposed suicide, and disposed of him straight away, Tom would have been in the tank for a month before Drake announced his plans. Her own written objection had been lengthy, and judging by the number of identical complaints from elsewhere in the town – although not from Cleveland Avenue residents themselves, Murray had noted – Caroline had provided cut-and-paste letters for serial planning objectors who could always be relied on to stick in an oar or two.

By the time Drake had finessed his application and re-applied, Caroline had already disappeared, fooling her family, the police and the coroner into believing she had committed suicide. Had she kept tabs on the planning site, just in case? Her objection – made in the name of Angela Grange – had been logged with an address of Sycamore, Cleveland Avenue. No one had noticed. No one had checked. Why would they?

So, according to Robert Drake, both Mark and Anna were in London. Neither car was on the driveway, so the couple must have travelled separately. Murray tried to remember whether Anna had told him her plans. No – only that her friend had been driving. It was good that she had people with her, Murray thought. Nothing like the discovery of a body to put a dampener on your New Year's Eve plans.

In the centre of the garden, where the patio met the grass, was a white tent. DS James Kennedy stood by the entrance, through which the ghostly figures of two Crime Scene Investigators could be seen.

'It's him,' James said, as Murray joined him. 'Signet ring matches the description on the original missing person report.'

'Rookie error,' Murray said wryly.

'The body's well preserved – the tank's dry and underground, and with the entrance sealed, it was a pretty good makeshift morgue – and he's got a hefty head wound. Hit over the head, perhaps? A domestic gone wrong?'

'There are several jobs logged against the address over the years,' Murray said. 'Dropped calls on the nines, and a fear for welfare from the neighbour, Robert Drake, after he heard shouting coming from the address.'

'Did we attend?'

Murray nodded. 'Both Johnsons denied any domestic had taken place, but Caroline Johnson was described as being "emotional" by the attending officer.'

'You think this could have been self-defence?' James said. Inside the crime scene tent, the manhole cover had been bagged and tagged, and the narrow neck of the tank could just be seen. Tom Johnson's body had already been removed from the tank by the Specialist Search Unit and transported to the mortuary, ready for the post-mortem that would hopefully tell them exactly how he died.

'Could be. Or could be she's the violent one,' Murray said. It never paid to assume. Taking things at face value was precisely how Caroline Johnson had got away with her crimes in the first place. 'Who's looking for her?' He wondered if she'd head back towards Derbyshire, not knowing that Shifty had already sold her out.

'Who isn't? Her photo's been circulated, and there's an all ports warning out for both Caroline Johnson and Angela Grange, although for all we know she's been using other names, too. We've got CCTV of a woman matching her description arriving at Eastbourne train station late on the twenty-first, and a taxi driver who *thinks* he might have dropped her off at the Hope hostel that night, but can't be certain.'

'What have they said at the Hope?'

'What do you think they said?'

'Get to fuck?' Staff at the Hope were fiercely protective of their residents. Great when a victim was housed there; less helpful when there was a suspect in their midst.

'Pretty much.' James rubbed the side of his nose. 'Derbyshire have lifted your man Shifty, but last I heard he'd gone no comment throughout.'

No surprise there, thought Murray, particularly given the snippet of intelligence with which landlady Caz had provided him, when he and Sarah had checked out of the Wagon and Horses.

'It's not only flats he hooks people up with, you know.'

Murray had waited.

'Weed. Coke. Crack.' She'd ticked off the items on her fingers as though she were checking off groceries. 'Guns, too. Just be careful, duck, that's all I'm saying.'

'The super's authorised a road check on all routes out of Eastbourne,' James said, 'but no joy so far. Mark Hemmings has followed his partner to London – he's not answering his phone, so presumably he's still driving. As soon as I have an address, I'll get a Met unit around there to debrief them. Find out if Caroline's been in touch, get hold of a list of people she might have made contact with.'

Murray wasn't listening. Not to James, at any rate. He was listening instead to the replays in his head of the conversations he'd had with Anna Johnson, Mark Hemmings, Diane Brent-Taylor . . . He was responding to the misgivings in the pit of his stomach, to the prickle on the back of his neck.

As far as they knew, Caroline Johnson had arrived in Eastbourne on 21 December, the anniversary of her supposed death, and the day Anna Johnson had gone to the police with claims that her mother had been murdered. She'd been adamant that Murray re-open the case, yet less than a week later she had screamed at him to drop it. Murray had attributed the change of heart to the swinging emotions of a grieving daughter, but it now felt horribly, dangerously clear that he'd been wrong. Finally, he pinpointed what had struck him as odd when he had visited Anna at home to ask about her mobile phone. She had been home alone, she'd told him. Yet there had been two mugs of tea on the kitchen table.

'I'm in the car. My . . . a friend's driving,' Anna had said earlier.

That hesitation – why hadn't he picked up on it earlier? He had been so intent on being the one to tell Anna her father's body had been found, so keen to prove that he was still a detective at heart.

'We need that Putney address,' Murray said. 'And fast.'

FIFTY-EIGHT

ANNA

I think back to all the action films I've seen, in which someone is in a car against their will.

I am not bound and gagged. I'm not bleeding or semi-conscious. In films, they crawl through the back seat and open the boot; kick through the back lights and wave for help. They signal for attention; send Morse code messages with mobile phone flashes.

I am not in a film.

I sit meekly behind my mother as we leave the motorway and make our way through the streets of south west London. We slow at a set of lights, and I contemplate banging on the windows. Screaming. There is a woman in a Fiat 500 in the filter lane to our right. Middle-aged. Sensible-looking. If she calls the police, follows me till they get to us . . .

But what if she doesn't? If she doesn't notice me, or she dismisses my shouts as idiocy, or doesn't want to be involved? If it doesn't work, I anger my mother for nothing.

And right now, she's on the edge. I think back to when I was a child, when I would be able to read the signs and know when I could interrupt to ask if I could play out, or to wheedle extra pocket money, a late pass for a Brighton gig. I would approach slowly, see the pulse throbbing in her temple, and know to leave it till later, when the stresses of the day had retreated and she was relaxing with a glass of wine.

Even though I know the child locks are on, I move my hand slowly to the inside of the door and press the button to open the window. There's a dull click as the mechanism registers the action and blocks it. In the rearview mirror, my mother looks up.

'Let us out.' I try again. 'You can take this car, and Ella and I will go home . . .'

'It's too late for that.' Her voice is high. Panicky. 'They've found Tom's body.'

A shiver runs through me as I think of my father in the septic tank. 'Why?' I manage. 'Why did you do it?'

'It was an accident!'

In her car seat, Ella wakes with a start and stares at me with unblinking eyes.

'I . . . I was angry. I lashed out. He slipped. I . . .' She breaks off and screws up her face, as though pushing away whatever images are inside her head. 'It was an accident.'

'Did you call an ambulance? The police?'

Silence.

'Why come back? You'd got away with it. Everyone thought Dad had committed suicide. You too.'

She chews on her lip. Checks her mirrors and moves into the right-hand lane, ready to turn. 'Robert's extension. He'd been planning it for months, but I didn't know he'd need to dig up the sewers, otherwise we'd never have . . .' She stops short.

'We?' Fear wraps itself around my insides.

'I tried to block it. He was refused permission, and then he went to appeal. I put in an objection, but I needed to see . . . I needed to see . . .'

'You needed to see what?'

The response is a whisper. 'If there was anything left of the body.'

Bile rises in my throat. 'You said *we*.' I think of the Mitsubishi. My mother's fear was real. 'Who was following us? Who are you so frightened of?'

She doesn't answer.

The sat nav sends us left. We're almost there.

I start to panic. Once we're in the flat, escape will be impossible.

Surreptitiously I unbuckle Ella's straps so I can grab her the second Mum opens the car door. I picture the underground car park beneath Mark's Putney flat. The electric door opens with a code and closes automatically, rolling slowly shut with a creaking groan that used to set my teeth on edge when I visited Mark here. The space for his apartment is on the opposite side of the car park. How fast does the door close? I think back, remembering the way the natural light shrinks as you walk from the car to the lift, disappearing altogether as the door clunks to the ground. There will be time. I'll have to be fast, but there will be time.

Blood is thudding so fiercely in my head I'm convinced I can hear it out loud. I slide one arm under Ella. I daren't pick her up too soon, daren't give my mother any reason to believe I might make a run for it. She'll come after us, of course, but even out of shape and with a baby, I can run faster than her. I can make it. I have to be able to make it.

My mother hesitates, unsure where the sat nav is taking her. I can see the entrance to the underground parking but I say nothing. I don't want her to know I've been here before and that I'm familiar with the layout. I need every advantage I can get.

She crawls forward, peering at each entrance until she sees the right one. It takes her three attempts to enter the code Mark gave her on a slip of paper, her fingers shaking so much they slip from the keys.

Slowly, the metal door slides upwards. It's slower than I remember, and I'm glad, because it will descend at the same pace. I picture the distance between the parking space and the exit, mentally preparing myself for the sprint, imagining Ella in my arms.

The car park is dark, lit only by sporadic fluorescent lamps in the absence of daylight. The roller door grinds as it opens.

We are through the entrance and down the ramp before I hear the clunk of the door hitting the top of the mechanism. There's a pause, and then the grinding resumes. The door is closing.

I can't help myself. 'I think the space is over there.'

She manoeuvres the car to the next row, and along to the bay. I start to lift Ella from her car seat. She stiffens, complaining, and I silently beseech her to comply. My mother hesitates, contemplating whether to reverse in, then changes her mind and slots the car neatly into the space.

Ella is in my arms. Mum's out of the car. Come on, come on! I glance behind, see the rectangular shaft of open air squaring off as the door descends.

Her hand on the car door handle.

Come on!

There must be twenty metres between the car and the exit. Ten seconds before the gate hits the ground. It's possible. It has to be possible.

She opens my car door.

I don't hesitate. I kick out, hard. The door slams into my mother and sends her flying backwards. I scramble out of the car, Ella clutched to my chest, and run.

FIFTY-NINE

I would have let them out. Anna and Ella.

When I stopped the car, and told Anna to get out, I really meant it. Not just because I could have gone – disappeared somewhere too far to be found – but because I never wanted either of them to get hurt.

Now it's too late. I'll have to keep them. As insurance. Collateral.

If only I'd got rid of your body on my own, this wouldn't have happened. But I couldn't.

I kneeled on the floor, your blood seeping into my jeans. I was feeling for a pulse – looking for the rise and fall of your chest – even though the bubble of blood between your lips told me everything I needed to know. There was no coming back from this. For either of us.

I couldn't have told you whether I was crying for you or for me. Maybe it was for both of us. All I know is I sobered up fast. I put my arms either side of you, tried to heave you into a sitting position, but my hands were slick with blood, and you slipped from my grasp and smashed once more against the tiles.

I screamed. Rolled you over and saw the tissue between the crack in your skull. Vomited once. Twice.

And it was then, when I was sitting there covered in your blood and crying in fear of what they'd do to me, that the door opened.

SIXTY

ANNA

Carrying Ella throws me off balance. I lurch from side to side as I run, like a drunk chasing the last bus. Behind me Mum moans as she picks herself up. She's hurt.

I hear her shoes – comfortable flats to suit the frumpy persona she acquired as Angela – slapping against the floor as she breaks into a run.

The car park is punctuated with grey concrete pillars. Fluorescent lights flicker beneath dirty plastic casing, throwing twin shadows of each pillar onto the ground between them. Disorientating me. I focus on the square of freedom directly ahead of me; the square that – even as I watch – is changing dimensions, as though someone has tipped the rectangle of the open door on its side.

Separating the rows of parking bays are half-height walls I had thought I would hurdle. They're higher than I remember – wider, too – so I scramble over the first one, skinning my knee through the rip in my jeans, and almost dropping Ella in the process. I clutch her tight to my breast and she opens her mouth and lets out an air-raid siren of a scream that bounces off the car park walls and comes back to me ten-fold.

I glance over my shoulder but I can't see my mother. The absence makes me check my pace. Has she given up? But I hear a sound and look to my left. She's veered off to the side. It doesn't make sense, until I realise there are no walls that way,

332

no columns to dodge. Her path is longer than mine, but it is clear. She will get to me before I reach the door. Unless . . .

I sprint faster. There are two walls between me and the door, and no time to stop and climb over them. I shift Ella to under one arm, which increases her screams but frees my torso to lean into my run. The first wall looms in front of me. When did I last hurdle something? A decade ago?

Three paces.

Two.

I lift my right leg, extending it forward as I push off with the left, tucking it up behind me to clear the wall. My foot clips the concrete but I'm over the wall and sprinting, sprinting.

The door mechanism grinds. Metal against metal. The bottom of the door is a metre from the ground, the shaft of night air shrinking back from the darkness of the garage, as though it's as afraid as I am.

The final wall.

Three.

Two.

One.

I take off too early.

The wall sends me hurtling forward and to the left, and I only just manage to twist Ella to one side as I smash onto the bonnet of a Mercedes.

The air leaves my body in one sharp breath.

'Don't make this hard, Anna.'

I'm light-headed with lack of air; with the pain in my stomach and chest. I lift my head – my body still sprawled across the bonnet – and see her standing there. Between me and the exit.

I give up.

The garage door is still closing. The thick metal bar across its bottom is lower than my waist, but higher than my knees. The lights call to me. There is time.

But she's standing right there.

And although her hand shakes, and although she swore she wouldn't know how to use it, I can't bring myself to ignore the shiny black barrel of the gun.

SIXTY-ONE

I wish you were here. That's ironic, isn't it?

You'd know what to do.

You'd put your hand over mine, and you'd lower my arm until the gun was pointing at the floor. You'd take it out of my hand and even though I'd yell at you to leave me alone, like I yelled when you tried to take the vodka, like I yelled when you told me I'd had enough, I would let you. I would let you take this gun.

I don't want it in my hand. I never wanted it.

He came around with it. Shifty. Chased me for that week's rent, then put it on the table and said he thought I might want this. Two grand.

He knew money was tight. Knew that cleaning toilets – even at a posh girls' school – didn't earn that kind of cash, and that everything I'd brought with me I'd given to him in rent.

But he knew I was scared, too. He offered me a loan, with interest rates that made my chest tighten, but what choice did I have? I needed protection.

I took the loan. Bought the gun.

I felt better knowing it was there, even though I never thought I'd use it. I used to imagine what would happen if I was found; imagined diving for the drawer where I kept the gun. Aiming. Firing.

My hand's shaking.

She's your daughter. That's your granddaughter!

What am I doing?

I hear the faint strains of a siren and half hope it will get louder, but it drifts away. I need someone to stop me.

I wish you were here.

But I suppose, if you were still here, I wouldn't need you now.

SIXTY-TWO

ANNA

I want to look at her – to see if her trembling hand means she's as scared as I am – but I can't take my eyes off the gun. I wrap my arms around Ella, as though they could stop a bullet, and I wonder if this is it: if these are the last few seconds I will spend with my daughter.

I wish now I'd banged on the car window. Shouted to the woman in the Fiat 500. Tried to kick out the glass. Something. Anything. What kind of mother doesn't even try to save her baby?

Years ago, when I was walking back from a friend's house, someone tried to pull me into a car. I fought like an animal. I fought so hard I made him swear.

'You fucking bitch,' he said, before he drove off.

I didn't even have to think about it. I just fought.

Why aren't I fighting now?

She jerks the barrel of the gun towards the corner of the car park. Once. Twice.

I move.

It isn't just the gun. It's because of who she is, because of how I'm programmed to be with her. Like a best friend who suddenly turns on you, or a lover who throws an unexpected punch, I can't reconcile what's happening now with the person I thought I knew. It is easier to fight a stranger. It is easier to hate a stranger than your own flesh and blood.

From outside I hear a noise like a distant machine gun, drumming on the sky. Fireworks. It's still an hour till midnight – someone's celebrating early. The car park is deserted; all the residents either out for the night, or settled at home.

The lift opens onto a carpeted landing. Mark's flat is at the end of the corridor and as we walk past his immediate neighbour, there are raucous screams. Chart music blares from inside the apartment. If the door is on the latch – for people to come and go from the party – I could open the door and be inside in a second. Safety in numbers.

I'm not aware that I've checked my pace, that my entire body is gearing up for this final attempt to save my life – to save Ella's life – but I must have done because there's a hard jab against my spine and I don't need to be told that she's holding the gun to my back.

I keep walking.

Mark's apartment is a far cry from the way I remember it. The leather sofa is scratched and torn – the stuffing exploding from a rip on one arm – and there are cigarette burns all over the wooden floor. The kitchen has been cleared of the garbage left by the previous tenants, but the smell has been slower to leave. It catches the back of my throat.

There are two armchairs facing the sofa. Both are filthy. One is covered in what could be paint. The soft woollen throws Mark used to keep folded over the back of each one are scrunched into a heap on the other.

We stand in the centre of the room. I wait for her to give me an instruction, to say something – anything – but she just stands there.

She doesn't know what to do.

She doesn't have a clue what she's going to do with us, now she has us here. Somehow, I find that more frightening than knowing this is all part of a grand plan. Anything could happen.

She could do anything.

'Give me the baby.' The gun is in both hands now, clasped together in a parody of prayer.

I shake my head. 'No.' I hold Ella so tight she lets out a cry. 'You're not having her.'

'Give her to me!' She's hysterical. I want to think someone will hear her, knock on the door and ask if everything's okay, but next-door's party is throbbing through the walls, and I think even if I screamed no one would come.

'Put her on the chair, then get over to the other side of the room.'

If she shoots me, Ella will have no one to save her from this situation. I have to stay alive.

Slowly, I move towards one of the armchairs and lower Ella onto the pile of soft throws. She blinks at me and I make myself smile, even though it hurts so much to let her go.

'Now move.' Another jerk of the gun.

I comply, never taking my eyes off Ella as my mother picks her up and cradles her against her chest. She makes shushing noises, bounces up and down on the balls of her feet. She could be any devoted grandmother, were it not for the gun dangling from one hand.

'You killed Dad.' I still can't believe it.

She looks at me as though she'd forgotten I was there. She walks from one side of the room to the other – back and forth, back and forth – but whether it's to soothe Ella or herself it isn't clear. 'It was an accident. He . . . he fell. Against the kitchen counter.'

I cover my mouth with my hands, stifle the cry that builds at the thought of Dad lying on the kitchen floor. 'Was he . . . was he drunk?'

It changes nothing, but I'm searching for reasons, trying to understand how my baby and I came to be imprisoned in this flat.

'Drunk?' Mum looks momentarily confused, then she turns away and I can't see her face. When she speaks, she's trying not to cry. 'No, he wasn't drunk. *I* was.' She turns back around. 'I've changed, Anna. I'm not the person I was back then. That person died – just like you all thought she had. I had a chance to start again; not to make the mistakes I made before. Not to hurt anyone.'

'This is what you call not hurting anyone?'

'This was a mistake.'

An accident. A mistake. My head is spinning with the lies she's told, and if this is the truth, then I'm not sure I want to hear it.

'Let us go.'

'I can't do that.'

'You can, Mum. You said yourself: this has all been a big mistake. Give me Ella, put down the gun, and let us go. I don't care what you do after that – just let us go.'

'They'll put me in prison.'

I don't answer.

'It was an accident! I lashed out, lost my temper. I didn't mean to hit him. He slipped and . . .' Tears trace the outline of her face and drop onto her jumper. She looks wretched, and despite myself – despite everything she's done – I feel myself weakening. I believe her when she says it was never meant to be like this. Who would want this to happen?

'So, tell the police that. Be honest. That's all you can do.' I keep my voice calm, but at the mention of the police her eyes widen in alarm and she resumes her pacing, even faster and more frantic than before. She pulls open the sliding door to the balcony and a gust of icy air rushes in. There are cheers from somewhere on the street – seven floors below us – and music competing from every direction. My heart pounds, my hands suddenly clammy and hot despite the open door. 'Mum, come back inside.'

She walks out to the balcony.

'Mum – give me Ella.' Trying to keep my voice calm.

The outside space is small – designed more for cigarettes than for barbecues – protected by a toughened glass surround.

My mother crosses the balcony. She looks down and I don't even know what I cry out, only that it leaves my mouth and makes no impact, because Mum's staring down at the street with horror on her face. Ella's tight in her arms, but so close to the edge, so close . . .

'Give Ella to me, Mum.' I move slowly, one step at a time. Grandmother's footsteps. 'You don't want to hurt her. She's just a baby.'

She turns around. Her voice is so faint it's a struggle to hear her against the noise of the city below us. 'I don't know what to do.'

Gently, I take Ella from her, resisting the urge to snatch her and run, to barricade myself in another room. Mum doesn't resist, and I hold my breath as I reach out one hand. She must know this has to stop.

'Now give me the gun.'

It's as if I break a spell. Her eyes snap to mine, as though she's just remembered I'm there. Her grip tightens and she pulls away, but my hand is already around her wrist and, although I'm seized by terror, I can't let it go. I push her arm away from me – away from us – towards the night sky, but she's trying to turn back towards the apartment and we're both using every ounce of strength we have. We tussle like children over a toy, neither letting go; neither brave enough to do more in case it—

It doesn't sound like a gun.

It sounds like a bomb. Like a building collapsing. Like an explosion.

The glass surround shatters. An echo to the gunshot, to the fizz of fireworks overhead.

I let go first. Step back from the edge of the balcony, where there's nothing now between safety and the night sky. My ears are ringing like I'm in a bell tower, and above the ringing Ella is screaming, and I know it must hurt her because it's hurting me too.

My mother and I stare at each other, eyes wide in mutual terror at what just happened. What could have happened. She looks at the gun in her hand, holding it flat in her palm, as though she doesn't want to touch it.

'I don't know what to do,' she whispers.

'Put down the gun.'

She walks inside. Puts the gun on the coffee table and paces the flat. She's muttering something, her face twisted and her hands on her head, fingers grabbing at her hair.

I look down from the balcony, Ella held safely away from the edge. Where are the people? Where are the police cars, the ambulances, the crowds running to see where the gunshot came from? There is nothing. No one looking up. No one running. Revellers on their way from one bar to another. A man in an overcoat, talking on the phone. He walks around the shattered pieces of glass. Drunks, litter, broken glass – just another unwanted consequence of New Year's Eve.

I shout, 'Help!'

We are on the seventh floor. The air is filled with snatches of music as doors open and close, a continual thump of bass from somewhere a few streets away, fireworks from party-goers too impatient to wait for midnight.

'Up here!'

There's a couple on the pavement below. I glance back at my mother, then lean over as far as I dare and shout again. She looks up; he does too. He raises one arm – what looks like a full pint glass in his hand. And the tinny cheer that drifts up to me tells me my shouting is pointless.

I'm about to turn away, when I see it.

Parked on the street, oblivious to the double yellows, is a black Mitsubishi Shogun.

SIXTY-THREE

MURRAY

Murray and DS Kennedy had decamped to the kitchen of Oak View, where an unofficial incident room had been established.

'Check the voters' register for Mark Hemmings.' James was standing up, issuing actions to a young DC, who was furiously scribbling them down, ready to relay them to control room. His phone rang and he took the call, listening intently, then covering the microphone as he updated the detective sergeant.

'Anna Johnson's car pinged automatic number plate recognition cameras twice leaving Eastbourne. There are several cameras on the A27, but they didn't trigger any of them.' Murray's heart sank – had Caroline taken Anna and the baby somewhere else entirely? The DC was still talking. 'They picked up the car again in London – the last ping was just after half ten on the South Circular.'

James looked at Murray. 'Anything from Hemmings' phone?'

'Still ringing out. I'll keep trying.'

'I've asked for cell site on Anna's phone.'

Murray pressed redial. Nothing. He had already left a message, but if Mark had switched his phone to silent for the drive, it could be another hour before he responded. In the meantime, who knew what Caroline had planned?

'Sarge, there are tons of Mark Hemmings on Voters. Do we have a middle name?'

While James rooted through the pile of post abandoned on

343

the kitchen table, in the hope of finding at least an initial, Murray brought up Google.

It was, he thought, the online equivalent of good old-fashioned policing, the sort that didn't rely on police intelligence systems, or databases, or data protection waivers. It was the equivalent of knocking on doors, asking real people what they knew.

He searched for 'Mark Hemmings, Putney' and got too many hits to be useful. He closed his eyes for a moment; remembered what he knew about Anna's partner. Then he allowed himself a slow smile. Mark Hemmings hadn't only *lived* in a flat in Putney; he had *worked* there.

'Flat 702, Putney Bridge Tower, SW15 2JX.' Murray spun the phone across the table to James, the listing of accredited counsellors open at: *Mark Hemmings, Dip.ST, DipSTTS, MA (Psych), UKCP (Accredited), MBACP.*

'Nicely played.'

Murray listened as James passed the address to control room. As soon as the call was finished, Sussex would pass the information to the Metropolitan Police, who would whir into action; the CAD Room despatching officers left, right and centre. *Silent approach . . . All officers to hold at the RV point.* Firearms officers waiting for threat assessments, authorisations. An ambulance en route. Negotiators on stand-by. Scores of people, all working towards the same aim.

All hoping to get there in time.

'That's that, then,' James said. He put down his mobile. 'I hate these cross-border jobs. We do the legwork and MetPol get the collar.' He gave a rueful shrug. 'Frustrating, you know?'

Murray knew. Only he realised that, right now, he didn't feel frustrated. He didn't want to be there for the collar, for the body count, for the tea and medals.

He wanted to go home.

He cared what happened to Anna and Ella – of course he did – but he had finally understood what he should have realised a long time ago. Crimes weren't solved by a single detective: they were solved by a team. Murray had been a good detective, but he wasn't indispensable. No one was.

'Murray.' James was hesitant. 'It was my team who dealt with the Johnson suicides originally. It was me who signed off the coroner's files.'

'We all miss things, James. Caroline did a proper job – it was practically watertight.' Caroline. Murray's brain wouldn't switch off. How had Caroline got Tom's body into the septic tank on her own?

'I was newly promoted. Wanted to get stuck in to GBHs, sexual assaults, you know? Real crimes. I was too quick to get things off my desk.'

Murray remembered his own early days on CID. He remembered the buzz when a 'good' job came in; the collective groans when stretched resources were tied up with investigations going nowhere. If he'd been in James's shoes, who was to say he wouldn't have done the same thing?

He let the younger man off the hook with a light touch on his arm, his mind still on Caroline. 'It doesn't get much more real than this.'

Who had helped Caroline dispose of the body?

'I'm going to take the team back to the office. You're welcome to join us – wait for an update?'

'Thanks, but I'm going to head home. See in the New Year with Sarah.' Murray looked out into the garden, where the tent had been zipped closed and a uniformed officer stood sentry, a thick black scarf wound around his neck.

'Don't blame you. I'll let you know as soon as we hear from the Met.'

They stood up. On the wall, next to Murray, was a corkboard, and he looked idly at its contents as he waited for James to gather his paperwork. A pregnancy scan had pride of place in the centre. A wristband from some festival or other dangled from a pin on the frame, a relic from Anna's life before the baby. There was a wedding invitation – evening reception only – and a thank-you note from Bryony for the *lovely flowers – filled two vases!*

And at the bottom, on the right-hand side, was a flyer.

That was it.

The final piece of the puzzle.

It wasn't euphoria Murray felt. Just relief – that his previously sharp memory hadn't failed him. He had finally remembered what he had seen on Diane Brent-Taylor's noticeboard. And – more importantly – he knew exactly what it meant.

'One last thing,' he said to James, as the two men walked towards their respective cars. He wondered, as he said it, if he might subconsciously want to hang on to the information – to check it out himself and claim the credit when everything fell into place – but he found that he didn't. In fact, he was glad to let it go.

'Yes?'

'I know who helped Caroline Johnson get rid of the body.'

SIXTY-FOUR

ANNA

There's a noise from the landing. The quiet 'ping' of the lift as it announces its arrival. I look at Mum, but her eyes are fixed on the door.

'Who is it?' I whisper, but she doesn't answer.

Could it be the police?

Mark would have called them as soon as we left Eastbourne; they know we're here. And now that they've found Dad's body, they must know what she did – they must realise who I'm with . . . I pin my hopes on Mark and Murray, on them adding two and two and making four.

'Open the door. I know you're in here.'

The rush of relief makes me so heady I almost laugh. Not the police, but the next best thing.

Mum doesn't move, but I do. I've been stupid. The black Mitsubishi Shogun wasn't chasing us; it was trying to make Mum stop. I run to the door and yank it open, because suddenly we're two against one and I feel invincible.

'Thank God you're here.'

I'm braced for attack from behind, not in front. It catches me square in the chest and forces me backwards, where I just manage to hold Ella aloft as I trip and land on the floor. I let out a moan. My head is trying to catch up with what my eyes are telling me is happening.

This is no rescue.

Laura shuts the front door and bolts it. She's wearing skinny black jeans with high heels and a shimmery top, dressed for a party she won't be attending. Our New Year's Eve party. Her hair falls in loose curls around her shoulders and her eyes smoulder with glittery greys and greens. She ignores me, directing her anger at Mum, who is backing slowly away towards the balcony.

'You double-crossing bitch.'

SIXTY-FIVE

I can still remember Laura's face.

She stood in the doorway, her features frozen in horror.

'I rang the bell. The door was open, so . . .' She stared at your body. The blood was congealing. The ceiling lights were reflected in the sticky gloop on the floor – a halo of silver around your head. 'What happened?'

I've thought a lot about that moment. About what I said. Would things have been different if I'd explained to her it was an accident? That I'd lost my temper, lashed out? That drink made me do things I hadn't planned to do?

'I killed him.'

The colour drained from her face.

I felt my muscles spasm and I realised I'd been in the same spot since I . . . since you fell. I straightened. Remembered I was still holding the neck of the bottle. I dropped it, and it fell with a thud. Rolling, not breaking. It made Laura jump.

The sound jolted me into action. I picked up the phone but didn't dial. My hand shook.

'What are you doing?'

'Calling the police.' I wondered if being drunk made it better or worse. An aggravating factor to be under the influence, or mitigation that I didn't know what I was doing?

'You can't call the police!' Laura crossed the kitchen and took the phone out of my hand. She glanced at you again and I saw her wince as she took in the seeping mess from behind your ear. 'Caroline, you'll be arrested! They'll put you in prison.'

I sank onto a chair, my legs suddenly unable to support my weight. There was a strange smell in the kitchen, a metallic, sour odour of blood and sweat and death.

'You could get life.'

I imagined what it would be like to live my life in a prison cell. I thought of the documentaries I'd seen. I thought of *Prison Break* and *Orange Is the New Black*, and wondered how close they were to the truth.

I thought, too, of the help I might get.

Because you were right, Tom, it was no way to live. I kidded myself that I didn't have a problem, because I didn't wake up shaking, or sit in a park with a can of Special Brew. But I shouted at you. I taunted you. I hit you. And now I'd killed you.

I had a problem with alcohol. A big problem.

'I'm calling the police.'

'Caroline, think about this. Think carefully. Once you make that call, there's no going back. What's happened is . . .' She shudders. 'God, it's awful, but you can't undo it. Going to prison isn't going to bring Tom back.'

I looked at the series of photographs printed on canvas and hung above the Aga. You, me and Anna, lying on our stomachs wearing blue jeans and white T-shirts. Laughing. Laura followed my gaze. She spoke quietly.

'If you go to prison, Anna loses both of you.'

I said nothing for a while. 'So . . . what?' I felt myself sliding away from what was right, what was good. Did it matter? I had already committed a crime. 'We can't leave him here.'

We.

That was the moment. The moment we became a team.

'No,' Laura said. Her jaw was set tight. 'We can't leave him here.'

It took two of us to move the terracotta pot away from the manhole cover. You had put it there when we'd moved in, and

I'd planted a bay tree we'd been given as a housewarming gift. The cover was ugly, and there was no need for access – the septic tank was a hangover from when the town boundary was half a mile to the west, and this cluster of houses a rural outlier.

The key was a fat metal baton, about three inches long. It had lived in the dresser drawer for as long as we'd lived at Oak View, but it slotted into the hole in the cover as neatly as the day it had been made.

Inside, a narrow tunnel, like the entrance to a sloping well. The air was stale but not fetid, the contents of the tank long since dried up. I looked at Laura. We were sweating from the effort of dragging you out from the kitchen, and from the blind fear of what we were about to do. What we'd already done. If we stopped now, it would be too late. It would be obvious we had tried to hide your body. The damage had already been done.

We put you in head-first. I cried out as you slid halfway into the tunnel and stuck fast, as your belt caught on the metal surround. Laura pulled hard on your jeans, and you made a sound. An involuntary groan as air was forced from your lungs.

I couldn't watch. I turned away and heard the heavy drag as you travelled into the tank; a loud, dull clunk as you hit the bottom.

Silence.

I had stopped crying, but my heart ached with loss and guilt. If the police had arrived right then, I think I would have told them everything.

Not Laura.

'Now we need to clean up.'

It was Laura's idea to fake the suicide.

'If we report him missing, they'll see you as a suspect. They always do.'

She made me go over the plan again and again, then she left. I didn't sleep. I sat in the kitchen, looking out of the window

351

at the garden I'd turned into a grave. I cried for you, and – yes – I cried for me, too.

Laura drove to Brighton as soon as it was light, waited for the shops to open and bought a mobile phone. An untraceable SIM card. She called the police; said she'd seen you go over the cliff edge.

Every day I expected the police to come. Every day I jumped when the door went. I couldn't sleep; couldn't eat. Anna tried to tempt me with scrambled eggs, scraps of smoked salmon, tiny bowls of fruit salad, her eyes full of her own grief, even as she tried to lessen mine.

But the police didn't come.

The weeks went by and you were declared dead, and no one pointed a finger or asked a question. And although I saw Laura often, and although we'd never agreed it, we never spoke of what had happened. What we'd done.

Until your life assurance paid out.

SIXTY-SIX

ANNA

I pull myself up to a sitting position and get clumsily to my feet. The ringing in my ears hasn't lessened but Ella's screams have become whimpers. What will this do to her? She won't remember this night, not consciously, but will something be buried deep in her subconscious? The night her grandmother held her hostage.

Laura.

'I didn't know he'd need to dig up the sewers,' Mum said in the car, 'otherwise we'd never have . . .'

Laura knew. Laura helped her.

The two women stand facing each other, Laura's hands on her hips. Mum glances to the table, where the gun lies innocently where she left it. She's too slow. Laura follows her gaze, moves fast.

Fear pounds in my chest.

Laura pulls her sleeve over her hand, wrapping the fabric around her fingers as she picks up the gun. She's methodical. Careful.

Terrifying.

'I didn't double-cross you.' Mum's defensive. I want to tell her to calm down, but I can't find my voice.

'You owed me, Caroline.' She walks to the sofa and sits on the arm, the gun held steady in her hand. 'It was all quite simple. If I hadn't been there you would have been charged with Tom's murder. I saved you.'

'You blackmailed me.'

353

Pieces of the story slot into place.

Not Dad threatening Mum, but Laura. Not Dad who tracked her down. Laura.

'You?' I can't comprehend it. 'You sent the anniversary card?'

Laura looks at me for the first time. She takes in Ella, my dishevelled hair, the shock that must surely register on my face. 'You were supposed to dismiss it as a crank. Nothing more sinister than the crackpot letters you got when Tom died.' She shakes her head. 'It was a message for Caroline, really, to make her realise who she was up against. I sent her a copy.'

'And I suppose the rabbit was a message too, was it? And the brick through the window? You could have killed Ella!'

Laura looks momentarily confused, then she smiles. 'Ah – I think you'll find that came from a little closer to home.'

I follow her gaze, to where Mum has her face in her hands. 'No . . .'

'I just wanted you to stop digging into what had happened to us. I knew that if you found out the truth, she'd come after you too, and—'

'You threw a brick through the nursery window? Onto your own granddaughter's cot?' The words sound as though they're coming from someone else, hysteria making them shrill and uneven.

'I knew Ella was downstairs – I'd seen her from the garden.' She takes a step towards me, one arm outstretched, but Laura moves faster. She stands, holding the gun in front of her. She jerks it to the left. Once, twice. Mum hesitates, then steps back.

Who are these women? My mother, who could hurt her own daughter? Her own granddaughter? And Laura – how can you know someone all of your life, yet not know them at all?

I turn to Laura. 'How did you know where Mum had gone?'

'I didn't. Not at first. I just knew she hadn't killed herself.' She looks at my mother, who is sobbing noisily. 'She's very predictable.' Her tone is patronising, scathing.

A wave of revulsion hits me as I think of the way she consoled me after his death; how she helped me through the memorial service. Dad might have died at Mum's hands, but it was Laura who hid his body; who masterminded the suicide; who concealed the crime. I remember her insistence that I go through Mum and Dad's study – her generous offer to do it for me – and realise now that she was searching for clues to where Mum had gone.

'I've got a copy of that photograph too, you know. You and Mum, in that shitty B&B in the arse end of nowhere.' Just for a second, there's a crack in Laura's voice. The tiniest hint that underneath this steely control is something more. 'She never stopped talking about it. How much you'd laughed. How it was a world away from real life. From *her* life. She loved it.' Her shoulders slump. 'She loved you.'

Slowly, she lowers her arm. The gun hangs loosely by her side. This is it, I think. This is where it stops. Everyone's said what they need to say, and now it ends. Without anyone getting hurt.

Mum takes a step towards her. 'I loved her too.'

'You killed her!' Instantly, the gun is raised. Laura's arm is ramrod straight, her elbow locked in place. The glimpse of vulnerability I saw has vanished. Her eyes are narrow and dark, every muscle rigid with rage. 'You married money and you left her in that damp shit pit of a flat and she died!'

'Alicia had asthma,' I say. 'She died from an asthma attack.' Didn't she?

I feel a flash of panic that this, too, is a lie, and I look to my mother for reassurance.

'You didn't even go and see her!'

'I did.' Mum's close to tears again. 'Maybe not as often as I should have done.' She screws up her eyes. 'We drifted apart. She was in London; I was in Eastbourne. I had Anna and—'

'And you didn't have time for a friend with no money. A friend who didn't speak like your new friends did; who didn't drink champagne and drive a posh car.'

'It wasn't like that.' But her head drops and I feel a wave of sadness for Alicia, because I think it was. I think it was like that. And, just like the way she treated Dad, she's seen it too late. I make a sound – not quite a cry, not quite a word. Mum looks at me, and everything I'm thinking must be written in my eyes because her face crumples and she's begging silently for forgiveness. 'Anna and Ella should go. They've got nothing to do with this.'

Laura gives a humourless laugh. 'They've got *everything* to do with it!' She folds her arms across her chest. 'They've got the money.'

'How much do you want?' I don't mess around. Whatever she wants, she can have.

'No.'

I look at Mum.

'That money's for your future. Ella's future. Why do you think I ran away? Laura would have taken it all. Maybe I deserved that, but you didn't.'

'I don't care about the money. She can take it. I'll transfer it all to whatever account she wants.'

'It's simpler than that.' Laura's smiling.

The hair on the back of my neck stands up, a prickling sensation creeping down my spine.

'If you give me all your money, people will ask questions: Billy, Mark, the bloody tax man. I'd have to trust you to keep quiet, and if I've learned one thing from this,' she glances at Mum, 'it's that you can't trust anyone.'

'Laura, no.'

I look at Mum. She's shaking her head, one step ahead of me.

'As far as anyone else is concerned, I came here to save you and Ella,' Laura says. 'Mark helpfully told me where you'd be when he cancelled the party, and my sixth sense told me you were in terrible danger.' She widens her eyes as she acts out her pantomime, hands raised, fingers splayed on the hand not

356

wrapped round the gun. 'But when I arrived, I was too late. Caroline had already shot you both and killed herself.' She pushes the corners of her mouth downwards in mock dismay, then turns to me. 'You've seen Caroline's will. You were there when it was read. *To my daughter, Anna Johnson, I leave all financial and material assets, to include all property in my name at the time of my death.*' She quotes verbatim from Mum's will, spitting out the words.

'Mum left you money, too.' Not a fortune, but a healthy inheritance that honoured Mum's long-standing friendship with Alicia; her duty to Laura as godmother.

Laura continues as if I haven't spoken. '*In the event that Anna has passed away before the execution of this will, I leave all financial and material assets to my goddaughter, Laura Barnes.*'

'It's too late,' Mum says. 'The will's been read – Anna's already inherited.'

'Ah, but you're not dead, are you?' Laura smiles. 'Not yet. The money still belongs to you.' She raises the gun; points it at me.

My blood freezes.

'If Anna and Ella die before you, I inherit the lot.'

SIXTY-SEVEN

MURRAY

Hard as Nails.

Sarah would have got it sooner. She'd have noticed the name in a way that Murray hadn't; would have stopped to read it out. To talk about it.

What a terrible name for a salon.

He imagined her jabbing a finger at the pocket notebook entry that meticulously noted the names of those present when police broke the news that Caroline's husband had killed himself.

Laura Barnes. Receptionist at Hard as Nails.

I hate it when businesses try to be funny . . . Murray could hear Sarah's voice as clearly as if she were sitting in the car with him. *You may as well call it No More Nails, just because it's catchy, and it has 'nails' in it, and that would be a ridiculous name, too . . .* Murray laughed out loud.

He caught himself. If talking to oneself was the first sign of madness, where did holding imaginary conversations rank?

Still, Sarah would have remembered the name. And if she had talked to Murray about it, he would have remembered it too. And then, when he'd left Diane Brent-Taylor's house, wondering who had stolen her name, the flyer on her noticeboard would have leaped out at him, and he would immediately have made the association between Laura Barnes and her former place of work.

In Murray's experience, inventing an alias was surprisingly

difficult. He used to laugh at the green kids from the estates, looking like rabbits in headlights as they tried to come up with something convincing. Invariably they'd use a middle name, the name of a kid at school, the name of their street.

Laura had panicked. Hadn't bargained on having to give a name at all, perhaps; thought she'd just ring on the nines and report a suicide, and that would be that.

'What's your name?'

Murray could picture the call-taker, headset in place, fingers hovering over keys. He could picture Laura, too: out on the cliffs, the wind whipping the words from her mouth. Her mind a blank. Not Laura – she wasn't Laura. She was . . .

A customer. Picked at random.

Diane Brent-Taylor.

It had almost been perfect.

When Murray pulled into his street, it was half past eleven. Just enough time to find his slippers, pop the champagne, and sink onto the sofa with Sarah in front of Jools Holland and his hootenanny guests. And at midnight, as they welcomed in the New Year, he would tell Sarah that he wouldn't be going back to work; that he was retiring again, and properly this time. He remembered an old detective inspector, who worked his thirty years then worked another ten. Married to the job, people used to say, although he had a wife at home. Murray had gone to his retirement party – when he'd eventually had one – had heard all the DI's plans to travel the world, learn a language, take up golf. Then he'd died. Just like that. A week after he'd turned in his ticket.

Life was too short. Murray wanted to make the most of it while he was still young enough to enjoy it. A fortnight ago he had been feeling every bit deserving of his bus pass; today – even at this late hour, and after the day he'd had – he felt as spritely as the day he'd joined the job.

Someone in the next street was letting off fireworks, and for a second the sky was lit up with blues and purples and pinks. Murray watched the sparks burst outwards, and then fade to black. The cul-de-sac split into two at the end, and Murray slowed down before he turned left into his section of the road. His neighbours were mostly elderly, and unlikely to be celebrating New Year's Eve by dancing in the street, but you never knew.

There were more fireworks as he turned the corner, the sky glowing blue and—

No. Not fireworks.

Murray felt ice in his stomach.

There were no fireworks.

It was a light, revolving silently; bathing the houses, the trees, the people who stood outside their houses, in soft blue.

'No, no, no, no . . .' Murray heard someone talking; didn't realise it was him. He was too intent on the scene unfolding in front of him: the ambulance, the medics, the open front door.

His front door.

SIXTY-EIGHT

ANNA

'You wouldn't.'

Laura raises an eyebrow. 'That's a brave challenge for someone on the wrong side of a gun.' She screws up her face. 'Can't you stop her crying?'

I rock my arms from side to side, but Ella's too fractious and I'm too on edge to make the movement smooth, and it only serves to make her cry harder. I lay her horizontally across my body and lift my top to feed her. The room goes mercifully quiet.

'She's just a baby.' I try to appeal to Laura's maternal side, although to my knowledge she's never wanted children. 'Whatever you do to me, please don't hurt Ella.'

'But don't you see? That's the only way it works. You and Ella have to die first. Caroline has to kill you.'

Somewhere in the depths of the building I hear a dull thud.

'No!' Mum's been quiet until now, and the sudden shout makes Ella start. 'I won't.' She looks at me. 'I won't. She can't make me.'

'I don't have to make you. I've got the gun.' Laura holds it aloft, the fabric of her shimmery top still wrapped around her fingers. 'It's got your prints on it.' Slowly, she walks towards Mum, the gun pointing directly at her. I look at the door; wonder if I'd make it. 'No one will ever know it wasn't in your hand the whole time.'

'You won't get away with this.'

She raises one perfectly plucked eyebrow. 'There's only one way to find out, isn't there?'

There's a roaring in my ears. Ella feeds hungrily.

'As it happens, I have an insurance policy of my own.' She smiles. 'Should the police be suspicious, I just have to point them in the right direction. I'll remember that I overheard you both talking about Tom's life assurance policy; that you clammed up when you saw me coming. The two of you were in it together from the start.'

'They'll never believe that.' There's more noise from somewhere inside the building. I listen for the 'ping' of the lift, but this is something different. Something rhythmic.

'And when they dig a little deeper, they'll discover that the phone used to report Tom's suicide was bought in Brighton . . .' she pauses for effect, 'by none other than Anna Johnson.'

The rhythmic sound grows louder. Faster. I stall for time. 'I always saw us as family.' I move slowly across the flat until I'm standing next to my mother. Facing Laura.

'The poor relation, I suppose.'

I know what this noise is.

Laura's consumed with anger, spitting out thirty-three years of resentment. 'It was just normal for you, wasn't it? Big house, clothes allowance, skiing in the winter, France every summer.'

The noise is that of feet, running on stairs. Police boots. Stopping two floors below and continuing more quietly than a lift that announces its arrival.

Laura's eyes snap to the door.

I start to shake. It was Mum who bought the gun; who brought Ella and me here. Mum who killed Dad and hid the body. They don't even know Laura's involved. Why wouldn't they believe her story? She'll get away with it all . . .

'That's not my fault, Laura. And it isn't Ella's.'

'Just like living on benefits in a damp flat with a sick mother wasn't my fault.'

Outside the door, there's a whisper of a noise.

Laura's hand moves. Just a fraction. Her finger, closing around the trigger of the gun. Her face is pale, a pulse throbbing in the side of her neck. She's scared, too. We're all scared.

Don't do it, Laura.

I strain my ears and hear the quiet shuffle of feet outside the door. Will they burst through, the way they do in films? Shoot first, ask questions later? Adrenalin's coursing through me and, as Ella pulls away, I feel my whole body tense.

My mother is breathing hard. She's cornered; nowhere left to run, no more lies to tell. She backs slowly away from Laura, away from me.

'Where are you going? Stay where you are!'

Mum glances behind her, at the unguarded balcony with its seven-floor drop. She looks at me with eyes that plead forgiveness. Like a television playing mutely in the corner of a room, my head fills with scenes from my childhood: Mum reading me stories; Dad teaching me to ride a bike; Mum at dinner, laughing too hard, too long; shouting downstairs; Dad shouting back.

What are the police waiting for?

A rabbit on the doorstep; a brick through the window. Mum holding Ella. Holding me.

Suddenly I know what she's thinking, what she's going to do. 'Mum, no!'

She carries on walking. Slowly, slowly. From the apartment next door comes a burst of shouting, as the party guests count down to midnight. Laura looks wildly between the front door and Mum, distracted by the shouting, not knowing what to do, where to look.

'Ten! Nine! Eight!'

I follow Mum onto the balcony. She knows it's all over. She knows she's going to prison for what she's done. I think what it will be like to lose my mother for a second time.

'Seven! Six!'

There's a dull clunk of something heavy from the landing.

363

Laura moves the gun. Points it directly at me. Her finger tightens. Behind me, Mum is crying. The wind whistles across the balcony.

'Five! Four! Three!' The cheers from next door grow louder. Around us, more fireworks, more cheers, more music.

'Don't shoot!' I scream it as loudly as I can.

The sound is extraordinary. A thousand decibels. More. The door off its hinges, crashing to the floor, and a hundred armed police running over it. Noise – so much noise – from them and from us and—

'Drop the weapon!'

Laura backs towards the corner of the room, the gun still in her hand. My mother's feet graze the broken glass at the edge of the balcony. The hem of her dress flutters. She looks into my eyes.

And then she goes.

I scream – on and on until I don't know if it's only in my head or if everyone else can hear it too. Her dress billows like a failed parachute and she spins over and over, plummeting downwards. Fireworks explode overhead, filling the sky with gold and silver rain.

A police officer, by my side. Mouthing words I can't hear, a face full of concern. Wrapping a blanket around me. Around Ella. He puts a hand on my back and guides me inside, not letting me check my pace as we walk through the apartment and out to the landing, even though I can see Laura lying on the ground, a police officer kneeling beside her. I don't know if she's dead or alive, and I don't know if I care.

In the ambulance, I can't stop shaking. The paramedic is cheerful and efficient, with blonde hair in two thick plaits over her shoulders. She puts a shot in my arm that, seconds later, makes me feel as though I've drunk a bottle of wine.

'I'm breastfeeding,' I say, too late.

'You're no good to her if you're having a panic attack. Better she's a bit sleepy, than hyper on second-hand adrenalin.'

There's a clunk as the back door of the ambulance opens. I think I recognise the police officer with the blanket, but the drugs have made me woozy and everyone in uniform looks the same.

'Visitors,' he says, and steps to one side.

'They wouldn't let us past the police tape.' Mark clambers into the ambulance and half sits, half falls onto the bed next to me. 'No one would tell me what was going on. I was so scared you were . . .' He breaks off before his voice lets him down, and instead wraps his arms around Ella and me. She's asleep, and I wonder again what babies dream of, and if she'll ever have nightmares about what happened tonight.

'Been in the wars, Annie?' Billy tries for a smile but fails. Worry is etched on his face.

'Laura . . .' I start, but my head feels too heavy; my tongue too big for my mouth.

'I've given her something for the shock,' I hear the paramedic say. 'She'll be feeling a bit groggy for a while.'

'We know,' Billy says to me. 'When Mark cancelled the party, he told me what had happened. About Caroline's cousin and her violent ex. It didn't sit right with me. Caroline never mentioned a cousin Angela, and then there was the Shogun Laura had borrowed . . .'

Just hours ago, I was lying across Ella's car seat. Keeping out of sight, terrified I'd be seen. It's as though I'm recalling a film, or a story that happened to someone else. I can't recapture the fear I felt, and I wonder if it's just the drugs making it feel unreal. I hope it isn't.

'I picked up Billy and we got here as quickly as we could.'

There's something different between them – no more tension; no more verbal rutting – but I'm too tired to analyse it, and now the paramedics are gently ushering them both outside, and lying me down on the bed, and strapping down Ella, too. I close my eyes. Give in to sleep.

It's all over.

SIXTY-NINE

MURRAY

Sarah's eyes were closed, her face as peaceful as though she was sleeping. Her hand felt heavy and cold, and Murray gently rubbed his thumb against her papery skin. His tears fell unashamedly onto the white hospital blanket, each forming dark spots like the onset of a summer shower.

There were four beds in this section of the ward, all but Sarah's unoccupied. A nurse hovered discreetly in the corridor, giving him solitude at this most private of moments. Seeing him look up, she came to his side.

'Take as much time as you need.'

Murray stroked Sarah's hair. Time. That most precious commodity. How much time had he and Sarah spent together? How many days? How many hours, minutes?

Not enough. It could never be enough.

'You can talk to her. If you like.'

'Can she hear me?' He watched the gentle rise and fall of Sarah's chest.

'Jury's still out on that one.' The nurse was in her forties, with soft dark eyes and a voice filled with compassion.

Murray followed the tubes and wires that snaked across his wife's body, to the myriad machines keeping her alive; to the IV drip with its soothing morphine.

They would increase the dose, the consultant had explained. When it was time.

*

366

The ambulance had taken only minutes, but they were minutes too long. In the days that had followed – in the blur of nurses and consultants and machinery and paperwork – Murray had made himself relive those minutes as though he had been there. As though this had happened to him.

There had been an upturned chair in the kitchen; a broken glass where Sarah had fallen by the sink. The phone, beside her on the tiles. Murray forced the images through, one after another, each one like a blade dragged against his skin.

Nish had begged him to stop. She'd arrived with something foil-wrapped, still hot from the oven, catching Murray in the brief space between hospital visits. She had listened to Murray tell her in agonising detail what no one knew for certain had happened, then she had put her hands around his and cried with him. 'Why are you torturing yourself like this?'

'Because I wasn't there,' Murray had said.

Nish's tears left tracks down her cheeks. 'You couldn't have prevented this.'

Cerebral aneurysm, the doctor had said.

Coma.

Hope for the best. Prepare for the worst.

Then: *I'm sorry. There's nothing more we can do.*

She wouldn't feel anything, they had insisted. It was the right thing to do. It was the only thing to do.

Murray opened his mouth, but nothing came out. There was a pain in his chest and he knew his heart was breaking. He looked at the nurse. 'I don't know what to say.'

'Say anything. Talk about the weather. Tell her what you had for breakfast. Have a moan about work.' She put a hand on Murray's shoulder, squeezed gently, then took it away. 'Say whatever's in your head.'

She moved away to the corner furthest from where Murray sat with Sarah, and began folding blankets and tidying the contents of the metal cupboard beside the empty bed.

Murray looked at his wife. He ran a single finger over her forehead – its worried furrows now smoothed flat – and along the bridge of her nose. He skirted the plastic mask that held the tube in Sarah's throat, and stroked instead her cheek, her neck. He traced the curve of her ear.

Say whatever's in your head.

Behind him, the steady burr of machines continued, rhythmic sounds that formed the language of the ICU.

'I'm sorry I wasn't there . . .' he began, but the words were sobs and his eyes were streaming and he could no longer see. How much time had they had together? How much time would they have had left, if this hadn't happened? Murray pictured Sarah on their wedding day, in the yellow dress she had picked in lieu of white. He remembered her joy when they bought their house. As he held Sarah's limp fingers, he saw instead the nails filled with dirt; her face not pale against a hospital pillow, but flushed from a morning's gardening.

It hadn't been enough, but the time they had spent together meant the world to him.

It had *been* his world.

Their world.

Murray cleared his throat. He looked across at the nurse. 'I'm ready.'

There was a pause. Murray half hoped she'd say *not yet – in an hour or so, perhaps*, yet at the same time he knew he couldn't bear it if she did. More time wouldn't make this any easier.

She nodded. 'I'll get Dr Christie.'

There was no more talking. They removed the tube from Sarah's throat as gently as if she had been made of glass; pushed away the wheeled machines that had been keeping the beat of a heart too weak to work alone. They promised to be right outside, in the corridor, if they were needed. That he mustn't feel afraid; he mustn't feel alone.

And then they left him.

And Murray rested his head on the pillow beside the woman he had loved for half his life. He watched her chest rise and fall with a movement so slight he could barely see it.

Until it wasn't there at all.

SEVENTY

ANNA

'Anna! Over here!'

'How do you feel about your mother's death?'

Mark puts a hand in the small of my back and steers me across the street, all the while talking to me in a low voice. 'Don't make eye contact . . . keep looking forward . . . nearly there . . .' We reach the pavement and he takes back his hand to tip the pram wheels up and over the kerb.

'Mr Hemmings – what first attracted you to the millionairess Anna Johnson?'

There is a ripple of laughter.

Mark takes a key from his pocket and unlocks the gates. Someone has tied a cellophaned bunch of flowers to the bars. For Dad? My mother? For me? As Mark slides the gates open – just wide enough for me to push the pram through – a man from the *Sun* steps in front of us. I know he's from the *Sun* because he has told me so, every day for the last seven days, and because he has a dog-eared identity card dangling from the zip of his fleece, as though this hint of professionalism negates the daily harassment.

'You're on private property,' Mark says.

The journalist looks down. One scuffed brown boot is half on the pavement, half on the gravel that covers our driveway. He moves it. Only a few inches, but he is no longer trespassing. He thrusts an iPhone in my face.

'Just a quick quote, Anna, then all this will go away.' Behind him stands his sidekick. Two cameras lie like machine guns across the older man's body, the sagging pockets of his parka stuffed with lenses, flashes, batteries.

'Leave me alone.'

It's a mistake. Instantly there's a rustle of notebooks, another phone. The small crowd of hacks surges forward, taking my broken silence as invitation.

'A chance to put your side of the story forward.'

'Anna! This way!'

'What was your mother like growing up, Anna? Was she violent towards you?' This last with a raised voice, and now they're all shouting. All trying to be heard; all desperate for the scoop.

Robert's front door opens, and he comes down the steps in a pair of leather slippers. He nods briefly to us, but his eyes are fixed on the reporters. 'Why don't you just fuck off?'

'Why don't *you* fuck off?'

'Who is he, anyway?'

'Nobody.'

It's enough of a distraction. I shoot Robert a grateful look, feel Mark's hand on my back again, pushing me forward. The pram wheels crunch on gravel, and then Mark's pulling the gates closed, turning the key. There are two, three, four flashes.

More photos.

More photos of me looking pale and anxious; more photos of Ella's pram with a privacy blanket pegged to the hood. More photos of Mark, grimly escorting us in and out of the drive, when necessity demands that we leave the safety of the house.

Only the local paper still has us on the front page (the nationals have already relegated us to page five), with a photograph taken through the railings, as though we were the ones behind bars.

Inside, Mark makes coffee.

They wanted us to stay somewhere else.

'Just for a few days,' Detective Sergeant Kennedy said.

I had just finished giving my statement, the result of almost eight hours in a windowless room with a female detective who looked like she'd rather be anywhere but there. She wasn't the only one.

Back home, the kitchen – the scene of my dad's murder – had been cordoned off, white-suited forensic officers swabbing every inch of it.

'It's my house,' I said. 'I'm not going anywhere.'

They found traces of Dad's blood in the grout between the tiles, despite the bleach poured on the floor by Laura and Mum. Blood beneath my feet, for all those months. I feel like I should have seen; should have known.

It was three days before we were allowed full use of the kitchen again; another twenty-four hours before they finished in the garden. Mark has pulled the curtains across the glass doors from the kitchen, so I can't see the piles of earth that now pass for our lawn, and closed the shutters at the front of the house, to avoid the telescopic lenses of the headline-hunters in the road.

'There aren't as many today,' he says now. 'They'll be gone by the end of the week.'

'They'll be back for the trial.'

'Let's cross that bridge when we come to it.' He hands me a steaming mug of coffee, and we sit at the table. I've moved things around; re-positioned the table and switched the two armchairs. Small changes that I hope – in time – will stop me remembering; stop me picturing what happened here.

Mark sifts through the post, leaving most of it unopened and putting it in a pile for the recycling, along with the notes from reporters that litter the driveway until Mark picks them up.

Cash waiting in exchange for exclusive rights to your story.

There have been offers from publishers and literary agents. Approaches from film companies and reality TV shows. Sympathy

372

cards, funeral leaflets, letters from Eastbourne residents shocked to discover that Caroline Johnson – campaigner, fundraiser, committee member – had murdered her husband.

They all go in the bin.

'It'll die down soon.'

'I know.' The hacks will move on to the next juicy story, and one day I'll be able to walk through Eastbourne without people whispering to their friends. *That's her – the Johnson daughter.*

One day.

Mark clears his throat. 'I need to tell you something.'

I see his face and my stomach lurches, a lift dropping to the ground floor without buttons pressed for pause. I cannot take any more announcements, any more surprises. I want to live the rest of my life knowing exactly what is happening each hour, each day.

'When the police asked about the appointment Caroline made with me . . .' He stares into his coffee; falls silent for a while.

I say nothing, my heartbeat a drum roll in my ears.

'I lied.'

I feel that shift again, the ground beneath me cracking, splitting, moving. Life, changing with a single word.

A single lie.

'I never met your mother.' He looks up, his eyes searching mine. 'But I did speak to her.'

I swallow, hard.

'I didn't make the connection, not until after your first session with me. I looked through my diary and there it was: your mother's name. And I remembered her phone call; remembered her telling me her husband had died, and that she needed help working through it. Only she never showed up, and it didn't enter my head again until that moment.'

'Why didn't you tell me?'

Mark lets out a breath like he's just run a marathon. 'Patient confidentiality?' There's a question mark in his voice, as though he knows it sounds absurd. 'And because I didn't want you to leave.'

'Why not?' I say, although I already know the answer.

He takes my hand and rubs his thumb across the inside of my wrist. Beneath his gentle pressure the skin pales, blue-green veins just visible, like the tributaries of a river. 'Because I was already falling in love with you.'

He leans forward, and I do the same. We meet in the middle, awkwardly bent across the corner of the kitchen table. I close my eyes, and feel the softness of his lips, the warmth of his breath on mine.

'I'm sorry,' he whispers.

'It doesn't matter.'

I understand why he did it. He's right: I would have gone somewhere else. It would have felt too strange to unburden myself to a man my mother had chosen for her own confessions. And if I'd gone elsewhere, Ella would never have been born.

'No more secrets, though.'

'No more secrets,' Mark says. 'A fresh start.' He hesitates, and I think for a second there's something else he wants to get off his chest, but instead he reaches into his pocket and pulls out a small, velvet-covered box.

He holds my gaze as he slips off his chair and onto one knee.

SEVENTY-ONE

MURRAY

'One more, please.'

It was an awkward pose for the camera, standing side by side with their hands mid-shake, and Murray's framed commendation held between them.

'All done.'

The photographer finished, the chief constable shook Murray's hand again and smiled with genuine warmth. 'Celebrating tonight?'

'Just a few friends, ma'am.'

'You deserve it. Good work, Murray.'

The chief stepped to one side and allowed Murray a moment in the limelight. There were no speeches, but Murray put his shoulders back and held his commendation in front of him, and as the chief began to clap, the room filled with applause. A few tables back, Nish gave him a double thumbs-up, a beam on her face, before resuming her wild clapping. From near the door, someone cheered. Even dour John from the front counter at Lower Meads was applauding.

Briefly, Murray pictured Sarah sitting in the audience. She'd be wearing one of her brightly coloured, voluminous linen dresses, a scarf draped around her neck or tied around her head. She'd be grinning fit to burst, looking around the room, wanting to catch someone's eye, to share her pride with them.

His eyes were stinging. He turned the commendation around

and held it away from him so he could look at it, blinking hard until there was no more risk of his eyes watering. He had been picturing Sarah on a good day, he reminded himself. There was every chance that Sarah might not have been in the room at all; that she'd have been at Highfield, or at home under the duvet, unable to face accompanying Murray today. To his final work commitment.

C6821 MURRAY MACKENZIE IS COMMENDED FOR THE DEDICA-TION, TENACITY AND INVESTIGATIVE SKILLS THAT ENSURED THE DETECTION OF THE MURDER OF TOM JOHNSON, AND THE IDEN-TIFICATION OF BOTH SUSPECTS. HIS CONTRIBUTION IS AN EXCEPTIONAL EXAMPLE OF SUPPORTING FORCE VALUES.

The identification of both suspects. It had been carefully worded. Murray felt a twinge of regret that they'd been unable to bring Caroline Johnson to justice. She had jumped from the balcony of Mark Hemmings' seventh-floor flat, landing in front of a crowd of onlookers who would for ever be haunted by the sight of her body hitting the ground, taking with her any secrets that hadn't already been shared with her daughter.

Laura Barnes was on remand pending trial. She had made no comment during interview, but the body-cams worn by the arresting officers had recorded a series of admissions made by her in the heat of the moment. The recordings, together with the case DS James Kennedy and his team had built against her, meant Murray was confident of a guilty plea. Laura had covered her tracks well, but ANPR showed her car in Brighton at the time of the Fones4All purchase. A voice recognition specialist had confirmed that the call to control room from 'Diane Brent-Taylor' matched Laura's voice, and would appear in court as an expert witness to that effect.

Not that Murray would be around to see it.

The applause had died away. Murray gave a nod of appreciation to the audience, then stepped off the low stage. As he made his way back to his seat, to listen to the chief make her closing address, he saw Sean Dowling sitting with their old DS – now a colleague of Sean's at the High Tech Crime Unit. As one, the two men stood up. They began clapping again, slowly this time. The rest of their table joined them. And as Murray walked down the centre of the room, there was a scraping of chairs and a swell of movement as, one by one, the friends and colleagues he had worked with over the years gave him a standing ovation. The drumbeat of clapping sped up, faster than his footsteps but not as fast as his heart, which was bursting with gratitude for the people in this room.

His police family.

By the time Murray reached his seat, he was blushing hard. There was a final cheer, and then more shuffling of seats as the chief wrapped up. It was a relief to have all eyes looking somewhere other than at him, and he took the opportunity to read his commendation again. It was the third he had received in his police career, but his first as a civilian. His first and last.

'Well done, mate.'

'Nice one.'

'Beer some time?'

Dismissed from the formal part of the evening, Murray's former colleagues were heading for the buffet table at the back of the room, clapping him on the back as they passed. It was rare to see food at an internal function; police nature to make the most of it when it happened. Nish pushed through and put her arms around him, whispering so only he could hear.

'She would have been so proud.'

Murray nodded fiercely, not trusting himself to speak. Nish's eyes were shining.

'If I could cut in for a moment . . .' Leo Griffiths, in uniform and holding a Diet Coke. A fleck of sausage-roll pastry on his tie suggested he'd been first in line for the buffet.

Murray shook the hand Leo proffered.

'Congratulations.'

'Thank you.'

'This is quite some do.' Leo looked around the room. 'The last commendation ceremony I attended served warm orange squash and a strict limit of one biscuit each.'

'It's a joint do. Part commendation, part retirement. Economies of scale,' Murray added solemnly, using one of the superintendent's favourite buzz terms. Nish suppressed a laugh.

'Quite. Actually, that's what I wanted to talk to you about.'

'Economies of scale?'

'Retirement. I wondered if you'd seen the advert for civilian investigators on the Cold Case Review Team?'

Murray had. In fact, no fewer than seven people had pointed it out to him, including the chief constable.

'Right up your street, I'd have thought,' she'd said. 'A chance to put those investigative talents of yours to good use, and skill up some of the less experienced members of the team. Officially, this time,' she'd added, with a pointed look. The positive outcome of the Johnson job had meant that Murray's breaches of protocol had been glossed over, but he had been left in no doubt that – had he wished to stay in post – they must never, ever happen again.

Murray didn't wish to stay in post. He didn't want to stay in the force at all.

'Thanks, Leo, but I've handed in my ticket. I'm going to enjoy my retirement. Do a spot of travelling.' Murray pictured the shiny new motorhome on which he had paid a deposit and would be picking up the following week. It had swallowed a large chunk of his pension, but was worth every penny. Inside there was a kitchen, a tiny bathroom, a double bed and a comfortable living area with a foldaway table, plus a huge steering wheel that made Murray feel like he was driving a truck.

He couldn't wait. His police family had been good to him, but it was time to cut the apron strings.

'Fair enough. You can't blame us for trying to keep you, though, can you? Where are you off to?'

In the weeks since Murray had shared his plans for retirement, several people had asked him this question. Murray's answer hadn't changed. For years he had lived his life by someone else's clock. Sarah's spells at Highfield. Her good days; her bad ones. Early shifts, lates, nights. Overtime, weekend working. Briefings; debriefs. In Murray's retirement plans, there were no clocks. No calendars. No plans.

'Wherever I feel like going.'

SEVENTY-TWO

ANNA

The smell of freshly mown grass fills the air. It's still cold, but the promise of good weather is just around the corner. I've swapped Ella's pram for a pushchair, and she babbles happily as I strap her in. I call Rita and put on her lead.

'I'm going to get out of your way. I'll be on my mobile if you need me.'

'No worries, love. Anything in the kitchen you want us to leave out?'

Oak View is a hive of activity. There are five removal men, each in a different room, and a mountain of boxes already packed.

'Just the kettle, please.' In my car is a box of essentials – tea, loo roll, a few plates and mugs – to save unpacking when we get to the new house.

I chat to Ella as we walk, pointing out a cat, a dog, a balloon caught in a tree. We pass the forecourt of Johnson's Cars, but pause only to catch Billy's eye. He waves and I lean forward to take Ella's hand to wave back. He's busy speaking to a new rep, and I don't want to disturb him.

The forecourt looks good. The Boxster sold with the first hint of spring. It's been replaced by another two sports cars, their tops optimistically down, and their bonnets gleaming. Uncle Billy finally let me bail out the business, so I put in a cash injection that will keep the wolf from the door for a while, at least. Mark thought I was mad.

'It's a business, not a charity,' he said.

Only it isn't just a business. It's my past. Our present. Ella's future. Granddad Johnson took over from his father, and Billy and Dad took over from him. Now it's down to me and Billy to keep things afloat till business picks up. Who knows if Ella will want to continue the tradition – that's up to her – but Johnson's Cars isn't going under on my watch.

We walk along the seafront. I look at the pier and think about walking here with my parents, and instead of the anger that has filled the last three months, I simply feel overwhelmingly sad. I wonder if that's progress, and make a mental note to mention it in my next counselling session. I'm 'seeing someone' again. Not someone from Mark's practice – that would have felt too weird – but a thoughtful, gentle woman in Bexhill who listens more than she talks, and leaves me feeling a little stronger each time we meet.

Down a side street, leading away from the seafront, is a row of small terraced houses. The pushchair bumps on the uneven pavement, and Ella's babbling increases. She's making noises that sound almost like speech, now, and I remind myself to write down each milestone, before I forget it.

We stop at number five, and I ring the bell. I have a key, just in case, but I'd never use it. I'm already bending down to take Ella from the buggy when Mark opens the door.

'How's it going?'

'Organised chaos. I know we're early, but we were getting under their feet, so . . .' I give Ella a kiss, holding on to her for as long as I can, before handing her to Mark. I'm still not used to it, but every time feels a little easier. There's nothing official, no every-other-weekend-and-a-day-in-the-week arrangement. Just the two of us, still parenting jointly, despite our separate lives.

'It's no problem. Do you want to hang out here for a bit?'

'I'd better get back.'

'I'll drop her off at the new place tomorrow.'

'You can have the grand tour!'

We lock eyes for a second, acknowledging everything that's happened, how new and strange this feels, then I kiss Ella again, and leave her with her dad.

It was easy, in the end.

'Will you marry me?'

I didn't speak. He waited, expectantly. Hopefully.

I imagined standing at the altar with him, Ella a toddling flower girl. I imagined turning and looking at the congregation, and I felt fresh loss at the absence of my father. Billy would give me away, I supposed. Not my dad, but the nearest thing I had to one. I was lucky to have him.

There would be friends, neighbours filling up the pews.

No Laura.

I felt no grief about that. Her trial date had been set, and although the thought of testifying against her was already giving me nightmares, Victim Support had talked me through the process. I'd be alone on the stand, but I knew there was a team of people behind me. She'd be convicted, I was sure of it.

She'd written a couple of times, begging forgiveness. Remand prisoners were forbidden from making contact with trial witnesses, and the letters had come via a mutual acquaintance, too blinded by friendship to believe Laura had truly done the things of which she'd been accused.

The letters were long. Effusive. They played on our shared history, on the fact that we only had each other. That we'd both lost our mothers. I kept them as insurance, not out of sentiment, although I knew I'd never show them to the police. Laura was taking a risk, writing to me, but it was a small one. She knew me too well.

I felt no grief, either, that my mother wouldn't be at my wedding. Thinking of her forms a hard ball of hatred in my heart that no amount of counselling will lessen. But it isn't Dad's murder I hate her for – although that is where it starts. It isn't even for the lies she told in faking her death, in abandoning me in my grief. It's for the ones she told afterwards; the story she spun from the half-truths of her marriage to my father. It's for making me believe that he was the alcoholic; that it was he who hit her, not the other way around. It's for making me trust her again.

'Well?' Mark had prompted. 'Will you?'

I realised the 'no' on the tip of my tongue had nothing to do with who would or wouldn't be at our wedding.

'If we hadn't have had Ella,' I said, 'do you think we'd still be together?'

He paused – a fraction too long. 'Of course we would.' I held his gaze and for a moment we stayed that way. He broke away, gave a tiny smile that didn't reach his eyes. 'Maybe.'

I reached for his hand. 'I don't think maybe's enough.'

Oak View sold quickly, to a family with three children who accepted the house's history in exchange for a price far below market value, and who will, I hope, fill the rooms with laughter and noise. Mark's Putney flat is on the market, and for now he's staying in Eastbourne, so we can continue to bring up Ella together.

I cried when the SOLD sign went up, but only for a moment. I had no desire to stay in Cleveland Avenue, where the neighbours looked at me with morbid fascination, and tourists went out of their way to walk past the house and gawp at a garden they couldn't even see.

Laura and Mum had disposed of the broken glass in the septic tank, along with Dad's body. Mum's prints were on the neck of the wine bottle; Laura's on the pieces of glass she'd so carefully picked up and thrown in the tank.

The tank is long gone. Robert's extension is underway, his thirty-grand sweetener a carrot dangled before the new owners in exchange for the inconvenience. They don't plan to replace Mum's rose beds, though; a football goal and climbing frame are on their shopping list instead.

I walk back towards Oak View, my hands feeling empty without a buggy to push. Rita strains at the lead as a black and white cat crosses my path, and I just manage to stop myself from pointing it out to an absent Ella. I wonder if I'll ever get used to her not being with me all the time.

The house I've bought is as different to my family home as it is possible to get. A neat modern box, with three bedrooms and an open-plan ground floor, where, as Ella starts to crawl, I can keep an eye on her from the kitchen.

Back at Oak View, they're loading the lorry. They'll leave my bed, and Ella's cot, and tonight we'll sleep in a near-empty house, ready for the big move tomorrow. It's only a mile down the road, but it feels so much further.

'Nearly done, love.' The removal man is sweating with the effort of heaving furniture into the van. I've left the heavy wardrobes, the long kitchen table and the big hall dresser for the new family, who were delighted to be saved the expense. They're too big for my new house, and too tied up in memories I no longer want. The removal man wipes his brow with the back of his hand. 'Post came. I popped it on the side for you.'

It's on the dresser. Hand-delivered by Laura's friend, again. I wonder if she'll still be so supportive after the trial, once all the evidence has been laid out for the world to see. The charges stack up. Concealing a crime; hiding Dad's body; threats to kill.

The envelope prompts unwanted images. Laura with a gun in her hand. My mother, edging closer towards the edge of the balcony. I shake myself. It's over. It's all over.

I pull out the letter. A single sheet. None of the effusive apologies of her previous letters. My failure to respond – to withdraw my support for the prosecution – has clearly hit home.

I unfold the paper, and suddenly there's a buzzing in my ears. Blood singing; my pulse racing.

A single line, in the centre of the page.

Suicide?

The letter shakes in my hand. Heat envelops me and I think I might pass out. I walk through the kitchen – through the boxes and the removal men moving like worker bees back and forth from house to van – and open the back door.

Suicide?

I walk into the garden. Make myself take deep, slow breaths until I'm no longer dizzy, only the buzzing won't leave my ears, and my chest feels tight with fear.

Because this time I don't need to look elsewhere for the answer.

It wasn't suicide this time, either.

My mother didn't jump.

AUTHOR'S NOTE

Like many people around the world, I was gripped by the apparently miraculous reappearance in 2007 of John Darwin, who, five years previously, had been declared dead after what was believed to have been a canoeing accident in north east England. His wife Anne later confessed that John had continued living with her in the family home, before the couple embarked on a new life in Panama.

I was fascinated by the story, and by the sheer audacity of John Darwin, who had adopted a disguise in order to move undetected around his hometown, and who had frequently eavesdropped on his two grown-up sons as they visited their supposedly distraught mother. I wondered how it must feel to discover your parents had deliberately caused you the pain of bereavement, and how you would begin to rebuild a relationship with them. I found it hard to understand how any parent could treat their children in such a callous manner.

As I wrote *Let Me Lie*, I found the following publications particularly valuable for the detail behind the Darwins' extraordinary story: *Up the Creek Without a Paddle* (Tammy Cohen) and *Out of My Depth* (Anne Darwin). However, the events and characters in *Let Me Lie* are fictional products of my imagination, and not based on any stories I have read or heard about.

In researching suicides at Beachy Head, I was very moved by *Life on the Edge* (Keith Lane) – the autobiography of a man whose wife jumped to her death from the Sussex cliffs. Keith Lane dedicated the next four years of his life to patrolling the cliffs, preventing twenty-nine people from taking their own lives.

The Beachy Head Chaplaincy Team provides more than 100 hours of patrol on Beachy Head each week. They support the police and coastguard services in search and rescue endeavours, and specialise in suicide and crisis intervention, saving around two thousand people since their inception in 2004. The team relies entirely on public support, so please do follow them on Facebook at @BeachyHeadChaplaincyTeam and support their work if you can.

According to the charity Mind, one in four of us will experience mental health problems this year, and more than twenty per cent of us admit to having had suicidal thoughts at some point in our lives. Every day, sixteen people in the UK will die by suicide. If you've been affected by any of the issues raised in this book, or would like to speak to someone about how you're feeling, I encourage you to call the Samaritans. They're available any time, from any phone, on 116 123.

ACKNOWLEDGEMENTS

My former police colleagues are unfailing in their encouragement and support, and I am grateful to them all for cheerleading my books, even when I stray from procedural accuracy. In writing *Let Me Lie*, I am particularly grateful to: Sarah Thirkell, for forensic advice; Kirsty Harris, for answering questions about inquests; Di Jones, for clarifying the procedure around 999 calls; and Andy Robinson – again – for more mobile phone advice. One day I'll write a book that doesn't require your help.

My thanks to Heather Skull and Kaimes Beasley, of the Maritime and Coastguard Agency, who were generous and creative with their advice around tidal activity and body recovery; and to Becky Fagan, for her advice on Borderline Personality Disorder and the mental health system. I apologise to all of the above for any liberties I have taken with the truth; all mistakes are mine, and mine alone.

Marie Davies was the winner of a competition run by animal charity Love Cyprus Dog Rescue, who do wonderful work rehoming abandoned dogs. I was delighted to include Marie's very own rescue dog, Rita, in *Let Me Lie*, and hope I have done her justice.

Ten years ago, social media would hardly have featured in an author's life; now I can't imagine being without my fabulous Facebook, Twitter and Instagram followers. You have commiserated with me when writing was hard, cheered my good news, helped with research, and propelled my books into the bestseller lists. Thank you.

I am fortunate to have the most amazing people working with me. Sheila Crowley and the Curtis Brown team continue to be there every step of the way – I couldn't wish for a better literary agency – and I have wonderful publishers around the world. Special thanks go to Lucy Malagoni, Cath Burke and the Sphere team; to Claire Zion and her gang at Berkley; and to the Little, Brown Rights team. Thank you all – I love working with you.

There are too many book bloggers, retailers and librarians to thank individually, but please know that I value everything you do, and am so grateful for your reviews, recommendations and shelf space, whether virtual or otherwise.

A big thank you to all those in the crime scene; to Kim Allen for keeping me organised and to my friends and family. Rob, Josh, Evie and George: you are my world. Sorry I'm so grumpy.

Finally – but so importantly – thank you for picking up this book. I hope you enjoyed it.

Exclusive to this edition

Read on for a bonus scene from *Let Me Lie*,
featuring Murray and Sarah

'In open order . . . right . . . DRESS!'

At the barked command, the eyes of sixty-four men and seventeen women snapped to the right. Each with one arm raised to the side, the newly qualified police officers shuffled into neat lines, precisely one arm's width apart, before standing once more to attention, white-gloved hands tight against tunics.

Murray kept his eyes trained on Staff Officer Henderson. Like many of their trainers at police training college, Henderson was a former military man, and right now, his grey moustache twitched in anticipation of the next command.

'By the left . . .' Henderson drew breath. Murray felt himself tense, even though they'd drilled these precise movements so often he sometimes woke to find his feet marking time beneath the itchy blanket issued to each new recruit. 'Quick . . . MARCH!'

Knees high and heads higher, the class of June 1982 marched across the parade ground in time with the brass band, which was just loud enough to be uncomfortable for anyone who had celebrated a little too heavily the previous evening. *Never again*, Murray thought, remembering the enthusiasm with which he had poured double measures of whiskey into plastic cups purloined from the canteen. At the time, the celebration had seemed like a good idea. This morning, with boots to bull and a shirt to iron, Murray had wished he'd taken the advice of his sergeant and gone to bed early.

'Parade . . . SHUN!'

The sun was in their eyes, and Murray tried not to squint, as he – and the majority of his peers – stood to attention in the centre of the parade ground. A small delegation, hand-picked from the cream of the intake, marched to the front of the ground to present the flag to that afternoon's VIP. They had been promised a Royal, and there had been much discussion about who it might be, with Steve Bridges running a book with Princess Diana at odds of ten to one. Murray had put a quid on the Queen Mother. He wondered now if anyone had plumped for the Duke of York, and who would collect the winnings if nobody had.

Prince Andrew gave a rousing speech about Robert Peel, the 'people's police', and the weight of responsibility that now rested on the new recruits' shoulders. Murray felt a burst of pride. Come Monday morning, he would be walking the beat in Brighton, catching criminals and putting into practice everything he'd learned in the classroom.

Each newly qualified officer had been allowed four tickets for family members. Murray had sent two to his parents, and passed the others to WPC Claire Woods, who had a big family and a persuasive manner. Now, Murray scanned the rows of raked seating at the front of the parade ground until he found his parents. His father, stiff in a borrowed suit and his wedding tie, gave Murray a proud smile as their eyes met, and it was all Murray could do not to grin back. Murray's dad had been PC 27 Mackenzie until his retirement three years ago, and although he'd left Murray free to choose his own path, Murray couldn't have been prouder to be following in his footsteps. He looked at his mother, but she was gazing at Prince Andrew with a look usually reserved for newborn babies and puppies.

'Parade . . . stand EASY!'

In unison, eighty-one officers brought up their left legs to a ninety-degree angle, before stamping their feet hard onto the ground, six inches to the left of where it had been. From the stands, Murray's attention was momentarily caught by a flash of luminous pink and a shock of yellow hair gathered like the top of a pineapple, half-hidden amid the sea of muted suits and hats.

'Parade . . . to your duties . . . DISMISS!'

They fell out, free to find their families and queue for the force photographer, who would immortalise the day with a cardboard framed image for mantelpieces of proud parents and partners.

It was another hour before Murray saw the luminous pink jumper again. His dad was talking to a chief inspector he'd known since way back when, and his mother was interrogating Staff Officer Henderson about the facilities in the single quarters into which Murray would be moving on Sunday.

The wearer of the pink jumper – which Murray now saw was flecked with glittery thread, and had sleeves that stretched from cuff to hem without going anywhere near an armpit – was by the buffet table. She was somewhere around Murray's age – perhaps nineteen, perhaps twenty-one – and looked like a strong gust of wind might blow her over. Bright turquoise eye shadow extended up to each eyebrow, and a dozen or more bangles jangled on her forearm as she reached for the vol-au-vents. She put two on her plate, looked up to see if anyone was watching, then picked the prawns out of three more and popped them into her mouth. Murray grinned, and as the girl looked up again, their eyes met. Far from being embarrassed, the girl grinned back, pinched another prawn, and put it in her mouth.

'Macca!' Jim Ryder clapped Murray on the back. 'Top night, mate.'

'I'm paying for it now,' Murray grinned.

'Hair of the dog?' Like a magician with a rabbit, Jim produced a hip-flask from inside his tunic, and sloshed a generous measure of vodka into Murray's orange juice before doing the same with his own.

'Any idea who the blonde in the pink jumper is?' Murray

nodded towards the buffet table, where the girl was peeling the smoked salmon from a mousse ring. As she did so, she glanced at Murray, a mischievous look in her eyes, and he had the distinct impression her buffet table antics were – at least partially – for his own benefit.

'She was with Ralphy and his folks last time I looked.'

Sure enough, the girl carried her plate over to the corner of the room, where Karl Ralph was introducing his parents to one of their sergeants. As the girl approached, Karl put his arm around her. Murray turned away.

'Give us another slosh of that vodka, will you?'

'Soon as the 'rents have all gone, I'm heading into town – get a real party started. You up for it?'

'Try stopping me,' Murray said, shaking off the fleeting disappointment he'd felt when he'd seen Karl Ralph with the girl in the luminous pink jumper. Good luck to them. He didn't know Ralphy very well, but the lad was nice enough, and the pair made a good couple. Murray had been single throughout training college, with the exception of a brief fling with a WPC that they were both pretending hadn't happened. Perhaps once he was settled in his nick he'd meet a few more girls.

The quiches and pâtés had been cleared from the buffet table and replaced with arctic rolls and black forest gateaux. Murray was just helping himself to the latter when a jangling arm reached out and nabbed the glistening cherry from the top of his slice. Murray's mouth twitched. He waited until the cake was safely deposited on his plate before turning around, his features arranged in what he hoped was a perfectly neutral expression.

'I'm Sarah.' She put the cherry in her mouth. A speck of whipped cream found its way from her fingers to her upper lip.

'Murray Mackenzie. You've got something . . . there.' He touched his own face. Sarah poked out her tongue and retrieved the cream.

'Gone?'

'Gone.'

'Cool parade.' She marched on the spot, huge silver earrings swinging above her shoulders. 'Last time I saw Karl look so smart, he was at Nan's funeral.' Her smile was a bright flash. Blink-and-you'd-miss-it. Close up, Murray could see dark circles beneath her eyes. The sleeves of her voluminous jumper were pulled down over her hands, and as they spoke she tugged them down further. Murray caught a glimpse of collarbone as the neckline moved; milky skin and a silver cross.

Nan's funeral . . .

'Ralphy's your . . .' he let the question hang in the air, and she held back the answer just long enough to let him know she was playing with him.

'My brother, yes.'

Murray tried to be casual. 'Oh.'

'Oh,' Sarah repeated, drawing out the vowel as though she was blowing cigarette smoke. They were both smiling, now; each silently challenging the other to make the next move.

'Do you have a—'

'Boyfriend?' Sarah shook her head.

'Me neither.' Murray flushed. 'Girlfriend, I mean. Well, either. Neither.' Christ, he was shit at this. He wracked his brains for chat-up lines, but could only remember the one about tumbling from heaven, and Sarah clearly wasn't the kind of girl to fall for cheesy pick-ups. In fact, Sarah wasn't like any girl Murray had ever met.

She held his gaze, but there was a beat before she spoke again. 'You know I'm mental, right?' Her smile was broad, but her eyes told a different story, and her chin jutted forwards defiantly. 'Karl's told you?'

Murray gave a shrug that could have meant anything from *sure, I know*, to *I don't give a damn*. Despite Sarah's unwavering, almost mocking, smile, Murray didn't join in. It didn't feel like something to smile about. He didn't recall Ralphy mentioning a sister at all, let alone outlining the specifics of her mental health.

'Borderline Personality Disorder.' An even broader smile, accompanied, this time, by a roll of the eyes. 'It sounds worse than it is, I promise.'

'What does it mean?' Murray asked, feeling stupid for not knowing.

'You can go and talk to someone else, if you want.' She shrugged. 'Go and eat your cake. Find someone normal to talk to.' Her tone was casual, not defensive, but nevertheless it tugged at something inside Murray. He felt absurdly protective of this girl he'd only just met; a girl who was clearly perfectly capable of looking after herself.

'I don't want to talk to—' Murray broke off. *Someone normal*, he'd almost said. Sarah's eyes twinkled. 'I don't even want the cake.'

'Mind if I eat some, then?' She took the fork out of Murray's hand, and poked around in the cake until she found a cherry. She speared it, the plate pushing down in Murray's hand. 'I have good days and bad days,' she said, putting the cherry in her mouth, and returning for a second. 'Ups and downs.'

'Don't we all?'

Sarah nodded as she chewed, conceding the point. 'I can get scared. Paranoid.' She looked up at him, and for the first time since they'd started talking, the spark went out of her eyes.

'Well,' Murray said gravely. 'You know what they say: just because you're paranoid, it doesn't mean they're not out to get you.'

Sarah burst out laughing. 'Where are you going to be stationed, PC Mackenzie?'

'Brighton.'

'I live in Hove.'

'Oh.'

'Oh.' That twinkle, again. The same rounded 'o' of her lips, as she stretched out the word. Murray took a deep breath.

'Would you like to have dinner with me sometime?'

Sarah raised one eyebrow, as though the suggestion was entirely unexpected. She contemplated Murray, and tapped the fork against the fingers of her free hand. 'Even though I'm a bit mad?'

Murray looked at her. He took in her luminous pink jumper; her hooped earrings and turquoise eyeshadow. He saw the way she bounced on her toes, as though she was about to take off. He thought about how he'd felt when he'd caught sight of her on the parade ground, and the mischievous look in her eyes when she was pinching prawns.

He grinned. 'Precisely *because* you're a bit mad,' he said.

The sensational *Sunday Times* bestselling debut novel from Clare Mackintosh, and winner of the Theakston Old Peculier Crime Novel of the Year 2016

A tragic accident. It all happened so quickly.
She couldn't have prevented it. Could she?

In a split second, Jenna Gray's world descends into a nightmare. Her only hope of moving on is to walk away from everything she knows to start afresh. Desperate to escape, Jenna moves to a remote cottage on the Welsh coast, but she is haunted by her fears, her grief and her memories of a cruel November night that changed her life for ever.

Slowly, Jenna begins to glimpse the potential for happiness in her future. But her past is about to catch up with her, and the consequences will be devastating . . .

AVAILABLE NOW

The second gripping psychological thriller and number one bestseller from Clare Mackintosh

You do the same thing every day. You know exactly where you're going. You're not alone . . .

When Zoe Walker sees her photo in the classifieds section of a London newspaper, she is determined to find out why it's there. There's no explanation: just a grainy image, a website address and a phone number. She takes it home to her family, who are convinced it's just someone who looks like Zoe. But the next day the advert shows a photo of a different woman, and another the day after that.

Is it a mistake? A coincidence? Or is someone keeping track of every move they make . . .

AVAILABLE NOW